AGAINST THE DARKNESS

AGAINST THE THE DARKNESS

KENDARE BLAKE

HYPERION
Los Angeles   New York

First Edition, April 2024
10 9 8 7 6 5 4 3 2 1
FAC-004510-24025
Printed in the United States of America

This book is set in Minion Pro, Bourbon/Fontspring; Aurelia Pro/Monotype
Designed by Tyler Nevins
Stock images: moon and clouds chapter ornament: 2035892681/Shutterstock

Library of Congress Cataloging-in-Publication Data
Names: Blake, Kendare, author.
Title: Against the darkness / by Kendare Blake.
Description: First edition. • Los Angeles ; New York : Hyperion, 2024. •
   Series: Buffy: the next generation; book 3 • Audience: Ages 12–18. •
   Audience: Grades 10–12. • Summary: Frankie Rosenberg, the world's first
   Slayer-Witch, finds herself fighting evil alone as the threat of Darkness
   grows; she must lead the charge to reunite the fragmented Scooby gang,
   save the slayers, and defeat the Darkness.
Identifiers: LCCN 2023039635 • ISBN 9781368075084 (hardcover) •
   ISBN 9781368075213 (paperback) • ISBN 9781368075725 (ebook)
Subjects: CYAC: Witches—Fiction. • Vampires—Fiction. • Werewolves—
   Fiction. • Demonology—Fiction. • Paranormal fiction. lcgft •
   LCGFT: Novels.
Classification: LCC PZ7.B5566 Ag 2024 • DDC [Fic]—dc23
LC record available at https://lccn.loc.gov/2023039635

Reinforced binding
Visit www.HyperionTeens.com

AGAINST THE DARKNESS

PROLOGUE

The vampire's footsteps thudded against the pavement as he chased the girl through the back alleys and dark streets of New Sunnydale. She was fast, but that was all right. It was good, even: Running got the heart pumping, so her blood would practically fly into his mouth when he bit. And he was so very hungry.

He'd been hunting this particular girl for a few nights. He'd even spoken to her once, pretending to ask directions to a restaurant. He'd leaned just close enough to give her the creeps. He liked to give them the creeps. He liked how it felt, when they edged away and the bashful look that rose to their faces, like they felt silly for feeling afraid. Almost like they wanted to apologize to him for it.

That was his favorite part. How bad they felt, about fearing for their lives.

He chased the girl down another alley (they always went down alleys), and the sound of her ragged breathing was music to his ears. He just wished she would scream. She hadn't screamed when he approached her in the park; she'd tried to give him her wallet. He'd had to show her his true face to get her to run.

The girl hit a dead end and stopped. Her shoulders heaved under her thick, knit sweater, and she put her hands out like she was feeling for cracks or a secret passageway through the twelve-foot cinder block wall.

"May as well turn around," he said. "There's nowhere left to go."

"Please," she gasped, too scared to turn and face him. "I don't have much money."

"I don't want your money." He stopped. "Actually, that's a lie. I am going to rob you, too. Right after I kill you." He bared his fangs and roared, ready to bite into the tender skin, to feel her struggle like a butterfly in a spider's web, her little fists beating a rhythm against him that grew weaker and weaker.

But someone pushed him from behind, and instead of his fangs sinking into a nice, soft girl, they smacked into a hard cement wall. Then a foot connected with his back, and he fell to the street. He pushed himself up just in time to glimpse his pretty blond dinner, scampering back toward town to safety.

"Hey. Fang Face."

The vampire spun. A different girl stood behind him. And this one held a stake.

"I hunted that for three nights!" he shouted.

"That's not very efficient."

He blinked his yellow eyes. "Maybe not. But it does mean I'm still hungry. So I guess you'll have to do."

"I'll have to do? Look, if I'm going to be eaten, I'm going to be the first choice on the menu, you know?"

He attacked and caught her by the wrist when she tried to dodge. The sound of the breath leaving her body when he slammed her into the cement wall was delightful. Part of him didn't even want to bite her. He just wanted to kill her. He saw her fist coming and grinned—only when it connected with his cheek his head lit up like it was on fire. He let go and backed off with a cry, hand pressed to his steaming face.

"Crosses! Your rings are crosses!"

"One on each finger."

He pulled away a bit of burned skin and threw it on the ground, where it withered to ash. "That's dirty pool."

"Dirty pool? Who says that? Where are you from?" The girl shook her head. "Never mind. I forgot I don't have to do that stupid demon census anymore."

Before he could even form the words "Demon census?" the stake sank into his chest and pierced his heart. It didn't hurt at all when he disintegrated.

"God, vampires are stupid," Hailey said. "One girl in their sights and all the blood rushes right out of their brains." She brushed a sprinkling of vamp dust from the shoulder of her black T-shirt, then tucked her thumbs under her suspender straps and turned. "So, how'd I do?"

Aspen stepped out of the shadows behind a dumpster. The leader of the Darkness cocked her head and shrugged. "You got yourself pinned and almost dropped your stake."

"But the rings were good, right?" Hailey wiggled her knuckles, admiring the small silver crosses. They even worked with her outfit. The whole slayer gig worked with the Goth aesthetic, to be honest. A brooding, nighttime existence spent courting the possibility of death. More slayers ought to look like her, not like Buffy Summers, or Frankie, who patrolled in soft pink hoodies and joggers with pockets stuffed full of stakes.

Or like Aspen, who even in chill weather insisted on dressing like she was headed to Coachella.

"I admit," Aspen said, "the ring crosses were a good idea. Your nerdy demon ex-boyfriend would be proud."

Hailey frowned. Sigmund *would* be proud. *He would kiss both of her cheeks and tell her she was brilliant. But only her cheeks. Because Sigmund didn't want to be with her anymore.*

"Half demon," Hailey corrected. "And yes, he would. He'd wish he'd thought of it. But he chose sides, and he didn't choose mine. So to hell with him." *To hell with him,* she thought for real. *It was easy to pretend to be angry with Sigmund. Because she was. The hard part was pretending to hate Frankie for killing Vi, and pretending to be broken inside over Vi's death, when really Frankie had only murdered Vi's fake mirror twin, and the real Vi was off with Sigmund's mom, Sarafina, having wacky road-trip adventures.*

"We should get out of here." *Aspen looked up the alley.*

"Don't worry about getting spotted by Frankie. Little Miss Goody Two-Shoes doesn't patrol past one a.m. on school nights."

That was true, but Aspen still stuck to the shadows as they walked back the way they'd come. Hailey checked the time on her phone. She shouldn't be patrolling after one a.m. on school nights either. At least Frankie had slayer constitution to get her through the lack of sleep. Hailey had black coffee and slapping herself in the face every few minutes.

I miss you, Frankie, *she thought. This double agenting thing . . . it sucks.*

"Come on!" *Aspen called.* "We can grab some food from the diner before we head home."

Home was a bedroom with flowered curtains at the Rosenbergs', not the smelly motel she was currently squatting in. But Hailey grinned and nodded. "Good idea, I'm starving."

PART ONE

SCOOBY-DOOBY-DOO,
WHERE ARE YOU?

CHAPTER ONE

WELCOME TO LOVELORN, POPULATION TWO

Sigmund's hybrid idled silently as he and Frankie sat in the lot of Valley View Park. So silently Frankie wouldn't have known it was still running were it not for his hand, tense on the gear shifter in case Jake texted them to relocate in a hurry. He and his boyfriend, Sam, were running a bait play somewhere in the park. Jake would use his werewolf senses to sniff out demons, and Sam would linger enticingly nearby in an effort to draw them out. Once they were out, they would give the signal, and Frankie would arrive to slay them.

"This thing is really quiet," she said, referring to the hybrid in the opening to their saddest small talk of the night.

"My next one will be even quieter," Sigmund commented. "I'm hoping to go full electric, just for you." He smiled without showing teeth. She did the same. Then she sighed.

"I miss Hailey."

"So do I," Sigmund admitted. "I don't like thinking about her all alone for so long in that fleabag motel."

"There are no fleas," Frankie said. "Just roaches." And water damage, and structural issues, and a smell that was hard to describe. The motel itself was kind of like a roach. It had survived the Spikesplosion. It was unable to be killed.

"She could have stayed anywhere. She didn't have to go . . . there."

Frankie shrugged. "Vi's room was paid up for the month. And subsequent months were the cheapest around." She prodded the half Sage demon in the shoulder. "You know she could have just moved in with you, if you weren't being such a butt."

"I've never in my life been a butt, Frankie." He sat up straighter, mock offended. "And even if Hailey and I were still together, wouldn't her staying with me have given away the plan?"

"We could have had you be neutral. Like Switzerland. Are they still neutral?"

"It's one of the main principles of their foreign policy." He sighed again, harder. "But I do wish . . . I just miss her."

Frankie glanced into the trees. They weren't that far from Vi's "grave." After the fight in the warehouse, when Frankie sunk the Scythe into Vi's double's stomach and then obliterated the Scythe into particles, they'd hoisted Vi's double's corpse between them and taken it to the forest. It was a long, disturbing walk, and Vi was no help—she couldn't touch her double without reabsorbing it, and she kept trying to make them do jokes from *Weekend at Bernie's*.

Sigmund followed Frankie's gaze. "I see her sometimes at the grave site." He stopped by to monitor it, since it was a Sage demon mirroring spell that was used to create the double.

"That doesn't count as 'seeing,' Sig; that counts as stalking. Have you been taking lessons from Grimloch?" But Frankie was no better—once she'd seen Hailey coming out of a coffee shop and tailed her for three blocks, unable to stop herself.

10

"At the grave," Frankie continued. "Does she seem upset? She shouldn't really be upset; Vi's not really dead, she's probably having the time of her life gallivanting around with your mom—" But Vi really was gone, and Hailey really was alone, even if it was only pretend.

Sigmund half smiled. "But I shouldn't be able to tell, should I? If it's real or not. Not if she's doing her job."

Frankie frowned. He was right, of course; Sigmund usually was. "I just want this to be over. No one's seen Aspen or any of the rogue slayers since the night at the warehouse. Maybe they really are gone. And then we're sitting around Hailey-less and miserable for no reason.

"Well," she amended, "I guess *I* have no reason. You have that Sage demon reason that I wouldn't understand. Isn't that what you're always saying?"

"I shouldn't have said that. That you wouldn't understand. What I meant was that I didn't want to explain."

"Oh." Frankie waited and held very still. Of course, he didn't have to explain. But if she stayed quiet long enough, he might crack under the silence.

"I broke up with Hailey because it seemed inevitable," he said.

"Inevitable?" Frankie's brow furrowed.

"One day I'll be expected to pair with another demon. And it felt like Hailey and I were getting too serious."

"But you're in love with her. So what if it might not last forever? You guys were . . . so happy."

"Aren't you in love with Grimloch?" Sigmund countered.

"Grimloch is carrying a torch for my mortal enemy. And no. I'm not in love with him."

"Well, you're in something with him," Sigmund said, and Frankie laughed.

"In something? Pretty inarticulate for a Sage demon, Sig." But okay. She was in something with him. She just didn't know what. Crushing on Grim had been messed up enough when he was only mourning the loss of his slayer. Now that his slayer was alive and also rogue and the ultimate evil? And that was saying nothing of the whole mortal/immortal problem. There were so many obstacles. So many complications. But Jake and Sam had complications, and they still managed to make being together look easy . . .

Frankie shut her eyes. She didn't want to think about Grim. She didn't want to think about his voice, or how he hid the tips of his fangs when he smiled. She didn't want to think of the way his eyes flashed blue when he was intrigued, or how those fangs felt when they nipped her lower lip. "Dammit, focus!"

She opened her eyes, and Sigmund grinned.

"Did I lose you for a moment there, Frankie?"

"Sorry."

"I suppose Jake and I aren't the best when it comes to girl talk . . ."

"No, you're great." She put her hand on Sigmund's knee. "I love you guys. It just . . . none of this feels right without the Scoobies. All of the Scoobies."

Sigmund put his hand over hers. Then he slapped it bracingly. "Want to pack this in and go get some frozen yogurt?"

"Sure," Frankie said. "Right after we save Sam."

"What?"

"Sam." Frankie pointed through the windshield to the park below as Sam ran past the base of the green, sloping hill, screaming as he was tailed by three vampires. Jake wasn't far behind, and as he passed, he turned to the car and shouted.

"Frankie! Get your slayer butt down here!"

"Well." Frankie opened her door. "I guess that's the signal."

12

"It was so subtle; are you sure?" Sigmund asked, deadpan.

Frankie raced down the slope, parallel to the nearest pursuing vampire, and launched herself onto his back. The pair of them went down rolling, and ahead, Jake followed her lead, leaping upon the next vampire with a snarl. With Sam acting as bait there was no time for fancy footwork, so she pulled out a stake as she and the vampire rolled, eventually angling it up between them, toward his chest. When she rolled on top his yellow eyes opened in surprise, and then she fell through his dust to the ground.

Frankie sprang up and looked around for Jake.

The vampire he was grappling with was much larger than he was, which was saying something.

"Jake!"

"I'm okay!" He waved her away. "Sam. Go after Sam!"

She turned, eyes following Sam as he wheeled around the park, screaming loudly so they'd always know where he was. He was in trouble, but he was fast, and Frankie couldn't leave Jake. The full moon was weeks away; the time when even Whoops Werewolf Babies were at their weakest. The super-sized vampire grabbed Jake by the shoulder and leg and lifted him high overhead.

"Put him down!" Frankie shouted.

"Or what?" the vampire asked.

"Or he's going to tag me in and I'm going to break a folding chair across your back."

The vampire growled and threw, and Frankie collapsed under Jake's weight.

"I don't remember you being so heavy."

"I'm not this heavy," Jake said as they helped each other up. "It just feels that way because a vampire threw me at you."

"Fair enough," said Frankie. "Let's kill him."

They ran in together, but their offensive quickly became

13

defensive as they ducked the broad sweep of his arms. The vamp knocked Frankie's stake out of her hands so hard that splinters flew in several directions.

"He broke my stake!" said Frankie, aghast.

"You take that arm, I'll take this arm," Jake said, and together, they wrestled them behind the vampire's back.

"Now what?" Frankie asked as the vamp struggled.

"Do I have to think of everything?"

Frankie grimaced. The vampire was so tall; too bad there wasn't a high-speed ceiling fan around. She looked farther into the park, toward the playground.

"Jake," she ordered. "Get him to the swings!"

Still listening to Sam's distant screams, they maneuvered the enormous vampire past the monkey bars to the swings, where Frankie quickly wrapped one of the chains around his neck. Even with her slayer strength it took some doing, but eventually the chain cut through. The vampire's head was parted from his body and both dissolved to dust to mix with the playground sand.

Frankie and Jake looked at each other tiredly, hands on their knees. "You're right," Jake panted. "Playgrounds are dangerous at night."

"AAAH!"

They jumped up. Sam had circled the park and was heading back in their direction, with the last vampire quickly closing in.

"Go," Frankie shouted, but even as they took off she knew: They weren't going to make it in time.

The vampire chasing Sam raised his arms to attack. Then he made an *urk* sound and stumbled forward as an arrowhead appeared through the front of his chest. He looked down at it sticking out of his heart, then evaporated in a puff of dust. Sam slowed and came to a halt, and Frankie and Jake blinked as Sigmund righted himself behind the open door of the hybrid sedan with a bow in his hand.

"Sigmund!" Jake shouted as the half Sage demon came down from the parking lot. Jake gave Sam a quick kiss, then hugged Sigmund so hard he lifted him off the ground. "You've been practicing."

"I only dared the shot because you got yourselves stranded so far away." Sigmund adjusted his glasses on his nose, but Frankie thought he looked pleased.

"You okay, Sam?" She put an arm out to steady him. He was breathing hard, eyes bright.

"Nothing like almost having your throat ripped out to remind you you're alive." He slipped his hand into Jake's. "It's kind of exhilarating."

"Try not to get used to it," Frankie said wryly. Sam nodded, and Jake pulled him closer. They were cute, those two. Frankie had never really seen Jake up close in a relationship. She wondered if he'd been this sweet to all of his cheerleaders. She hoped so, but she couldn't imagine him growling and scruffing around with a cheerleader the way he did with Sam. Watching Jake be affectionate was kind of like watching a puppy love on a shoe.

"Hey, Frankie, you okay?"

She looked up. The boys were all staring at her. "Yeah. Sure, I'm okay."

"You missing Hailey?" Sam asked.

"We are, too," said Jake. "It's just not the same without her running in and clobbering vampires with disturbing intensity."

"How long are we going to wait for the Darkness, anyway?" asked Sam. "Before we decide they've just given up and slunk away on their disloyal, rogue slayer bellies?"

"I don't know." Frankie sighed. "It would be easier if Mom, Spike, and Oz had figured out how to get Buffy and the other slayers back. More slayers on the good side would give us some breathing room. I knew I should have Scythed the Darkness to death in the warehouse when I had the chance."

"But slayers don't kill non-demons," Jake noted as they walked back to the car. "So you'd have had to capture them instead."

"And then they'd be prisoners with no due process," added Sigmund. "And you don't want to be Frankie Guantanamo Bay."

"We could stash them in a hell dimension," Sam suggested. "Like they did to Buffy and the others."

"Or use black magic to wipe their memories and give them a do-over," said Jake, and Sam laughed.

"Nothing at all disturbing about that," said Frankie.

As they walked, Frankie listened and laughed along with them. But before she got into the car, she looked back at the park, hoping she'd see a flash of tan skin and ink-black hair between the tree trunks. She loved her Scooby boys. But she missed Hailey.

CHAPTER TWO

STRAIGHT OUT OF
THE WATCHER'S HANDBOOK

The next day, Hailey wasn't in class. Again. When the bell rang, Mr. Toivola caught Frankie before she could dart through the door.

"Is Hailey out sick again?" he asked.

"Yeah," Frankie lied. She didn't know what excuse Hailey had used, or if she had bothered to report her absence at all. "She's fighting off an end-of-winter bug." She gave Mr. Toivola her brightest, most Frankie-like smile, but he only pursed his lips. With his stylish fade and dark skin, he suddenly reminded her of an older version of Sigmund. But just when she was ready to buckle under his scrutiny, he looked away and handed her a stack of papers.

"Worksheets for extra credit. Her work is good, but if she misses more classes . . ."

"It's not her fault," Frankie blurted. "She's really sick sometimes, like, really sick. She says it's coming out both ends." She winced, then tried to nod knowingly. She could practically hear Hailey's voice in her ear: *Coming out both ends? Classy improv there, Rosenberg.*

"Well, thank you for that . . . unnecessary information. But I suppose if she gets a doctor's note, I can give her an incomplete and she can make it up over the summer."

"Thank you, Mr. Toivola!" Frankie squeaked. She spun on her heel before she said anything else that was terrible, hurrying to meet the other Scoobies in the library for one of their after-school Slay & D sessions. Days when Hailey didn't make it to school should have been easier. At least then they didn't have to pretend to shoot daggers at each other with their eyes. But really they were worse. Without Hailey there, people seemed far more eager to pull Frankie aside and ask her what was going on. Last week, Jasmine Finnegan had asked if she and Hailey weren't friends anymore because Frankie had started dating Sigmund.

"And she arrives," said Spike as Frankie pushed through the double doors and plopped down at their usual table with her arms around her books. "You're late, Mini Red."

"I was trying to keep Hailey from flunking out. Mr. Toivola is not happy about her lack of biology attendance."

"Same." Sam raised his hand. "I had to cover for her in calc."

"Someone ought to talk to her," said Sigmund. "Tell her she's carrying the illusion too far. She can look upset without costing herself a diploma."

"So far she's just costing herself a few months of summer," Frankie said optimistically. "But you're right. Something must be up. Maybe there's been an Aspen sighting."

"I've checked our drop spots for messages." Sigmund shrugged. "All empty."

"Did you check the laundry bin in the boys' locker room?" Jake asked.

"We agreed that wouldn't be a drop spot, Jake."

"Well, it should be."

"Maybe it's too soon for her to make contact," Frankie suggested. "If Aspen is back, she might be watching Hailey extra closely. Which would explain the dramatics and missed classes."

"I'll have a word the next time I see her," said Spike. "Principal Jacobs stopped by this morning and asked if I'd give her extra help after hours. Study sessions, or what have you. Seemed worried about the girl's home life."

"That was nice," Frankie said. "She's actually a really good principal. I hope she doesn't get eaten by a gigantic snake demon."

"Or by your uncle Xander," muttered Spike.

"Huh?"

"So what did you tell Principal Jacobs?" asked Sam. "About Hailey's home life?"

"That Hailey's sister-slash-guardian was out of town but she'd been placed in the capable care of the Rosenbergs. As long as she doesn't get suspicious enough to tail Hailey back to that fleabag motel"—Sigmund shot Frankie a knowing glance and mouthed "fleas"—"she should be none the wiser."

"When's the last time you saw Hailey, Jake?" Frankie turned to the werewolf and was surprised to see him lost in the pages of a book. "Jake? Are you reading? You don't read."

"I do too read." He flipped the cover to show her: *A Global History of Lycanthropes.* "Part of my training with Oz. He wants me to understand our werewolfy roots."

"And then he'll teach you to control your werewolfy sprouts?" Sam teased, running his knuckles along Jake's jaw.

"That's the plan. But it's taking forever." Jake went back to the book, turning it upside down and sideways. "You'd think there'd be a way to just—" He made mojo-like motions with his fingers. "Think you could find a spell for that?"

"I don't think you want me mixing magic with your wolfiness," said Frankie. "And what's with the hurry?"

"Just that I'm tired of being locked in a cage three nights a month and waking up with no memory. Three nights a month times twelve months a year times seventeen years is . . ." He narrowed his eyes. "Well, it's a lot of nights."

"But it's always been that way," said Frankie.

"Yeah, and that's another thing. I'm a super special werewolf baby, so shouldn't I get to advance faster?"

"I don't think that's how it works. Oz studied for years to get his level of control."

Jake shrugged dismissively. "Jordy did it in a few months in Weretopia."

"I don't think you can call what Jordy does 'control,'" Frankie said, eyebrow raised.

Jake gave her a glare, and Sam lightly slapped the table.

"Hey, hey," he said. "No real fighting."

"Right," Frankie said. She turned to her Watcher, who was outfitted in a very snappy number of three-piece tweed. "So, Uncle Spike. What's the what? What are we meeting for?"

"Training." Spike's brow, furrowed by Willow's glamour of aging, furrowed still further. "That's what we always meet for. Training, so you're ready when the Darkness re-rears their ugly, rogue slayer heads."

"So Sam and I can go to practice, then," said Jake, and he slammed his book shut. Following the recent drop in student athlete murders, the lacrosse season had been reinstated. Though it had resumed with less urgency, since after the games they'd had to forfeit they had even less a chance of making the playoffs than usual.

"Wait," said Spike. "Don't you want to see what I did?"

Frankie and the boy Scoobies watched as Spike strode to the four walls of the library and tugged down cloths that had been covering targets. Then he took another target and hung it from a hook suspended from the motion sculpture in the ceiling.

"It's straight from *The Watcher's Handbook*," he explained. "The slayer throws weaponry into each target while fending off attacks from an opponent. Each target must only be hit at the command of the Watcher. You see—"

As Spike explained, hands gesturing eagerly, a shadow outside the window caught Frankie's attention. And not just any shadow. A shadow shaped like the Hunter of Thrace. Grimloch was skulking around in the bushes outside of her high school. She stifled a snort, and when Grim peered in and saw he was caught, he gestured for her to come out.

"It's meant to hone concentration amid the distraction of battle," Spike was saying. "But in Frankie's case, she'll have to hit the targets with traditional weapons"—he unveiled a case of silver scalpels—"and with her mind."

"Very nice." Sigmund nodded. But Frankie was already gathering her things.

"Very, very nice," she said. "But can we do it tomorrow? I just remembered I have to get home. Mom wants me to clean out my closet . . . Donation and recycle time . . ."

"What?" Spike stepped toward her. "No, we can't do it tomorrow, I spent my whole lunch hour setting this up—"

"And it's great. And it'll be just as great tomorrow!"

"Frankie!"

"Spike!" Frankie felt her magic flare, and all at once the scalpels rose out of their velvet-lined case to float in the air.

"Duck," Jake said to Sam, pulling him behind some shelves.

Frankie rubbed her fingers together and felt the increasingly familiar click as her magic and her slayer strength linked like two fitting puzzle pieces. She threw her arms out.

Each scalpel sliced through the air and embedded itself into one of the targets. The one that embedded in the hanging target hit so hard that it spun around in a loop.

Spike blinked as Frankie jumped and clapped her hands. "Did you guys see that?" she asked as Jake and Sam emerged from the stacks, speechless.

"That was excellent," said Sigmund.

"But it wasn't the point," Spike objected.

"Bye, Uncle Spike!" Frankie waved as she left the library. "See you tomorrow! When we'll totally do this again!"

$$) \,) \, \bigcirc \, (\, ($$

Frankie was careful to keep out of Spike's line of sight as she made her way through the bushes. She could see him in there, walking dejectedly from target to target, pulling the scalpels out and putting them back in their box. She felt bad. He'd put a lot of thought into that. And when it came to Watching, Spike was vehemently anti-establishment, so if he was looking in *The Watcher's Handbook*, it meant he was pulling out all the stops to prepare her to face the Darkness.

Frankie would just have to make it up to him. With fresh blood and cookies. Or freshly baked blood cookies. No, that was disgusting.

"Grim!" she hissed. "Grimloch!"

She made her way farther into the shrubbery, and even though she knew he was there, she jumped a little when he stepped out from behind the far corner of the building. She put her hands on her hips to cover her surprise. "What's up? Why are you here?"

"I caught wind of a demon," he said, walking closer. "And trailed it here."

"What kind of demon? Do I need to go back and grab a sword, or Mr. Stabby—"

Grimloch looked down and smiled. Frankie narrowed her eyes.

"So there is no demon."

"Only the one standing in front of you."

"Jake was right. You are a stalker."

Grimloch chuckled. "It's in my nature."

"Well, you should add self-preservation to your nature." Frankie grabbed him by the sleeve and tugged him away toward the nearest copse of trees. "You can't just go sneaking around a school. You're going to get yourself arrested." She led him through the trees to emerge on the shaded sidewalk that led to downtown New Sunnydale. Where he still stood out, but not in a way that screamed Stranger Danger.

"So what *were* you doing there?" she asked. "Outside my school library, where you know I do my slayer training?"

"I was looking for you. I missed you, Frankie."

"You can see me whenever you want."

"If I have information to share. About a demon, or the Darkness."

"I said 'whenever you want.'"

"It doesn't feel that way."

"Well, how should it feel?" She stopped and turned to face him. Her hands rose to her hips again, but she let them drop. She wasn't trying to start an argument. It seemed like that's all they did since the fight with Aspen and the Darkness, since she'd found out that Aspen wasn't only the leader of the rogue slayers who murdered Faith and so many others, and who imprisoned Buffy and the survivors in some kind of torturous hell dimension—she was also the slayer that Grimloch loved. It really made one question his taste.

"We're allies," Grimloch said.

"Are we? You still don't know whose side you're on."

"It's not that easy."

"It seems to me it's a choice between sunshine and sustainable living"—she pointed to herself—"and the ultimate evil!"

"Aspen is not the ultimate evil. She's misguided. She's suffered. She can change—"

"Yeah. If we get Buffy back and she decides to put her in slayer rehab—"

"And I do love her," Grimloch said loudly, and Frankie shut her mouth. "I will always love her. But not in the way that I once did."

"What does that mean?"

"It means," he said, again in a normal speaking voice, "I believe she can be forgiven. But it won't take back what she did, or that there are consequences. And one of those consequences is the loss of my heart."

Frankie pressed her lips together. "Pretty big consequence. I almost feel bad for her. Are you sure? Are you okay?" She tugged on the edge of his sleeve. "Are you sure you're okay?"

"I will be."

They resumed walking, and Frankie fought the urge to slip her hand into the crook of his arm. She also fought the urge to cheer him up by doing something bouncy and ridiculous. She could just be quiet and be there. That was enough.

For a few minutes, at least.

"So you missed me, huh?" she asked, and he smiled, that little smile that hid his fangs. "What did you miss the most? The bubbly optimism with which I dispatch vampires? The way I seem to pop right back up when I get thrown into a headstone, like one of those inflatable balloon guys in front of car dealerships?"

"You do make me laugh," Grimloch replied. "But you also make me feel . . . hopeful."

Hopeful. That was nice.

"And young."

"Young?" Frankie shoved him. "Gross, why don't you go buy a sports car or bleach highlights into your hair. *Young.*" She made a face, and Grimloch laughed.

"That's not what I meant. It's hard to explain. It's not that you make me feel young. You make me feel . . . like I'm here. Like I could belong in this time."

Frankie fell back into step beside him. "That's not a terrible answer."

They walked in silence for a few moments before Grimloch spoke again.

"Frankie, how old do I seem to you?"

"Um . . ." She looked up at him. Was there a number to describe agelessly gorgeous? "Well, you look like you're twenty. But you dress like you're thirty." She tugged the edge of his button-down shirt's sleeve again, and this time let her fingers slide into the curve of his elbow. "But you *seem* . . ." She sighed. "About five hundred."

"Five hundred." He nodded. "Five hundred is practically a pup."

Frankie laughed. She rested her head against his shoulder and felt a thrill rise into her chest as he covered her hand with his own. "Uh-oh," she whispered. "This is going to get complicated. Again."

CHAPTER THREE
EARTH TO BUFFY

With a deep and cleansing breath, Willow eased herself down onto the pillows. There were at least ten, embroidered and fringed, velour and sateen, plus one of each of hers and Frankie's bed pillows. Almost every pillow in the house, which she had brought onto their back patio and arranged into a nest. A Willow nest of creams and rusty oranges, browns and deep greens, comfy enough to sit in and meditate for as long as she had to. Hours, maybe. Until dawn.

She looked up at the stars beyond the patio. She'd been trying to contact Buffy, sending her mind out into the night, and into the day, and into her lunch hour, when she had the energy. Her consciousness skipped and rolled through every metaphysical layer, coolly and casually seeking out the shy edges of dimensions and searching for any trace of Buffy inside them. But she'd had no luck. No luck at all, despite having been plugged directly into the *right* dimension during the botched window spell with the Scythe. She had heard Buffy's voice. They'd heard each other. But now, no matter how loudly Willow called, Buffy didn't answer.

It was starting to piss her off.

She settled into the pillow nest and cleared her mind, listening to the low chirp and hum of early springtime insects. Perhaps she could do a spell? For extra luck.

No. She had to focus. These things couldn't be rushed.

Except these things *had* to be rushed. Buffy and the last of the surviving slayers were imprisoned in a hell dimension. Maybe with Andrew. And the only people who knew which dimension they were in were from an evil organization that had tried to kill them. Sure, the Darkness said the explosion was an accident, but who believed that? And sure, Aspen insisted they would let Buffy and the others go as soon as their reckless plans were complete, but who believed that either?

"Quiet, brain," Willow whispered.

She sat with legs crossed, her hands resting softly on the knees of her most comfortable pants. She'd left her hair loose to keep any elastics or bobby pins from pinching and poking her scalp and was surrounded by the gentle scent of her lemon trees. She'd also made herself a soothing cup of tea to sip from. Only now she kind of had to pee.

With a soft push, Willow sent her consciousness forth on invisible wings, gone in a flash, much farther from Sunnydale than her physical body had ever been. Somewhere out there was Buffy Summers. Her best friend.

Of course, also somewhere out there was her sixteen-year-old daughter, probably slaying something that was trying to kill her.

Willow's consciousness jerked back toward home.

No. Focus. Find Buffy.

But finding Buffy was hard. Finding Frankie was easy. She would have even had an easier time finding Sarafina and Vi, who were who knows where in hiding, and probably fighting something, too, if Willow knew Sarafina DeWitt.

Willow's eyes opened, her consciousness once again firmly plopped into the nest of varied pillows.

"I just wish you were here," she said to the sky. "All the things that have happened, with Frankie, and with Sarafina . . . you're the one I want to tell most."

"Hey, Red! You around?"

Willow raised an eyebrow toward the cosmos. "Instead I have Spike." She heaved herself off the pillows and went inside to find the vampire in the kitchen, unloading paper sacks of takeout.

"There you are." He reached into the sack and pulled out pale brown to-go containers. "Stopped by the diner. Got some burgers and things, and a couple of those blooming onions."

She looked at the food and walked to the refrigerator to grab some O negative. "You want a blood bag to dip your fries in?"

"Obviously." He unloaded more food as she set up the double boiler and turned on the stove.

"Aren't you supposed to be training with Frankie at the library?" Willow asked.

Spike snorted. "If she had any interest in training. That girl gets more distracted every bleeding day." He crushed a napkin in his fist. Whatever had happened, he seemed pretty indignant about it. Almost hurt. He plopped a white cup with a red straw onto the countertop. "And I got milkshakes."

"Spike? Are you okay?"

"I'm fine," he snapped. He craned his head into the hall and peered toward the patio and the nest of pillows. "What's that there?"

"That's nothing." Willow plopped down on a stool, opened a container, and took a big bite of red meat. Spike gave her a look, but she still ate burgers sometimes. Like when Frankie wasn't around or when she couldn't find her best friend no matter how many dimensions she combed through. "It's a big, tangly, stupid ball of nothing."

"Hey, don't cook my blood." Spike went to the stove and turned off the burner, then poured his warmed blood into a tall, clear glass. She wished he'd used a mug. She'd been around vampires most of her life, but she still didn't enjoy watching them eat. The sight of him wiping off his blood mustache was gross enough. "You trying to reach out to Buffy again?"

"Again. And again, with absolutely no progress. I need more magic."

"Don't you have . . ." He turned to look at her. "*All* the magic? You've been getting stronger and stronger since popping out of witchcraft retirement." He returned to the stool beside her and sat down to eat.

"I guess," she said. "But Frankie destroyed the Scythe because she thought I could find the surviving slayers without it." Willow frowned. "What if she was wrong?"

"She hasn't been wrong so far. She was right about the Amulet of Junjari, right about Aspen, right about the Countess—even right about the Loomer of Thrace."

"Don't you mean the Hunter? And can't you just call him Grimloch?"

"No, and no." Spike dipped a fry into his blood cup. "The point is, I trust Frankie—when she's not flitting about shirking her training duties—and she trusts you. With reason."

Willow watched Spike eat his fries, trying to pretend the red stains were ketchup. He'd had his soul for a long time—decades—but it was still a little strange to hear him say things that were kind. Even with a soul, Spike could be kind of a deviant. So when he was kind, she should reward the behavior.

"Thanks, Spike." Willow leaned forward to pull him into a hug, at the precise moment that he stood up to get something from the kitchen. So instead of her arms wrapping around his shoulders, they landed farther south, and her hand bumped dangerously close to—

"Buffy!"

Spike jumped back. But that had been Buffy. Just for an instant, when Willow had touched Spike, she felt a ping, like a wavelength stretching between their minds.

She pointed at his pants. "What was that?"

"That's exactly what you'd expect to find," the vampire said, and squared his shoulders. "My pants tend to have that effect on people."

"It's not your pants." She raised her brow. "It's what's in them."

"Well, yeah—"

Willow grabbed for his pants, searching for more of what she'd just felt.

"Red! Hey!"

Her fingers dug into his pockets. There it was again. *Buffy.*

Willow stood, and Spike backed away, nearly knocking over his chair.

"What's in your pants?" she demanded.

The vampire blanched. "It's Buffy's cross."

Buffy's cross. The one engraved with her mother's name, Joyce, on the back. The one that had fallen through the window to the prison dimension when the Scythe spell had gone kablooey.

"You keep it in your pocket? Aren't you afraid it's going to accidentally burn your . . . downstairs area?"

Spike made a face. He stuck his hand into his pocket and pulled out the cross, carefully contained in a piece of cloth. "I have it double wrapped."

She took it from him and folded back the cloth. Even hovering an inch above its surface, the skin of her hand began to tingle. She studied the delicate engraved letters.

A little bit of help here, Joyce, she thought.

Willow laid her palm flat over the cross. Her head jerked back.

"Red?" Spike asked.

Impressions came to her in a rush. She heard Buffy's voice in her ears, the echoes of past conversations. "It's a sham, but it's a sham with yams. It's a yam sham."

"If the apocalypse comes, beep me," Willow repeated. Flashes of her friend rose behind her eyelids: The satin red of Buffy's homecoming dress. A triumphant smile. A sheepish *oops.* The stance she took when she drew her stake.

Buffy was everywhere on that cross.

"We are so stupid!" Willow exclaimed. She held the cross up, right under Spike's nose, and he jerked away from it without its protective cloth overlay. "This is Buffy's and she held it and it was in the other dimension!"

"So?" the vampire asked.

"So what do you want, a map? Come on!" Willow bolted for the patio and kicked through her carefully made nest of pillows. She waved her hand and lit four pillar candles on the railing. But candles weren't right. She needed open air. She needed the night and stars.

Willow raced into the yard and brought the candles floating with her, lit and circling her in an increasingly fast orbit.

"Can you tell me what you're doing?" Spike asked, ducking under the magically revolving flames.

"No time."

"But you're the one making the time!" He eyed the candles, moving so fast now that they had become one bright blur, trapping them in the center of the grass. Overhead, the sky was clear and dotted with stars, and to Willow they looked like any number of possibilities. She opened her palm and sent her consciousness into the silver cross. It began to hover in the air.

The cross spun slowly, and Willow whispered, soothing it. Then she blew it wide open. Figuratively speaking.

As they watched, the cross took on a glow, soft and silver at first, then growing in intensity until it rivaled the light of the sun. Spike raised his hand to shield his eyes. Willow reached out and grabbed it.

"Buffy?"

She waited. They both waited, interminable seconds.

"Willow?"

Willow's heart leapt. Relief hit her so hard at the sound of that voice—it felt like her rib cage would cave in on itself.

"Buffy, oh my god," she breathed. "We've been looking and looking for you. Are you okay? Is everyone okay?"

"We're okay. We were getting nervous. We haven't seen anyone in days. Where are you? I can't see you, I can just . . . hear you."

"We're here! I mean, we're at the house in Sunnydale. We're trying to get you back, we just . . . don't know which dimension the Darkness imprisoned you in. Do you know?"

"Well . . ." Buffy's voice trailed off, and Willow had the impression she was talking to someone else. "Right, right, but when Aspen came through she came through that door, and that door only. So maybe it's about that door?"

"What door?" Willow asked. "Buffy, I can't hear anyone else. Just you."

"So she can't hear me?" Spike asked, and Willow couldn't tell whether he was relieved or disappointed.

"Sorry, Will," said Buffy. "There are a lot of us here, and ALL OF US ARE TALKING."

"Wait, how many of you? Who's with you?"

"Rona and Chao-Ahn, Flora, Dominique . . . okay, okay. Kennedy says hi."

"Uh, hi," Willow said, and smiled.

"She also says get us out of here, Goddess. A sentiment that I actually second. This place is not welcoming. And we're locked in a building. Cages, that feel underground. Like an old prison, but the walls are made of dirt and leak slime. Also, Aspen was evil, but she did occasionally feed us. Now that she's gone we've got water, but not much else."

"Don't worry, we're on it. We're going to get you out of there."

"But what is Aspen doing? Are you safe?"

Willow looked at Spike, who sucked his cheeks in proudly. "Frankie kicked her ass and sent her packing."

"Frankie? Wait, your Frankie? Little, eco-witch, A-plus Frankie?"

"She's a slayer, Buffy."

Willow waited. She wasn't sure how Buffy would feel about that.

"Then I need to get home, to show her the ropes."

Willow grinned. "And Spike's her Watcher."

"Oh jeez," Buffy groaned. "Now I really need to get home."

"Hey," said Spike.

"Where's Giles? Is he safe?"

"He's safe," Willow replied. "Xander and Dawn have been in contact with him."

"Xander and Dawn." Buffy said, and Willow heard her exhale. "What about everyone else? Aspen said they were all dead, but that can't be—"

Willow looked at Spike. Her silence answered for her.

"What about Faith?" Buffy asked, and Willow shook her head before remembering Buffy couldn't see her.

"No," she said softly.

Buffy paused. When she spoke again her voice was low and angry.

"You have to get us out of here, Willow."

"It won't be long now, I promise."

"Good. Because it feels like we've been here for weeks."

Willow glanced at Spike, wondering if she should tell them they'd actually been missing for most of a year. He shook his head.

"And if we start to starve, we're going to eat Andrew."

"Buffy—" Willow stopped as bright pain exploded in her head. She felt the cross drop from her hand and faintly heard Spike shout, and then there was darkness, and nothing.

CHAPTER FOUR

THE WOLF IS, LIKE, A STATE OF MIND, MAN

J ake sat quietly at the kitchen table while Oz messed around in the kitchen, brewing a blend of herbal tea that smelled like lawn clippings and rotten leaves.

"You want me to drink that?" His nostrils flared. The smell was awful. So bad he wanted to run out of the room. But Oz didn't even seem bothered by it. Actually, he seemed to like it. He leaned over and took a big whiff of steam.

"It's not that bad," said Oz.

"Not that bad?" Jake sniffed again as Oz added another ingredient. "What is that now, some kind of mushroom?"

"Okay, it is that bad." Oz took the pot off the stove and poured the tea into a Sunnydale Razorbacks mug. He slid it onto the table in front of Jake. "But you get used to it."

Jake peered down into the cup, the contents of which resembled a tiny, dirty pond. "Could we at least strain it?"

"Eventually. For now, you need to drink the herbs for potency." Oz sat down across from him and lit a large, cream-colored candle as Jake reached for the cup. His palms were wrapped in prayer beads, and they clinked against the sides of the ceramic mug.

"Bottoms up," he said, and took a drink. Then he took another. And another, until the cup was empty except for a nasty little trail of wet green and brown flakes.

"Does it still work if I throw it all up?"

Oz snorted. "No."

Jake sat back. Now came the truly hard part: meditation. So much meditation. Letting his mind go slack. Shouldn't have been that hard, considering his mind's rather natural slackness.

"Am I supposed to feel anything?"

"Do you feel something?"

"I don't know. Kind of jittery. And I still kind of want to yak."

"You're fine. Just . . . give it some time."

Give it some time. That was Oz's only motto these days. He should have it painted on the side of the van. But Jake tried again. Breathed in. Breathed out. Stared at the candle. Looked at the tiny little flame until it went all blurry.

"Hey, Oz, don't you want any tea?" When he spoke, Oz startled, and Jake felt a surge of jealousy for how easily his uncle could slip into the meditative state.

"I don't need it anymore."

"Well, how long will I need it? How long did you have to drink this stuff before you could control your wolf?"

"It's different for everyone." Oz closed his eyes again. "You've only been taking the tea for a week. But by the time the full moon comes, don't be surprised if you have moments of lucidity in your wolf form."

All of the relaxation snapped out of Jake's body. "Like I'll be aware? As the wolf?"

"It'll be fleeting. But it can be pretty overwhelming. Hence the meditation." Meditation. And after the meditation there were chants. Long, rumbling, melodic chants that made Jake feel like a complete bozo.

"How long was it before you were, you know, *you* all the time?"

"Years."

"Years?" He knew how Oz's process worked. First, the wolf receded, like it had been placed on a leash, and for the first time in his life, Jake would see the full moon, walk around underneath its bright, silvery glow, all Jake-shaped. Then, slowly—apparently very slowly—the wolf consciousness integrated, until they were one in the same. Jake and wolf. Wolf and Jake. Subconscious, meet conscious; id, meet super ego. Or so Oz said.

"But it could be different for me, right?" Jake asked. "Since I was born this way?"

Oz looked at Jake calmly, and Jake tried to be quiet. He knew he was being a pain.

Oz's phone buzzed from the kitchen counter.

"That's an X against you, bro," said Jake as his uncle went to answer it. "Meditation rule number one is to put our phones on silent."

"I set it to do not disturb, so Willow can call twice and get through if it's an emergency." Oz squinted at the screen and picked up. "Spike? Everything—" He paused. "Okay, slow down. Does she need an ambulance?"

"Ambulance?" Jake got up. "Is it Frankie?"

"Okay, we're on our way." Oz hung up and grabbed the keys to the van. "Come on."

"Oz! Is it Frankie?"

"No," his uncle replied as he headed for the door. "It's Willow."

☽ ☽ ○ ☾ ☾

By the time Frankie and Grim turned lazily up the street that led into New Sunnydale Heights, the sun had long since gone down. They'd taken a leisurely detour through the cemetery but found no demons, and most new vampires preferred to rise a little later. Later and later, actually, as the days turned longer heading into summer. Soon even the early risers wouldn't claw their way out until midnight.

"Do vampires hate summer?" Frankie asked. "I mean, the nights get so much shorter. There's way less time for carousing and ripping throats out." She shrugged. "I never thought of that before."

Grimloch smiled. "Would you . . . come to the tent tomorrow?"

"The tent?" Frankie looked up at him innocently. "For what?"

"Training," Grim replied, and cleared his throat. "Obviously, training."

"Right. Obviously." There was no reason to turn down free training. And if it was only training, there was no reason to tell anyone about it either. "Sure. I can come tomorrow."

"Good. Then I'll see you tomorrow." He slipped out of her grasp and walked backward a few steps before turning to eventually melt into the trees.

"He's so good at that," Frankie murmured as she swung toward home. Just once, she'd like to see him trip on a root.

She was almost to her house when she heard a screech of tires and looked up to see Oz's van careening into the driveway. Surprised, she stopped short, until Oz and Jake piled out and Jake saw her and shouted, "Frankie! It's your mom! Come on!"

"Mom?" She raced across the grass, cutting through lawns and jumping over Mr. Briggs's shrubs to meet Jake on their front walk. "What do you mean it's my mom? What happened?"

But before he could reply, Spike burst out onto the porch.

"Frankie! Jake! Get your backsides inna kitch!"

38

"Were those words?" Jake asked as they hurried inside.

When she burst through the door, Frankie found Willow lying on the kitchen floor. Oz knelt beside her head as Spike paced back and forth.

"We were in the backyard," the vampire said. "She was doing a spell, and then she just went down. I moved her in here, but I didn't know—" He ran his hands over his platinum hair, then leaned down to shout into Willow's face. "Red! Come on, Red, wake up!"

"Mom!" Frankie pushed gently in next to her mom in front of Jake.

"She's still breathing," Spike said quietly. "And her nose only bled that little bit."

That little bit was a drying rivulet running from her left nostril down into her hair.

"What kind of a spell was it?" Frankie asked.

Oz got up and headed for the open back door. "Was there a spellbook?"

"Hold up," Jake cried. "She's coming around!"

Willow's eyelids fluttered open, and Frankie breathed a sigh of relief.

"Frankie?"

"I'm here, Mom."

Willow struggled to sit up.

"I'll get a pillow," Jake said and dashed to the living room. "Where are all the pillows?"

"I made a nest," Willow muttered. "It's okay, Jakey. I'm . . ." She sat up and pressed her palm to her forehead. "Ow."

"Mom," Frankie said sternly. "What were you doing? Why were you casting big spells with no one here?"

"Hey," said Spike. "I was here."

"I say again," Frankie said, eyeing her Watcher, but teasingly.

39

"I thought I could do it," Willow replied. "I guess I got a little overexcited. Is there any tea?"

"I'm on it." Jake got up and bounded to the stove, while Frankie and Oz helped Willow into one of the dining room chairs. Frankie fetched a wet cloth and used it to wipe the blood from Willow's nose and cheek.

"Want to tell me what you were up to?" Frankie asked after the tea was ready and her mom's hands were wrapped around a nice hot mug.

"Not really," Willow teased. Then she looked down guiltily. "I was trying to contact your aunt Buffy."

"Mom." Frankie was about to launch into a full-on lecture when she noticed the smile creeping across her mother's face.

"And it worked."

Frankie looked at Jake. "It worked? What do you mean 'it worked'?" Willow looked at Spike, so Frankie did, too. The vampire reached into his pocket and pulled something out, then partially unwrapped it. Buffy's cross. The one she dropped through the portal that opened during the Scythe spell.

"I heard her. I talked to her. She's *okay.*"

Frankie smiled. Buffy was okay. And they'd reached her. They could find the slayers. They could really find them.

Willow reached for the cross, and Spike quickly pulled it away.

"Not a chance, Red."

"But I want them to hear her. I want them to know—and you—that it wasn't just in my imagination."

"This spell just knocked you out cold," said Oz. "Maybe you should give it a few days."

"I can do it." Willow looked at them stubbornly. "It was just a little nosebleed."

"And maybe a little concussion when you hit the ground," said Spike. "And a little stroke."

"I can do it." Willow reached for Frankie's hand. "If Frankie helps me."

Frankie swallowed as every eye in the room settled upon her. Talking to Buffy. Being able to hear Buffy's voice? She wanted that more than anything. But this spell had just knocked down her mother, who was known the world over as the Big Bad Witch. She looked at the silver cross lying in Spike's open palm.

"Okay, let's try it."

Frankie shook out first one hand and then the other as Spike, Oz, and Jake flocked to the other chairs around the table. She and Willow sat at the head, with Buffy's silver cross resting between them on the wood, the faint etching of *JOYCE* like a whisper of encouragement.

Willow picked up the cross and took a deep breath.

"If you both hit the floor," Jake said with his phone in hand, "I'm calling an ambulance."

"Let's make the connection." Willow held out her hand, and Frankie took it. Instantly she felt the rush of her mom's superior magic like an electric shock. The sensation seemed slightly unhinged, and Frankie suddenly felt full of static electricity. A coppery taste rose to the back of her tongue. "Send it back," Willow whispered.

Frankie gave her magic a small push. It crept out to meet the current of her mom's, and then she felt a great whoosh, like being swept out to sea.

"There we go," Willow said as Frankie gritted her teeth. "Hold on."

"Holding," said Frankie, as her mom closed her fist around the cross.

"Buffy?"

Frankie waited.

"Is it not going to work this time?" Jake whispered. "That is so unfair."

But Willow didn't seem discouraged. She smiled like she was listening to something none of them could hear.

"What," she said, clearly not to them. "Like you have so many other things to do in a hell dimension?"

Frankie leaned forward. "Mom, is she there? Is she talking? We can't hear her!"

Willow grimaced slightly and tightened her grip on Frankie; Frankie felt more of her magic leave in a wave. "Okay. Buffy, can you say something else?"

"Hi, guys."

"Oh my god!" Frankie squealed.

"This is one, Buffy Summers, broadcasting from our lovely neighborhood prison dimension. The weather inside is currently a balmy eighty degrees with a northwest wind coming through Andrew's armpits. We would very much like to come home now, please."

"Holy shit," Jake breathed, and he and Oz grinned at each other. Spike crossed his arms and looked down, listening.

"Buffy!" Frankie exclaimed.

"Frankie?"

"It's me!" She was a little short of breath. The spell stretched across dimensions, far bigger than any spell Frankie had ever cast, even when she destroyed the ancient slayer Scythe.

"I heard you have some news. Some, you're a slayer now, news."

Buffy knew she was a slayer. "Is it . . . is that okay?"

Buffy paused.

"It's more than okay. It's amazing. I can't wait to get back there and see how you throw a punch."

Frankie grinned.

"Terribly," Jake said, leaning in and grabbing the cross like a microphone. "She throws them terribly."

"Shut up, Jake," Frankie said, shoving him. There were a million other things to say, a thousand other questions, but they flew right out of her mind. "Sorry, that was Jake. Uncle Spike's here, too—" She gestured for Spike to come closer, but he hung his head and backed away. "Oh. He says next time, I guess—"

"Bollocks." Spike strode forward and grasped Willow's fist. "Slayer," he said. "You hanging in there?"

"We're hanging. This isn't my first time being trapped in a hell dimension, you know."

Frankie started to say more, but the magic was waning. She felt the spell begin to slide through her fingers, and she and her mom had both started to pant.

"I think we have to go now," she said. "But we're going to get you out, okay? Right now we just have to . . . try not to have strokes."

"Strokes?"

"Bye, Buffy! Bye, slayers!" Frankie nodded to her mom. "Nice and slow. On three." She counted down with their breaths, and Willow loosened her hold on the cross. Even with the shock spread between them, Frankie still felt the moment when the connection broke like someone had set of an air horn right beside both of her ears.

"Wow, that hurt," she said, and her words sounded like talking underwater. She opened her eyes and saw Jake's mouth moving with no sound coming out. Then the ringing started, fierce and fast.

"Frankie! Are you okay?"

"Yeah, yeah." She blinked. The pain and ringing had already begun to fade. "Mom?"

"Not even a little blood," Willow declared, touching her nose. She looked down at her fingertip. "Well, maybe a little blood." Frankie handed her the damp cloth.

"So what does this mean?" Frankie asked, looking at her mom and Spike.

"They don't know where they are," he said. "So we just have to keep searching."

"But now there's a way to contact them at least, if we need them to, I don't know, do something on their end." Jake shrugged.

"Searching for Buffy, tracking the Darkness . . ." Frankie sighed. "It's a lot. And right after midterms."

Willow put her hand on Frankie's. "You let me worry about this."

"Mom?"

"I can find Buffy. I know I can. You have enough to worry about."

Frankie looked at her Watcher. She did, honestly. And her mom was by far the most qualified to do the searching. "If you're sure?"

"Sure I'm sure. And I'll loop you back in the minute I find something."

CHAPTER FIVE

ROACHES AND RENT CONTROL

There was a cockroach on the edge of the sink. Hailey noticed it when she was taking her makeup off. One minute the sink was its usual rusty, roach-free self, and then one swipe of makeup remover pad later, there it was. A roach.

Hailey stared at it as she made one more pass with the remover pad, the surface pitch-black after sponging away her mascara and eyeliner and glittery silver shadow. She glanced up, in case more roaches were waiting to parachute down from the ceiling, but it appeared to be a loner, like her.

It was a polite sort of roach. It stayed on the far side of the soap dish and didn't move much, unless you counted its two little feelers, which wiggled back and forth. If it had been a rude roach and scurried across her makeup brushes, it would've found itself promptly squished.

"Do you need some eyeliner?" she asked it, and it waggled its thin antennae. She sighed. She preferred her friends have fewer legs. But here in the motel, she was willing to make exceptions. "I will call you Sassafras. And in return for this name, you will stay out of my mini fridge and not give me any horrible diseases."

The roach seemed amenable and raised one small foot. Not that Hailey was going to shake on it.

She jumped when a knock sounded at the door. When she looked back at the sink, Sassafras had scurried back to wherever she'd come from.

"So you're not a guard roach."

Hailey went to the door. On her way past her dresser, she grabbed a stake, unsure who she was going to see. The hotel-owner-slash-manager, with his hand out for next month's rent. Or a friend of the vampire she'd slayed in the alley.

Hailey swung the door open.

The leader of the Darkness leaned against the door frame holding a pizza box.

"I've got double cheese and all the meats," Aspen said, opening and closing the box like a mouth as if the pizza was speaking for itself. She slid past Hailey without waiting for an invitation. That was slayer protocol, she'd said. Waiting for invitations was for vamps.

However, not waiting was kind of pushy.

Aspen hopped onto the bed. She tried to bounce a little, but like everything else in the motel the springs were totally shot. And the mattress had a smell that Hailey feared would stick to her forever if she stayed much longer.

"Come on. Get it while it's hot."

Hailey took a slice. It was from Giovanni's, definitely the best place to get pizza in New Sunnydale. Last November, Giovanni's had been their Thanksgiving dinner: the Thanksgiving Special, a pizza topped with stuffing, cranberry sauce, mashed potatoes, and gravy, modified for Frankie with slices of tofu-turkey.

46

"I can't believe there's actually a decent pizza place in this town." Aspen took a bite and her eyes rolled back.

"Sunnydale's not so bad. There are lots of good restaurants here."

"You're right. And it's not like I haven't been to worse places. At that last Slayerfest that Andrew planned, everything on the menu had pine nuts in it." Aspen smiled a little, but it faded. "I liked Andrew, you know. He wasn't everyone's cup of tea, but I thought he was all right. I wish he hadn't . . ." Aspen set down her slice as Hailey carefully kept chewing. Aspen always said she never meant for things to go as far as they did. That she never meant for slayers to die, that she wished none of it had ever happened. Sometimes Hailey almost believed her. "But at least he's alive," Aspen said, brightening. "He's in the prison dimension, and pissed as hell. But he'll get over it after we let them out." She took a big bite of sausage and cheese.

"You really think they'll get over it?" Hailey asked.

"Eventually. I mean, I can hope, can't I?"

"Your actions caused the deaths of their friends. Whether you meant for that to happen or not, that's not something you just forgive."

"Hey." Aspen's brow knit. "I know, okay? I didn't mean to imply that you were going to be able to forgive Frankie."

"Good." Hailey grabbed another slice of pizza and got up off the bed, turning away so she would seem mad, and also to stuff half of her pizza into her face. She was so hungry. There were a ton of unforeseen consequences to this double agenting thing. Isolation and mortal danger cozying up to a psychopath, sure. But also, no access to Jake's weekly brunches.

"Why don't you just let them go now?" Hailey asked.

"I can't. Not until we're finished. Your misguided baby slayer friend—"

"Ex-friend."

"Sorry. *Ex*-friend Frankie may have destroyed the Scythe, but there has to be another way to give up our powers. It's what they're all hoping for," Aspen said softly, meaning the other members of the Darkness, the rogue slayers she led. "They're depending on me to give them their lives back. And we're this close." She reached in between the buttons of her blouse and fished out a dark green gemstone embedded in a fat gold setting. The Amulet of Junjari, which according to Sigmund's research could harness the power of an army. In this case, a slayer army. "The amulet can draw our slayer powers out. All we need is a door to shove it through. And lock the door behind, if I have anything to say about it."

"And after that, you'll let them go?"

"Sure." Aspen picked off a piece of pepperoni and popped it into her mouth. "They'll be angry, but we won't be slayers anymore, and while Buffy Summers can't be trusted to do anything else, I know she won't break her rules to come after us. We'll be safe. We'll be free."

And all it cost was the lives of dozens of young women.

"Well, you'd better hurry up," Hailey said, nodding to the amulet. "Because that thing is gaudy as hell."

Aspen laughed and let it drop, hidden again beneath her shirt. "I know, right? But I'm starting to warm up to it. It's vintage."

☽ ☽ ○ ☾ ☾

It had taken almost three weeks for the leader of the Darkness to take the bait. Three long weeks of moping around and fake mourning until Hailey's face hurt from the fake sobs. She'd put on the last twenty minutes of *Marley & Me* so she could leave her motel room coated in fresh tears so many times she'd become desensitized. If

Aspen had waited much longer, she'd have had to resort to watching the part in *Inside Out* when Bing Bong dies.

But just when she was ready to give up, the act paid off. She'd been visiting Vi's grave—her fake grave, only it wasn't entirely fake because there really was a dead mirror-twin Vi down there under the dirt—when the toes of Aspen's stylish black boots appeared on the grass beside her.

She'd apologized about Vi. She'd actually wept. And the whole time she was lamenting Hailey's fallen sister, saying how she wished she hadn't changed sides at the end, how she wished Vi had never been involved at all, Hailey fought to keep herself from trembling. Plotting to be a spy was one thing. Being alone with Aspen and keeping up the lie was another. Aspen was a slayer, and a rogue one. She killed demons as easy as she ate breakfast, and then one day she decided to try killing people and discovered that wasn't so bad either.

Before they'd said their goodbyes, the Scoobies had planned out all sorts of creative ways to communicate the intel that Hailey would learn. Hand signals. Discreet drop locations for notes. But with Aspen actually there, it all seemed ridiculous.

Now, Hailey jumped at the sound of a snapped twig beneath Aspen's foot. They'd left the motel to patrol, just a short one, Aspen said, to burn off the pizza, even though she had a slayer metabolism and actually should have eaten the whole thing by herself. Aspen just loved to patrol. She loved to slay. When she had her hands around a demon's neck, a light came into her eyes. If Hailey occasionally had doubts about Aspen's true motives—maybe she really didn't mean to hurt the slayers, maybe she did want to give her powers back—seeing that look in her eyes put them to rest.

But even though Aspen enjoyed the kill, she never lost control with demons. Only with people. Once, during a slay, Aspen had grabbed Hailey's wrist to show her a move. Hailey'd spent the night in the motel icing a purple bruise in the shape of a hand.

When Aspen realized what she'd done, she was sorry. She hadn't meant to. Except she had meant to, a little bit. That's what frightened Hailey the most. Aspen wasn't in pain, she wasn't working out her issues on the faces of a couple of vamps. Aspen just liked being stronger than other people. And Hailey sensed that she'd always been that way, even before she got her powers.

Hailey knew she should tell Frankie that Aspen had made contact. That she was here, in New Sunnydale. But every time she thought about it, she felt Aspen's eyes drift to her like she was somehow capable of telepathy. And Hailey was afraid.

"It's too quiet out here," Aspen muttered as they walked. They were on the south side of town, near the bus station, where Frankie rarely patrolled and there were plenty of places to hide if she suddenly felt they might be spotted. "Too bad we can't go to the busier parts of town."

"We probably could if we wanted. It's late. Frankie's probably asleep by now, dreaming sad dreams about your ex-boyfriend."

Aspen chuckled and pulled the hood of her T-shirt hoodie farther over her hair. She walked with her hands stuffed into the front pockets, the Amulet of Junjari clinking against a bright silver cross suspended from a drop chain.

"Who says he's my ex?"

"You think he's not? He seemed pretty into Frankie to me."

Aspen snorted. "Frankie's just a kid. I'm a woman, and I'm a hero, and I'm his equal."

"Frankie might have started out a kid, but slayers grow up fast. And what about after this is over? When you're not a slayer, and not a hero?"

"Then I'll still be his equal," Aspen said, a little sharply. "But you have a point. The faster I take care of this and get Grimloch away from New Sunnydale, the better."

"How long—" Hailey started, and caught herself. Talking to Aspen was surprisingly easy. Sometimes she forgot that there were questions she probably shouldn't ask. Areas she shouldn't pry into.

"Aw." Aspen nudged her with her shoulder. "Are you getting attached to me?" Hailey made a *pft* sound, and Aspen laughed. "Well, it won't actually be much longer. I have a lead."

"A lead?" Hailey asked. This could be it. Something she could give to the Scoobies that was big enough to blow up Aspen's plans and let Hailey go home to the Rosenbergs. "What kind of lead?"

"Want to find out?" Aspen asked. "You can come with me when I meet them tomorrow night."

"Really?"

"Sure. After what she did to your sister you deserve to be there. I wouldn't cut you out of that." She put her hand on Hailey's shoulder, and despite herself, Hailey felt a surge of fondness. Aspen was magnetic. And she could be so effortlessly warm and kind, sometimes.

"You know, after we do the spell and use the amulet, Frankie Rosenberg will be just another person. One punch from you, and she'll fall down and cry." She looked at Hailey, and Hailey forced a bark of laughter.

"That's hard to imagine," Hailey said. "But it's *fun* to imagine."

"Well, she'll have it coming. It'll be good, to bring her down off her high horse."

"And she'll be better off, really," Hailey noted. "Not being a slayer anymore. No more burden of the world. No more having to be the guardian of the Hellmouth."

"Yeah, I guess." Aspen cast her a cockeyed smile. "But just because it's better for Frankie doesn't mean I'm not going to do it, so don't ask."

"I know." Hailey kicked at a rock. "Hey, why don't you want to be a slayer anymore?"

Aspen glanced at her. There was a slight edge to the look, and Hailey kept her eyes carefully on the ground, watching the street roll by like she was barely interested in the answer. "I know you said how hard it is, and that you're tired. But you seem so . . . tough and not tired?"

Aspen brightened. "I hide it well. And I did want to be a slayer at first. I tried to follow all their rules and be a good little soldier. Then their orders got my best friend killed. Geraldine. She was a few years older than me. She was amazing. Funny. Great taste in music. Now she's dead, because Buffy Summers made a bad call. Because Buffy Summers thinks her way is always the right way. Like Frankie did, when she made the choice to kill your sister.

"I know me and the Darkness . . . we don't want to be slayers anymore. But some slayers never deserved to be slayers in the first place."

"Like Frankie," Hailey said. "I'm ninety-nine percent sure that one was a mistake."

"Right?" Aspen laughed. "God, she's the worst. Flailing around and flapping her arms." She did an impression that was surprisingly close to the mark, and Hailey laughed for real. She felt so immediately bad about it that she couldn't disguise her frown.

"Sorry," she said quickly. "It just sucks that I don't have anyone here anymore. All the people I thought were my friends took the side of that idiot."

Aspen nudged her gently. "You don't have to stay here. You could come with us. Now that your sister is gone, we could be your sisters. We could be that for each other."

"Maybe," Hailey said, and Aspen smiled.

CHAPTER SIX

HUNTING PRACTICE

The next day, Frankie headed to the woods behind Marymore Park as soon as classes ended. Only when she got to Grim's tent, it was empty except for a note, which she unfolded and read.

Hunting practice.

Frankie smiled. She stepped out of the tent and looked around. Signs of Grim were everywhere, which made sense. It was where he lived. "So how . . ." She scanned the trees. A flash of blue caught her eye. A length of ribbon. Frankie walked to the branch and grabbed it. She looked past where it hung, and her slayer senses caught on stomped ferns and bent branches leading southwest, where the woods were denser, the hills steeper, and a creek ran in a zigzag through the trees, creating muddy banks her shoes would be sucked into. Once, not so long ago, she'd tumbled down a ravine over there and gotten a hole in her sock.

That was where she'd first seen Grim. He saved her from a vampire that day. He'd told her she wasn't ready.

But she was ready now.

53

Frankie took off into the trees. She ducked branches and jumped ferns, following the trail Grim had set. As she half ran, half slid down the side of the ravine, much more gracefully than she'd gone down it the first time when she'd roll-bounced down like a cartoon coyote, she reached up to grab another length of ribbon. Then she swung off a low branch to get over the fallen log that crossed the creek.

This was the place. The exact spot where she'd skewered two vampires like a vampire kebab but missed the second one's heart. She lowered into a crouch. A branch cracked, and she turned just in time to see Grimloch smile and set something on the ground before he took off farther into the forest. Frankie raced after him, bending low to pick up what he'd left: an open, empty white box.

"Grim! You're littering!" She ran faster, trying to close the gap. It was hard going, fighting through the dense underbrush with her shorter legs. She couldn't seem to gain ground. "*Damn* you're fast," she called a little breathlessly. And he was in slacks and a button-down. She'd hate to see how he could move in something stretchier, like a tracksuit.

Fed up with the ferns, Frankie leapt up onto a low branch. She jumped from branch to branch and tree to tree, tracking Grimloch from above, and caught him just as he neared the clearing. She swung from the last branch like it was a parallel bar and flipped right onto his back.

"Got you!" she cried as they tumbled to the grass. They rolled to a stop, and Grimloch laughed.

"No slayer can catch the Hunter of Thrace."

"Well, this slayer just did."

"I must have let you." He stood and helped her to her feet as she brushed leaves from her pants and tried to pick the twigs out of her tangle of red hair.

"Whatever you have to tell yourself." Frankie held up the ribbons, and the empty box. "What's with the garbage? If I were the parks authority, I would fine you."

"It's all compostable," he said, and Frankie held up the ribbons, impressed. They were so shiny. "And they're meant to house this." He held up his hand. A delicate gold chain of tiny interlocked hearts dangled from his fingertips.

"What's that?" Frankie asked, flummoxed.

"Give me your wrist."

She held it out, and he carefully fastened the bracelet around her. It was so light that it tickled.

"In my time, successful hunters were honored with many tributes. This is mine to you."

Frankie held her arm up and gazed at it.

"It's upcycled," Grimloch said, in a tone that told her he'd just learned that word.

"Hang on, this is real gold? Was it . . . too expensive? Do I need to give it back?" She lowered her wrist. "Just what do you do for money, anyway? The slayers have the Watchers Council Investment Fund, but I've never seen you behind the counter at Doublemeat Palace."

"You've heard of 'new money' and 'old money,' " he said, and shrugged. "Well, I'm—"

"Super old money?"

"*Ancient* money," he said, and gave her a look. He reached out, wiping away a bit of dirt on her cheek.

"Well, however you bought it, no one's ever given me anything like this. No one's even gotten me flowers." She frowned. "No one's even gotten me *gum*. So . . . thank you."

"You're welcome." He cocked his head. "Are you all right, Frankie?"

"Sure, why? Did I stop smiling? I didn't think I stopped smiling." She tried to smile again, but it wouldn't stick.

"Being the slayer is a heavy burden," Grimloch said.

It was. Sometimes she felt like she'd gotten the hang of it, like she could totally stick her flag in the Hellmouth. And other times it felt like . . . a lot.

"Buffy did it. She did it her whole life. Save the world and go to school. Date and slay. Have friends. Have jobs. Work in the shadows, live in the sunshine." Frankie shrugged. "She was the one."

"You could be that, too," said Grimloch. "You are like her."

"I am not like her. Have you seen me fight? My favorite move is this—" She made a *V* with her fingers and poked for his eyes; he put his hand up to his nose to block them.

"Stop that."

"It works if they don't know it's coming." Frankie sighed. "I'll just be happy when she's home. When the senior slayers are home, and this junior slayer can work up to her apocalypses gradually. But this is Sunnydale and I just said the word 'apocalypses,' so another one should be arriving any minute."

"You'll be ready. And I'll be here, to help you."

"I know. And I have the Scoobies. And my mom. And Spike's teaching me some new—" Frankie's eyes widened. "I have to go."

"What?"

"I was supposed to meet Spike in the library an hour ago!"

☽ ☾ ○ ☽ ☾

"I'm sorry, I'm sorry, I'm sorry!" Frankie burst through the library doors and rushed to the table. She threw her backpack onto a chair and started to stretch, kicking and swinging her arms, warming up to train. Not that she needed to, after her mad dash across town. "I just meant to run over and get us all coffee, but the line at the café was out of control! Apparently the foamer broke and then some guy had a corporate order . . ."

"But where's the coffee?" Sigmund asked, and Frankie looked down at her empty hands.

"Yeah." Jake shoved a thick book far away from him on the table. "After all this reading about lycanthrope history, I could really use some."

"It . . . took so long that I finally gave up and came back," Frankie lied. "Where's Sam?"

"He went to practice."

"You're skipping practice?"

Jake raised an eyebrow and gestured to the werewolf book, flipping the cover back open. "Priorities, Oz says." But he didn't sound too happy about it. Frankie turned her attention back to the library, searching for Spike. He came out from behind the stacks carrying a short wooden ladder that he was using to take down the targets he'd set up for her *again*.

"Hey, no—Uncle Spike, I'm here! I'm ready! Let's telekinesis some scalpels and throw some axes. Let's telekinesis some axes!"

But her Watcher didn't even look her way. "Don't 'uncle' Spike me," he said. "You forgot."

"I didn't—"

"And you're lying. And you didn't tell me where you were going, and you're not taking your training seriously, and you're making me sound like bloody Giles!" His voice got louder and louder, and on the word "Giles" he raised the last target in the air like he was about to smash it on the floor. Frankie braced for impact, but then he sighed, and tucked it back under his arm.

"Spike, I'm sorry."

"Hailey wasn't here again today," he said as he breezed past her into his office. "Not that you care. But someone had better go and talk to her before this little spy plan of yours causes her to repeat the eleventh grade."

"I'll go, Mr. Pratt," Sigmund said, which he only called Spike when he knew he was upset.

Frankie took a step toward Spike's office, but he closed the door.

"Just go home, Frankie," he said from inside. "Or don't. Go do whatever it is you're going to do."

Frankie's face fell as Sigmund and Jake gathered their things.

"Come on," Jake said and threw an arm around her shoulders. "We'll take you for pizza and veggie burgers."

"And you can tell us the real reason you were so late," Sigmund added as they walked out the door.

CHAPTER SEVEN

GIRLS JUST WANT TO HAVE DESTINIES THAT LEAD THEM TO LOSS AND PAIN

Hailey checked her makeup in the mirror of her compact while she waited for Aspen in the motel parking lot. But that was just a nervous habit. Her makeup was flawless, as usual. She'd outlined her mouth in crimson liner, then filled it in with a rich, bloody shade from a recyclable aluminum tube: a gift from Frankie. The makeup was like armor, a disguise for her disguise. It made her feel safe around Aspen, like the makeup could conceal her nerves, hiding vulnerabilities beneath shimmer and double luxe lashes.

They were going to meet a contact, Aspen said. Someone with information on how she could move forward with her plan to free the rest of the Darkness from their slayer powers. She hadn't mentioned whether that contact was human, and Hailey hadn't asked. She kind of assumed they wouldn't be.

She idly checked her phone—for the time, for notifications, for something to do with her hands. The lot of the motel was empty except for the nineties-model pickup truck in emerald green that always sat in the parking space near the rental office. It didn't belong to the owner, and she'd never seen it move. It was just another relic, like the motel itself.

Hailey checked her phone again, then stuffed it into her pocket. Maybe Aspen wouldn't show. And maybe that would be for the best. She wanted to go home to the Scoobies, and not just because the leader of the Darkness was a frightening psychopath. She wanted to go home because something about this life—skipping school, being alone, hustling for her dinner—suited her. She could get used to it. And she didn't want to get used to it.

"Ow." She pressed her palms to her temples to quiet her thoughts. This must be what Jake meant when he said thinking made his head hurt.

"Hey."

Hailey looked up as Aspen approached along the sidewalk. She never let a rideshare drop her at the motel. She always scoped it out first.

"Let's get going," Aspen said. "This guy is twitchy, and if we're late, he'll bail."

"Okay. Are we walking, or . . ." Hailey pulled out her phone, but Aspen placed a hand on her shoulder. She stared at the emerald-green pickup parked across the lot.

"Think that thing still runs?"

"No," Hailey said, following as Aspen walked to it. When she tried the driver's side door of the pickup it was unlocked, and she looked at Hailey and shrugged. They got in and did the obligatory key search above the visors. "Well, I guess that's that," Hailey said when they didn't find any, but Aspen just snorted and got to work. Dressed in ripped jeans, boots, and a slouchy gray tank top beneath a cardigan, Aspen looked more fit for a wellness retreat than for crime, so it was weird to see her hotwire the truck. Less weird to hear her triumphant whoop when it started.

"Time to go," she shouted over the drone and sputter of the engine, putting on a pair of sunglasses she found in the center console. Hailey rolled down the window as Aspen threw the truck into reverse and gunned it backward, then shifted into drive. And just like that the abandoned emerald truck lurched onto the highway, coughing on old gas.

"If this thing doesn't break down in a mile it'll be a miracle," Hailey said.

"If it does, we'll be walking for nineteen."

"We're going twenty miles out of town?" Hailey glanced at the signs beside the road. She should have guessed: Aspen wouldn't want Willow to catch wind of anything mystical within Sunnydale limits.

"Don't worry; it's not like a cave or anything."

That wasn't exactly an answer, but Hailey'd gotten used to that. Besides, there was no need to be open about everything, no need to wear your heart on your sleeve, show all your cards, or whatever other annoying platitudes that meant not protecting herself. She should have protected herself better with Sigmund instead of letting her heart do whatever it wanted. The heart was a moron, all muscle and blood. She should have listened to her head. Love with your head. That should be the saying she lived by. She ought to print T-shirts.

"Hey." Aspen glanced at her from behind the wheel. "You okay?"

"I'm fine."

Aspen gave her a knowing look. "What are you thinking about?"

"Nothing."

"You thinking about the Scoobies?" She cocked her head and

pushed her sunglasses back on her head. Hailey rolled her eyes.

"No."

"Maybe about one Scooby in particular? A freakishly-hot-for-a-nerd half demon whose name begins with an S?"

Despite herself, Hailey smiled. "He's not freakishly hot."

"Come on!" Aspen reached over and shoved her, a little hard. "He's so hot, every time I look at him I feel like I've just committed a felony. There's no chance he's, like, one of those twenty-five-year-old high school students, is there?"

Hailey laughed.

"Or even just a twenty-two-year-old student teacher. That wouldn't get me arrested."

"Okay, okay. Let's just . . . stop thirsting. It's weird."

Aspen grinned. It was weird, but it was true. Sigmund was freakishly hot, and damn, Hailey missed him.

"I thought he was supposed to be super smart, though," Aspen said. "So what's he doing, taking Rosenberg's side and breaking up with you?"

Hailey shrugged. "Really it was over before that." She pressed her lips together. She hadn't meant to say that. But now that she had . . . "It wasn't even hard for him. He just called it quits."

"See," Aspen said gently. "Sounds pretty stupid to me."

"Yeah." Hailey snorted. "Except not. He had reasons. I just don't think those reasons should have mattered. Or they shouldn't have mattered enough to break us up. Or maybe just that it shouldn't have been easy to walk away."

"He's the kind that loves with his head, maybe. Not his heart."

"Yeah," Hailey said. "I'd just been thinking that. He's fifty percent demon and fifty percent head. Good for him."

"And good for you," Aspen said. "Even though it doesn't feel like it right now. Because who needs that kind of love?"

Hailey watched Aspen quietly as she drove on, fingers wrapped tightly around the wheel. *She's playing you,* Frankie's voice said inside her head. But Hailey didn't think she was. At least, not all the time.

The truck ran rough, and Aspen kept one eye on the gauges on the dash, driving with one hand while her other fiddled with the buttons and knobs of the old-style radio, more for the novelty, it seemed, than actually trying to get it to work.

"Where did you learn how to hotwire?" Hailey asked. "You don't seem like the type who would have needed to."

"I wasn't. Back when I had a life. And tennis lessons. And a pony, named Pickles. But all of that changed when slayville came calling." She stopped messing with the radio and smacked it until it turned off, cracked and likely to never turn on again. "It was Andrew. He made all of the slayers take survival courses. Starting fires, tying knots, cooking in urban and wilderness situations. What berries to eat and not eat. How to pick a lock when you don't want to bust down a door. How to hotwire a car."

"Seems practical."

"Yeah, but he didn't make himself and the other witcher-Watchers do it. He's still as useless as Buffy used to say he was." The truck began to slow, and Aspen took a turn off to the right. "There it is."

Hailey leaned forward. "It" was a small brick building with a tin roof, with no road leading to it. Aspen had to take the pickup into the ditch and drive through the brush.

"I know I don't leave Sunnydale often, but I don't remember seeing this from the road."

"That's because it normally isn't here. It moves around, with the guy inside."

"The guy?"

"Yeah. The witch guy."

"The witch guy," Hailey muttered as she got out of the truck.

When they walked into the brick building, Hailey expected it to be magical, bigger on the inside than it was on the outside, or at least done up in fancy silk curtains. But it was just as advertised: small, brick, and plain. There was a fireplace that housed a small fire, some cupboards, a table, and a chair. Well, and the witch guy.

He looked old. Hailey guesstimated his age to be anywhere from ninety to several hundred. He wore a little visor even though they were indoors, and his white T-shirt was covered in stains. Grease stains. Sweat stains. A few paint stains in pretty colors, like he'd been working on a sunset landscape.

"You're late," he said.

"Not according to my watch," said Aspen, even though she wasn't wearing one. "Want me to pay extra?"

"Extra never hurts." He turned his eyes—which were surprisingly sharp and clear—to Hailey.

"So, witch guy," Hailey said as the old man stepped up to her. "Do you have an actual name?"

"Witch guy will do," he replied as he sniffed all around her and even wafted the scent of her hair toward his nose like she was a cup of coffee.

"Hey. Creeper." Aspen tugged Hailey away and stepped between them. "I'm not paying with her." She pulled out cash, and he took it.

"Good," he said, and sniffed the money. "I don't take payment in girls." He rolled his eyes back to Hailey. "Not even Potential Slayers."

"Huh?" Hailey's brow knit. "I'm not . . . what is he talking about?"

"What *are* you talking about?" Aspen asked. "I'm here to ask about the missing slayer Scythe. And if it can be recovered."

The old man waved his hands. "You're here for answers. And answers I've got. To questions you asked and questions you didn't." He shuffled away and started to riffle through drawers and the doors of his cupboard. "The Scythe, the Scythe," he muttered. "If you wanted it back, you shouldn't have blown it into smithereens!"

"I didn't." Aspen crossed her arms.

"You didn't do it," he said. "But that doesn't mean you didn't do it."

"Huh?" Hailey said again. The witch guy had started to hum and fill a bowl with odd ingredients.

"The Scythe, the Scythe." He set the bowl before them and placed his hands on either side. "You can have it back."

"That's amazing." Aspen sighed. "How much?"

"I'll do it for free."

She and Hailey traded a look. Nothing was ever free. "When can I have it?" she asked.

"One hundred years."

"One hundred years? What good is it to me in a hundred years?"

The witch guy threw up his arms. "Then you shouldn't have blown it up! Now hold still. And brace yourself."

"For what?" Hailey asked.

"For the smell."

She glanced at Aspen. The slayer tensed but didn't move to stop him, instead giving her a *let's wait and see* raise of her eyebrows.

The old man placed a long, pale snakeskin onto the table beside a small green pod that looked like a leaf. "Shed of snake and chrysalis, too," he muttered. "To light the aura of the new." Then he produced a dry sprig and what looked like the bare stem of a rose. "Tumbleweed and rosebush thorn. To indicate the fresh reborn." He reached in for the final ingredient in the bowl. "And an egg."

Hailey's brows knit. "Pretty blunt ending to an incantation."

"Here comes the smell," the witch declared, a little too gleefully, she thought, as he threw the ingredients into the fireplace.

"Whoa." Aspen put her hand over her nose and mouth. "He wasn't kidding."

The spell smelled like rot: rotten snakes and rotten eggs, and maybe an extra dose of Limburger cheese.

"What is that?" Hailey asked, gagging.

"It is a spell to show your potential."

"If by 'potential' you mean my rising potential to vomit—" She covered her mouth. "There's no need to check."

But as the smell cleared, a glow rose in its place, starting in the fire and moving out, a small, bright orb encased in a hazy aura.

As the orb began to move, Aspen stiffened, and Hailey backed up a step. It darted forward, and she darted farther back.

"This wasn't what I paid you for," Aspen growled. "Hailey, you don't have to do this!"

"She doesn't have to *do* anything!" The old man shrugged. "It's informational."

Hailey backed up to the wall. She'd come for intel that would help the Scoobies, not to find out her lifelong destiny. Sure, being a Potential might seem nice in theory, and she'd wished since she was a kid to be like Vi, to have a mission, to be strong and able to do backflips. But the orb was different. This wasn't a daydream, it was real. "Get it away from me!" Hailey dashed around the table, but the orb dashed, too, chasing her wherever she went.

"Stop it," she heard Aspen order, and saw her draw a knife to hold against the old man's neck. "Call it back!"

Hailey turned, trapped, and the orb hit her right in the chest. It exploded in a gold cloud and sank in, leaving a sensation like putting on a warm sweater right out of the dryer. But nothing about Hailey felt warm and fuzzy.

"What does that mean?" she asked Aspen, and no amount of shadow or liner could conceal the fear in her eyes.

"It doesn't mean anything." Aspen took her by the arms. "It doesn't have to mean anything, do you hear me?"

"What it means is that the time for Potentials has come again," the old man said, his eyes bright.

"You leave them alone!" Hailey heard Aspen shout as Hailey shoved out of the shack and back into the night air.

She walked through the desert on shaky legs, back toward the pickup and then right past it. She needed to breathe. She couldn't think about getting into that cramped cab right now.

"Hey," Aspen called as she ran to catch up. "Hey, are you okay?"

"What does that mean?" Hailey asked. "Does that mean—" *That I'm a slayer, holy shit, I'm a slayer!* "Does that mean that if Frankie dies, I'm going to—"

"No." Aspen held out her hands like she was trying to corral a runaway horse. "If it's even true—that's not how it works, okay? There's no way to know which Potential would be activated if Frankie died."

"I don't want her to die," Hailey cried. She swallowed hard. She tried to calm down and remember her job. "I hate her. She killed my sister. But I don't want her to die."

"I know."

"I don't know if I'd even *want* to be a slayer!"

"I know that, too," Aspen said, but for a second something in her eyes changed, like she didn't quite believe it. "The good news is there's no way to make you one, because we can't get the goddamn Scythe back for one hundred freaking years!" She stomped her boots into the dirt. She screamed a little and pressed her fists to her eyes, then hovered a hand over the Amulet of Junjari like she wanted to tear it off her neck. "So what the hell am I supposed to do now?"

They looked at each other, defeated.

"Listen, I just need to walk for a while," Hailey said. She turned around and headed for the road.

"No, come on. It's twenty miles back to Sunnydale. I'll drive you."

"I'll get a rideshare closer to town."

"On the freaking lost highway?" Aspen held out her arms to showcase the absolutely no traffic, but Hailey kept walking.

"I just need to think, okay? I'll see you later." Hailey waved and jogged back to the highway without looking back.

If she had, she might have seen the little old man walk out of the shack and shove a canvas bag into Aspen's hands.

"What is this?" Aspen asked.

"It's what you paid for," the old man replied. "The question you asked."

Aspen opened the bag. Inside were chains. Golden chains, with manacled ends. They'd been engraved with mystical symbols. "Shackles," she said. "To hold what?"

"To hold the thing that can help you in your quest." All of the mirth was gone from the old man's eyes. He licked his lips, and she saw that his teeth had sharpened to points. "The oracle who spoke to the red witch."

CHAPTER EIGHT

BURGERS WITH A SIDE OF CLAW

J ake set a burger down in front of her, but Frankie was still feeling guilty about forgetting Spike's training session. Far too guilty to eat.

"Come on, it's your favorite. Plant meat and avocado, mayo, and triple fake bacon." He nudged it toward her. "Don't make me turn the bun into a mouth." He hinged the bun top open and said in a deep voice, "Eat me. Eat me, Frankie, I'm full of protein that slayers need. Yum-yum."

"Like that ever worked," she said glumly. But she did want to eat it a little more now. She picked it up and took a big bite, then spoke with her mouth full. "There. You happy?"

Jake grinned and folded his gargantuan slice of pizza before shoving half of it down his gullet.

"Spike will get over you missing training today," said Sigmund, with his book bag in his lap.

"Yeah, you know how he is." Jake had already tuned partially out, pizza in one hand and his phone in the other to text Sam. "But what has been up with you lately? You're normally so goody two-shoes about training."

"I am not."

"Are too," Jake said, still only half listening. Frankie gave him a punch, and he mouthed "ow" and set down his phone.

Across the table Sigmund waited patiently for their childish antics to end. "But it's true, Frankie. You have seemed distracted."

"I'm not distracted," she said, and they looked at her. "Okay, I'm a little distracted. But there are distractions!" She took another bite of her burger. "I just wish I knew what the Darkness's next move was. I can't focus. And until I know, yes, training does feel a little pointless. Like . . . riding a stationary bike. Sure, you're keeping yourself tuned up. But are you really going anywhere? And does it prepare you for real hills?"

"Sam loves his stationary bike," Jake mused around a mouthful of pizza. "Trains on it all the time during the off-season." He waggled his eyebrows. "Says it really builds his quads."

Sigmund chuckled, but Frankie sighed.

"I really wish I knew what Aspen was up to."

"So do I," said Jake. "Then maybe Hailey could come home."

"And stop flunking out of school," Frankie added. "Sig? Aren't you going to eat something?"

"I'm going to grab a few sandwiches to go." He stood and put his bag over his shoulder. "I told Spike I'd find Hailey and try to convince her to stop skipping. I realize it's part of her plan, but she may not know how close she is to being held back."

Frankie frowned. "Give her the secret signal that means we say hi," she said.

"What signal is that?"

Frankie frowned deeper. "I don't remember."

Sigmund smiled. "I'll just tell her, then. We're not supposed to seem angry with her. A few hellos won't do anything to compromise the ruse."

"He'll convince her," Jake said confidently, watching Sigmund leave. "He's got that spice demon mojo thing."

"Yeah," Frankie said, staring after him, too. She wished she could go see Hailey. Even if it was just to stage a fight or something. Staging a fight could even be fun, they could pie each other in the face or—

"Hey, is your name Frankie?"

Frankie looked up. One of the table bussers peered down at her. "Someone left this for you." She set down a white box, secured with a blue ribbon.

"Who?" Jake asked.

"Just some guy." The girl shrugged. "Dark hair, kind of long. Looked like an—"

"Underwear model," Jake supplied. "Yeah. Got it." He took the box and placed it in front of Frankie, and the busser walked away. "So what is it?"

Frankie opened the box and smiled. "It's gum."

Jake leaned over to look. "Big spender," he said. "A whole pack of it. Why is he so weird?" But Frankie happily put it into her pocket.

"It's not weird. It was something I said to him before. He—" Frankie looked at Jake and froze as he lifted the last of his pizza to his mouth. He held it gently, folding it to fit it all in, and his hand was tipped with razor-sharp claws.

"Jake. Your hand."

He glanced down and startled hard, dropping the pizza into his lap. "Uh . . ." He grabbed a napkin and wrapped it around his claws.

"It's not the full moon," Frankie whispered. "What's happening?"

"It's okay," Jake said, though he didn't sound sure. "Oz said this might happen. It's the herbs he's got me on, and the chanting; he

71

said the wolf might kind of know what we're up to and try to"—he grinned nervously—"rattle the cage. The only thing to worry about is if I start to fully transform."

"What if you fully transform?" As Frankie watched, a fine shadow of fur began to grow on Jake's cheek. And his face was definitely starting to get snouty.

"You have to slay me?"

"That's not funny. What do we do, Jake? How do you stop it?"

"I have to chant." He paused and closed his eyes, like he was trying to remember the words. Frankie scanned the restaurant. It wasn't that crowded. If it came down to it, she might be able to contain the Jake wolf inside one of the big folding umbrellas over the outdoor tables.

"Frankie?" Jake's eyes were wide and terrified. "This isn't working."

"It's going to be okay. Hey. Look at me. Just keep your eyes on me and focus. Breathe."

Jake took a shuddering breath. His incisors were twice their normal length. "I'm starting to have doubts about Oz's method."

"Me too." Frankie put her hand on Jake's arm. He started to rock back and forth. "It's okay, Jake. It's okay, Jake wolf." She paused. The Jake wolf. It knew her. She'd been calming it since they were kids and it was a puppy! Frankie took Jake's hands and felt his claws wrap around her fingers. "Once upon a time," she said. "There were three delicious little pigs."

Jake stopped rocking and stared at her.

"Three delicious, stupid little pigs, who built terribly break-downable houses and seasoned themselves with dry rub like it was going out of style . . ." Jake's claws receded. The fur on his face began to retreat. Frankie went on, telling the whole, wolf-friendly tale, all the way to the end when she listed every pork product the wolf was able to make with those three little fools. Pork chops and back bacon. Pickled little pigs' feet. She told the whole thing, holding Jake's hand until it was only a hand.

"Thanks, Frankie."

She patted him. "Anytime." She picked up the pizza he'd dropped into his lap and set it back on his plate. "But you know, just to be safe, maybe I'd better start teaching Sam some of these stories."

CHAPTER NINE

SECRETS ARE LIES

Sigmund drove his car through the empty parking lot of the motel, looking for Hailey's room. He didn't actually know which one was hers, but that wouldn't matter. Hailey seemed to be the motel's only inhabitant, so he could just knock on every door. He parked and got out, sheepishly peeking through gaps in the curtains to try to spot signs of life or a few of Hailey's belongings. There was a whole lot of nothing, and then an obvious break: a window strung with sagging, unlit Christmas lights. Sigmund took a breath and mentally reviewed his checklist: *I'm not here to judge you, Hailey, but I'm concerned about your academic future; I know I'm not the face you'd most like to be seeing right now, but I am the authority among the Scoobies when it comes to academics; I miss you and I love you, Hailey, and I don't want you to come to harm.*

He cleared his throat. He'd probably skip over that last one.

He knocked on the door to with a number nine sign, which promptly detached and flipped around to read six.

"Oh. Oh dear." He fiddled with it, trying to get it to hold the nine position, when he heard Hailey's voice ring out behind him.

"Sigmund!"

He turned. "Hailey! I was . . ." But he didn't get the chance to finish telling her why he was there, because Hailey ran straight into his arms. "Hey, it's all right. It's all right, I'm here." He held her tight. What a nonsensical thing to say. He was here. He was only a half demon scholar, what could he do to help? "Are you hurt?"

"No." Hailey drew back. She wasn't injured, but she had been crying. Her makeup had run down her cheeks.

"You have . . . raccoon eyes." He said it to cheer her up, but she only turned away and said "shit" under her breath.

"I'm fine, Sigmund. What are you doing here?"

"Hailey, you're clearly not fine, and whatever I was here for can wait—"

"Just get out of here, then," she said, and brushed past him to open her door. It wasn't even locked. "It locks okay from the inside," she said when she saw the horror on his face. "So go. I'm fine."

"I'm not going anywhere."

"Sigmund! Will you just get out of here?" She pointed her arm in the direction of his car. But he planted his feet. Her jaw clenched, and her fists. But he knew if he waited long enough she would buckle. Angrily, but she would buckle.

"Fine," she snapped. "Get inside, at least." Her eyes rose to his. "I don't want Aspen to see you."

Aspen. Sigmund's pulse quickened, and he looked over his shoulder before ducking into the room.

"So she's here," he said gravely. "She's back in Sunnydale."

"If she ever left," said Hailey as she closed the door.

Sigmund peered around the sad, gross little room. He heard

skittering coming from the direction of the bathroom, and somewhere in a wall a pipe groaned for no reason. The floor seemed uneven, which made him suspect that the old foundation hadn't survived the Spikesplosion in as good a shape as the owner hoped.

"If she comes around, she's going to know you're here by your car," Hailey said. "If she asks, I'm telling her you were coming to beg me to take you back."

"She would never believe that," Sigmund said reflexively, and Hailey looked hurt. "I mean, she's shrewd, and she would know that I wouldn't, that I couldn't—"

"It was a joke, Sigmund."

She crossed her arms. She looked smaller somehow when she did that, and with the tear streaks down her tan cheeks, she seemed fragile. This Goth girl who punched vampires in the fangs and flirted with death, who agreed to get close to a known murderer. He wanted nothing more than to dry her tears and to kiss her until she forgot what caused them.

Sigmund went into the bathroom and wetted a washcloth. He pressed it to Hailey's cheek, and her hard eyes turned softer until she sank down on the bed. He sank down, too, and held her hand.

"This isn't my charm," he said.

"I know. I can tell the difference." She took the washcloth and wiped her face. "If it was your charm, I would have jumped you by now." She looked up at him with large, brown eyes.

"Hailey," he said. "Tell me."

And so she did. When she was finished, Sigmund sat in a state of numb shock.

"You're a Potential," he said quietly.

"Yeah. Whatever that means."

He raised his eyebrows. "It would explain why you've been so naturally good at slaying. Better than Frankie, even, when it comes to basic skills."

"Don't say that." Hailey got up off the bed. "I mean, it's true. But I don't like how it sounds now. Now that I'm . . ."

"In line after Frankie's death?" Hailey gave him a look, and he flinched. "Sorry. I'm saying the absolute wrong things tonight. I had a checklist . . ."

"I didn't want it, you know. I wasn't going around asking. I just went along with Aspen to see this witch guy so I would know what she was planning."

"What is she planning?"

"The same thing she was always planning. To use the Amulet of Junjari to return the Darkness's slayer powers."

"And funnel them into herself," Sigmund added.

"I don't know."

"You don't know?"

"I don't know anymore!" Hailey started to pace. "She's not like I thought she was going to be, all right? Maybe we were wrong about that part. It was only Frankie's hunch."

"Frankie's hunch? Hailey, Aspen and the Darkness murdered other slayers—"

"*By accident*, maybe. She's not all bad, all the time, is all I'm saying. And even if she was, it's not like she doesn't have a point. Why should one person be able to shove this destiny on someone who doesn't want it?"

Sigmund sat silently while she hugged herself. She didn't know what she was saying. She was confused. He'd seen Aspen firsthand, and there was a reason she'd become the leader of the Darkness. She was charismatic. She had magnetism, and her lies sounded righteous. She used the right words, and she used them over and over.

And he was sure she could be kind. That would be the worst of it. Her deadliest trick. To make you believe that this powerful young woman was on your side, and that she was your friend.

Plus, let's face it, Aspen was gorgeous. The kind of gorgeous that could make even someone as beautiful as Hailey feel like they ought to just fall in line.

"Hailey," he said softly. "I think it's time you came back to the Scoobies."

"No." Hailey's eyes opened wide. "Sig, I can do this. Aspen is kind of cool to hang around with sometimes, but Frankie and the Scoobies . . . and you . . . Frankie is my best friend. I promised her I'd find out what the Darkness's plan was, and I will."

"Why didn't you tell us the moment Aspen made contact with you?"

"I wanted to. But she's kind of terrifying." She sat down beside him and put her hands on his chest. "I can do this. If you trust me."

"Of course I trust you, Hailey, I—" *Love you. I still love you.* But he couldn't say so. It would have been unfair. He was still a demon, and she wasn't. He would still have to marry from one of the acceptable Sage demon clans, and how could he ever stand to do that if he could have been with Hailey instead?

He cleared his throat. "But you have to promise to come back to school. Principal Jacobs has started hassling Spike. She says if your attendance doesn't improve she'll have to hold you back."

"Hold me back?" Hailey asked, horrified. "Why didn't you tell me sooner?"

Sigmund smiled. Then he took her hand and kissed it before he could stop himself. "I should get going, before I'm seen."

"Okay." Hailey sat with her hands in her lap as he went to the door, one finger unconsciously tracing the place where he'd kissed. "Sig?"

"Yes?"

"How's Frankie?"

"She's fine. She misses you, she says hello."

Hailey smiled. "Tell her I say hello, too. *Don't* tell her I'm next in line after her death."

Sigmund chuckled. "There's no way for us to know that," he said, and he walked out the door.

CHAPTER TEN

WATCHER CARE

On Monday, Frankie was at the Scooby meeting early. And she'd brought a present.

"Bourbon balls!" She held them out to Spike in a glass container.

"What are these for?" The vampire took them and peered through the clear bottom like it might be hiding something.

"No reason," Frankie said. "I just wanted to say thank you for being such an amazing Watcher. I would have rather gotten you a bottle of bourbon, because, you know, you like that, but I'm too young to buy alcohol. So I made these instead. Bourbon balls!" She followed him into his office. "My mom had a bottle in the cabinet. I've never made them before, and I tried one, and it was actually pretty gross. But I think that's how they're supposed to taste?"

Spike set the container on his desk, and Frankie waited while he sucked in his cheeks.

"That's very sweet of you, Mini Red."

Frankie beamed. "I'm sorry about last week. I will not take your training for granted anymore, I promise. You have one hundred percent of my attention." She stood up straight, shoulders back. "So, what do you got?"

"Well, nothing actually. I didn't even know if you'd be here—"

"Helloooo!"

Spike said no more as Jake howled his way into the library with one arm across Sam's shoulders. "Did our slayer-witch actually show up today?"

"Of course I did." Frankie and Spike emerged from the office and headed for their usual table. "And so did Hailey—did you see her?"

"Totally," Sam said. "I even sat with her during study hall, as an acceptably neutral party."

"Is she okay?" Frankie asked.

"She seemed a little nervous. And maybe tired? But other than that, yeah. Okay."

"I saw her, too," said Spike. "She came in before that study hall to get the extra assignments I'd collected from her teachers. So it's nice to know that she was hard at work on them and not chatting away with Sam."

Sam grimaced. Jake sat and put his feet up on a chair, then leaned back to look around the stacks. "Where's the spice?" he asked.

"I haven't seen him all day." Frankie craned her neck, like Sigmund must be there somewhere and she'd just missed him.

Spike stood at the head of the table. "Report. Anything odd happen since our last meeting?"

Jake caught Frankie's eye and shook his head. There'd been no more instances of spontaneous claws since that afternoon over burgers and pizza. And he'd sworn to her that he was drinking nothing but Oz's herbal teas and listening to nothing but recorded calming chants through his earbuds. "Fine," she mouthed at him. "I won't tell."

"Why don't *you* report?" Jake asked the Watcher. "What's up with Buffy and the slayers in the prison dimension? Are we any closer to springing them?"

"I know the answer to that one," Frankie said. "No. And it's not for lack of my mom trying." The few times she'd seen her mom in the last few days, Willow had looked absolutely harried. Her eyes were all wild, and her hair was all wild, at one point standing up and looking singed at the ends like she'd stuck her finger in an electrical outlet. "I even think she's started taking days off work. You don't think . . . ?" She looked at Spike. "You don't think she's using too much magic?"

Spike stood still while the new Scoobies stared at him. "What are you looking at me for?"

"Because you're the adult," Jake said. "Sort of."

"And because you're the only one who was alive when my mom was doing too much magic. You know what it looks like."

"I missed most of that, actually," Spike said. "I was off getting a soul. By the time I got back your mum was just your mum again, and Dark Willow was a story they told to evil little warlocks who deserved to lose their skins." He nodded to Frankie. "But I'll keep an eye on her. I'm sure Red's fine. She just needs more time to do what she has to do and get Buffy back." When he said that last part, Frankie's slaydar gave a very soft ping. Maybe Spike wasn't the best person to watch out for Dark Willow. Maybe he was willing to let her mom go a little too far, if it meant he got his slayer back.

Frankie gave her slaydar a mental tap on the hand. No. That wasn't fair. And it wasn't fair to her mom either. *I trust you,* she thought, looking at her Watcher. *And I have faith in you both, that you can do this.*

"Well," Spike said, taking up his green jadeite mug, "if there's nothing else to report, then let's get started—"

The Scoobies' attention redirected to the door as Sigmund came shoving through it. Frankie sat upright and thought she heard Spike mutter, "Oh bugger . . ."

"Sorry I'm late," Sigmund said. "I went to see Hailey last week as we discussed—"

"We know," said Jake. "She's back at school."

"Good job," said Sam, giving him a thumbs-up.

"I'm glad she held up her part of the bargain. That's why I've stayed away all day." The half Sage demon adjusted his glasses and looked at Frankie. "I've been trying to decide if I should hold up mine."

"Yours?" Spike asked.

"I've been going over and over our conversation, and I realized it was never actually said out loud. She never swore me to secrecy—well, not about that part, anyway—it was only implied."

"Sig," Frankie interrupted him. "You're rambling, and you're starting to look hot."

"Sorry." He took a breath and calmed his nerves; the Sage demon charm mojo receded, and he looked like normal old attractive Sigmund again.

"Thanks, Frankie," Sam said, and wiped a bit of drool from the corner of his mouth.

"No problem."

Jake cocked his head, annoyed, and tugged Sam closer. "All right, spice rub. Out with it, then."

"Aspen's back."

"Whoa." Jake, and everyone else, half rose out of their chairs. "I changed my mind. In with it. I meant, in with it, then."

"Too late, I'm afraid."

"How do you know?" Frankie asked.

"She's been in contact with Hailey."

"Just like we hoped she'd be," Jake said calmingly. He made chill-out gestures to Frankie, who realized that she must look ready to kill. Her fingers had hooked into claws and dug into the top of the table.

"I'm fine," she said. She willed herself back into her chair. "This is good news."

"Hailey's going to stay on the mission," Sigmund went on. "She feels certain that she'll discover Aspen's specific plans soon."

"Is that the best idea?" asked Spike. "It was all well and good when it was talk. But Aspen's a rogue slayer. A killer."

"If Hailey says she can handle it," Sigmund said, "then I believe her."

Sigmund believed her. But Sigmund loved her. He had the demon love goggles. Frankie sat quietly as her slaydar ricocheted off her insides like a pinball in one of those machines that lit up and had sound effects. There was only one person who knew Aspen well enough to predict whether Hailey was safe. Frankie stood.

"I have to go!" She beelined for the door.

"Hey!" Spike shouted. "Frankie! You can't just run off to your looming boyfriend! There are more important things—What about training?"

But in Frankie's mind, there was no time to lose.

☽ ☽ ○ ☾ ☾

Frankie's impulse was to bust straight into Grimloch's place. It was a tent, after all, it wouldn't have been hard. But she restrained herself and shouted from outside.

"Grim!"

It only took a moment for him to emerge. "Frankie?" He glanced around for danger, but except for her, the woods were quiet. "What's wrong?"

"Have you seen her?"

"Have I seen who?"

"Aspen. Apparently, she's back in town."

"No, I haven't seen her," Grimloch replied. He looked into the trees again, more cautiously this time.

"Are you lying?"

He stiffened, and his eyes flashed blue. She saw him just barely grind his fangs.

"No," he said again.

"Sorry. Had to ask. And that's not why I came. I came for your advice. No. Insight. I need your insight. Can I come in?" He nodded, and she walked past him through the flap. Inside, it was like it always was: sparsely furnished but surprisingly homey. She searched a little, but her eyes detected no lingering traces of Aspen. "You've got to move out of this tent." She touched the canvas. "This thing only gives the illusion of privacy." Grimloch walked back inside and closed the flap.

"How do you know that Aspen has returned?"

"Sig says Hailey's seen her." Frankie crossed her arms. Then she changed her mind and put her hands on her hips. "Is she in danger?"

"You knew that she would be, if your plan worked."

Frankie looked down. They'd all known that. It was just . . . different when it was actually happening. "But how much danger?"

"It's difficult to know. It may be that I never knew her as well as I thought—"

"Will she kill her?" Frankie demanded.

"If she has to," Grimloch replied. "But that doesn't mean she will."

Frankie paced the length of the tent. Hailey was tough, and the spy plan had been worth a shot. But this was going too far. "I'm calling her home. We'll take Sigmund's car, and go to the motel, and get her tonight."

"And then what?" Grimloch asked. "Hailey hasn't uncovered the specifics of Aspen's plan. You'll be no more able to fight the Darkness than you were before."

"I don't care. We were wrong to risk Hailey. If I have to fight Aspen, I will. And if I have to kill her, I'll do that, too."

Grimloch looked at her quietly. "No, you won't."

No, she wouldn't. But she could, almost. "It isn't fair that she has the advantage just because she's a murderous psychopath."

"She doesn't have the advantage. You have the advantage." He touched her temple. "Of clear thoughts. And true friends. Hailey is brave—"

"Yeah, sometimes too brave."

"And she's clever. Let her find what she will find. When you made the decision to do this, you acted as the leader. She went because she trusted you. Are you going to go back on that now? Out of fear?"

"No," Frankie said, and sighed. "I do trust Hailey. I don't trust your murdering ex-girlfriend."

Grimloch trailed his hand down to her wrist, where the delicate gold bracelet glittered. "I can keep an eye on Hailey if you wish. Track her from the shadows."

"I don't know if I want you around Aspen either. What if you get caught?"

But the demon only smiled, as if the idea amused him. "I like that you worry about me. It's quaint."

"Quaint?"

"Perhaps that's the wrong word." He thought about it. "No. That's the right word."

Frankie gave him a small shove. "You're insufferable. Is that the right word?" Grimloch laughed. "It's just . . . sometimes it feels like the Scoobies aren't an advantage. Like I'd be better off alone so I wouldn't have to worry that something . . ." She looked down. "How do I balance being a leader with being a protector? How do I trust them and still keep them safe?"

"All leaders feel that way," Grimloch said.

"Yeah. I don't like it."

Grimloch stepped closer. He touched her chin.

"I was alone, you know," she said, "before I was called. Before the Scoobies formed up around me like the kids from *Captain Planet*. Well, except for Jake. Jake's been tailing me since preschool. But I don't know how to do any of this leader stuff."

"You're doing just fine."

"I thought the fighting was going to be the hard part. Can't I just . . . ?" Frankie made a *V* with her fingers and poked for his eyes.

"No." He stopped it with his palm. "Stop that."

She sighed. "Maybe you're right. Maybe I'm worrying too much. Hailey is a great person. Maybe being around her will make Aspen realize what she's doing. She'll be reformed, and a good slayer again, and we can work with the Darkness to find solutions instead of killing each other. And then my mom will find a way to rescue Buffy and the others—without using too much magic—and Spike will be happy, and we'll all just eat pie and never have an apocalypse again."

Grimloch's eyes wrinkled at the corners. "Have I told you how much I enjoy your optimism?"

"What?" Frankie asked. "It could happen. It's not like I said

Jake's lacrosse team was going to win a championship." She shrugged. She felt better. Calmer. Maybe she really was overreacting. Maybe Hailey was perfectly safe with Aspen, and everything was going to be okay.

The oracle didn't bother to struggle against her bonds because she knew it would do no good. Or because she'd already seen her fate. Aspen wasn't sure. Was that how oracles worked? Did they see all? Know all? And if they did, what was the impetus to keep on going? To wake up every morning with nothing left to chance, no excitement, no wonder, truly nothing to look forward to because you knew how it would turn out? To be so devoted to the intangible force of the universe that you strayed not one foot off the prescribed path, even when that path ended with you in chains.

Aspen looked at the oracle, suspended from the ceiling by golden manacles at her hands and feet. Loops of thick gold chain wrapped tightly around her waist. They were in an abandoned building way out of Sunnydale. There'd be no chance she would be interrupted. And no chance for little Hailey to stumble in and see it either.

Little Hailey. Aspen smiled. She hadn't meant to, but she liked that kid. She was pretty, and scrappy, and a smart-ass. She went a little heavy on the eye makeup, and despite being mad at Frankie she was still obviously trying to pump Aspen for information to feed the Scoobies, but she was cool. In another life, they could have been friends for real.

Of course, now Hailey was a Potential. That was a surprise. When the witch guy had done that stinky spell, and the ball of light hit Hailey, part of Aspen had wanted to grab the Amulet of Junjari and smash it straight through Hailey's rib cage to see if it could absorb some power directly. There hadn't been a Potential since the red witch had activated them all. The last thing Aspen needed was more Potentials, snapping at her heels. But she could figure that out later. For now, from surprise would come opportunity: She could use Hailey's special status to drive an even bigger wedge between her and that pesky baby slayer.

"I can't figure it out," she said to the oracle, hanging from the ceiling. "If you letting yourself be captured was brave, or stupid. I mean, if you saw yourself meeting this end, and kept going anyway, that's kind of brave." She tapped the tip of her knife against her temple. "But it's also pretty stupid." She touched the tip of the blade to the oracle's chin and pressed until the oracle's eyes rose to hers. "Maybe I just don't get how oracles work."

The oracle stared at her. Strange silver blood seeped from cuts inflicted by the manacles and pooled upon the floor like bright splashes of mercury. When she'd first arrived, appearing in the chains courtesy of the summoning spell the old witch guy had performed, the silver stars upon her blue skin had been still and serene. Now the stars writhed and rippled. They moved in fits and starts across her surface like they were trying to escape the very body they adorned.

"This is not my end," the oracle whispered.

Aspen raised her eyebrows. "I'll keep that in mind. But now, is it not because you told me it wasn't, or because it never would have been?" Aspen shook the knife back and forth as if it were her index finger. "That's the trouble with prophecies." She stabbed the knife into the oracle's gut, just half an inch. "Causality."

She removed the knife and studied the tip. Since the oracle's blood was silver, it was almost invisible against the blade.

"Actually, I feel silly asking you these questions, when you must already know what I'm going to ask. Should we cut out the middleman and you can just tell me what you're going to tell me?" She waited. Despite the pain she was in, the oracle didn't seem afraid or angry. It was kind of fascinating.

Aspen sighed. "Fine. You know why I brought you here. Because you were the oracle who came to Sunnydale to visit with the red witch. What did you tell her?"

The oracle swallowed. She breathed in and out.

"Tell me." Aspen pressed the blade to the oracle's throat. When that didn't work, she twisted the chain near the oracle's left wrist, making the manacle cut in deeper. There. That got a flinch. But still no words. "Did you tell her I was coming? Tell her what to expect? How did she destroy the Scythe? How can I get it back?"

"You cannot get it back," the oracle said, and Aspen caught the hint of a smile.

"That weapon was eternal," Aspen spat. "There must be a way to restore it."

"Nothing is eternal," the oracle said, "but eternity."

Aspen stepped back. She wanted to slap the oracle across the face. "Nothing is eternal but eternity. What is that, the oracle motto? Do you have it tattooed on your ass?"

"Why don't you look and find out?" The oracle bared her teeth in a grimacing smile.

Aspen smiled, too. It was better when they fought, when they had some spunk in them. She walked forward slowly and dragged her knife across the oracle's stomach. That got a scream. But it was also too close. The last thing she needed was to spill the oracle's guts all over the floor. If she did that, she'd have to summon another one to read the prophecy laid out in the entrails.

"Just tell me what I want to know. If you know that this isn't your end, then you must also know that you eventually talk. Because if you didn't, I would eventually kill you." She placed the knife back to the oracle's throat. "So stop wasting my time."

91

"Time." The oracle laughed. Then she coughed. No matter how flippant she wanted to seem, she was becoming exhausted. "Slayer. Lower being. Always obsessed with time."

"I am not a lower being," Aspen growled. She dug the blade in just a little, and the thought crossed her mind that she should go ahead and kill this one after all. There were other oracles in the world. Oracles she wouldn't have to torture. Some oracles just wanted to get paid.

But this was the one who knew the red witch. This was the one who held her answers.

The oracle began to grin, as if she could read Aspen's mind. The stars on her skin slowed and dripped to the front of her face. Another cluster collected on her neck around the point of the knife, like they could protect against it.

"Do you know when I'm bluffing?" Aspen asked. She stepped back and removed the knife, then grabbed the oracle's hand and set the blade to her fingers. "If you know when I'm bluffing, then I can't bluff. I need to make up my mind to really do it—"

"The thing you seek is still here," the oracle said.

"The Scythe is still here?"

"The Scythe is no more. But the Scythe is not the thing you seek. You seek the gate. The gate through which the slayer power flowed. And the gate is still here. In Sunnydale."

"The gate through which the power flowed," Aspen repeated. "And if I open that gate, I can channel the slayer power through it and into the Amulet of Junjari?"

"I have told you all you will need to know. Now let me go."

Aspen frowned. She wanted to ask more. She wanted a written booklet of instructions on gate opening and a map with a big X on it that said "Here's your gate!" But she respected that oracles never made things simple.

"Of course I'll let you go." Aspen ran her fingertips lightly across the edge of her knife. "This isn't your end, like you said. But perhaps it is the end of your prophecies. What is it that seers need in order to see?" She pointed the knife at the oracle's eyes, and the oracle jerked backward, bucking in the chains, spilling more of her own blood from her wrists and ankles. "Oh come on, I'm doing you a favor. Without those eyes, you'll be free. I wish someone had done the same thing for me."

The oracle squeezed her eyes nearly shut, but Aspen could still see the whorls of glittering blue and silver, racing around her pupils. Aspen raised the knife, and the oracle began to scream.

"Don't be scared," Aspen murmured. "Two little pokes, and it's all over."

PART TWO

NOBODY EVER TELLS
THE SLAYER ANYTHING

CHAPTER ELEVEN

WHAT DOES HE WATCH NOW THAT THERE'S NO MORE *PASSIONS?*

W illow had never actually been to Spike's place before. She hadn't realized that until she was traipsing down the cement steps to his new basement apartment and was surprised by the bright redness of the door. She'd thought it would be black, like his fingernails. Or let's face it—she thought it would be old wood, like a crypt.

But inside was nice. Cool and dim, because, hello, basement apartment—but completely furnished, with soft white rugs and coffee tables, overstuffed leather furniture—Frankie wouldn't like that—and art on the walls.

"Can I get you anything?" the vampire asked from his open-floorplan kitchen. He looked like his old self today, not his library self, in black pants and a black shirt, unbuttoned to show pale immortal abs.

Spike reached into the refrigerator. "I'm making Bloody Marys."

"With real blood?"

"Of course. But I could hold it for you." He peeked out from behind the open door and winked.

"Isn't it a little late for Bloody Marys? That's a brunch drink. Where's Frankie? Are you meeting her for patrol later?"

"Frankie," he said irritably, "has run off to Grimloch." Spike raised his head above the door and regarded Willow seriously, eyebrows raised. "You should put a stop to that."

"Why? Did he turn evil?"

"He's the kind of demon girls lose their heads over. The kind that makes them do crazy things and cry their eyes out. He's like me." He set out jars of garnish: olives, pickles, stalks of celery, and even tiny balls of white cheese. He threw some chopped heirloom tomatoes into his Vitamix.

"You're pretty full of yourself."

"Red, I speak only from experience."

"Well, I think Frankie can handle it. And if it's a mistake, then it's a mistake she's going to have to make, like we all did."

"Fine. Just don't come crying to me when she's locked in her room listening to Adele."

Willow narrowed her eyes. "You know, you're still kind of a jerk sometimes."

"Yeah, well." He skewered the olives and cheese. "I may not be a villain anymore, but I'm still bad."

Willow smiled. "That's just what I was hoping you'd say."

☽ ☽ ○ ☾ ☾

"You want to tell me where we're going?"

Spike followed a step behind Willow as they walked through the quiet nighttime streets. They'd left her car a few blocks away.

"Do I need to? You know Sunnydale as well as I do." And he probably knew this part better. They were headed for the airport.

More specifically, Cargo Bay 2. Where the shadiest of shady deals went down.

Not that they were all shady deals. Sunnydale did have legitimate businesses. It just had more than its share of less-than-legitimate ones.

Willow tugged on the edge of her sweater. Behind her, Spike looked just how she'd wanted him to look: like a vampire in a big, black coat. Like muscle. But she still felt vulnerable. Her magic couldn't keep her safe from everything. Not from a well-slashed claw, or even a blade to the throat. Sometimes she remembered what it felt like to be dark, the rush and invulnerability that followed in the wake of sucking a volume of black magic dry.

"I don't miss it."

"What?" Spike asked.

"Nothing. Now be quiet." He looked a little hurt, and she made herself soften. She was doing it again. Being snappish. Wanting to cut corners. It was because she was frustrated. A little more magic would make things so easy.

Willow pursed her lips. Even after all these years, the need for magic—the desire for it—never really went away. It was exhausting, and when she was exhausted, giving in started to seem okay.

But that wasn't what she was doing. This was for Buffy. This was important.

They reached the boundary of the chain-link fence, and Willow motioned for Spike to wait as she studied the planes. She knew the aircraft registration by heart. And she knew what the plane would look like. It was a small Cessna Citation.

"There!" She pointed, double-checking the combination of numbers and letters in her mind against the ones painted on the private jet's tail. It had landed. And it was open, and empty. "Perfect. Climb!"

"Why?" Spike asked, but he followed her lead as she dug her toes into the chain link and hauled herself over the top to drop down on the other side. She heard a rip and felt a sharp burn; she'd torn the leg of her pants and cut herself.

"You're bleeding." Spike knelt to check her injury, but she brushed him away and ran across the tarmac, staying low and wishing she had more close-fitting and stealthy-colored clothing.

"Now's no time to get hungry," she hissed. "We have to get on that plane!"

They scurried toward it like shadows and hid for a moment behind the nose and front wheels. Willow scanned for movement. There was no one outside, nor visible through the windows of the cockpit. "Let's go!" She tugged Spike's sleeve, and they stole beneath the belly of the jet and up the airstair.

Inside, it smelled like the odd combination of cigars and new car. Willow quickly headed for the back.

"Willow," Spike said as soon as they were on and found it empty. He tilted his head, looking at the crystal decanter and silver tray. "What are we bleeding doing here?"

"Keep a lookout." Willow fell to her knees and rifled through the cargo. She knew it was here, the thing that would help them bring Buffy home; she could feel it like a tingle in her fingers. It wasn't in the metallic envelope marked by a pentagram. It wasn't in the walnut box with the silver lock that burned when she touched it. It was— "There."

The box was cardboard. Weathered, water stained, and covered with smudges. A few of the corners looked like they were ready to bust wide open.

"That's come a long way," Spike said, peering over her shoulder. "What is it?"

Willow tore the box open and reached into the padding of

wadded up newspaper. Her hands jerked the moment she touched the cover, sensing the heft of the magic inside, or perhaps the whispers of some long-ago curse. "I can't believe it. I wasn't even sure it was real, and then when Willy called and said it would be in Sunnydale . . . that it was being sold right here in Sunnydale . . . I thought he was just, you know, on the take."

"You've been hanging out at Willy's Place?" Spike asked, referring to the coziest demon bar in town. And actually it was Willy's Other Place, as the original Willy's went down in the Spikesplosion with most everything else.

"No," said Willow. "I just pay him to keep an ear out for anything useful." She moved the newspaper away and looked down at the cover. *The Black Grimoire.* One of the strongest books of magic in the world.

"Better hurry up," Spike said, his eyes to the window. "Someone's coming."

"Okay, okay." She wanted to take it out, to feel the leather and stroke the spine. But she did as she was told and packed it back up, then picked up the box to carry it home. She looked out the window. Three dark-jacketed figures were walking to the plane. "Too late!" She looked at Spike. "Hide!"

He gave her a *hide where* shrug, then dove to the floor behind the front row of seats as she pressed herself to the shadowed side of the cargo closet with the box hugged to her chest. She heard the box's owners come up the stairs and squeezed her eyes shut.

"He'll be here in twenty minutes. He's never late."

"Never?"

"Just relax. Have a drink. This is a two-hundred-thousand-dollar payload. He's not going to cock it up."

Willow chanced a look around the side of the closet. The man doing most of the talking looked like a man, though she doubted that anyone dealing in this kind of black magic smuggling was really *just* a man. The one he was speaking to, the one who sounded nervous, was a demon with green skin. Four short black horns studded his forehead. The third figure . . . Willow blinked. She couldn't see him. She retreated into the closet and took a breath before peeking out for another look.

Right into the third man's chest.

Willow winced as he grabbed her by the neck and yanked her out of hiding. "Stowaway," he said.

"Uh . . . flight attendant had a shift change?" Willow suggested as Spike burst out from behind the row of seats.

He threw a few good punches, taking full advantage of the element of surprise. "Willow, move!"

She tried, but the man holding her, who actually wasn't a man at all but a vampire, bared his teeth to sink them into her neck. "Spike!"

Spike launched himself across the small space and pulled a stake out of his duster.

"A vampire with a stake and a woman after *The Black Grimoire*," the human dealer said. He looked at Willow. "It's you. You're the red witch of Sunnydale." His eyes widened. "Don't let her touch that book!"

The demon with the green skin lowered his studded horns to charge and Spike tackled him off course.

"All this for a book?" Spike shouted at Willow. "And since when do you steal things?"

"You heard what they said," she shouted back. "Two hundred thousand dollars; I don't have that kind of money!"

She cried out when the vampire Spike had failed to dust knocked the box from her hands. She dropped to her knees to crawl after it. Spike was starting to lose the fight; he went sailing overhead and came up with a face full of fangs and blood running from his nose. Having had enough of staying on the sidelines, the dealer drew an orb from his jacket. He whispered to it, and the air went thick and Jell-O-like. Willow felt it changing even inside her lungs, the air she'd already breathed becoming solid.

"Willow!" Spike shouted. "Forget it! We have to go!"

"No!" She felt her magic rise in a wave. Her magic fought the dealer's spell and the air became air. The orb in the dealer's hand cracked and then shattered, slicing into his palm. "Spike! You have to get it! It's for Buffy!"

Spike pressed his lips together and gave her a look, his nostrils flaring. He dove for the box just as the green-skinned demon did and caught a sharp horn in the side of his face for the trouble.

"I've got it," he said, wiping at his blood with the back of his hand. "Now let's go!" He scooped Willow up with his other arm and dragged her down the steps. As they ran across the pavement, she heard the dealer scream, "Kill them! Kill them, now, dammit!"

Willow stopped short. Her vision shaded black as she took the box from Spike and reached for the book inside. He asked her what she was doing, but she ignored him and opened the cover. She laid her hand upon the first page she came to. She didn't need to look at it. She didn't need to read.

"Aigis pyrko."

It was only a whisper. But the Cessna Citation exploded in a ball of flames. The blast knocked Willow and Spike onto their backs.

"You blew up a plane!" Spike cried.

"I didn't mean to!" She got up, hugging *The Black Grimoire* under one arm and helping him to his feet with the other. "But just the same, we'd better get out of here."

"It's a book," said Spike, unimpressed as Willow fluttered her hands over the cover. "You used me to get a book."

"It's not just a book." They'd brought it home, and she'd immediately removed it from the box and set it on the kitchen counter. It was large almost to the point of being unwieldy, like a thick, leather-bound photo album.

"So what does it do?" He leaned over it, a cloth pressed to the horn wound in his face.

She opened it and leafed through. The pages were heavy, the edges brittle. The writing appeared to have been done by several hands, in several inks. Some had certainly been done in blood. And some of the diagrams and illustrations were . . . disturbing, to say the least.

"This is *The Black Grimoire*. Or sometimes it's called the 'Book of Wants,'" she heard herself say. "The spells inside are myriad, knowledge and power gained over generations—"

"Hang on, this isn't some black-market family heirloom? Is someone going to be coming after this? Someone with teeth?"

Willow paused. She hadn't thought of that. Or maybe she had, and she'd simply ignored the danger. She shut her eyes and stepped back from the counter as the room tilted. What she'd done tonight was reckless. She'd willfully pushed thoughts of consequences away. She'd put Spike in danger . . .

He wasn't really in danger. He's a vampire. A Big Bad, he said it himself—

"Red."

She felt his hands on her shoulders, cold but solid. She opened her eyes.

"I'm sorry," she said. "I don't know. If anyone does, we'll use what we need and give it back." She was doing it again: talking herself into things. She could hear it, and she could see that he did, too. "Whatever you want," she said, looking at the book, "whatever it is you have to accomplish, you can find it in the pages of *The Black Grimoire*."

"And what are you hoping to find?" he asked.

"A spell to tear down the walls between dimensions." She watched him weigh it in his mind—Buffy's return against the risk—and she knew what he would choose.

"That's a big spell. A Dark Willow kind of spell."

"Not a Dark Willow kind of spell. An *old* Willow kind of spell. The good old Willow kind of spell! I did the ritual to activate the Potential Slayers and I turned to the light, not the dark! I'm a white hat now, dammit!"

"This is different." He pointed to the grimoire. "This is black magic. It's screaming and blood. It takes away the will of the subject and it rebounds on the practitioner more times than not, and don't shake your bloody head at me, Willow! You know it as well as I do."

"Oh, come on." She heard her voice change, the hint of manipulation. The meanness. "Don't go all ensouled on me now. Do you want her back, or don't you?"

Spike stared at her hard. He looked like he wanted to throw something, or smash something on the floor.

"If this goes wrong . . ." he said.

"It won't go wrong." She reached out and playfully tugged on the end of his sleeve. "I promise."

"You'd better be sure that it doesn't. Because if it does go wrong—if *you* go wrong . . ." The vampire sighed. "Frankie will never forgive me."

CHAPTER TWELVE

SHINY HAPPY FUTURE SLAYER

Aspen put down the tailgate of the green pickup and climbed up to lay out a blanket while Hailey waited, holding the bag of burgers and fries. They'd driven out to the desert. Miles from Sunnydale. A dinner under the stars, Aspen called it. Hailey would have preferred the diner. Even with the blanket in the bed of the truck, sitting on the hard metal grooves was killer on the backside.

She handed Aspen the bag and stepped onto the tailgate while Aspen grabbed the drinks and started to unload food.

"Chocolate banana milkshake." Aspen handed it to Hailey and stuck out her tongue. "Blech, you are so gross. Bananas." She sat down beside Hailey and reached into the paper bag to start crunching on fries. "I stopped by the motel the other day. You weren't there."

"I went to school," Hailey said. "Apparently, I'm *this close* to having no future."

"I know what that's like." Aspen unwrapped her burger. "But

there's still hope for you. Frankie's still alive. I think if we just keep her alive for another ten, twenty years, you'll be in the clear."

Hailey smiled. She unwrapped her own burger: mushroom and Swiss with garlic mayo. She'd almost ordered a plant-based patty because she was missing Frankie, but she had to keep up appearances.

"I guess this means I'll never get my vengeance," she said, then took a big bite.

"Is that what you really want? To kill Frankie?"

Hailey stared at her burger. She had to be careful here. She tried to imagine what she would really want, if Frankie had killed Vi. Even if she'd had to, wouldn't Hailey hate her just a little bit?

"Didn't you want to kill Buffy after what happened to Geraldine?"

"I told you," Aspen said, a little sharply. "The explosion in Halifax was an accident." Then she sighed. "But it's okay, you know? If you don't get vengeance. Turns out vengeance isn't all it's cracked up to be."

"What do you mean?"

"I mean look at me." She gestured to herself. She had on a white tank under a lace leaf kimono and torn-up jeans, and she wore a floppy hat even though the sun had long since gone down. Between her fingers she held a keychain and twirled a bright gold key in a circle before letting it rest against her palm. Hailey studied it. The key was old-fashioned, with an intricate looped bow that circled and twisted in an almost dizzying pattern.

"You look fine to me," Hailey said.

Aspen laughed. "Thanks. I'd hate to look like I'm in the back of a pickup in the middle of the desert, eating greasy burgers with a girl who's just as alone and trapped as I am."

"I'm not trapped," Hailey said. Only she realized that she kind of felt like she was. Being a Potential Slayer was a predetermined path. It closed the door on everything else. She wanted it—she'd always wanted it—but now that she had it, she understood what Vi had been talking about. And even what Aspen was talking about. Choices.

"You're right," Aspen said. "You're not. And you don't have to be alone either. Those Scoobies of yours still love you. You could go back any time, if you wanted." Aspen looked at her. "Maybe you should."

Hailey was so surprised she almost choked on her fries.

"Look," Aspen said. "I know what I think about being a slayer. About the way it works and what was done to us. But I'm not here to tell you what to think about it. All I want, for me, and for all of us, is the choice. To make that choice for ourselves." She smiled. "And I'll be the first to admit that right now, I am not what you would call a slayer role model. You need to figure out what you want, Hailey. And Frankie, and Willow, and Spike—even though he's a terrible Watcher—they're the ones who can help you understand what being a slayer means."

"You . . . you think I should go back?" Hailey tensed. This wasn't the plan. But maybe they didn't even need the plan anymore. What Aspen was saying wasn't wrong. "What about Vi?"

"I'm not saying you should forgive them. I just know that if I'd had people like them, preparing me for this, things might have gone a whole lot differently." Aspen looked out across the desert, lit by the growing moon and stars. There were insects out there but they sounded distant, and everything seemed so still. "You know, the Potentials came out here once to seek guidance from the original slayer."

"Vi told me about that," Hailey said. "There was like, a fire and a lot of gourd hokeypokey."

Aspen snorted. "Maybe if someone played gourd hokeypokey with me all of this would have made more sense." She paused and made a face. "That sounds wrong."

Hailey smiled. "So you really think I should just go back?"

"I really do." Aspen took the first bite of her burger and frowned before setting the rest down uneaten. "It got cold." She clapped her hands to free them of sesame seeds.

"I don't know if I want to tell Frankie that I'm a Potential," Hailey said honestly. "I don't know how she'd feel about that."

"So don't tell her. Not until you're ready. But I'm sure she'd take it fine. Take you right under her wing, no drama. Just being around her will help, Hailey. Maybe it would help me, too." Aspen reached under the fabric of her tank top and drew out the Amulet of Junjari. "Because I've just about reached the end of the line with this thing. Without a way to draw our slayer powers into it, it's not even a talisman, it's just an accessory. And green and gold do not go with every outfit."

"I wasn't going to say anything," said Hailey, and Aspen laughed and gave her a shove.

"You know, if Willow and Frankie could just understand what I'm trying to do, they wouldn't even try to stop me. And Willow must know a way . . ."

"She would be the witch to ask."

"But you can't ask them. If you gave so much as a hint that you agreed with me, Frankie would turn on you in an instant."

Hailey snorted. "No, she wouldn't." Only . . . would she? Frankie had disliked Aspen from the moment she saw her. She was like Jake when he first met Sigmund, all growling and raised fur.

"I just don't think you should mention me," Aspen said. "But you do believe me, don't you? That it was an accident? That all I'm trying to do is get us back to what we were?"

"I don't know," Hailey said honestly. "There's been a lot. People have died."

"I know."

"But I do believe that you should have a choice."

Aspen's eyes brightened. "Then maybe, if you see something, or hear something that might help—" She stopped short when Hailey swallowed. "I won't ask you to betray your friends. Only to keep it in mind, what I'm trying to do. We're all trying to do the same thing, if you think about it," she went on, turning a cold french fry before her. "Free the slayers. We're just going about it in different ways."

Hailey looked down at her mostly uneaten burger and took another bite. Hers had gotten cold, too, but she didn't care; she was hungry.

"So that's it, then," she said. "I'm going back. No more roach motel . . . no more . . . whatever that smell is that's starting to stick to my clothes . . ."

"I wasn't going to say anything," said Aspen, and it was Hailey's turn to laugh. She laughed so hard that she didn't see the way Aspen's smile sharpened, or how lovingly she rubbed the Amulet of Junjari with her thumb before dropping it back into her tank top.

☽ ☽ ○ ☾ ☾

Frankie stood at the kitchen island, carefully paging through the book of black magic her mom and Spike had acquired. She didn't want to touch it much; it was old and delicate, and also kind of stained, spattered with faded red and black that Frankie didn't want to think about.

"So what does it do?" she asked as her mom paced nervously behind the breakfast stools.

"It's called the 'Book of Wants.' Or *The Black Grimoire*. Any spell you need, any magic you want, you can find it inside. Magic to solve any problem. Those blank pages, they just fill up according to the needs of the user. It's like the grimoire itself is a spell."

"What about the spells that are already in it?"

"Those are the spells that other people have needed."

"Needed, or wanted? You said 'wants.'" Frankie looked down at the book suspiciously. "And there's strong enough magic here to tear open doors between dimensions?"

"According to its reputation, there isn't a whole lot *The Black Grimoire* can't do."

Frankie frowned and turned a page, and then another, her eyes moving over the spell texts.

"Spells to manipulate time, spells to alter memory, a spell to make the subject obey every command of the holder of this book. Mom!" Frankie slammed the grimoire shut. "Every spell in this book is evil!"

"The only evil is in the will of the witch who casts it," her mom said, but she didn't sound the least bit convincing. Frankie flipped toward the back of the book, where the spells remained unwritten.

"And these blank pages just . . . fill in?" Frankie asked.

"Yes, but don't touch those!" Willow jumped forward, hands up, stopping just shy of snatching the grimoire away. "See, you just lay your hands upon it, and poof! A spell to address whatever you want."

"What happens when it runs out of blank pages?"

"It never runs out of blank pages. No matter how many spells it gives you, there are always more."

Frankie narrowed her eyes. "How much research did you do on this before you went and got it? What happened to the book's other users?"

"I did a lot of research." Her mother went to her laptop, which was open on the table, and shrank down slowly to hide behind the screen. "But I've known about the Book of Wants for ages. I just never thought I'd find it."

That made Frankie's slaydar ping. The Book of Wants was strong. Even Frankie's less-developed magic could feel it. The book kept reaching out to prod her witchiness and give it a soothing shoulder rub: *Come on, open me up. There's super nice stuff in here, and candy . . .*

Disturbed, Frankie shoved the grimoire away and gave it a small spank. She was even more disturbed when she felt the air around it shiver, as if the book had liked it.

"And you and Spike just happened to find a black magic dealer who had it in their inventory?"

"Yes," Willow said. "Well, sort of. Just . . . stay away from Cargo Bay Two at the airport for a while, okay sweetie?"

"Mom! Did you steal this book?"

Willow rolled her eyes. "Can you really steal an evil book? Can it even ever really be owned?"

"Yes, and yes." Frankie nodded and stomped her foot. "Mom—"

"Hello, Rosenbergs! Anybody home?"

Frankie stopped talking, and she and Willow looked at each other in surprise. That was Hailey's voice, pitched low and calling to them from just inside their front door. With matched expressions of glee, the two witches bolted from the kitchen to slide into the entryway and skid to a stop on the rug.

"Hailey?" Willow asked.

"Seems like." Hailey set down her duffel bag and shrugged, lingering in the open door like she wasn't sure she was going to be welcomed back.

"What—" Frankie started. "What happened?"

"Well, Aspen's in Sunnydale, which from the not-surprised look on your face I guess Sig told you. And she says I should come back and give you guys another chance."

"She said that?" Willow's brow furrowed.

"Yep. So here I am." Hailey held out her arms. "Ready to do that fake forgiveness for killing my fake sister thing. And to move back into my old room, if it's still available."

Frankie and Willow looked at each other. Of course it was still available. They hadn't touched it since she'd left, except for some light dusting. Frankie stepped forward and folded Hailey in a hug.

"Sorry I ruined the plan," Hailey said over Frankie's shoulder. "When she said I should come back here, I couldn't think of anything to say to convince her I shouldn't."

"Well, I'd be lying if I said I was sorry it was over. We missed you." Frankie looked Hailey over, from her jet-black hair and black long-sleeved T-shirt to the ripped-up knees of her jeans. "We were worried you were starving or something. But you look good. I'm digging this whole First Nations Jessica Jones vibe."

Hailey grinned. "Thanks. That's just what I was going for."

"Let's get you back upstairs!" Frankie bent and picked up Hailey's duffel. "Mom!" she shouted when Willow made to slink back to *The Black Grimoire*. "We still have more talking to do about that book." She gave her mother a serious look. But that could wait. Right now she was too happy to have Hailey home. And she couldn't wait to go back to school together tomorrow and have the first real, fully attended Scooby meeting in ages.

CHAPTER THIRTEEN

MAYBE HE SHOULD CHECK
THE DOSAGE ON THAT TEA

W hen Frankie sent out the text for an early morning
library meeting, no one whined about it. They were
all too excited to have Hailey back in the fold. Well,
except for Jake, apparently, who despite Frankie's tapping foot and
repeated texts remained absent. Sam's chair was empty, too, but
that was understandable; Sam hadn't known Hailey as long, and
Frankie'd made it pretty clear that the meeting wasn't an emergency
with a capital E. Sam wasn't obligated to get up before the butt
crack of dawn. But Jake? Jake should've been there.

She looked across the room into the open door of Spike's office,
where Hailey was dabbing some cover-up and foundation onto the
bridge of the vampire's nose and blending out around the yellow
bruises surrounding his eyes.

"Good thing you're back," Spike said, holding still so she could
finish. "Or I'd have had to miss another day of work."

"Since when do you like work?" Hailey asked, smirking.

Spike jerked away and stalked out of the office. "Next time I'll
just have Frankie glamour it."

"You know what Frankie says about that, putting a glamour over an existing glamour," said Sigmund.

"Like putting a hat on a hat," said Frankie, and the three of them stifled their giggles as Spike scowled. He pulled out his chair at the head of the table and sat down.

"Let's just get started."

"What about Jake?" Frankie asked.

"I'm sure we'll miss his usual contributions of yawns and making googly eyes at Sam," Spike muttered. He nodded to Hailey. "What's the word on Aspen and the Darkness?"

"Word is no word." Hailey shrugged. "She just said I should come home."

"And that's it?" Spike cocked an eyebrow.

"Well, I'll still see her, I guess," said Hailey. "It's not like she sent me away while throwing rocks at me and crying about how I was born free."

"Is it wise to see her, though?" Sigmund asked. "If you're not seeing her with a purpose? Is it worth the risk?"

"Who says I'm not seeing her with a purpose?" Hailey asked back and chucked him under the chin with her finger. "I can still spy. It'll just be easier now. I won't have to pretend. I can see you guys without doing weird hand signals; I can go to school so I don't flunk out and doom myself to another year of direct Hellmouth exposure."

Sigmund's eyes went briefly glassy. "A study on the effects of prolonged exposure to the Hellmouth would be extremely fascinating."

"But wait." Frankie looked between Hailey and her Watcher. "So that's it? We know she's here and we know where to find her, and we don't attack? Are we slayer neighbors now? Do we wave to each other over the hedges?"

Spike sat back. "I know it feels wrong," he said. "But Aspen isn't currently a threat, and she is still dangerous. Even for you, Mini Red. So we wait and see what Hailey finds out."

"The goal was never to attack her," Sigmund added, "but to gather information on her plan."

"A very Watchery response." Frankie drummed her fingers on the table, eyebrow cocked at them both. "But is it right? I mean, it doesn't feel like we can attack her when she's not doing anything, but shouldn't we? For all the past bad stuff? The explosion? The deaths?"

"Maybe not," Hailey said quietly. "Maybe it *was* an accident, and if it was—"

"An accident?" Frankie blinked. "You don't really believe that."

"Of course she doesn't," Spike interjected. "And even if it was, Aspen killed slayers. By accident or on purpose, she has to pay."

"Like you paid for the slayers you killed?" Hailey asked.

Spike's eyes widened.

"Hey," Frankie said. "That's not fair. Spike feels that guilt every day."

"So guilt is enough? You just say, 'oh, I feel bad,' and all is forgiven?"

"No, but—"

"Look." Hailey took a breath. "I'm not saying it isn't complicated. And I'm not trying to go after Spike. He went and got a soul, for eff's sake. You can't repent much harder than that. All I'm saying is if we believe in redemption and real change for him, then we should believe in it for other people."

"Like Aspen," said Frankie. She didn't like the turn the conversation had taken. She wanted a warm, fuzzy Scooby reunion, not an argument on redemption arcs.

Hailey shrugged.

"Maybe the difference is that there's a process?" Sigmund suggested amid the tension. "As a demon Spike struggled and failed with morality—and with common decency—for years before the Spike we know regained his soul. Aspen attacked the slayers less than a year ago. And just two months ago, she seemed more than willing to harm Frankie if it meant she got what she wanted. Is that enough time to be redeemed?"

"She was backed against a wall," said Hailey.

"A wall she made!" Spike half shouted, pushing his chair back to lean on the table.

"Or maybe a wall that Buffy and Willow made," Hailey said, standing to lean on the table, too, "when they unleashed the slayer line and let it fly willy-nilly over little girls who—"

Frankie and Sigmund looked at each other. But just as they'd silently agreed that Sigmund would grab Spike around the waist and Frankie would grab Hailey, Sam burst into the library holding Jake's letter jacket. Spike and Hailey promptly stopped arguing, and Frankie rose out of her chair at the look on Sam's face. He was pale and out of breath. Shaky.

"Sam? What's going on?"

"I don't know." He looked down at Jake's jacket and squeezed it. "Jake was supposed to meet me before the meeting, and he never showed. I went looking for him, and I found this." He held up the jacket. It was destroyed. The sleeves dangled in ribbons. "I'm not trying to worry, but it looks like . . ."

"Like he shredded out of it," Frankie whispered.

"That doesn't make sense," said Sigmund. "It's more than a week until the full moon." Immediately, he and Hailey and even Spike pulled out their phones to check their moon trackers, like they might have made a mistake. They didn't know that Jake had been having trouble with his wolf. Frankie was the only one who'd seen him partially transform in the middle of the afternoon the other day.

"I'm going," she said. "Get word to Oz and have him meet me at Marymore Park. Sig, monitor the Sunnydale hashtags and flag anything that references big dog sightings or any posts that tag Sunnydale Animal Control."

"I'm on it," Sigmund said, grabbing a tablet.

"I'll patrol the grounds of the school," said Spike, slipping out of his tweed jacket. "Which just happens to be the only place I can patrol this time of day without frying crispy."

Frankie nodded. "Sam, you should stay with Spike."

"No way." He stepped close. "I'm going with you."

"Spike has just as good a chance of finding him at school as I do in the woods." She took Sam's shoulders. He was scared. Terrified. "Sam. Werewolves are attracted to teenage hormones. And the Hellmouth. Both of which the school has in spades. Spike is going to need your help to calm Jake down and to cover for him if Spike finds him. He wouldn't want anyone at school to know."

"Okay," Sam said. "Okay, I'll stay here, just in case."

"Good." Frankie turned to Hailey. "Hailey, I hate to ask you to miss class after only a few days of showing up again, but—"

"Can I go to your mom's and see if she can do a tracking spell?" Hailey was already gathering her things. "No problem."

"Get the tranq gun from the safe," Frankie said. "Just in case he heads home in search of snacks." She glanced at Jake's shredded jacket, still clutched in Sam's hands. "And, everybody, be careful."

"You too, Mini Red," said Spike. "You get bitten, and you'll be the world's first slayer-witch-werewolf."

Hailey smiled wryly as she backed out of the library doors. "Isn't that known as the Sunnydale triple threat?"

𝄃 𝄃 ○ 𝄂 𝄂

Frankie met Oz in Marymore Park at the edge of the woods. He handed her a tranquilizer gun, and both wore similar gritty frowns as she checked the sight and hefted it over her shoulder. "Do you have any idea where he could have gone?" Frankie asked.

"If he started to change at school then he would've run as far from people as possible. Your instinct to come to these woods was good. We going to swing by the tent and grab Grimloch?"

"I think he could help." Frankie glanced at Oz. His face bore his usual lack of expression, but he was scared. A faint line creased the space between his eyebrows, and his jawline trembled like he was clenching and unclenching his teeth. "Oz, I know you've been helping Jake learn to control the wolf. He says you've been using teas and chanting—did you have any idea this could happen?"

"No," Oz said, and Frankie was sorry for even asking. "But I should have been more careful. Jake's werewolf wasn't turned, it was born. There was really no telling how he would respond to any of it."

"Let's just find him."

They walked together into the forest, senses on high alert. It seemed to take forever to get to Grimloch's tent, but at least he heard them coming and met them outside.

"Frankie," he said. "What's wrong?"

"Jake is missing. He might be in his werewolf form despite it being daytime. And not a full moon. Also, you have to get a phone; this is ridiculous. Can't you use some of that 'ancient money' and at least get a burner?!"

Oz sniffed the air. Following his lead, Grim did, too. Frankie knew that as a werewolf, Jake had his own special scent signature. She was both happy and sad that she couldn't smell it.

"Now that we're together," said Oz, "we should split up. I know how that sounded," he added when Frankie and Grim gave him a look. "But we'll cover more ground."

Frankie nodded. "We'll take the ravine and head southeast to the clearing. Oz, you backtrack on the north side. Keep your phone handy; Sig's going to text with leads, and so will my mom if she manages to cast a tracking spell." She took the tranquilizer gun down from her shoulder. "If you need backup, howl."

"What if you need backup?" Oz asked.

"Grim will howl."

"Frankie, if Jake's hurt, or if he's hurt anyone—"

"Don't think that. It'll only slow you down. The important thing is finding him."

Oz smiled at her. With just the corner of his mouth.

"It's good to see you like this," he said. "You remind me of her."

☽ ☽ ◯ ☾ ☾

Hailey was almost to the front doors of the high school when she realized she'd left her phone in the library. She wheeled around and dashed back, then popped through the doors just in time to surprise Sigmund.

"Hailey," he said.

"Forgot my phone. Why do you look like that?" He was the only one left in the library, and the expression on his face was decidedly shameful. "Did I catch you mid naughty internet search? You know you're supposed to be looking for Jake—" She reached across the table and grabbed her phone, quickly looking at it to make sure she hadn't missed any messages from Frankie.

"Oh no, that's—" Sigmund started, but he was too late. Hailey had grabbed his phone by mistake. The screen wasn't locked, and what she saw when she looked down were pics and messages from a very pretty girl who appeared to be named Natasha. A very pretty, very Sage demon girl, if one was to judge by the twisting set of horns.

"Oh," Hailey said softly.

"That one's mine," said Sigmund as she handed it back. He pulled her phone out of his pocket. "I was going to give it to you the next time I saw you."

"Great, thanks." She looked down and was mortified to find her vision had begun to blur. She was going to cry. She was actually going to cry, just because of a few photos, a few messages. A few heart emojis. She held up her phone and tried to act triumphant. "Now you don't have to."

"Hailey . . ."

"Gotta go." She walked backward. "Gotta get to Willow's so she can do the mojo . . ."

"Hailey, it's not—"

She waited, but of course he didn't finish. Because what was he going to say? That it wasn't what it looked like? It was exactly what it looked like. And Sigmund wasn't one to lie.

"It's great, Sig," she said, horrified by how froggy her voice sounded. How impossible it felt to smile. "I'm happy for you."

"Hailey, wait."

Hailey didn't wait. She turned and walked as quickly out of the library as she could, and waited to wipe the tears from her cheeks until she was out of the parking lot.

$$\text{)} \text{)} \bigcirc \text{ (} \text{ (}$$

"I wish people would stop saying that," Frankie said as she and Grimloch picked their way down the ravine. "That I remind them of Buffy."

"I think he means that you are a real slayer now," Grimloch replied. "That you've grown into the responsibility."

"I know. And I wish they would stop it."

"Why?"

"Because it doesn't feel like I have. It feels like I'm pretending half the time. Faking it but not making it." She adjusted her grip on the tranq gun. She didn't like guns. Not even when they were loaded with darts. Holding it was making her palms all sweaty.

"Have you told your Watcher this?"

Frankie shook her head. She didn't want Spike to feel like he was failing, and honestly, she was ashamed. She bet Buffy never felt this way.

"If you had a choice," Grimloch said, "if the Darkness wasn't evil and it was truly possible to return your slayer powers . . . would you choose to decline this calling, and go back to being Frankie, not Frankie the Vampire Slayer?"

"Just Frankie." She snorted. "Just Frankie was nobody. She didn't have Scoobies. She certainly didn't have a hot demon boyfriend in a billowy coat."

"What's with the billowing coats? Everyone notes that, and I wear jackets."

"It's because of an old boyfriend of Buffy's. I'll introduce you sometime. You'd probably like him." Frankie cocked her head, teasing. "He's old, too."

"How old?"

"About as old as Spike?"

"An infant," Grimloch said, and sniffed.

"Anyway . . ." Frankie sighed. "If I wasn't a slayer, what about me is there to like? So hell no, I wouldn't give it up." They walked on, ears attuned to the sounds of snapped twigs or snarls. Before she was a slayer, Jake had been the only one looking out for her, all the way back to when they were little witch and little wolf. She wasn't about to let him down now.

"Frankie," Grimloch said quietly. "There's plenty about you to like. It's true I wouldn't have known that if you weren't a slayer, because I wouldn't have been watching. But that would've been my loss. And if no one saw you before you were called, then that was their loss, too."

Warmth spread in Frankie's chest. She smiled.

"Jake saw me. And he annoyed me. If anything's happened to him, or if he's done something . . . it'll wreck him." She let the tranquilizer gun droop and scanned the quiet woods. "Where the heck did he go?"

$$\quad \Big) \; \Big) \; \bigcirc \; \mathbb{C} \; \mathbb{C}$$

All the way to the Rosenbergs', Hailey couldn't get the messages on Sigmund's phone out of her head. Natasha. What kind of a name was that, anyway? A pretty nice one, that's what. Why did Sage demons get to have all the good names? Sigmund, Sarafina. Natasha. So much more musical than "Hailey," which sounded like something that grew in a field, or like a shouted greeting to a person named Lee. *Hey! Lee!*

"And I bet she wears, like, colors," Hailey grumbled as she walked up the front steps.

Inside, the house was quiet. She called for Willow a few times and popped her head into the basement. She checked the garage and found the Prius, parked and present.

"Willow?" Hailey jogged up the stairs and knocked on the witch's bedroom door. "Willow? Are you in there?" She thought she heard something from behind the wood, some kind of humming or softly playing music. She tried the knob. Locked. And locked tight. The knob wouldn't even wiggle, as if it had been sealed by magic.

"Willow!" Hailey pounded on the door. "I don't want to interrupt whatever you're doing in there, but Frankie and Jake need help!" She pounded on it again. "Willow!"

But Willow didn't respond. And behind the door, the strange music kept on playing.

$$\quad) \;) \; \bigcirc \; (\; (\quad$$

There was no end to the power contained within *The Black Grimoire*. So many spells, performing so many functions. And so many pages. Willow's eyes watered from the strain of reading all of the differing, scrawling scripts as her index finger led her gaze down spell after spell. She was tempted to simply sink her fingers into the pages and take all of the grimoire into herself. But she didn't, and whether that was a testament to her willpower or to some protective enchantment on the book, she wasn't quite sure.

"Willow!"

She heard her name being called, but it seemed far away. She heard it again, along with some pounding.

"Willow, are you in there?"

That sounded like Hailey. Hailey, calling from somewhere. But that hardly mattered when she had so many pages left. Nearby, in her bag, or maybe on the table, she heard a familiar tune, and it took a moment for her to place it: the ringtone on her phone. How annoying that she should hear it now, when she was in the middle of something so important.

All she'd wanted was an hour or two to herself to try to find a way to rescue Buffy. She didn't know that was going to be so unreasonable. She glanced out the window. The light didn't look right. It should have been the soft light of morning, not the bright sun of midday.

She looked down at the book. How long had she been there, reading? How much time had she lost to it, and had she lost anything else? Who, she wondered, had been reading whom?

But that was ridiculous. The Book of Wants was merely that: a book. And books were good things. Books were safe.

But not all books, cautioned a voice in her head, a voice that sounded curiously like Giles.

I'm backsliding, she realized. *This is backsliding.*

And immediately after, a part of her whispered, *I don't care.*

CHAPTER FOURTEEN

EVIL PEOPLE DON'T GET TO HELP

The scream that cut through the forest didn't belong to Jake. But Frankie could guess that Jake was probably the reason for it. "Move!" she said, and she and Grimloch started to run, following the sound. She pulled her phone out of her pocket to call Oz, but the uneven terrain made it impossible to hold steady and run at the same time. She could barely unlock it. "Grimloch! Can you howl or something?"

"No," he said.

"Grim, this is an emergency!"

He growled a little and plunged through the undergrowth. Unfortunately, with Frankie so close behind, that resulted in a lot of branches and ferns smacking her in the face.

She slung the tranq gun over her shoulder and swung onto a low branch, doing her trick of leaping from branch to branch. Ahead, the screams continued, so at least whoever Jake was after wasn't dead. Yet.

As the trees thinned the clearing began to come into view, and from Frankie's elevated vantage point she saw the Jake wolf, on all fours and swiping at what looked to be a hollowed-out tree trunk. And the tree trunk was shouting.

"Help! Please somebody help me!"

She was going to have to tuck and roll, and hope she was stealthy enough that Jake wouldn't hear her coming. Or at least that he would be too preoccupied with his tree-boxed lunch to care. But just as Frankie reached the last branch, another slayer burst into the clearing and hit Jake with a spinning kick.

The werewolf yelped, and it didn't matter if he'd been about to eat a hiker; Frankie hated that sound. She hated it, and Aspen was the one who'd caused it.

Aspen advanced on Jake. He was disoriented from the kick, and it was easy for her to dodge his claws. Her fists connected with his stomach and the side of his head. She kicked him, and he dropped to the forest floor and cried like a puppy.

"Leave him alone!"

Aspen straightened, surprised when Frankie tumbled onto the grass, all of her smooth tucking and rolling forgotten in the heat of her temper.

"What do you mean 'leave him alone'? It was about to murder that hiker!"

"Don't you touch him again!" Frankie flew at the other slayer, and the feeling of her fist connecting with Aspen's jaw was delightfully satisfying.

"Stop it!" Aspen shouted, but Frankie simply jumped and drove the heel of her foot into Aspen's chest to knock her flat on her back. Aspen rolled to her side and got up, her pretty face a grimace. "Grimloch! What the hell is wrong with your girlfriend?"

"The werewolf is Jake Osbourne," Grimloch said. He'd emerged from the trees and stood frozen.

"Well, I didn't know that," Aspen spat. "Also, who the hell is Jake Osbourne?"

"You might not have known it was Jake, but you did know it was a werewolf," said Frankie. "So human for most of the month!"

"Yet I thought it was a special case, considering there's no full moon and it's completely daytime!"

The two slayers glared at each other. Frankie was about to fling another insult when the Jake wolf tackled her into the grass.

"Frankie!" Grimloch shouted, but she couldn't respond—she was too busy dodging snapping teeth. She looked up at the wolf through squinted eyes. He looked different. Not like he usually did when she visited him in his cage. He still had his pretty, red-gold coat, and the same brown eyes. The same snarling snout panting meat breath inches from her face. But his face had . . . expression. And that expression was Jake's.

"Jake?" Frankie said. "Can you understand me?" She wrenched on his shoulders to keep him at bay. "If you can understand me, then stop . . . trying . . . to kill me." For a second, the Jake wolf looked at her desperately, and his whole body froze. Then Aspen grabbed him around the midsection and threw him into a tree trunk.

"No!" Frankie cried.

"What is your problem?" Aspen cried back. "Have you considered a thank-you? Why, you're welcome, slayer junior, I'm happy to keep you from becoming werewolf chow."

"All I needed to do was tell him a story!" Frankie shouted, and Aspen looked at Grim like she suspected Frankie was suffering some kind of a breakdown.

"Frankie!"

Oz had appeared at the edge of the clearing. His werewolf ears must have been able to hear all the fighting, and the screams. He pointed past them, to the hollow log that the hiker had climbed into to get away from Jake. In the hiker's efforts to climb back out of it, it had come loose from where it was wedged and started to roll. Straight for another ravine.

Oz leapt toward it, and Frankie glanced at Grim.

"Go," he said, turning to face Aspen as the Jake wolf shook his head and started to get to his feet.

"Yeah, go," Aspen agreed. "We'll take care of your wolf until you get back."

Frankie scowled as she raced away. She didn't like that. But she had to save the hiker.

Oz reached the log first. It had gained momentum, and his first attempt to grab it resulted in nothing but a broken-off branch. He snarled and partially transformed, using his claws to crack through and grab on to the trunk just as Frankie flipped over the top and leaned against it to stop the roll. Her legs braced as the toes of her shoes skidded through the mud and moss.

"This is a big frickin' tree," she groaned as it came to a halt. Oz punched through more of the bark to reveal a very frightened, fairly dizzy hiker, his cheeks smeared with dirt and his clothes covered with sawdust. He was wedged in there pretty deep.

"Are you okay?" she asked after she'd pulled him out.

"I think so?" His eyes were wide and his voice shaky as he looked around, and Oz deftly hid his hands as the claws and fur receded. "What was that?"

"Bear," Frankie quickly supplied. "We're from the parks department; we'll get it handled."

"There are bears here?"

"Well, not usually. Sir, were you bitten?"

He shook his head. "I got into the tree pretty fast. It couldn't reach me."

Frankie figured he was right; there were no slash marks in his clothes and no visible blood. But he was also in a bit of shock, so she took the liberty of feeling up and down his arms and turning him around to check his back.

"Hey, what—"

"Sorry," Frankie said. "Just a routine injury check. You'd better get out of here. And if you get home and discover any bites or open scrapes saliva could have gotten into, I want you to go immediately to the Sunnydale Emergency Room." Sigmund could hack into that system and keep an eye on it.

"For a scratch?" the hiker asked.

"This species of bear has been known to carry infectious diseases," Oz said. "Better safe than sorry."

"Okay." They got the hiker on his way and waited until he was safely on the trail before racing back to Jake.

"Can you believe they buy that 'parks department' stuff?" Frankie asked as they ran, gesturing down to her pale blue T-shirt with a happy planet on it. "Like, who do they think the city is employing?"

"Sunnydale goggles," Oz replied. "Just be glad it works."

When they reached the clearing, Grim and Aspen were trying to subdue the Jake wolf. Grimloch held him down, his hands on the wolf's shoulders and his knee resting on his back. Aspen was getting up after being tossed a short distance away. When she saw Frankie, she jogged over and plucked the tranquilizer gun from her shoulder.

"Wait!" Frankie cried, but Aspen aimed and fired, and the Jake wolf went limp. "You didn't have to shoot him!" Frankie said as Grimloch got up.

"It's only a dart," Aspen said. "He'll be fine."

"He'll have a headache," Frankie growled as she knelt. She knew how she sounded—unreasonable and cranky. But that's also how she felt.

Aspen gave the tranquilizer gun to Oz, who hurried to join Frankie at Jake's side. He pulled out the dart and the fur disappeared, until it was just naked Jake lying on his stomach. Frankie took off her gray hoodie. "Take this," she said, handing it to Oz so he could wrap it around Jake's waist. "And give it back after many washings."

Jake's eyelids fluttered. "Oz? Frankie?"

"We're here," said Oz. "It's gonna be okay, Jake."

Aspen stepped closer. "Is he going to be all right?"

"He should be," said Oz. "Thanks."

"Thanks for nothing," Frankie spat.

"I was just trying to help," Aspen said.

"You don't get to help. You turned in your helping card. So get out of here." Frankie's eyes rose to the other slayer's. She was surprised by how angry she felt. She hadn't felt nearly so hostile even when she'd been preparing to fight Aspen in the warehouse. But this was different. Aspen was putting on a show. Making herself seem good. Harmless. Helpful. It was the same show she must have put on for Hailey, only Hailey didn't see it. Judging from the uncomfortable looks on Oz and Grimloch's faces, neither did they, but Frankie didn't know how. Her slaydar was clanging like a fire bell.

"Whatever," Aspen said, and turned to leave. Before she went, she gave Grim a look that was kind of pitying. *Poor Grim,* it seemed to say, *to have to deal with this angry, unreasonable little slayer.*

"Frankie," Oz said. "You okay?"

"I'm fine. Let's just get Jake back to my house."

☽ ☽ ○ ☾ ☾

131

Sam and Spike were pulling into the driveway as Frankie, Oz, and Grim unloaded a semiconscious Jake from the van.

"Jake? Jake! Is he okay?" Sam called as he ran to help. Spike, steaming from the midday sun under a fire blanket, dashed up the front steps to hold the door open.

"Get him onto the table," Oz ordered, and Grimloch quickly cleared the kitchen table of obstacles with a sweep of his arm that sent their salt and pepper shakers crashing to the floor.

"You found him, thank god." Hailey came out of the living room with her phone in hand.

"I texted Sig already," Frankie said. "He's on his way." Frankie rushed around the kitchen and wrapped an ice pack in a towel, then rolled another towel to place beneath Jake's head. The wolf in him had faded entirely, seemingly taking the effects of the tranquilizer with it. Jake was starting to come to.

"Jake?" Sam held his hand and kissed it, leaning over him. "Are you okay?"

"Yeah, bro, I'm good," Jake whispered, his voice a rasp, and Sam laughed.

"Stop calling me that; I'm your freaking boyfriend."

"But you're still my bro." Jake grinned. "Now you're just my hot bro."

"Clearly Jake's fine," Hailey said with a smile. "So what happened?"

Jake struggled to sit up just as Sigmund burst through the door.

"Hey! Watch the daylight!" Spike leaned out of the way.

Sigmund quickly closed the door. "Thriller! Thank god."

"Spice rub," Jake said with the ice pack pressed to his head. "I didn't know you cared."

"Of course I care, you big oaf," the Sage demon replied. "Though now that you're safe, my mind turns to science. How did this happen with no full moon?"

"And before lunch," Hailey noted, cocking her head toward the kitchen windows, the curtains drawn tightly shut to preserve Spike.

"Spontaneous transformation is possible in the early stages," said Oz. "I'd hoped you could control it."

"I tried," said Jake. "And when that failed, I ran. As fast and as far as I could, while I was still me."

"Do you remember if something upset you? For me the transformation was always an emotional response."

Jake thought a moment, then shook his head. "I don't remember."

"Do you remember Aspen?" Frankie asked. Every head in the kitchen turned her way. She didn't know whether it was that she said Aspen's name, or the way she said it. Her voice was sharp as a knife. Aspen made her feel like hitting something, like lashing out, and she didn't know why. Well, she knew why. Aspen had killed slayers. She'd hurt Buffy and was holding her captive. She was a liar and an all-around ass. But this felt like more than that. Frankie took a deep breath.

"Aspen was there?" Hailey asked.

"She helped," Frankie said curtly. When Sigmund, Sam, and Spike looked confused, Oz explained.

"She kept Jake distracted and out of trouble while Frankie and I rescued the hiker he'd treed. Literally."

Sigmund, Sam, and Spike still seemed confused. But Frankie's eyes were on Hailey. "You don't seem surprised," Frankie said.

Hailey shrugged. "She's a slayer at heart, right? She won't *always* do the wrong thing. When it comes to werewolves she'd follow the same rules as everyone else."

"Why would she follow those rules when she didn't follow the ones about not killing people?" Frankie countered.

"Look, she's not a total psycho is all I'm saying. She has a wrong idea. But also kind of a right idea."

"Kind of a right idea?" Frankie asked. "I can't believe what I'm hearing."

"Oi." Spike stepped closer, in between the two girls. "What's going on? As far as I know, you two have never said a word out of lockstep." He peered at Hailey. "You didn't go and get yourself brainwashed, did you? Pretend to turn on the Scoobies only to actually turn on the Scoobies?"

"No," Hailey said, offended. "Never. Frankie's my best friend. And if anyone asks me to take sides, I'm taking hers."

Frankie's cheeks warmed. The knots in her belly loosened, just a little bit. Maybe that was all she needed to hear.

"But I *am* a friend." Hailey looked at Frankie, and the knots snapped tight again. "And friends have to say what's on their minds. I think you might be quick to judge Aspen's motivations, because of what happened at Slayerfest—"

"Well, duh," said Frankie.

"And because of her history with Grim."

Frankie's mouth dropped open. "That is not—" She turned to the other Scoobies for support and found them all wearing sheepish expressions. "That is not what this is! I'm telling you, she's bad news. She's going to use the Amulet of Junjari to suck all the slayer powers into herself just like we thought—" She stopped. They doubted her. And she couldn't blame them. Especially Oz and Grim, not after how she'd behaved in the woods.

"It did seem like you were immediately angry," Oz said.

Frankie took a deep breath. No one was going to believe her if she didn't calm down. "I was," she admitted. "Because I sense something. You have to believe me. Hailey—"

"I've just spent more time with her than you have," Hailey said. "I've seen some things, and understand some things, that aren't all bad."

"Not all bad? She's holding Buffy in a hell dimension! She exploded the slayers! Our whole mission was defeating her, and you're defending her instead?"

"That's not—" Hailey looked away, disappointed. "This is just how she said you'd react."

Frankie's mouth dropped open. It was happening right before her eyes. Aspen was turning her Scoobies away from her. She had that kind of magnetism, the kind that Frankie had never had. *Given enough time, even my mom would like her better,* she thought irrationally, just as Willow came down the stairs.

"Hey," Willow said. "What's everybody . . . oh my god, Jake!" She rushed through the kitchen and touched both sides of his face, and the top of his head, and all down his body for breaks and bruises.

"Wait, you've been up there the whole time?" Hailey held up her phone. "I was pounding on the door and calling and texting nonstop."

"I—" Willow stiffened. "I was . . ."

Spike pointed a finger. "You were with the book!"

"What book?" Oz asked.

"The evil book," Frankie said, and looked at her mother. "Mom!"

As the kitchen devolved into shouted accusations and exclamations of innocence, peppered with cries of "Someone tell me what's happening, I've been a wolf for three hours" from Jake, Spike went to the light switch and flickered it on and off.

"Emergency Scooby meeting," he bellowed, and everyone

quieted. "Underwear model, get out. This is all starting to unravel, and we're having a meeting RIGHT bloody NOW."

"Uncle Spike—"

"I'm the Watcher! And the one benefit of tweed is when I say 'meeting,' meetings happen." He gestured to the living room. "So everyone who's less than ten thousand years old, get in there!"

PART THREE

SAY THAT YOU'RE HAPPY NOW,
ONCE MORE WITH FEELING

CHAPTER FIFTEEN

ON THE BUFFY PHONE, LONG, LONG DISTANCE

"I am, technically, less than ten thousand years old," Grimloch said quietly as Frankie said goodbye to him at the door.

"I know. But Spike's serious. He's looking all Giles-y. And Spike's right. The Scoobies are starting to splinter; we need to get back on the same page. I'll come find you later?"

"If I don't find you first," Grim said as he walked down the steps.

"That sounded like a threat, you stalker."

"I know. I heard it, too." He didn't turn around, and Frankie smiled and shut the door. When she went into the living room she found everyone seated except for Spike, who stood beside the weapons trunk with his arms crossed.

"Was there absolutely no other robe?" Jake asked. He was wearing one of Willow's, which was pink and fuzzy and embroidered with daisies.

"I have a black kimono with lilies on it, do you want that?" Hailey asked, and Jake shrunk deeper into the fuzzy collar. "Also, no one made you wear the matching slippers." She looked down at his pink-clad piggies.

"All right," Spike said. "Who goes first?"

"You called the meeting," Hailey said.

"Well, I didn't call it to run it. I just thought we needed to have one. Everyone was acting like a bunch of babies." He looked at Frankie. "Or magic fiends." He looked at Willow. "Or distracted, lovesick teenagers." He looked at Hailey and Sigmund. "And don't get me started on who's flunking out of werewolf school." He looked at Jake. "Have you all forgotten what we're supposed to be doing here?"

"I haven't," Frankie said. "We're supposed to be stopping Aspen."

"And rescuing Buffy," said Willow.

"And controlling our inner werewolf," said Jake.

"And some of us do have more things on our mind than romantic entanglements," Hailey said, with a glance at Sigmund.

"Well, if you'd just give voice to them," Sigmund replied, and suddenly everyone interjected with their own goals and why everyone else was going about it wrong, and the living room became a cacophony of bickering.

"All right, all right," Spike shouted, and everyone stopped what they were doing as he started to dig around in his pants. To their collective Scooby relief, all he pulled out of them was Buffy's silver cross in its protective wrapping of satin. "Have you all forgotten?" He shook the cross in his fist. "That there are slayers trapped somewhere? Heroes, trapped somewhere, who've saved countless lives—who've saved the world! And they're depending on *us*." He held the cross out to Willow. "Call her. Call Buffy. We need to remember what we're fighting for."

Willow took the cross.

"Can I help?" Frankie asked.

Willow smiled. "Sure, sweetie." Willow placed the cross in her palm, and Frankie lay her hand over it. The moment their fingers interlaced, the air in the room shifted. It sharpened, and a scent like sun-warmed rocks permeated the air.

"Something's going on here." Buffy's voice rippled through the room. "Willow? Is that you?"

"It's all of us." Willow looked around, then seemed to decide against individual introductions. The interdimensional phone calls through the cross weren't easy; already Frankie felt simultaneously energized and shaking. She was going to need a double shot later just to get through patrol.

"All of you?" Buffy asked. "Is everything okay?"

"Just checking in," Willow assured her. "Seeing how you are."

"We're okay. Still trapped in this hell dimension."

Frankie looked at her mom. To Frankie's ears, Buffy sounded like she always sounded: brave. But Willow would be able to hear the cracks. The weariness. Her mom's lips drew into a thin line.

Through the cross, Buffy's voice trailed off, and they heard her speaking to someone else. "Fine, Andrew. Andrew has a theory he wants to tell you. Is there a way for him to do that, or do I have to repeat everything that comes out of his mouth? Because my patience for that would wear thin quickly."

"I think we could hear him if he puts his hands on you?" Willow suggested. They waited a few beats. "Buffy? Did you hear me?"

"I heard you, Will. I'm just trying to decide which unappealing option to choose." She sighed, and a moment later, Andrew's voice flooded into the air of the living room.

"Oh my god Willow and Spike I am so happy you're here! Or not here, but *here*. When Aspen and those rogue traitors tried to blow us up and sucked us into this demon dimension I thought I'd never see you again."

"Which he still can't," said Spike. "Can someone prod him along?"

"Andrew?" Frankie asked. "Buffy said you have a theory?"

Andrew inhaled deeply. "Yes. Every time that little rat traitor Aspen came to visit us—and by visit us I mean taunt us and gloat about her *murders* and feed us our disgusting gruel slop—"

"Andrew," Buffy snapped, to get him back on course.

"Sorry. As I was saying. Every time that whiny little psychotic brat came to visit us, she came through a door. And usually it was the same door. But the last time I noticed that it didn't look like quite the same door, even though it was in the same place. And there was always a sound, of a key turning in a lock. So I think that maybe she has some kind of key, and maybe it unlocks any door. And turns it into a door into our prison dimension."

"Wait a minute," said Hailey. "I think I've seen that key." She rushed forward, and in her haste knocked Frankie's fingers aside to grasp Willow's hand over the cross. "Hey, did you ever see this key? Was it gold, with nine swirling loops on the bow?"

"What's a bow?" Andrew asked. "And who is this?"

"This is Hailey. I'm Vi's little sister."

"Oh my god, Vi's little sister! I didn't know Vi had a little sister. Also, why did your sister betray us and turn all evil?"

"Andrew," Buffy interjected.

"Well, it was a real slap in the face."

"Andrew, did you see the key?" Buffy asked.

"No. I only heard it in the lock."

"Okay. Interdimensional phone time over." They heard Andrew's muffled objections, and then it was only Buffy on the line again.

"Does that help?"

"Maybe," said Frankie, sliding her hand back onto the cross after Hailey released it, a bit sheepishly.

"And that's not the only lead we have," said Spike. He nodded to Willow. "Tell her."

"We also have another lead," Willow said. "Maybe another way to get you home."

"It's a big evil book," Spike interjected, even though Buffy couldn't hear him. "Tell her."

Willow looked at the vampire from underneath her brow. "I'm trying." She took a breath. "It's a . . ."

"Big . . . evil . . . book," Frankie prompted, and her mom scowled.

"A big evil book?" Buffy asked. "Willow?"

"It's not evil. Well, it is evil. But I'm going to use it for good, so I don't want you to worry about it, okay?" There was a heavy pause from the prison dimension. "Just sit tight. We'll have you out of there in what for you will feel like only a day!"

"Wait, there's a time distortion? Willow, how long have we been gone?"

But Willow broke the connection. She wrapped the cross and shoved it back into Spike's hands.

"Mom, why didn't you want to tell her about *The Black Grimoire*?"

"Because I didn't want her to worry. Like I don't want you to worry." She glanced around the room and settled on Oz. "And stop looking at me like that."

"Like what, Willow?"

"Like you're about to throw a yellow crayon at me. I'm fine." She stood and paced a few steps behind her chair, arms crossed. "And even if I wasn't fine, we don't have a choice."

"Is that true," Oz said quietly, "or is it an excuse?"

"Can *you* perform the spells in *The Black Grimoire*?" She turned to each of them. "Frankie, can you?"

"Maybe, if you'd let me try—"

"I didn't think so," Willow declared as if Frankie hadn't spoken.

"Wait." Sigmund cleared his throat and adjusted his glasses. "If we can get ahold of that key that Hailey saw . . . it certainly seems safer to unlock an interdimensional door than to try and perform any interdimensional spell from *The Black Grimoire*."

Spike snorted. "You can't go off something that Andrew bloody said. And even if we could, I don't know how much safer it'd be, trying to get a key from a psychopath." Frankie straightened. At least her Watcher saw Aspen for what she was.

"Still, it might be worth a chance," said Oz. "Since we have someone that she trusts." They turned to Hailey, who leaned back on the couch.

"Yeah, I don't know if I'm comfortable with that. I mean, I used to pick pockets a little, but not from someone who could squash me like a bug."

"So you think she'd squash you like a bug?" Frankie asked.

"No. But maybe she'd hurt me just on reflex."

"Fine." Frankie stood. "New plan. I'll go and find Aspen, beat her down, and take the key. No stealing necessary."

Spike peered at her. "Are you out of your bloody mind?"

"What?" Frankie looked around. "You all think she's so helpful, right? Reformed? Not a threat? So either you're right, and there's no danger to me going to fight her, or you're *wrong*, and it's a bad idea."

"Pretty sure it can still be a bad idea," said Sigmund.

"Why don't you just let me talk to her?" Hailey asked.

"Talk to her," Frankie repeated skeptically.

"I'm not going to try and steal the key. But maybe we can come to some kind of understanding."

Frankie looked around at the Scoobies. She didn't like this plan, but it was clear she was overruled.

CHAPTER SIXTEEN

IF YOU WANT GRIM'S BODY, AND YOU THINK HE'S SEXY, ASPEN'S GOING TO LET HIM KNOW

G rimloch heard her coming. He was the Hunter of Thrace, and he knew what being hunted sounded like. He heard her from so far away, in fact, that he had time to put on a pot of tea. When Aspen stepped through the flap of the tent, he held out a cup and offered it to her.

"Sugar?" he asked. "I don't keep any cream. No refrigeration."

Aspen made a sour face as she took it and held it while he added two lumps with a tiny pair of silver tongs. "Has anyone ever told you you're annoying?"

Grimloch smiled as he sipped from his own cup. "You would be less annoyed if you stopped trying to sneak up on me. What do you want?"

Aspen cocked her head playfully. "Just what every girl wants. The freedom to live the life she chooses and the love of an immortal hunter god."

"I meant what do you want today."

She set the teacup down and ran a finger across the cool surface of his table. "I guess I keep foolishly expecting that one of these days I'll show up and things can be just like they were." She tucked her long hair behind her ear and pushed the rest over her shoulder. There was a time when such a movement would have laid him bare. And he would be lying if he said he wasn't tempted to run his fingertips down her throat, to pull such a strong and wild creature closer. But everything was different now. He saw things about her that he hadn't seen before, and now the feelings she evoked were only memories. Dull reflections of the things he used to feel. The feelings that were bright and sharp were the ones he felt for Frankie.

It was strange to realize that. He'd been sure that he and Aspen would burn bright for the rest of her life, and long after into the endless years of his. But their time apart had changed them. What she had done, and who she had become to do it, had changed them.

And, of course, there was Frankie. Frankie had also changed things. What he valued. What he wanted.

"It will never be just like it was," he said. "But we don't have to be enemies. If you stop what you are doing and remember your purpose."

"My purpose." Aspen's jaw tightened. "Oh yes. To be an instrument in the fight between good and evil. To stick my neck out to save people who are just as likely to be destroyed by themselves or each other as they are by a demon." She sighed. "I've done that for years. Now I get an early release for time served. You should come with me. If you stay here with the new slayer, all you'll do is work, work, work."

He watched her as she slunk around the tent, arms out to run her fingers along the canvas.

"Is that why you're here? To say goodbye?"

"Are you ready to say goodbye to me, Grim?"

He wasn't. But goodbyes didn't really exist for a being like him, who could travel wherever he wanted, whenever he wanted, when he could find whomever he sought no matter how many years had passed. Goodbye wasn't real until they were dead.

"If you're going to stay in New Sunnydale," he said, "you have to stay away from Frankie and her Scoobies. You're upsetting her."

"I'm just looking for a solution to my problem. I'm not making trouble."

"And you have to release the other slayers."

"Can't." Aspen shrugged. "If I let Buffy go now, she'd kill me right and proper. I can't let them go until I'm beyond their reach. Until we all are."

"Where are the other members of the Darkness?" he asked, but she shook her head. She couldn't trust him. And he couldn't trust her.

"Grim, hey, are you—" Frankie ducked under the half-open tent flap and stopped midsentence. Aspen backed away from her teacup.

"I was just leaving." She slipped past Frankie and out into the woods.

"What was she doing here?"

"I don't know," Grimloch replied. "I think she came to talk."

"And you just let her in?"

He looked at Frankie and shrugged helplessly. "It's a tent. Frankie, we weren't—"

"I know." She crossed her arms and looked at her shoes. She looked so small. So overwhelmed. And there was only so much he could do to help. In the end, slayers were alone in their burdens. "I know," Frankie growled. "But she's making me crazy! And I can't seem to stop it."

CHAPTER SEVENTEEN

MACHO, MACHO WEREWOLF;
I WANT TO BE A MACHO WEREWOLF

wo nights after Jake's spontaneous wolfing, things had mostly gone back to normal. It wasn't as if the Scoobies had had a real fight. It had just been a disagreement. A bubble-up of emotions because they were all stretched thin. Only that's not all it was. Frankie could feel it, unease simmering inside them, covered over by forced smiles and too many jokes.

Frankie opened her dresser drawer and pulled out a thin long-sleeved T-shirt to wear on patrol. Spring was rolling right ahead, and the Sunnydale nights were starting to lose their crispness in favor of a mellower kind of cool. But the cemetery might still get chilly, if there were no vampires to chase after. Also, sometimes it was windy—a relatively new phenomenon starting after the Spikesplosion turned the city into a hole.

Frankie wandered into the hallway, twisting her red hair up into its usual bun. She stopped at Hailey's open door and peeked in. Hailey wasn't there, but Frankie lingered a minute anyway. The guest room of the Rosenberg house. That's what it used to be. But now it was solidly Hailey's bedroom. Frankie smiled at the knitted pillow of Animal from *The Muppets* and the studded collars holding back the relentlessly cheerful floral curtains. The black bedsheets that clashed with absolutely every other color in the pale-yellow Rosenberg-painted room.

"What?" Hailey asked, making Frankie jump as she padded in barefoot, long black hair still wet from the shower. "Have I made a mess already?" She picked up a few crumpled T-shirts and threw them in the corner.

"No. I was just thinking." Frankie leaned against the doorjamb. "How I hope this is your room for a really long time."

Hailey looked up from toweling her hair. "Me too. Though maybe we could repaint? All this yellow with all this black—it looks less Goth and more like I'm really into bumblebees."

"Could you get really into bumblebees?" Frankie asked. "Bumblebee Goth would be adorable."

Hailey laughed. "They do sting only once before dying. Tragic. But they're out too much in the day, and they're way too into flowers. Plus, I hear they like to cuddle."

"So," Frankie started. "I'm sorry I snapped at you the other day. About Aspen."

"I get it," Hailey said. "I just . . . I know her better? Which was kind of bound to happen . . ."

"I know. I guess I just wish that you didn't. Because I feel like we're going to have to make some hard choices when it comes to her."

"Maybe not," Hailey said hopefully. "When we get Buffy back, she can make the hard choices for us."

Frankie smiled, but only a little. When they'd first faced the Darkness, she'd thought the same thing. That if they could only get the other slayers home, they would take care of the problem. But Aspen was starting to feel like Frankie's fight. Which was something she couldn't say to Hailey, even though she wanted to.

"So how are things with you and Sig?" Frankie asked. "When you were gone, every night it was 'Hailey this' and 'Hailey that,' and I would have to be all, 'Excuse me, Sig, I am trying to fight the forces of darkness.'"

But instead of being happy to hear it, Hailey's face fell. "Yeah. I think he got over that. He's messaging some Sage demon girl now. I saw it on his phone."

"What? Since when? He hasn't said a word about it to me. I wonder if he told Jake."

"Don't know." Hailey tossed her wet towel into the pile with her T-shirts and slipped on a black jean jacket.

"But he loves you."

"Doesn't matter. I am not supernatural enough for the DeWitt clan. But you know, slayers are kind of part demon, so—" She stopped abruptly, and her eyes snapped to Frankie's like she'd said something wrong.

"No, it's fine," Frankie assured her. "Slayers are kind of part demon, with the demon essence of our powers. Besides, we like some demons. There is no blanket demon judgment."

"Right," Hailey said.

They walked together to the cemetery where they would meet up with the other Scoobies and Spike. Her Watcher had some kind of special training planned after they'd finished their usual sweep for fresh vampires. Sigmund was waiting for them at the entrance and waved.

"I, uh, need to retie my boots." Hailey bent down. "You guys go ahead."

Frankie frowned. "Go on, Sig! We'll catch up!" He nodded and disappeared inside. But he seemed sad about it. "Is this how it's going to be?" Frankie asked. "You avoiding Sig, Sig avoiding you . . . you take one apocalypse, he takes the next?"

"No." Hailey stood. "Or not always. Being broken up is fine, you know? It hurts, but I can handle it. Knowing he's already seeing someone else? That's a whole new kind of suck."

"You'll get to a place where it's okay. Where you can just be Sig and Hailey again."

"Well, I wish it would hurry up. Do you think he could say something horrible and misogynistic to me? So I'd get over him faster?"

"I don't think Sigmund would even know what that was," Frankie noted.

"Yeah, but he could ask Spike." They started to walk into the cemetery. "Speaking of guys who are too hot for our own good, is Grim coming?"

"No." Frankie looked away. She wasn't angry with him for talking with Aspen, alone, in his tent. But seeing her there had gotten under Frankie's skin. "He's, um, hunting. For tasty demon organs."

"Gross. I take back what I said about him being too hot. Frankie, are you okay? You seem like you want to tell me something."

"I do," Frankie said. "But I can't."

"I want to tell you something, too." Hailey scuffed the toe of her boot against the stones of the path. "But I can't either."

"So what does that mean? What are we going to do about it?" They looked at each other quietly. And then they walked on.

☽ ☽ ○ ☾ ☾

Jake and Sam met them where the path forked near the Meyer crypt. Well, Sam met them, anyway. Jake said hello and then trailed behind, messing around on his phone. Sam was wearing a bright aqua polo shirt over a pair of dark pants.

"Are you wearing that for the patrol?" Hailey asked. "To make yourself more bitable?"

"You think I'm not usually bitable?" Sam asked.

"Vamps do love bright colors," Frankie noted. She nodded to Jake. "How's he doing, since the whole daytime *rawr*?"

"He's okay. I've been doing a lot of comforting. In addition to being extremely bitable to vampires, I also make an excellent werewolf chew toy." They laughed, and Sam nudged Frankie with his elbow. "Thanks for finding him. And not letting the leader of the Darkness break his furry neck."

"She wouldn't have done that," Hailey muttered, but Frankie only said, "You're welcome. Who's he texting so much?"

"Jordy."

"His brother? As in the mostly feral, constantly troublemaking biter of Oz, starter of the whole werewolf family?" Frankie stomped over to Jake and pulled his arm down to snoop at his text thread.

"Hey!" Jake exclaimed. He tried to tug away, but slayer strength.

"Coming back for a visit?" Frankie read with horror. "No way, Jake, he is not coming back from Weretopia! We kind of have"—she gestured all around—"enough."

"He's not coming back." Jake gave a firmer tug, and she let go of his wrist. "It was just an idea we were floating. I thought it might be good to have another perspective on the whole taming your inner beast. Since Oz's has been . . ." He made a gesture with his hand depicting ups and downs.

"That's true," said Hailey. "Other perspectives, always good."

"But Oz knows what he's doing as much as anyone can," Frankie said.

"Really? Is that why I just wolfed out at school and nearly ate a Crave Case of classmates?"

"You only nearly ate one hiker. And Oz said the random transformation might happen."

"Yeah, he also said it would only be partial, like the claws or extra facial hair."

"Well, it's just that you're different, Jake. You're a Whoops Baby."

"Exactly. I'm different. So I'm exploring different options." Jake looked into the sky and glared at the growing moon. "I've been doing it Oz's way for weeks, okay? And it's going nowhere. It's going in the wrong direction."

"It takes time," Sam said quietly. "You said it would."

"I know. But there's no reason not to try other methods. Like Rhodacarthia tincture."

"Rhoda what now?" Hailey asked.

"It's an herb Jordy's been using. Says it let him take control really fast. He's sending me some. Express mail."

"Does Oz know?" Frankie asked, and looked at Sam. The expression on Sam's face told her that Oz didn't.

"Not yet," said Jake. "But I'm not going to hide it or anything. Hey, vampire."

Frankie spun just in time to see the vampire leap from behind the headstone. It was just a baby vamp, freshly dug from the grave, but it was already sprightly, and before she could draw her stake it caught sight of Sam in his bright aqua shirt and grabbed him.

"Sam!" Jake darted ahead, knocking Frankie back in the

process, but it was Hailey who got to Sam first. She shoved Sam's head down and twisted the vampire around by his shoulder to thrust her palm up into its nose.

"Ow." It staggered backward, hands to its face. "Why did you do that? Is my nose bleeding?"

"Um, let me see." Hailey went closer, to peer into the vampire's nostrils. "Nope, all good," she said, and staked it through the heart. Frankie bounded up for a high five.

"Quick thinking," she said. "And nice aim with the stake."

"I learned from the best," Hailey said, and when Frankie's face fell, added, "From you and my sister. Not Aspen."

"Of course," Frankie said. "I knew that." They walked farther down the hill, toward the older section of the cemetery where there were fewer fresh graves. Frankie saw Sigmund, waiting patiently with his nose in a book, a small penlight illuminating the pages, and Spike, standing on top of the Rimbauer crypt. "Uh-oh."

"What?" asked Sam.

"He only gets up there when he really wants to torture me."

"Mini Red," Spike said as they approached. "What took you so long?"

"Vampire," Jake explained. "Hailey dusted it."

"So, Watcher." Frankie clapped her hands together. "What brilliant piece of training do you have for me tonight?"

Spike gave her a look. Normally when a slayer said that kind of thing to her Watcher she was being sarcastic. "I do have something special, in fact. Say hello to my old friend—" He proceeded to rattle off an incomprehensible combination of consonants, glottal stops, and snorts. "But you can call him Steve." At the introduction, a man stepped out from behind the crypt. Or at least, he looked like a man. His head was entirely bald, and he had eyes that were an odd shade of brown. Almost yellow. He was dressed all in black, but on closer inspection, the skin of his torso was some kind of stretched, dark membrane. Frankie could see veins in it. And the pulse of Steve's blood running through them.

"You're a Nachanmuller demon," Sigmund said, adjusting his glasses and putting his pen light in his pocket to keep himself from inspecting every inch of Spike's friend. "It's an honor to meet you—"

Frankie and the other Scoobies blinked as Sigmund repeated the demon's name perfectly.

"You would know how to do that," Hailey said, impressed. "What's a Nachan . . . mewler?" she whispered to Frankie.

"They're a species of demon from western Europe," Sigmund supplied. "A clan, really. There are so few of them."

"They're mimics," said Spike, looking down at Frankie with his arms crossed. "They can flawlessly replicate whatever opponent they face, from the fighting style right down to the strength level. You need practice fighting slayers. And without Vi, we don't have anyone to practice on."

"So he's going to mimic *me*?" Frankie bobbed her head back and forth, and after a moment, so did Steve. "This is weird."

"You have to be ready, Mini Red. For whatever comes. It'll be just like that Sage demon mirror spell, except without the extra mirror strangeness."

"I think this is plenty strange," Frankie said, raising her fists into a fighting position. "Do I have to do anything? To get him started?"

"No way," said the demon, in a particularly Frankie tone. "I had your number the minute I saw you!"

Jake and Sam laughed. "He sounds just like you!"

"He does not," Frankie muttered. But, of course, he did.

"All right, Mini Red. On the attack. Don't hold back."

Frankie threw a punch, and the mimic dodged it easily. She swung her arm back in a reverse, and it dodged that, too. She tried to go faster, testing blows, not full strength but more than half speed, quick combinations that were blocked and returned. Eventually, Steve hit her in the face. Frankie staggered back. It felt like being hit by a slayer, all right.

"Again," Spike ordered, so Frankie went again. She was starting to feel looser, starting to have fun, and when she drove her heel into the side of Steve's knee he went down with a cry and rolled out of the way, right into a headstone. She winced.

"Don't stop, keep after him."

She did, and caught a kick to the stomach with an audible oof. After that, both she and Steve simply tried to dodge, leaning and ducking this way and that, with mutual exclamations of "yipes" and "whoa."

"Um, Spike," Hailey said, "I don't think this is exactly how most slayers fight."

"This is just how Frankie fights," Jake agreed. "And it's kind of embarrassing to see the pair of them."

"Yeah," said the vampire as he watched, squinting. "I maybe shoulda thought of that."

Frankie, however, thought it was fine fun, right up to the moment when Steve made a *V* with his fingers and jabbed her in the eyes. "Ow!" she cried, one hand to her face as she tried to feel around her with the other to keep from tripping over headstones. "My signature move!" How did he know that? And why did everyone seem to think it was such a bad one? It hurt like a mother, and her vision was totally compromised.

She couldn't lose to a mimic. That would be too humiliating. Like losing to herself. Did Steve's mimicry extend to magic? It was worth a shot. She swung her arm wide and sent her telekinesis out in a wave. She heard the Scoobies cry out as they were hit with it, too, some knocked over and others lifted into the air and dropped. But she held her focus and was able to feel the moment her magic wrapped around the demon. She closed her fist and sent her magic up.

Frankie blinked. Her eyes were still a little teary, but she'd done it. Steve was suspended in midair beside the Rimbauer crypt. Hovering and harmless.

"I did it!" she cried, just as the mimic demon raised its arms, and she felt herself thrown across the cemetery to land on her back.

Frankie opened her eyes to see Spike, Steve, and the Scoobies leaning over her.

"Don't feel bad," said Sigmund. "Nachanmullers are legendary. Nearly impossible to beat."

"Good to know."

Jake and Sam helped her up while Spike said his goodbyes to Steve, with an exchange of cash and what Frankie could swear was a couple of tabby kittens. "Hey," she snapped. "He's not going to eat them, is he? Because we can just give him more cash instead."

"I'm not going to eat them," Steve said, cuddling the furry bundle to his cheek. "I love them."

"Well, that's adorable," said Hailey as Steve and the kittens blinked out of existence.

Jake sighed. He stuffed his hands into his pockets. "So this was a less than successful training exercise," he said to Spike.

"No," said Frankie. "It was great. It was fun."

"It wasn't supposed to be fun," Spike said. "It was supposed to be a challenge."

"It was a fun challenge."

But the vampire refused to be cheered. "We're not done, Frankie. We're going to hit your training hard. Every day. Every day until the Darkness is gone, or Buffy comes back."

CHAPTER EIGHTEEN

I'M THE BAD GUY . . . DUH

Willow was on the phone with Frankie when she heard Oz's van pull into the driveway. "I am being safe, sweetie. Only one hour with *The Black Grimoire* before a mandatory tea break." She tapped her fingernails against the cover of the book. It rested beside her empty teacup on the kitchen table and she felt it tap her in return, as if it was just as anxious to get back to being read as she was to get back to reading it. Only Frankie kept on chirping in her ear. "Yes, I'm setting a timer. My eyes are eye colored. Hey, who's the mom here?" She looked down at the book and tuned her daughter out while she stroked it. "Mm-hmm. Mm-hmm. Huh? Yes I *am* paying attention! You just focus on your training, young lady, and stop worrying about me. That's Oz at the door right now, so I'll be fine."

She set her phone down as Oz poked his head in the door. "Willow?"

"In here. I was just talking to Frankie. She's taken it upon herself to become my magic addiction sponsor."

Oz came into the kitchen and eyed *The Black Grimoire*. His

nostrils flared slightly as he scented the air. *For what?* Willow wondered. Black magic didn't have a smell. Except that it kind of did, and it was warm and scorchy and caramelized.

"Frankie's just worried." He stopped short of saying that they all were, but she could see it on his face. It was touching, how much they cared. Almost as touching as it was annoying that they didn't think she could handle it. "Is she still at school? Jake didn't mention a Scooby meeting."

"Extra training with Spike."

"He's hitting it pretty hard."

"I could hear him bellowing in the background for her to get off the phone." Willow pursed her lips. "He's trying to be a good Watcher. Even after all this time, he still kind of sucks at it."

Oz snorted softly. "So how's it going with—?" He sat down and jutted his chin toward the grimoire.

"Fine. Making progress." She ran her hand over the cover again. Truthfully, all she and the grimoire had done was bond. Get to know each other. She'd read it, and it would read her. Eventually, it would suss out what she wanted most in the world—a way to bring Buffy and the other slayers back, plus Andrew, if there was time— and then the book would craft a spell to give it to her.

It was easy. And it was nice. It felt a little like falling in love, and in the same moment she also realized she couldn't remember the last time she'd thought about Sarafina.

Uh-oh.

"So how is Jake? Frankie says he's been talking to Jordy in Weretopia."

"Yeah. He got a package of Rhodacarthia tincture from him in the mail yesterday."

Willow tore her eyes away from *The Black Grimoire.* "Rhodacarthia? Isn't that dangerous?" Werewolves sometimes used

Rhodacarthia to subdue their wolf spirits, but it could backfire. She'd read about cases where the human was completely subsumed. Moon or no moon, only the wolf remained.

"It can be. If he uses it responsibly, he should be fine."

"But do you really want him—"

"I can't tell him what to do, Willow." Oz's expression, usually more open with her than with most people, closed off. "I'm not his father."

Willow frowned. She wasn't technically Jake's parent either, but she felt like it sometimes. She'd put Band-Aids on his scrapes, she'd fed him pizza and burgers and covered him up in a blanket when he fell asleep on her sofa. She'd been to more of his losing lacrosse games than Ken and Maureen put together, and the idea that somebody was putting her Jakey in danger upset her enough to punch briefly through even the haze of *The Black Grimoire*.

"Did he say that to you? Oz, he didn't mean it. Well, he did mean it, but . . . Jake knows how much you love him. He knows you've been there for him. Ken and Maureen know it, too. As for Jordy . . ."

"Jordy would never hurt his brother."

"Not on purpose. But no mess Jordy has ever gotten himself into was on purpose. Except that one time with the mailman." Willow's brow knit. Oz had never tried to interfere with raising Jordy and Jake. But everyone knew he was the Osbourne pack leader.

Oz gave her his best *I'm going to be fine* closed-lip smile. "So . . . what are you finding in that thing?"

"Nothing. This much magic is delicate." That seemed to put him at ease. It made it sound like she was being cautious, and she made a mental note to say more things like that.

"Have you talked to Xander lately? He and Dawn had any luck?"

"I talked to him yesterday, but I don't want to tell him about the grimoire until I know it'll be of use. He'd just worry. Besides, he's got enough on his plate: Dawnie's getting desperate. He says she's been talking about seeking out a shaman to turn her back into a dimensional key."

Oz cocked an eyebrow. "I was unaware that was a possibility."

"It's not. Pretty sure Dawnie was a single-use, one-door-only kind of a key." Of course, if they could press Dawn's hand into the Book of Wants . . . Willow gazed down at the cover. It was basically a genie in a bottle. Who knew what they could turn Dawn into, if she wanted it badly enough? She could become a dimensional skeleton key, and think of the possibilities—

"Willow?"

"Huh?" She turned. Oz had somehow gotten up from the table and gone to the refrigerator without her noticing.

"I asked if you wanted a sandwich?"

"Oh. Sure. Thanks." She'd drunk what felt like a few gallons of tea, but she couldn't actually remember the last time she'd eaten. That was bad. The way she felt about the grimoire, that was also bad. She wasn't denying that. But she was doing it for Buffy. She was doing it for Frankie. She just had to hold on to herself for a little longer.

$$ \mathcal{D} \; \mathcal{D} \; \bigcirc \; \mathcal{C} \; \mathcal{C} $$

Frankie got off the phone with her mom just in time to block a hit from Spike. "Hey!" she cried. He was only using a sparring stick, but still. "A little bit of warning?"

"No warning from the underworld," Spike said, and swung again. Frankie ducked it and spun back onto the training mat he'd rolled out in the middle of the library. The drill today was protecting eggs. Spike would give her a raw egg, and then he, Sigmund, and Sam would try to break it, with any combination of fists, feet, and weapons. Frankie was covered in raw egg and cracked shells.

"All right." She held her hands up. "That's enough. This is not a vegetarian-friendly exercise."

"You're an ovo-vegetarian," Jake called from the sidelines without looking up from his phone. "You eat eggs."

"Not this many."

"You could have saved them all, Mini Red. All you had to do was guard them." Spike tossed her a fresh egg.

"There are three of you!" Frankie cried. But she calmed. Re-centered herself. And used her telekinesis to send the egg high into the air to hover out of reach.

"Hey," Spike said. "That's cheating." Frankie shrugged. "And it won't work. Sigmund!"

"On it," Sigmund said, retrieving his bow and arrows.

"Sig, don't," Frankie peeped, zigzagging her egg around near the ceiling as he took aim.

"Hey, Frankie," Jake called. "Jordy says thanks for the undead meat."

"What?" Frankie turned, her concentration broken. Sigmund didn't even have to loose an arrow; her poor little egg dropped and went splat against the library floor. "Dammit, Jake."

"He also sent a yum-yum emoji." He turned his phone so she could see. She hoped he was joking. They'd sent the pieces of the Countess to Weretopia for safekeeping, not for eating. But just the thought of chewing on the pieces, the idea of Countess bits swimming in Jordy's stomach—literally swimming, doing tiny, meaty backstrokes—

"Blech." Frankie stuck her tongue out and shook her head. "That's it, training over. I'm going home to put some butter in a pan and scramble these clothes."

"I'll give you a ride," Sigmund said. He returned his bow and arrows to their case and eyed Jake as the werewolf unscrewed a glass vial and used a dropper to place several drops of brownish liquid on his tongue. "Is that the Rhodacarthia?" he asked. "How much are you taking?"

"Just enough," Jake replied. "Honestly, I already feel amazing. Like I'm part wolf all the time."

"You *are* part wolf all the time," Frankie said.

"Yeah, but like . . . more." He stood and stuffed the vial into his pocket. "If you and Sig are good to get home, Sam and I are going to hang with the guys from lacrosse. Sam! Let's go meet up with the guys."

"Excuse me, Cap?" Sam said. "I'm unused to being ordered around off the lacrosse field. Can I get that in the form of a question?"

Jake made an apologetic face and went to give him a pecking kiss. "What is, Sam would you like to go hang with the guys at Giovanni's?"

"What is, yes I would," Sam replied, and smiled.

"You guys are cute," Frankie said as the four of them walked out of the library.

"Hey!" Spike shouted from his office door. "Who's going to help me clean up these eggs?"

☽ ☽ ○ ☾ ☾

Hailey was alone in her room when Aspen tapped on the window. She'd left the Scooby meeting early to catch up on the mountain of classwork she'd missed while living at the roach motel and had just finished her hourly "snack break" to check on Willow and *The Black Grimoire* in the kitchen when she heard a distinct knock against the glass.

Not knowing what else to do, she got up and opened it. The slayer swung inside feet first.

"Did I scare you?"

"Sort of? I know you're a slayer, but it's still weird to see a face in a second-story window."

Aspen smiled, and for a moment the two stood in awkward silence. "I missed you. You're kind of my only company right now." She looked around Hailey's room, nodding approvingly at the studded collars holding back the curtains, raising her eyebrows at the pattern of the curtains themselves. "This is much nicer than the motel." She started to wander, to the dresser, to the closet, and Hailey's eyes flickered to the door. "I won't stay long," Aspen said, noticing.

"No, it's not that. You're totally welcome. Except that you're totally not welcome, you know?"

"I know," Aspen whispered. "So I'll keep my voice soft." She wore a cute white top with gathered sleeves and shimmery, delicate embroidery over a pair of loose gray pants. Her brown hair hung long and smooth down her back, and, of course, the Amulet of Junjari peered out from her collar, the dark green gem seeming to wink inside its gold setting. She didn't look right, in the room. She didn't feel right, in the house.

This is wrong, something inside Hailey whispered, and she wondered if it was her version of slaydar. Potential slaydar. But if it was, it was weak and not fully realized, so she shoved it aside and ignored it.

Hailey glanced at Aspen's pockets, wondering if the key she'd seen was in there somewhere, and if her pick-pocketing skills were good enough for her to swipe it without the slayer noticing.

But she hadn't been going to steal it. She'd been going to talk to Aspen about it. Reasonably.

166

As Aspen continued to nose around, Hailey did a quick mental inventory, making sure there was nothing in the room to suggest something they didn't want Aspen to know, like that Vi was alive. She also found herself worrying that it was too messy, and not cool enough. That her clothes weren't designer, and her makeup was all gross and used down to nubs. Frankie praised her for that: using everything rather than throwing it away. But she didn't get the impression that Aspen appreciated things that were "well-loved."

"So how are you doing?" Aspen asked.

"Fine, I guess. I may have eternal summer school, but—"

"I meant about what you are. About being a Potential."

"Oh." Truthfully, she'd tried not to think about it. To ignore it, in the face of more pressing issues, like missing slayers and being caught in a tug-of-war between her best friend and her best friend's mortal enemy. "Well, it doesn't really matter, does it? Being a Potential isn't even a real thing. It's just saying that something might happen in the future. I may as well get upset because someday I might be a chef or someday I might hike the Andes."

Aspen sat down on the bed. "It does matter. And it is a thing. It's a thing I wished I knew before I was called. I never had the chance to process what Potential meant. I was a freaky strong kid, and then I was found, and then I was conscripted, and then I was a slayer."

"That sounds . . ." Hailey searched for a word. "That sounds hard. But if I was ever called, it wouldn't be the same. I've known slayers a long time. I'm working my way up the ladder from the inside."

"Right." Aspen laughed a little. "That's true. You're, like, a legacy. Maybe I'm worrying for nothing."

"It is nice, though," Hailey said. "That you worry."

"So . . . have you talked to them yet? About helping me out with my gaudy accessory?" She tapped the Amulet of Junjari.

"Not yet. Frankie's not . . . well, she's not—"

"Finished unreasonably hating me yet?" Aspen snorted. "Yeah, I kind of got that."

"It's not that unreasonable. Not if she thinks you killed the slayers at Slayerfest on purpose."

"How many slayers do you think the leadership murdered, during their years of waging war on the vampires and demons?" Aspen asked.

"That's not the same."

"Isn't it?" Aspen asked. "Because I can tell you that it feels the same when your friends are dead." She turned to Hailey, and Hailey was surprised to see the sheen of tears gathered in her eyes.

"Listen, I haven't asked the Scoobies about it yet, but there is something that might be able to help. They have this book, it's called the 'Book of Wants,' and it pretty much gives—"

"Knock knock, Hailey. Sig's in the driveway. We thought we'd grab you and go out for—"

Aspen sprang to her feet just as Frankie opened Hailey's bedroom door.

"What is she doing here?" Frankie asked.

"It's no big deal, I can go." Aspen eyed the window, then sidled around Frankie toward the door instead. "Maybe just this way. It's an easier dismount."

"You brought her into our house?" Frankie demanded.

"She was at the window! I opened it. Also, what's all over your clothes?" Hailey and Frankie followed Aspen down the stairs and into the kitchen. Willow rose to her feet.

"What's going on? What's she doing here?"

"I think we need to seal the house against unwanted guests,

Mom," Frankie said, and Hailey stepped between the two slayers. Aspen was backing slowly away, but Frankie had her head low and her eyes narrowed.

"Okay, everybody, take it easy." Willow moved closer, eyes moving cautiously between her daughter and the leader of the Darkness. "Aspen, I think you should leave."

"No problem. I only came to make sure Hailey was okay. It's not easy finding out you're a Potential."

Hailey froze.

"Oh shit," Aspen said. "I thought you told them."

"Told us . . ." Willow and Frankie turned to Hailey. Their brows were knit and their faces stricken; she'd never seen them look so much like mother and daughter.

"I'm sorry," Hailey said. "I didn't know how to."

"You're a Potential?" Frankie asked. "Like a *Potential* Potential? Potential with a capital P, heir to the slayer line, next to be called after I *die* kind of Potential?"

"Nobody knows that," Hailey said. "Nobody knows how the line works. Or at least, I thought nobody did . . . Right—?" She looked for Aspen, and for the second time in mere moments, Hailey found herself frozen again.

Aspen was holding *The Black Grimoire.*

She'd been paging through it, and when she felt the eyes—and the power—of the witches rising, she gingerly shut the cover and set it back on the table.

"I was just having a look."

"A look at what?" Willow said, her voice low.

"I don't even know, okay? Hailey just said there might be some kind of book that could help us give our slayer powers back. That's all." Aspen stepped backward, toward the front door, but Hailey wanted to tell her to run. She knew that Willow was good, that

Willow was kind, that Willow helped Jake make after-school flatbread pizzas, but even she could feel the magic in the air.

"I'm not looking to cause trouble," Aspen said, almost to the door. "And I'm certainly not looking to have my skin removed."

"Get out of my house," Willow said.

"Easy, Mom."

Hailey looked at Frankie. She had her hand out as if she was trying to comfort a frightened or dangerous animal. If Frankie was afraid, Aspen really wasn't safe. If Frankie was afraid, maybe none of them were.

"Aspen, go," Hailey whispered. Aspen opened the door without taking her eyes off Willow, then darted out of the house to disappear into the night.

"Mom," Frankie said as Willow followed her. "Mom, don't do anything!"

"Raise a wall," Willow said as she stood on their front steps. Both Hailey and Frankie stumbled backward as magic burst into the air around them, forming a force field that engulfed the entire house.

"Nice," Hailey said, and took a breath. Willow spun and grabbed her by the arm. Her eyes had gone dark as pitch.

"Why did you bring her here?"

"I didn't, I swear!"

"Mom, let her go!"

Willow released her. Her eyes went back to normal, and she turned and walked back inside the house.

"Are you okay?" Frankie asked.

"Yeah." Hailey rubbed her arm. It hadn't hurt, it had just surprised her. She turned to Frankie. "I swear I didn't ask her to come. When she showed up, I thought I could talk to her about the key, like we said. I didn't mean—"

"It's okay," Frankie said. "Nothing bad happened. It could have, but it didn't."

"Hailey? Frankie? What's happening?" Sigmund stood in the driveway, half out of his car. "That was Aspen that ran off just now." He blinked in wonder at the force field Willow had raised around the house.

"I'll go try to let Sigmund in," said Frankie. "And then we'd better call the rest of the Scoobies."

☽ ☽ ○ ☾ ☾

Aspen smiled as she walked quickly out of the development of New Sunnydale Heights, past the boring, cookie-cutter houses and carefully manicured lawns. She cut through yards and hopped over fences, then waited until she was at least a mile away before reaching into her pocket and pulling out the spell she'd stolen.

The mind control spell.

Hailey was right about that book. It was going to help her, quite a lot.

CHAPTER NINETEEN

LOOK WHAT YOU MADE ME DO

"What do you mean she's a Potential?" Spike asked. They'd gathered in the kitchen around the table, with Hailey at the head. Willow had taken the chair nearest *The Black Grimoire*, and Frankie noticed that she never stopped touching it.

"Potential Potential?" Spike went on. "As in the pitter-patter of teenage girl feet constantly taking up space in the bathroom and eating all the Weetabix Potential *Slayer*?"

"Seems like." Hailey shrugged.

Frankie sat silently while Hailey recounted the details: meeting Aspen at the motel, the trip to the odd mobile magician, and the spell, the ball of light that struck her square in the chest.

"At least now we know why Hailey is so naturally good at kicking ass," Sigmund said, and Hailey gave him a weak smile.

Frankie noted the comfort that ran back and forth between Sigmund and Hailey in a warm red current. "You knew," she said to Sigmund. "Since when?"

"Since the night I went to beg Hailey to come back to school. She'd just found out. I'm sorry I didn't tell you." He turned to the Scoobies. "But it wasn't my secret to tell."

"I guess we still wouldn't have known," said Frankie, "had Aspen not decided to spill it."

Hailey stared at the table. "I just didn't know what to say."

"But we're sure about this?" asked Spike. "It's not just Aspen messing with you?"

"We're sure," said Frankie. Before the rest of the Scoobies had arrived, they'd performed the spell again. The ball of light had barely taken shape before it beelined for Hailey and set her ablaze in gold.

"Does it always smell like that?" Jake asked, nose wrinkled against the waft of rotten eggs. Hailey shoved her chair away from the table.

"I don't know why we're having a big meeting about this. It's no big deal." She looked at Frankie. "It doesn't mean anything."

"Of course it does," Frankie said. "It means something. And it is a big deal. But it's not a bad deal. We're all going to need some time to process, and we're all going to have feelings, but right now I think we can just be whatever you want us to be. Want us to be excited? Then we're excited. Want us to be scared? We'll listen. Want us to order pizza? Then someone's going to need to take the dome down from around the outside of the house."

For a moment, Hailey just stared at her. "Well, now I feel ridiculous. I should've just told you."

"Yeah, you should have." Jake gave Hailey a shove, and Frankie gave him a shove in return. "What? I can do that now; she's a Potential."

"She's always been a Potential, and no, you can't." Frankie

looked at Hailey. "Not to change the subject, but what exactly was Aspen doing here? You said she wanted you to talk to us about something?"

Hailey squirmed. Her lip curled sheepishly, but eventually she sighed and said, "She thinks if I just talk to you, you'll understand what she's trying to do and help her return the slayer powers through the Amulet of Junjari. After that, there's no reason for her to hold Buffy and the others. Aspen and the Darkness would be harmless. She'd let the slayers go, and—" Hailey made a poof gesture with her hands. "Two problems solved. Zero fighting."

"If we believe that's what she wants to do," Sigmund said, and Hailey gave him a sharp look.

"Which I don't," said Frankie.

"We can't trust her," said Spike. "And lest we forget, she murdered slayers."

"We haven't forgotten." Frankie leaned back and looked out the windows. Her slaydar was on full alert, but it was quiet. She didn't sense Aspen out there, watching, waiting. "At least we have her outnumbered. And when we get Buffy and the missing slayers back, we'll have her beat. I think we're safe for now. Mom, we should probably go take the force field down, before the neighbors start bouncing off it."

Willow's eyes moved to Hailey. "And if she comes back, you won't just let her back in?"

Hailey shook her head.

"Okay, then." Willow stood and came around the table to pat Hailey's hand. "I'm sorry for being so stern. But Aspen is dangerous. And I don't like any of my girls to be put in danger." She bent to kiss Frankie's head.

"Yeah, but are you more mad that we were in danger?" Frankie asked. "Or that she touched your book?"

"How are things going with that?" Spike asked as Willow went to the front door to remove the spell.

"Fine," she said. "Making some definite progress."

$$\begin{array}{ccccc}) &) & \bigcirc & (& (\end{array}$$

Grimloch was alone in his tent when Aspen arrived. He set the book he was reading aside on his table as she stepped through the flap.

"I would prefer you not come here unannounced," he said.

Aspen shrugged. "If you want better security, try not living in a tent."

He had considered whether to find a more permanent residence. And then he'd considered what that would mean. Did he really intend to remain in New Sunnydale? It was a nice enough place, and its proximity to a hellmouth made for good hunting. He'd ingested more varieties of demon entrails in the last six months than he had in decades. And Frankie was here. But surely she would leave for college, and what then? Would he follow her? Start hunting for game around her campus? Be mistaken for one of her professors?

"What do you want, Aspen?"

In response, she reached into a cloth pouch and threw a handful of something at him that sparkled and smelled like herbal oil. It stuck to his skin and clothes; he would never get all of it out. He touched his fingers to his cheek, and they came away twinkling. "I hate glitter."

"If you hate that, just hang on to your hat," she said, pulling a folded piece of paper from her pocket. The paper looked old and stained, and as she began to read from it, Grimloch's head started to swim. The spell filled his ears and the space of the tent, and he doubled over with his hands pressed to the sides of his head. His world went briefly black, but when he opened his eyes again, he was still standing, and Aspen was standing right in front of him.

"Grim?" she asked. "Grimloch, can you hear me?" He nodded, though her voice sounded far away now, or like his ears had filled with water. "Raise your hand and wave."

No, he thought as he felt himself doing it: his right arm bending at the elbow and his hand moving back and forth.

Aspen smiled. "That's perfect."

"What did you do to me?" he asked. "What was that spell?"

"It was the 'Mind Control Spell,'" she replied. "Or at least that's what it said when I tore it out. But after I held it for a while it changed. Now it reads 'Make the Hunter Do What You Want.'" She turned the paper around, to show him. "Isn't that fun? Your little girlfriend gave it to me. Imagine what she was going to use it for."

"Frankie wouldn't have used it. She—"

"Stop talking," Aspen said, and he did. "Now . . ." She tapped her chin and walked around him, looking him over as if he were a mannequin in a clothing store. "What do I ask for first? I feel like a kid at Christmas." He ground his teeth, and she inclined her head. "You may speak again."

"Aspen. What is this spell?"

"I already told you. Did you not listen? I get to make you do whatever I want. This spell grants the holder total control over the subject. I think that means that anyone who holds this spell can command you like it's a remote control. But don't worry." She folded it up and placed it back into her pocket. "I'm never giving it away. Besides the Amulet of Junjari, this is my new favorite possession. Tomorrow I'm getting it laminated."

"How do you end it? How long does it last?" His mind raced ahead, searching for loopholes, wondering if he could move fast enough to get it from her. He could feel the strength of the spell, working its way into his muscles, taking away his will, and the Hunter of Thrace was afraid.

"You don't," Aspen said. "And forever." She stepped closer. "Be good now, and don't attack me." She watched with fascination and growing glee as his arms jerked, trying to grab her, trying to take the spell. He couldn't even attack her with words. The spell was strong, and soon he was too weakened to try anymore. "This is amazing," she whispered. "They're never going to see you coming. But first, let's have some fun with your little Frankie."

CHAPTER TWENTY
LOVE BITES, LOVE BLEEDS

Sam checked his heart rate app as he jogged up the street toward the park: 140. Nice and low, nice and steady. Only that wasn't what it was supposed to be. He was supposed to be pushing it. Since Jake had started taking that Rhodacarthia tincture he'd been totally keyed up; The entire lacrosse team was on orders to get their butts in gear. STRENGTH! SPEED! STAMINA! Those were the bricks that paved the road to victory, boys! Or something like that. Sam had kind of zoned out. He loved lacrosse, but that inspirational dig-a-little-deeper, go-a-little-harder, unlock-another-level crap had always seemed to him like . . . well, like crap.

But this was for Jake. And for Jake, he would do a lot of things.

Sam turned into the park and lengthened his stride. At that speed it didn't take him long to run the whole of it, and he still wasn't tired. When the paved trail turned back toward the road, he swung left onto the dirt hiking paths that traversed through the woods.

Footsteps sounded behind him and he glanced over his shoulder in case he needed to make way, but whoever it was had turned off somewhere so Sam kept running. He would take the fork where the trail came out beside the creek and head back up toward the road home. Maybe his mom would make him a big bowl of jjajangmyeon. They had a standardized test coming up, and she loved to feed his brain.

Footsteps sounded behind him again and he moved over, but no one passed. He looked back. The trail was empty.

A few months ago, he wouldn't have thought anything of it. Back then, he was just another blissfully oblivious resident of New Sunnydale. But now? Now Sam knew he was being followed even before he saw the movement in the ferns and heard the sound of hungry breathing.

The distance that remained between him and the safety of the open street wasn't far. If he sprinted, he could be off the trails and onto the sidewalk in under two minutes.

Don't look back, he thought and took off, feet flying, arms pumping as whatever was chasing him began to crash through the underbrush. Almost instantly his legs began to fail. He'd already run so far, and the shaky, gassed sensation in his quads terrified him. What if he was too slow? What if he stumbled and fell? There was no Frankie covering his tail, no Sigmund tracking him with a bow and arrow. Sam was alone, and Scooby or not, he could die alone, torn apart and left for Frankie and Jake to find in the woods.

Go, GO! his brain screamed as the breath of the demon grew louder. The trail forked and he threw himself to the left, driving his legs up and up, grunting as he leapt over roots, racing for his life up the wood and dirt steps of the path.

His feet hit pavement, and he ran along the sidewalk for another fifty feet before he dared to turn.

There was nothing behind him. Whatever it was hadn't wanted to leave the woods.

Sam jumped when his smartwatch beeped.

"Max heart rate," he said, looking at the app. He laughed and bent over to lean on his knees. "Definitely max heart rate."

☽ ☽ ○ ☾ ☾

When Frankie got to school, she was surprised to find Sam waiting by her locker. And with not a single Jake in sight.

"Sam? Is everything okay?"

His handsome face scrunched regretfully. "Do I only show up to talk to you when something's wrong? I guess I haven't made an effort to just say hey." He put up a hand. "Hey!"

"It's okay," said Frankie as she went past her locker, which she never used, anyway, and Sam turned to walk with her to the library.

"No, it isn't. I've been kind of happily preoccupied with Jake, but it's been really cool getting to know you, too. Even if I'm just Jake's plus one and not a real Scooby, I hope that you and I could still hang out sometimes, if Jake and I broke up."

"Sam. You are not just Jake's plus one, and I don't like this kind of thinking," Frankie said. "We will totally still hang out. Look at Sigmund and Hailey—they broke up, but they're both still here." She and Sam smiled at each other awkwardly. Sigmund and Hailey were both still there, true, but things between them weren't great.

Sam put his hand on Frankie's arm. "So, remember when I said I only show up to talk to you when something's wrong?" He sighed. "I think something chased me through the trails behind Fall Creek Park. I was jogging, and I heard it kind of stalking me, snapping twigs and rustling ferns and stuff. I barely made it up the path and onto the street."

"Did you get a look at it?"

"I didn't see it. I just heard breathing. And chasing. And maybe growls?" He shrugged. "It could've just been . . ."

"Don't say a raccoon," said Frankie. "And don't say your imagination. This is Sunnydale."

"Yeah, that was also my thinking."

"Let's report this to the Scoobies. We can keep an eye out and put a patrol through Fall Creek Park."

They had started to head toward the library again when they were suddenly surrounded by a herd of water buffalo, i.e., a few members of the lacrosse team. Frankie pulled her appendages in close as they crowded around in a loud, bustling circle of letter jackets and slapping hands. Sam laughed as they jumped toward him for chest bumps, but if one mistakenly aimed for Frankie they were going to find themselves promptly bounced off a locker.

"Missed you at practice this morning," said O'Shay Thomas after he and Sam had done some kind of guy handshake.

Sam shrugged. "Wasn't mandatory. I don't know why we're pushing so hard, anyway, when the season's almost over."

"Because it's almost tourney time," O'Shay replied. "I don't blame you, though. Cap's been calling a lot of early practices. And you weren't the only one who missed—Perry was out, too. At the doctor getting stitched up; his dog bit him when they were playing ball."

One of the other players, Drew Rawson, mimed sad tears at Perry's expense. "Why is my doggy so mean to me?" he teased.

"Is the dog okay?" Frankie interjected, and the boys stopped laughing.

"Of course," said O'Shay. "Perry loves that dog. It was probably just an accident."

Frankie nodded, just as Jake showed up and all the high fives and jostling began anew. Frankie pulled her arms in again and found herself ping-ponged back and forth between O'Shay and a midfielder named Zach Connors. Sam had to step in and shield her with his arm. She was a slayer, but these lacrosse guys were rough. Half of them still had sod from the playing field under their fingernails, and they were covered in bruises and scratches.

She caught a familiar movement in the corner of her eye and craned her neck to see Grimloch standing awkwardly in the hallway.

"What's he doing here?" Jake asked, and maybe it was because he was surrounded by his teammates, but Frankie could have sworn he puffed himself up and broadened his shoulders.

"What am I, a mind reader?" she asked back, then squirmed free of the scrum to go see. "Grim? Everything okay?" He wore dark jeans and a gray short-sleeved shirt, not so different from some of the guys at school, but it was obvious that he was older. He had the muscle tone of a hunter god, for one. But mostly it was in his eyes. One look at them and it was clear that he'd seen things. Maybe that he'd seen all of the things.

"I think Aspen is preparing to bring the Darkness back to Sunnydale," he said.

"When? How do you know?"

"I'm not sure. It was something she said. She came by the tent again."

"Again," Frankie said. "You should start charging her rent. Tent rent. How much would that even be?"

"Frankie." He stepped closer, and she stopped grumbling and sighed.

"Okay. I know, this could be serious. Or maybe not. You said you weren't sure."

"But if she is, it could mean that she's found something to revive her plans."

"Come to the library. We should tell the others." Frankie started to lead the way and suddenly found them both surrounded by members of the lacrosse team.

"You okay, Frankie?" O'Shay asked. "This guy bothering you?"

"What?" Frankie blinked at them. Grimloch growled quietly, and she jabbed him in the ribs with her elbow. "No. He's a . . . He's almost like my . . ." She paused at the growing horror on O'Shay's face. "My mom's friend."

"Oh, cool. Sorry, man." He gave Grimloch a high five that was mostly unreciprocated. "For a minute I thought she was going to say 'boyfriend,' and I was like, whoa, going to report this. But I shoulda known. You're like, what, thirty years old?"

"He's twenty-one," Frankie snapped.

"Well, still. Twenty-one-year-old bothering with a sixteen-year-old . . . we'd have had to do something."

Frankie looked over O'Shay's shoulder to Jake for help, but Jake only cocked his head and mouthed, "See?"

"Anyway, my bad," said O'Shay. "You know, Frankie, for a long time I thought you and Jake might be a thing. Before Sam, I mean. You and he used to be joined at the hip, from way back."

"Gross," said Frankie.

"Ultra gross," agreed Jake. "I'm almost getting sick right now."

"But you're coming to the party on Friday, right, Frankie?" Zach Connors asked. "At Jake's house?"

"Friday at Jake's house?" She looked at Jake quizzically. So did Sam. Friday was the first night of the full moon.

"Full moon party," Jake said. "Everyone's invited." He nodded to Grim. "Even your mom's friend."

"We'll be there," said Grimloch. Frankie closed her mouth. She'd opened it to decline for him. "Later then, Francesca." Grim turned and walked away. So did Jake and the lacrosse players, leaving only her and Sam.

"Okay," she said. "What the heck is going on?"

☽ ☽ ◯ ☾ ☾

It wasn't until after school on Friday that Frankie realized she had no idea what to wear to a party. A party that Grimloch would be at. That almost made it like a date. "What am I doing?" she groaned to Hailey. "And why does every shade of lipstick I own look like Pennywise cosplay?"

"Probably better that you haven't found the right shade yet," Hailey replied. "You need a sandwich. Your slayer belly is starting to sound like a trio of bullfrogs." She walked over with a few options for outfits and held them in front of Frankie in the mirror—one midlength brown corduroy skirt, and another much shorter and black. Hailey, of course, was already dressed, effortlessly pretty in long black braids and a pair of black plaid pants.

"You don't think Grim was right about Aspen bringing the Darkness back to Sunnydale?" Hailey asked, and Frankie shrugged.

"I thought you might know more about that than me. But it seemed more like some kind of a trick. She just let it slip? That doesn't seem like her."

"It doesn't," Hailey agreed.

Frankie popped into her closet to change into the corduroy skirt. She paired it with a white shirt and some silver jewelry, and the result was not bad. She touched the shirt. "Maybe not white. I'm bound to spill something down the front of myself." She wheeled back into the closet and tried again, this time with a soft brown sweater. "Well, now I just look like a human turd."

Hailey got up from where she sat on Frankie's bed. She went into the closet, found nothing, left the room to go into her closet, and came back with a cute cropped black sweater. "Here. And here." She handed Frankie a black belt with an oval gold buckle. "Now we do gold tones, and all of this will look great with your hair."

"Thank you." Frankie hugged them to her chest. "Is this annoying? Are you ashamed of my complete fashion ineptitude?"

"Never. I just hope that deep in the forest, Grimloch is frantically thrashing around in that tent trying to look as good for this party as you do." Hailey sat back down on the bed and checked her phone. "So what's up with this party, anyway? I mean, I know it's a big deal for Jake—"

"His first view of the full moon," Frankie said. "His first ever. Outside of pictures and movies and stuff."

"You think the Rhodacarthia whatever is really going to keep him from transforming? He's only been taking it for like a week and a half."

"I think if it was dangerous, Oz would have put a stop to it. Besides, that's why all the Scoobies will be there. In case we need to tranquilize him." Frankie swapped out her silver jewelry for gold, including Grim's gold heart bracelet.

"So that's why Grimloch is coming? To help in the instance of werewolves?"

"I don't know." Frankie stopped. "It is a little weird. I didn't think he'd want to come, but he practically volunteered to bring the dip. Mmm. Dip." Her stomach growled. She really did need a sandwich.

"Okay." Hailey held up a handful of tubes of eco-friendly

lipsticks in neutral tones. "Which one of these? And do you want shoes with a low heel or some kicky boots?"

"Boots," Frankie said. "Spike says I have to patrol after the party because, you know, zero time off when it comes to preparing for slayer versus slayer fights."

"Maybe it won't come to that."

Frankie gave her a look. "I thought I was supposed to be the optimist. Is this going to end in an awkward tug of war with Aspen? She's my Potential! No! She's *my* Potential!"

Hailey chuckled. "I'm totally team Scooby Potential. Only . . . I am kind of on her side now."

"Huh?"

"Well, now that I am what I am, I definitely see the reasoning behind wanting a choice. I don't want something to happen to you and then all of a sudden just be thrust into your shoes."

Both girls fell quiet. "I think you mean thrust into my kicky boots," Frankie at last said softly.

"I'm sorry. I didn't mean to say that. Like your death is inevitable, or like it would just be some pain in the butt for me. I don't want anything to happen to you, Frankie. I never want to be a slayer, if that's what it costs."

Frankie stared at her. Then she hugged her. "I know that! What? You think I've been watching my back in case you're sneaking up with a knife? Sniffing my food to check for poison?"

Hailey grinned. "I guess not."

"Of course not. Now let's just go to this party so Jake can see his first full moon and I can make a fool of myself over a millennia-old demon."

"Okay." Hailey stood up and backed out of the room. "But first," she said in a low, creepy voice, "let me go make the slayer a sandwich."

$$\textrm{☽ ☽ ○ ☾ ☾}$$

"Thanks for coming early and helping me set things up, spice rub." Jake and Sigmund were handling the party prep at the Osbournes. Oz had already gone, agreeing to give Jake the run of the house until at least midnight. It hadn't been easy to convince him to let the party happen, but Jake had played every guilt card he had. Oz was still walking on eggshells after their fight about who controlled his werewolf destiny and how Oz wasn't the boss of the family. Jake felt kind of bad about that, but Oz would see. The Rhodacarthia was working. Everything would be fine. And Oz deserved a night off: He and Spike were headed over to Willow's for a big night of reminiscing about old battles, or playing Parcheesi, or whatever old heroes did when they gathered around for an evening.

"Happy to do it, Thriller," Sigmund replied. "There isn't actually much to set up." Sodas and bottled waters in the coolers, meat and cheese trays out of the refrigerator. Snack bowls filled to the brim.

"Don't forget the leaning tower of pizzas set to arrive in an hour," Jake said.

"Right." Sigmund glanced around. "I see you didn't bother to clean."

Jake shrugged. The Osbourne house wasn't dirty, per se, but it was definitely messy and cluttered.

"Maybe we should put Oz's guitars in a closet at least?" Jake suggested. "So the guys don't mess with them." He took Oz's acoustic off the stand. He hadn't heard Oz play it in a while, and he kind of missed the sound.

"You okay?" Sigmund asked.

"Yeah." Jake shrugged it off. "Things have been a little tense between me and Oz since I started talking to Jordy and taking the

Rhodacarthia . . . I screamed at him, actually. Told him to stop acting like my dad."

Sigmund's eyes rose. "Sounds a bit harsh."

"It was. I apologized right away. Oz knows he's my dad-uncle."

"Or your cousin-dad-uncle." Sigmund smiled.

"He's just overprotective. He's worried about the Rhodacarthia."

"We're all a little worried about the Rhodacarthia. Are you sure you know what you're doing, Jake? I don't want Frankie to have to tranquilize you in front of your entire lacrosse team."

"I'm fine," Jake said. The Sage demon adjusted his glasses, and Jake twitched a little under the laser-focused scholarly scrutiny. "There are just some things that only werewolves can understand. And one of those things is whether Rhodacarthia is working or not."

He grinned at Sigmund and placed the guitars in the entryway closet. Honestly, he was a little angry with Oz for not recommending Rhodacarthia sooner. It made him feel great. Energized. Untouchable. He'd been able to call up his claws at will and send them away just as easily. No more spontaneous partial transformations while eating burgers. No more spontaneous transformations, period. He was in total control. Though it did make him nap unpredictably. He'd wake up somewhere without remembering he'd fallen asleep. Sometimes he'd snap awake right there on his feet, with no one around him any the wiser. And when he did transform, he felt a little wild, and it hurt a little more than usual. But that was a small price to pay.

"Good," Sigmund said, then went back to shaking snack mix into a bowl. "Is . . . is Hailey coming tonight?"

"Of course she is. And so is the Hunter of Underpants. I invited him as a joke. I thought he'd say no." Jake jutted his chin in Sigmund's direction. "Something up with you and Hailey?" He walked back to their kitchen island and tossed a handful of pretzels into his mouth. "Frankie says you've been DMing with some new Sage demon chick."

"She's . . ." Sigmund said, and Jake was amused by how flustered he got. "She's not new. Natasha's an old acquaintance. We're reconnecting."

He nudged Sigmund in the shoulder. "Show me."

"No."

"Come on, man, show me." He leaned in, and Sigmund pulled up a few photographs. The girl was beautiful. Long black braids and deep brown eyes. Great smile. Nice set of horns. "Bet she's smart, too," Jake said.

"Of course she's smart; she's a Sage demon." Sigmund took the phone back and looked through the pictures himself. "I don't even like her that much. I mean, I like her. She's lovely."

"But she's not Hailey."

"No. She's not Hailey. Hailey calls to my human side. And I've never been more torn between my human side and my demon family."

"Family's tough. But you are human, and you are Sage demon, and you've got to love who you're going to love, man."

"If only it was that easy. But thanks for the advice, Jake. I'm sorry to be bothering you with this."

"Are you kidding? I love this stuff. This stuff is normal." He smacked the half demon lightly in the shoulder.

Sigmund cocked an eyebrow. "Your friends being torn apart because one is a demon and has to date other demons is normal?"

"In Sunnydale."

They traded a grin, and someone knocked at the door. "That'll be either the pizzas or Sam," said Jake. "And I'm equally excited about both." He went for the door, noting the sun starting to slant down in the sky. Only a few hours remained until sunset. And then only a few hours more before he could look up at that glowing white orb in the sky and remain himself.

CHAPTER TWENTY-ONE

LEADER OF THE PACK

The party at Jake's was wild and uncomfortable: The lacrosse players were wild, and the Scoobies were uncomfortable. Frankie, sitting on the sofa beside Grimloch and Sigmund, ducked a thrown Wiffle ball, which Hailey caught and lobbed back in between sips of her cola.

"Are they always like this?" Hailey asked Sam as Zach Connors and Perry Reilly tackled each other down the hallway.

"No?" Sam grabbed a wobbling bowl of snack mix before it could fall to the floor with the rest of the bowls that were already down there. "But they've never been invited to a party at Cap's house before."

"Well, they're going to trash the place." Frankie twisted around. "Jake!"

"Hey, Scoobies." He perched on the back of the couch, his red-gold hair wild and his eyes bright. "Having a good time?"

"Super," Hailey said, deadpan.

"You think you might settle things down?" Frankie asked.

"Huh?" Jake asked. Someone had turned on some music, and it blasted through the house. Another errant Wiffle ball winged through the air, and Sigmund jerked out of the way. It struck Grimloch cleanly in the side of the head.

"I said!" Frankie shouted. "Do you think—!"

Jake made a cutting motion toward his neck, and someone turned the music down.

Frankie took a breath. "Do you think you might ask them to settle down? This place is getting wrecked."

"Yeah," he said, but he didn't seem too concerned about it. "Definitely. But we'll be moving the party outside pretty soon, anyway." He gestured to the windows, which had begun to darken. "Moonlight football." And then Jake was gone again, taking Sam with him to attack more of the leaning tower of pizza.

"Francesca," Grimloch said, and stood. "We need to talk." He held out his hand.

"Okay," she said, taking it. He tugged her up off the couch a little too quickly. She barely had time to shrug to Hailey, who traded an awkward glance with Sigmund and went back to sipping her cola.

)) ○ ((

At the Rosenberg house, Oz and Spike reclined comfortably in the living room while Willow brought out the Parcheesi box and set it on the coffee table. "Parcheesi?" she asked, and both men leaned forward.

"Sounds good to me," said Spike, and she lifted the lid.

Of course, there was no Parcheesi inside the box. There was only a very old bottle of scotch. Oz set out three short, crystal tumblers and Willow poured, while the vampire rooted around among the rest of the detritus of time gone by. When he came up with a baggie of something, he raised his eyebrows and Willow snatched it.

"That's medicinal. And it's for spellwork." She smiled as she tucked it into her belt. "It's for medicinal spellwork."

"So," Spike said as they settled back with their drinks. "It's nice to gather around for a night. With none of the kiddies scampering underfoot."

"Mm-hmm," murmured Willow.

"No immediately impending apocalypse," the vampire went on. "No running out to save the world."

Oz nodded.

"The kids probably think we're hovering over our phones or trying to stop ourselves from driving by the house to spy," Willow said.

Spike scoffed. "Thinking we're sitting around being sad, playing board games. Like we don't know what to do with ourselves when there's no world to save."

"They're young," said Oz. "They've only gone through what, like, one apocalypse?"

Spike held up his tumbler. "Sometimes there's nothing better than a good scotch, good company, and a relaxing evening of *not* fighting the darkness."

"Hear hear." Oz leaned forward with his elbows on his knees while Willow drummed her fingers against her glass. "So do you think our place is totally trashed by now?"

"One hundred percent." Spike nodded.

"Nothing but rubble and potato chips," Willow agreed.

☽ ☽ ◯ ☾ ☾

Grimloch led Frankie out into the front yard, where the air was soft and orange and smelled far less like lacrosse boys and haphazardly applied colognes, and where the noise from the house was muffled enough that they could hear themselves think.

"Whatever it is we're doing, Francesca, it needs to stop."

Frankie turned. "What?"

"I don't know what I could have been thinking," Grimloch said. "That I could forge something lasting with someone like you."

"What are you talking about? I thought we were . . ." Frankie blinked as her brain tried to catch up with her ears. He couldn't be saying what it sounded like he was saying. "Did I miss something? I thought we were just . . ."

"You thought we were what?"

"I don't know."

"I'm not trying to be cruel."

Frankie swallowed. He wasn't trying to be, but it felt cruel anyway. The backs of her eyes started to sting and she clenched her teeth. No crying. It wasn't like she was in love with Grim—except that maybe she was, just a little—but she sure did like him a lot, and she'd thought he liked her, too.

"Where is this coming from?"

"I've been . . . considering it for a while now. We don't make sense, Frankie." He glanced back toward the house. "And everyone can see it."

Stupid O'Shay Thomas, Frankie thought, *putting stupid thoughts into our heads.* And Grim, he sounded . . . he sounded embarrassed by her.

"So it's just finished?" she asked.

He sighed. "It never really started."

Frankie closed her mouth. Everything Grimloch said landed like a punch to her stomach. And worst of all, he didn't seem to care.

"So how will this work?" she asked, her voice a croak. "Will we stop patrolling together? Will we not be friends?" She looked at him. "Will you leave?"

He looked down. Yes. He would leave.

"Dammit." She wiped a tear from her cheek. She heard him move, taking a step toward her, and for a second she thought he might change his mind.

But all he said was "Don't cry, Francesca. Go back in with your friends."

Frankie clenched her fists. "Don't talk to me like I'm a child!" she shouted, and she spun to face him. But Grimloch was already gone.

Frankie stood by herself in the Osbourne front yard. She didn't know how long she remained there, motionless, the echoes of their conversation swirling through her head. The sun disappeared below the horizon. The air grew a little cooler. And the crashing intensified inside the house.

Frankie squeezed her eyes shut. She didn't want to go back in there. She knew it was important to Jake, for them to be by his side beneath his first full moon, but all she wanted to do was go home and curl up under her yummy sushi blanket. Jake would understand. And they would have lots of full moons from now on, they—

"Frankie!"

She looked to the front of the house as Hailey, Sigmund, Jake, and Sam burst through the door and slammed it shut behind them. "Lock it, lock it!" Sam screeched as Jake fumbled with the keys. "Is the back door locked?" Sigmund asked. Jake threw the keys to him, and the Sage demon sprinted around to make sure.

"Guys? What's happening?"

"Uhh . . ." Jake ran his hands through his hair as Frankie jogged up. The Scoobies regarded her with bewildered expressions as she leaned over to peer in the windows. That close, she could hear the snarling and snapping, and knew what she would see even as her brain told her it was impossible.

As the sun went down, every last member of the lacrosse team had turned into a werewolf.

$$☽ ☽ ○ ☾ ☾$$

"So the rumors are true," Spike said as he and Willow and Oz sat at the kitchen table around the actual Parcheesi board. "This game is boring."

"Maybe I read the rules wrong?" Willow picked up the yellowed rules pamphlet and squinted at it.

"No," said Oz. "I think boring was the intention when they designed it."

The werewolf grew quiet, looking at the shadows cast upon the sidewalk in between the streetlamps.

"Not long until Jake will be gazing up in wonder," said Spike. Oz smiled. "Do you ever—?" He raised his eyes skyward.

"I remember the first time," Oz said. "It felt like I'd never seen it before. I can't imagine what it's like for Jake. Who really hasn't."

"Not that much difference between last night and tonight," said Spike.

"No, there is." Oz sighed. "There really is."

Willow leaned over and squeezed Oz's hand, and Spike leaned back from the board game and stretched. "So," the vampire said, "who's ready to get into some real trouble?"

"I am," the witch and the werewolf said together.

$$\supset \supset \bigcirc \mathbb{C} \mathbb{C}$$

"Jake. There are twenty werewolves in your house." Frankie turned from the window and Jake backed off, moaning and tugging at the ends of his hair.

"I know. I know! I don't know how this happened!"

"Don't you?" Sigmund asked. "Or do you, and could it perhaps rhyme with Wodaparthia Winkture?"

"I wouldn't . . ." He gestured to the house, and the absolute ruckus taking place inside. "How could I even do that? Bite twenty of my teammates without them noticing?"

"I saw a bunch of marks on the guys after practice the other day," said Frankie.

"Is that why you've been playing so rough?" asked Sam, horrified.

"I didn't do this!" Jake protested. "Or I didn't do it on purpose! I've been . . . well, I've been kind of blacking out sometimes. Oh god, what am I going to do? What are we going to do?"

"First off, we're going to leave the Jake blaming for later." Frankie turned back to the windows. "Right now we have twenty very hairy problems, and none of them are leash trained."

"Look on the bright side." Hailey patted Jake on the back. "You didn't bite Sam."

Jake looked at Sam with relief, and Sam winked. "And you certainly had plenty of chances."

"Also, the Rhoda-whatever seems to be working on you, at least." Hailey nodded upward, and Jake leaned his head back, his jaw dropping open at the sight of the rising moon, bright and silver, a full circle.

"Wow," he said.

"Jake!" Frankie snapped. "Your teammates!"

"Right." The Scoobies gathered around the window. "So what's the plan?"

Frankie surveyed the scene. Inside, the house was completely trashed as twenty werewolves tore through the closets and cupboards like bargain shoppers at a warehouse sale. Already the refrigerator lay open and tipped on its side, and most of a werewolf had dived in snout first, leaving only his hind paws visible.

"The good news is," Frankie said, "there couldn't be a better house for this to happen in. Jake's cage is in the basement, and the whole place has stashes of tranquilizer guns and plenty of ammo. The bad news is"—she tilted her head toward the house full of rampaging wolves—"all of that stuff is in there."

"We need a diversion," Hailey said.

"Right," said Jake. He ran for his moped and reached into the under-saddle storage compartment. He came back holding a bottle of pheromones that hunters used to lure big game. "Will this work?"

"Why do you have that?" asked Sam.

"I don't know, I just like to smell it sometimes."

Frankie looked at the bottle. "Okay. Jake, take off your shirt. Sig, Sam, I hate to ask, but you, too." The boys did as requested, and Frankie piled their shirts into a ball on the deck and poured the pheromones all over them. "That should do the trick. Each one of these shirts is like werewolf catnip. We just need to put them in places where the wolves will smell them and be distracted, but nowhere with an exit big enough for them to get through."

"The basement window," said Jake. "It's small, and it'll lure them downstairs close to the cage."

"Good. Sam, can you place one there?"

"I'm on it," said Sam.

"Try not to touch it too much."

"No problem there," he said, wrinkling his nose.

"Sig, Hailey," Frankie said. "Can you boost yourselves up onto the roof and get these down the chimney?"

"Can do." Sigmund took his and Jake's shirts, and Hailey nodded.

"Jake." Frankie turned, and he stepped up close. "You're the only one of us who's immune to bites. So as soon as the werewolves take the bait, you're with me. We get inside, get to the tranquilizer guns, and start shooting. Get every wolf you can into the basement cage. Does everybody know the plan?" The Scoobies nodded, and Frankie took one more look through the window. "Then let's go snare us a sled team."

$$) \;) \; \bigcirc \; (\; ($$

Spike and Oz cleared the kitchen table, banishing the Parcheesi board and setting down *The Black Grimoire* in its place, along with several lit candles and, of course, their mostly empty scotch glasses.

"Maybe this isn't such a good idea," Willow said.

"Oh, come on," said Spike. "Isn't it high time we made some headway on this? We blew up a plane for it; I wanna see how it works!"

"Yeah, but—"

"You don't have to do anything you don't want to do," Oz said. "But if there's a safe time to experiment, I think it's now. With the two of us here."

Willow looked at the grimoire. "Okay. But no more scotch; one more glass and Spike's going to start drunk cross dialing the prison dimension."

In reply, the vampire cocked his head and topped himself off. Oz opened *The Black Grimoire* and flipped to the blank sheets in the back. Willow raised her hand over it and prepared to place it palm down.

"I don't want to!" She took her hand back.

"Come on, Red. What are you so scared about?"

"This book is powerful," she explained. "It shouldn't be treated lightly, and what would you know about it?"

"What would I know about it? You act like I haven't cast my share of dark magic."

"You once kidnapped me to do a *love spell*." Willow narrowed her eyes.

"Okay." Oz placed his hands on the table between them, and on either side of the Book of Wants.

"Look, I'm just scared, okay?" Willow said. "I don't want to put my hand on that blank page because I'm afraid of the spell I'll see there when I do."

"You mean a spell like How to Drain the Black Magic of the Universe Dry to Become the Ultimate Evil?" Spike asked. "Even if that's what it showed you, Red, it wouldn't mean that's what you really want."

"It wouldn't?"

"No. It would mean this is a bloody evil book!"

Willow frowned.

"Spike's right," said Oz. "But even if he's right—a spell like that isn't exactly one we want to see in print." He and the vampire traded a look. "The spell the grimoire created for Willow would be too strong for anyone to possess."

"So what do we do?" Spike asked. "We can't let something like this just sit there. Not when we have to get the slayer back."

"She's not 'the' slayer," Willow said softly. "She's one of many, has been for years."

"Not to me she bloody hasn't," Spike mumbled, and took a drink. Oz looked at the vampire. He looked at him for a long time, in that quiet, constantly thinking way of his. "What?" Spike asked.

"Why don't . . . *you* put your hand on the book," Oz said.

Spike and Willow sat up straighter. Oz turned the book to face the vampire, and Spike raised his hand and set it palm down on the blank page.

In the space of a breath, the spell rose to the surface, the ink rising beneath Spike's fingers, drawing out all of his desires to craft them into something diabolical. He withdrew his hand, and the three of them leaned forward to read.

The Spell of Many Interdimensional Returns.

☽ ☽ ○ ☾ ☾

Frankie and Jake crouched beside the front door, waiting for Hailey and Sigmund to complete their phase of the plan and stick the pheromone-soaked shirts down the chimney.

"I'm really sorry about this, Frankie. I never should have taken Jordy's advice."

"He's your brother," Frankie said. Jordy had his issues, but he did love Jake. Even if he forgot to act like it sometimes. "I'm pretty sure he didn't mean for any of this to happen."

"Pretty sure?"

"Jordy would never hurt you on purpose. And you would never hurt your teammates on purpose either, Jake, so stop punishing yourself! Right now we have to navigate a very bitey obstacle course."

Jake chuckled. "It'll be just like when we used to play that the floor was lava. Only instead of lava, the floor is deadly werewolves."

"Yes," Frankie said, and sighed. "Just like that." Inside the house, one of the wolves, who she thought might be Zach Connors—his fur was the same pale blond as Zach's hair—raised his snout to the sky and sniffed before darting toward the fireplace. It wasn't long before three others joined him. Then four.

"Okay. It looks like the bait has been placed."

"Looks like Sam's got his through the window, too," said Jake, as several other wolves bolted for the basement. He nodded to Frankie, and she quietly cracked open the front door.

They crept inside, staying low, eyes on the wolves. The closest stash of tranquilizer guns was in the hall closet. But it would be safer to sneak into Oz's bedroom, where they might not be noticed and could arm themselves and load in peace. Frankie watched the gathering of werewolves as they snarled and snapped at the fireplace. They occasionally got angry at one another and erupted into small squabbles. But so far, the pheromones were holding their interest. She'd just rounded the corner into the hallway that led to the bedrooms when she heard a warning growl.

A werewolf that looked strikingly like O'Shay Thomas was staring at her from the overturned refrigerator. Apparently, he'd had his snout so deep in Oz's leftover pot roast that he hadn't detected the pheromone bait. But he definitely detected her.

"Jake," she said. "Run!" She darted for the bedrooms, but Jake didn't run. Instead, when the O'Shay werewolf leapt at her, he tackled it and brought it to the floor.

"Go, Frankie! I'll handle this!"

"No, you won't!" She ran back as they struggled, and two of the other wolves heard the chaos and turned to join in the fun. She ducked the claws of one and delivered a hefty kick to the ribs of another just in time to grab O'Shay and tear him off Jake. "Just because you're immune to the bites doesn't mean you're immune to being ripped apart!" she cried, and together they scrambled into Oz's bedroom.

$$\text{☽ ☽ ○ ☾ ☾}$$

"How do you think it's going down there?" Sigmund asked, hugging his torso as he stood in only his undershirt on the roof in the nighttime breeze.

"Pretty good, I'd say," Hailey replied. "I think I heard Frankie yelling at Jake just now."

Sigmund smiled. "Definitely a good sign. Listen, Hailey, about Natasha . . ."

"You don't have to tell me anything, Sig."

"No, I want to tell you," he said. "I need you to know . . . that there's nothing there." He shrugged. "I was trying to get over you, and she's an old friend. But . . ."

"But there's no getting over me, right?" Hailey teased, but Sigmund smiled and nodded.

"I'm starting to think not."

"What does that . . . Sig, what does that mean?"

"I don't know. But maybe after we cage all these lacrosse werewolves, we can sit down somewhere, over coffee, or dinner, and—"

"And you can explain to me again why it's so complicated?" Hailey asked, and Sigmund's face fell. It would have been nice to say yes, to go over it all again. But nothing had changed. They still loved each other, and they were still on different paths.

"So what's up with the werewolves? Are they going for the bait?"

Sigmund leaned over the chimney and shined the light of his phone down into it. "My shirt seems to be quite popular. I can see at

203

least three separate sets of claws working— Oh! No! Bad werewolf! Down! Down!"

"What?" Hailey cried as Sigmund turned and raced toward her across the roof.

"It's coming up the chimney," he called.

"Frankie!" Hailey screamed as she turned and started to run. "Angry reverse Santa Claus! We've got an angry reverse Santa Claus!"

☽ ☽ ○ ☾ ☾

Frankie held the loaded tranquilizer gun to her chest as Jake braced to open the door. He had a gun in his hand as well, a smaller model, with smaller darts. Frankie's would put a werewolf out on the spot. Jake's would take a few minutes for full effect.

"Open it."

Jake nodded and swung the door wide. The O'Shay werewolf was first through the door, and Frankie took him down midleap; he was followed by the Perry Reilly werewolf and an unidentified wolf with a shaggy gray coat. Frankie took them both out and reloaded, and then she and Jake stormed into the hallway. They fired shots left and right, dropping wolves onto the carpet to lie like drooling rugs. At the sight of their pack mates going down, the wolves near the fireplace smartened up and started to look for escape routes. Frankie winced when one of them jumped through the window. She'd hoped they wouldn't figure out that glass could break.

From down the stairs came a scream, and Jake screamed, "Sam!" then took off to help him.

"Jake!" Frankie almost went after him, listening to him snarl and roar. She heard the metal of the cage rattle. But she had to stop the one who'd jumped through the window.

204

She rushed out onto the front porch and saw it, getting to its feet on the grass, shaking its shaggy head. She took aim just as she heard Hailey scream.

"Frankie! There's one on the roof! It came up through the chimney!"

Frankie looked up at the roof. Hailey was panicked. She held her hand out.

Frankie turned between her and the werewolf on the grass. She threw Hailey the gun and raced after the fleeing werewolf on foot.

She caught up to him right at the edge of the road and tackled him to the ground. As they rolled together, she caught a glimpse of Hailey on the roof, taking aim over a ducking Sigmund to put down a charging werewolf with one shot.

"Yep, she's a Potential all right," she grumbled as the werewolf broke free from her grip. She scrambled after it and caught a kick to the face. He was getting away, and she had no tranquilizer gun to stop him.

"Hailey, I need that gun," she shouted, but before she could rise, a wolf with pretty red-gold fur jumped over the top of her. The redheaded wolf chased down the other werewolf in four impressive strides and knocked it to the pavement. It was weird to see a werewolf holding a tranq gun, and weirder to see it aim and fire a dart into the prone form of a packmate.

"Jake?" Frankie asked. She got to her feet as Jake's fur receded and he transformed back to himself, under the light of the full moon.

CHAPTER TWENTY-TWO

JAKE AND THE LACROSSE WEREWOLVES, LIKE JOSIE AND THE PUSSYCATS?

Scoobies both new and OG stood silently in the middle of the Osbourne basement, marveling at the many shades of fur in the piles of passed-out werewolves. They'd shoved so many wolves into Jake's cage that it was filled to bursting, and six more snoozed in Jake's locked bedroom.

"Looks like," Willow said, "quite a party."

"Jake," said Oz. "How did this happen?"

"I don't—" Jake started, and visibly swallowed the rest of that phrase. "It was the Rhodacarthia. I think it made me black out. I must've gnawed on the guys during practice, and I don't think Perry's dog is the one who bit him." He looked guiltily at Sam. "It was probably me who chased you through Fall Creek Park."

Sam's eyes widened. But after a moment, he took Jake's hand and kissed it. "Good thing I've always been faster than you."

Frankie looked around at the unconscious werewolves. There were so many. And they represented so many families, so many hard conversations, so many lifetimes of missed full moons. Of being afraid of losing control and hurting someone they loved. Only maybe it didn't have to be that way. It wasn't that way for Jake and Oz.

Oz stared into Jake's crowded cage, his face unreadable as usual. This was the largest werewolf turning Sunnydale had ever seen. It went against everything Oz believed in. It was a disaster. And it was Jake's fault.

He didn't mean to, Frankie wanted to say. She wanted to chime in, offer to help, brainstorm solutions. But she was a slayer, not a werewolf. This was werewolf business.

"I'll do whatever I have to do," Jake said. "Take whatever punishment there is. I'm so sorry, Oz."

Oz said nothing.

"I should probably go to Weretopia," Jake continued. "Get myself handled somewhere far away. Somewhere safe."

Frankie had to bite her tongue again to keep from shouting, *Jake can't leave!* Not her Jake. What would she do without him?

"You're not going anywhere," said Oz. He turned to Jake as Frankie's knees turned to jelly with relief.

"These new wolves are going to need someone to lead them. They're going to need *you*."

Jake blinked.

"Me? No way, not me. This is my fault!" He waved his hand across his teammates' sleeping forms. Some still had darts sticking out of their haunches. The O'Shay wolf's snout was crusted with pot roast gravy and bits of coleslaw. "They're going to hate me!"

"So they'll get over it," Hailey said, and smacked him in the arm. "Like we all do."

"You are already their cap, Cap," said Sam.

"Jake and the lacrosse werewolves," said Sigmund. "Has a nice ring to it. Like Josie and the Pussycats."

Jake's face paled as he looked over his new situation. Twenty new werewolves were a lot of responsibility.

Oz placed a hand on his shoulder. "You can handle it."

"But not on my own, right? I know they need a new pack leader, but—" He looked at Oz. "I still need mine."

"I'm not going anywhere."

"Right," Spike said. "Well, I am. This place smells like a cave of hibernating bears." The Scoobies started to file upstairs. There wasn't long until sunrise.

"Someone want to help me grab all the blankets off the beds?" Jake asked.

"What for?" asked Hailey.

"Have you heard of that show *Naked and Afraid*? Once the sun comes up, it's going to be filming in my basement."

Hailey raised her eyebrows. She turned to Frankie. "Hey, where'd Grimloch run off to? He missed out on all this zany werewolf fun."

"I don't know where he went," Frankie said, and something in her voice made them all pause. "He might not even be in Sunnydale anymore. We broke up."

"Oh, sweetie." Willow frowned. "I'm sorry."

"Yes. I'm sure both you and Spike are very sorry."

"I'm not sorry at all," the vampire said, and her mom smacked him. "Ow. What? He was a sod, and she's better off!" He looked at Frankie, grudgingly sympathetic. "You want me to bring you some cookies, or . . . ?"

"Yes," Frankie said. "Many cookies. And much distraction, with extra training, please."

When Grimloch returned to his tent, he washed his hands in his camping sink. He felt dirty after what he said to Frankie. She'd been so pleased when he'd said he'd come to Jake's party. And then he'd hurt her, and she didn't understand why.

"Is it done?" Aspen asked.

"It's done."

She got up from his cot. "Did she cry?"

Grimloch clenched his teeth.

"Tell me if she cried," she said, more sharply.

"Yes. She cried."

"Good." Aspen stood beside him, toying with the gem around her neck. "That was fun. I wish we had more time to mess with her. But now it really is time to bring the girls home." She touched his face. He remained motionless. She'd already ordered him not to flinch. "And I can't have her actually starting to hate you. You still need to have access. So you can go get me the one last thing I need."

CHAPTER TWENTY-THREE

I'M FINE, JUST GIVE ME
SOMETHING TO PUNCH IN THE FACE

O n Monday, Frankie and the new Scoobies sat on cement benches in the quad, watching the new lacrosse were-wolves as they hung out before first bell. They seemed . . . okay. They were less boisterous, less like happy water buffalo and more like watchful antelope. And every now and again they would glance at Jake, but Frankie couldn't tell if that glance meant *oh good, you have my back*, or *oh god, you guys stop looking at us*.

"They took it really well, all things considered," said Jake. "But I don't know if it's really sunk in yet."

"What," said Hailey, "you mean the fact that they'll have to come up with an excuse to have team sleepovers at your house every full moon?"

Jake's eyes widened. "I guess yeah. That."

"But only until they find a way to tell their parents," said Sigmund. "And have their own cages installed in their homes."

"Or until they figure out how to control their inner werewolves," said Sam brightly, when Jake started to look overwhelmed. "Like you did."

Jake's newfound control over his transformation was quite a wonder. Over the weekend's full moon, and under the watchful eye of Oz, he'd managed to become the wolf and then himself numerous times. And he could still do it even after the moon had passed. He'd shown off a little that morning, growing his claws and then whisking them away, saying, "Wolverine! No Wolverine!" over and over.

"This level of control might fade once the Rhodacarthia is out of my system," he said. "I'll have to be careful. But it feels like I know how to do it now."

"So something good came out of contacting Jordy after all," said Frankie. Jake's face fell. "What?"

"I texted Jordy yesterday. Asked him if he knew what might happen if I took the Rhodacarthia. And he said he did."

"Oh my god," said Hailey. "I know you said he was kind of feral, but seriously."

"I asked him why he didn't tell me," said Jake.

"And?" Frankie asked.

He showed them his phone. The reply from Jordy read: "I just didn't want you to completely neuter yourself like Oz." Frankie frowned, and Jake pulled the phone away, ashamed. "I'm still coming up with the appropriate outraged response." Sam put an arm around him, and Sigmund scratched Jake's shoulder with his knuckles in that way that sometimes made his foot kick.

"Frankie? How are you? Do you need some extra scratchies, too?" Hailey wiggled her fingers in the air. Frankie'd had the weekend to think over things about Grimloch, and she'd tried to sit with it, and really feel her feelings. Except that in this case, feeling her feelings totally sucked. She shifted uncomfortably on the bench. She was officially single again, but it didn't make her feel like a loner or a rebel. It just made her feel untethered, like a thread dangling from a sleeve that needed to be torn off.

"Frankie?" Jake nudged her with his shoulder.

"What? Me? I'm fine," Frankie said, and made a lot of dismissive, *what are you even talking about* facial expressions. No one seemed to buy it—their faces took on grave, shadowed looks like Frankie was about to crack.

"Are you sure you're fine?" Sigmund asked gently. "Because it's a lot."

"*A lot* a lot," added Sam. "If I broke up with someone as hot as Grimloch, I would weep for days. I did weep a little, actually, on your behalf."

"I do feel like crap," she admitted. "I wonder how long it'll last?"

"Not forever," Hailey said. "Though your limbic system may try to convince you otherwise."

Frankie smiled. "I really am okay, guys. I just need to get back to normal. Slaying, staking, hitting Spike in the face."

"That's the spirit," said Hailey. She clapped her on the knee. "Let's go find Spike, so you can start on the hitting."

"Work-and-school, work-and-school," Jake and Sam chanted supportively, pumping their fists as they stood.

"And of course," said Sigmund, wrapping an arm around Frankie's shoulders, "getting Buffy and the other slayers back."

Frankie took a deep breath. Thank goodness for the Scoobies. Thank goodness for the demons. There was more than enough on her plate to keep her busy, and for once it felt like a welcome distraction rather than the weight of the world on her shoulders.

Except when she started her free-period training session, her Watcher seemed determined to give her grief. At first, he didn't even want to train her.

"So now you're ready to learn something, since the Loomer of Looming Underpants is unavailable? I haven't been able to get you to concentrate on anything for weeks!"

"The Loomer of Looming Underpants," Frankie repeated. "What even is that? Also, I just got dumped; give me a break!" But Spike was unmoved. So Frankie lowered her overeager fists and resorted to whining. "Come on, Uncle Spike. I'm sorry I ditched you for Grimloch all those times. Honestly, I thought you'd be happy. He *is* an ancient hunter god. Training with him is like training with . . . it's like getting cooking lessons from Bobby Flay."

Her Watcher grumbled to himself, but he got out their sparring sticks and a box of scalpels for her to float. Eventually, he forgot that he was supposed to be mad, and they ran drill after drill: attack drills, defense drills, something with a blindfold where she had to hit him with a basketball. He even seemed to sense that Frankie needed something to pummel and let her get in a few extra whacks.

"Thanks, Uncle Spike," Frankie said when they had finished and were cooling down.

"It's what a good Watcher does," he replied, rubbing his shoulder. "Sorry what I said about the Loomer. Are you really all right, Mini Red?"

"I'm fine. I'll be better when we get Buffy back and she and I can run Aspen straight out of town. Maybe she'll even take Grimloch with her."

"You don't think the two of them have teamed up again?"

"I don't know. I don't care. I care so little that I'd buy them a new evil vase to furnish their new evil apartment. Mazel tov." She had no reason to suspect that Grim had broken up with her to go back to Aspen. He hadn't mentioned her, and every time he had he'd been pretty clear about what he thought of her actions. Still, Frankie couldn't shake the weird feeling she got about them. But was that weird feeling her slaydar or her bitter, bitter jealousy, like everyone else seemed to think it was?

"Speaking of slayer running slayers out of towns, we might have some good news." Spike reached into his office mini fridge for a cold pack of blood to drink and an actual cold pack to press to his bumps and bruises. "That evil book of your mum's finally gave us something to go on."

Frankie walked closer. "It did? Since when?"

"Since the night of your fancy werewolf party. We haven't mentioned it because your mum needed some time to work on the spell, and, well . . ." He cocked his head at her. "What with you being so down in the dumps . . ."

"I am not down in the dumps!" Frankie cried.

Spike took a long drink of cold blood. He only liked it cold after a good workout, and for some reason it being cold made it even more disgusting for Frankie to think about. "It was thanks to me, actually," the vampire said. "So you're welcome. I laid my hand on one of the blank pages, and poof! Spell to return the missing slayers. Guess we know who wants to bring Buffy back the most." He raised his eyebrows, but at the moment Frankie was uninterested in playing a game of Who Loves Buffy More.

"But what was it?" she asked. "What was the spell?"

"The Spell of Many Interdimensional Returns. Come on." He grabbed his tweed jacket from the back of his chair. "Let's cut the rest of the school day and go see what Willow has to say about it."

CHAPTER TWENTY-FOUR

EVIL SPELLS FROM EVIL BOOKS

Willow did not, in fact, allow them to cut the rest of the school day. She ordered them back to class via text before they'd even made it to the parking lot, and as punishment for their attempted delinquency said the Scooby meeting couldn't even start until after dark.

After school got out, Frankie sat at their kitchen table, tapping her foot as the sun sank lower, turning through the seemingly endless pages of magic kept within *The Black Grimoire*. The Book of Wants. Frankie was nervous just putting her hands on it. The spells inside had a reputation for changing themselves to suit the reader, and Frankie held her breath with each turned page, expecting that it might reveal her most secret desires and she would suddenly be looking down at a spell to whisk the clothes right off the body of a hunter god. Or maybe to make one fall madly in love with her.

Frankie frowned and flipped toward the back. To the last spell.

"The Spell of Many Interdimensional Returns."

"That's a pretty wordy name for a spell," Hailey said as she came into the kitchen. She opened the refrigerator and leaned in, then came out crunching a green apple. "Think it'll work?"

"If I'm reading it right, it should." Frankie shut the book. "Of course, it's also extremely dangerous." In the entryway, the front door opened and Sigmund and Jake walked in. They'd brought dinner, and poor Sigmund was sagging beneath the bulk of so many takeout bags. They came to the table and started to unload; Frankie grabbed her order of a double veggie burger with vegetarian chili fries. Plus a triple chocolate milkshake.

Hailey traded her apple for some fries and sat down. She stared at *The Black Grimoire* but stopped short of touching it.

"Worried about what you'd find in there?" Frankie asked. "Me too. I was afraid I'd find a spell to disrobe a hunter god."

"Gross," said Jake.

"And you're probably scared you'd find a spell to make you an instant slayer."

Hailey looked down, guiltily. Hailey hadn't talked about being a Potential much. But Frankie knew it was always on her mind.

"There's nothing inherently bad about either of those spells," Sigmund said. "Assuming Grimloch has no problem with nudity."

"Except that this book is evil," said Frankie. "The spell to disrobe Grim would probably take his skin with it. And the spell to activate Hailey would make me drop dead on the spot." She looked up as her mom entered the kitchen. Willow didn't seem pleased at the sight of them gathered around *The Black Grimoire*. She made a beeline for the table and scooped it up to cradle it in the crook of her arm. "Take it easy, we weren't going to get chili on it," Frankie insisted. "And even if we did, I get the feeling that it's been stained by worse things. Like blood. And entrails."

"Mm, entrails," Jake said, then bit into his chili dog. "So, Ms. R. What does this spell do, anyway? What does it take?"

"It takes a lot of power." Willow raised her eyebrows and hugged the grimoire tighter. "Which I have. But what it *does* is tear through a whole bunch of dimensions, opening doors to return misplaced things in the wrong dimensions back to their homes."

"Back to their homes. That sounds nice," said Hailey.

"Only, while the doors are open, it'll be pretty much an inter-dimensional free-for-all. Demons, hellbeasts, and it doesn't say exactly how many dimensional tears it's going to make."

"That sounds less nice," said Frankie.

Willow tapped the grimoire. "Evil book, remember? It wasn't going to be all wine and roses. But when the spell ends, the doors will shut. We just have to try to keep anything too big from . . . popping in."

"But what if something interrupts the spell?" Hailey asked. "What if it doesn't end?" Willow and Sigmund traded a look, but they didn't need to answer. If anything went wrong, the spell would continue. The interdimensional doors would remain open. Demons would keep on pouring through, all the way to the ends of worlds.

"Well, that's great," said Frankie, dismally.

"Should we even do this?" Hailey asked.

"We don't have a choice," Frankie said. "This is our chance to get Buffy and the other slayers back. We just have to make sure the spell won't be interrupted. And on that note—" She stood and stuffed the last of her veggie burger into her mouth.

"Where are you going?" her mom asked.

"I'm going to talk to Grim."

"What," Jake asked, "now?"

"Aspen knows about this book," Frankie said, and Hailey looked down. "I'm not saying that to blame anyone; it's just a fact. I need to know what her plans are. If she's coming for it. And we have to figure out a way to get rid of it."

217

Willow's fingers curled around the edges of the grimoire. "I don't want to get rid of it yet. We should keep it, in case this doesn't work."

"Mom, it's too dangerous." Frankie headed for the door.

"I think Spike might know a black magic dealer who can take it off our hands," said Sigmund, adjusting his glasses and thinking. "I'll ask him about it, when he arrives."

"Good. Also, when he arrives, get on the Buffy phone and let the other slayers know what's up. We're going to drop them through dimensions, into a nest of possible hellbeasts. They need to be ready to fight."

$$\text{)) } \bigcirc \text{ ((}$$

It didn't take long for the Scoobies to get Buffy on the line in the prison dimension—just as long as it took to wrestle Buffy's silver cross out of Spike's pants. The slayer sounded relieved to hear about their plan. But she also seemed worried.

"This is a big spell, Will. At least as big as the spell to activate the Potentials, and a lot more dangerous. Are you sure you're ready for this?"

"I have to be," Willow replied as she gripped the cross. "Don't I?"

"I want to get out of here as much as anybody," said Buffy, "but tearing open dimensions . . . Where's Frankie? What does she think?"

"She had to take care of something." Willow gripped the cross tighter. "But I think we can handle it."

"What about Aspen and the Darkness?" Buffy asked. "Are they going to be a factor?"

"Probably," Spike grumbled, at the same time that Hailey muttered, "Maybe not."

"Willow," said Sigmund. He placed his hand over hers on the cross when he spoke, probably just to be polite. "How long will the spell take to cast? From start to finish?"

"Who's this now?" asked Buffy.

"Sigmund DeWitt, Ms. Summers. An ally."

Hailey added her hand to the pile and said, "A new Scooby."

"Oh," Buffy said happily. "Can't wait to meet you."

"To answer Sigmund's question, I think the spell will take . . . maybe ten minutes?"

They fell quiet. A lot of demons could come through in ten minutes. And they could do a lot of damage. Buffy's voice sounded smaller when she said, "Presumably you'll have us not long after the spell starts."

Spike touched Willow's hand with his fingertip.

"Are you okay to fight, slayer? You've been starved and held hostage for quite a while."

"Bet I can still kick your ass, Spike," she said, and he smiled.

"What if we called in our reserves?" asked Hailey. "Sarafina and Vi."

"That's a good idea," said Willow.

"Okay then." On the other end of the Buffy phone, Buffy took a deep breath. "You tear a hole in the dimension, and we'll be ready to jump through."

$$) \,) \, \bigcirc \, (\, ($$

Frankie didn't make it to the tent to talk to Grim. She didn't need to. As she was leaving her development in the direction of Marymore Park, he was walking toward her down the sidewalk.

"Grim?" At first she thought he might be an optical illusion. A hallucination conjured by a witchy, love-starved mind. She also looked behind her to see if he was walking toward someone else. "What are you doing here?"

"I—" He seemed to be trying to say something, but no words came out. Eventually he stopped trying and settled on clenching his jaw. His eyes flashed blue in the dark.

"Are you mad at me?" she asked. "Because you kind of don't get to be."

"I'm not angry with you. Frankie, I—"

She waited, but again he struggled to find his words.

"I need to tell you something."

"What?" Frankie crossed her arms. When he failed to speak, she sighed and said, "Listen, I just need to know if you've heard from Aspen. Do you have any reason to believe she's planning to come after *The Black Grimoire*?"

"Yes."

"And why do you think that?"

"Because it's what I would do."

"And you two are so alike." They were peas in a pod, him and the leader of the Darkness. They professed their adherence to a warrior's code, but when it came down to it, morality schmorality, right? "If you're changing sides, I won't hesitate to fight you. I kind of want to fight you right now."

"You don't have to," Grimloch said. "That's why I've come. I still want to help."

"More help that I don't want." Like Aspen in the woods with Jake. But this was help that she needed. Frankie was strong, and the new Scoobies were strong. But against the Darkness they weren't strong enough to turn away assistance from the hunter god of Thrace. "Okay then. Just be ready when I call."

CHAPTER TWENTY-FIVE

THE SLAYERS ARE COMING

Hailey asked Sigmund to visit Vi's grave with her one last time, before the final pieces of the plan were in place and her real sister came back to help. "You know, in case something goes wrong and we bleed all the dimensions into one another," Hailey said as she and Sigmund walked through the woods on the way to Vi's fake grave site. "Or maybe it's stupid."

"It doesn't seem stupid to me," he replied. He held up a loose bouquet of wildflowers. "I brought these, didn't I?"

Hailey wrinkled her nose. "Yeah, but I mean, I'm going to see her pretty soon. The real Vi. Not—" She waved her hand toward the dirt. "Whatever's down there."

What was buried in the grave wasn't really Vi. Vi wasn't really dead. But she felt dead sometimes, since she was gone and was pretty unreachable. And there was a piece of her buried under all that dirt. The empty, twin corpse of Vi, with a massive Scythe wound in her belly. Maybe that's what Hailey was saying good-bye to.

"Is there such a thing as being effectively dead, or functionally dead?" Hailey put up air quotes with her fingers. "Like, 'dead'?"

"I suppose so," replied Sigmund thoughtfully. "Though I don't think that's an apt term for what we're visiting. The mirror twin we put into the ground is a piece of your sister, and that piece *is* dead. But it might not even be decomposing. Or maybe it is, and Vi will never be able to reabsorb it. Or perhaps reabsorption would be possible, yet fatally toxic. It would be a fascinating subject of study." When Hailey gave him a look, he raised his own air-quote fingers. "I mean, 'fascinating.'"

They reached the small clearing where they had buried Vi—or rather, fake, mirror-spell twin Vi—and stepped up to the grave, an oval mound ringed with stones, to mark it and so no one visiting would step on her by accident. All through the spring Hailey had trimmed the grass by hand, making uneven cuts with a knife and pulling up weeds by the roots. She'd added more stones, too, to keep the border from becoming overgrown.

"You know, I worried at first that the ground over the mirror twin would turn sour," said Sigmund. "That the dead, magic flesh would cause the grass to wither or turn black, maybe eventually cave in—" He stopped when he saw Hailey's horrified face and raised another set of air quotes. "I mean . . . 'worried.'"

Hailey knelt at the head of the grave. Sigmund knelt beside her and placed his bouquet, pretty blooms of white, pink, yellow, and purple against the green. She wondered if she would always feel compelled to visit this place, even after Vi came back. Maybe when Vi and Sarafina got back, she would bring Vi here, too, to lay her own bouquet.

"This is a big spell Willow's trying to pull off," she said. "With everything that's going on, I mean with Grim and stuff—do you think Frankie's ready?"

Sigmund's brow creased. "I've never heard you doubt her before."

"I don't mean to doubt her," she said quickly, except she had, a little bit. "I'm just worried."

"Well," Sigmund said. "That's why the Scoobies will be there. Willow and I will handle the magic, so you and Jake and Spike, and my mother and your sister, and Frankie, can handle all the beasts of the hell dimensions." He watched her as she stared off into the distance.

"You're thinking it might be helpful if we had just one more slayer," he said. "Perhaps a Potential who's been in the fight all along."

Hailey paused. She shook her head. "No, Frankie's right. Even if *The Black Grimoire* could activate me, it would come at a cost. But it's tempting sometimes, you know? I'm this close to being awesome. This close to having all that strength."

"You're already pretty awesome, Hailey," Sigmund said, and she felt his charm mojo surge as he awkwardly cleared his throat.

Hailey gazed at the grass, where her dead, mirror-spell sister lay only a few feet down. No animals had gotten at the grave; she'd never found any evidence of digging, or clawing. Maybe Sigmund was right and the body was just lying down there, not decaying. "What do you think, dead Vi?" she asked, speaking to it as she did sometimes.

Under the dirt, dead Vi didn't seem to have an answer either. Until she did.

"Dig me up and find out."

Hailey and Sigmund leapt up from the grave, as Vi and Sarafina emerged from behind a tree, laughing. Vi held her arms straight out, miming the undead.

"Raise me from the grave, Hailey," she said in a slow, low voice.

"Vi! You dumbass!" Hailey said, running to hug her. "How did you know we were here?"

"You mean you're not always by my grave, weeping and lighting candles?" Vi smirked. "Sarafina called Willow, and she told us where you went."

"And since you are the two people we wished the most to see," said Sarafina, walking to Sigmund and placing her hands on his cheeks, "we came here first. How are you, my son?"

"I'm well, Mother." Sigmund smiled. "It's good to have you back."

"Called back for a battle, isn't that always the way?" Vi cocked her head at Sarafina. "And just when we were about to bust the head vampire of the Everglades."

"It would have been a mess anyway," Sarafina replied. "So much mud."

Hailey looked back and forth between them. They looked good. Which was nothing out of the ordinary for the great Sarafina DeWitt, but Vi looked good, too. In a way that she hadn't looked in a long time.

"Being dead really suits you." Hailey prodded Vi in the shoulder of her black button-down shirt. Vi had changed her hair again, stripped the dark brown dye and lightened it a little, to a pale, only-slightly-strawberry blond, even lighter than Jake's.

"Weren't you supposed to be lying low?" Sigmund asked. "Not attracting attention to yourselves and to the fact that Vi was Vi and still alive?"

"Are you lecturing me?" Sarafina asked, but she did so with a smile.

"Only when a lecture is warranted," Sigmund said, smiling back.

Vi threw an arm casually around the elder Sage demon. "You know how it is with slayers: Trouble finds us. And besides, we worked in the shadows. We were like dual Batman."

"Being like Batman is not laying low," said Hailey. "He uses a frigging bat-signal, for Pete's sake."

Vi shrugged. "The point is, we're here, and still a surprise for the Darkness. So let's sneak over to the Rosenberg house and keep it that way. Hey, you were just asking dead me for advice. Living me is here now, so, about what?"

Hailey glanced at Sigmund. He kept his face carefully neutral, but what the heck, she was unlikely to get a better opening to spill the beans.

"Well, turns out I have some news. Remember when you were a Potential?"

"Yeah," Vi said, suspiciously.

"Well, guess what. It runs in the family."

Sigmund winced, but Vi was her sister. She was used to the bluntness.

"You mean—"

"Yep," said Hailey, keeping her voice as upbeat as possible. "We did the stinky glow ball spell and everything." She waited. She refused to squirm under Vi's stare. But Vi had a really good stare. "So . . . what do you think?"

"This isn't what I wanted for you," Vi said.

"But I guess it's what the slayer line wanted."

"The slayer line is greedy," said Vi. She was starting to get that haunted look again, like she used to have when she went out at night to patrol, or when every Slayerfest came around.

"Vi? Are you okay?"

"Are you?"

Hailey shrugged. It was a lot to process, this whole being a Potential business. But she was surrounded by people who knew how to help.

"I think I am," she said, and smiled when she realized it was true. Vi smiled back.

"Then so am I."

$$) \,) \,\bigcirc\, (\,($$

Frankie sat by the window of her bedroom, watching the sun slant across the lawn and trying to meditate. It was hard now that Vi and Sarafina were back. Since they'd returned a few days ago, Vi had been camping out in their basement and Sarafina was coming around on the regular to see Willow. Their house was constantly loud. Not to mention that every time Frankie's mind went slack, thoughts of Grimloch rose in the void. *Frankie and Grimloch, first ever slayer-witch and hunter god of Thrace, alas, we knew them well.*

She sighed. They were casting the spell tonight. The spell to bring Buffy back, the Spell of Many Interdimensional Returns. In just a few hours they would all be reunited, and if the house felt crowded now, once the missing slayers were added to the mix, Frankie would literally be tripping over people.

This was the biggest spell any of them had ever attempted. She had to be ready. She had to be her best. She certainly couldn't be her regular. They were about to fight a battle with interdimensional hellbeasts. She imagined making a *V* with her fingers and blinding some evil, snarling demon, laughing as it held its face and screamed, "My eyes, my eyes!" in some indecipherable demon language. It was funny until an image of Spike rose in her mind, and he did not look pleased.

She shook her head and tried again to meditate. She let her mind go slack, let her magic stretch, and immediately saw Grimloch's smile flash behind her closed eyes.

There had to be a way to make all of this easier.

Slowly, her eyes traveled across the carpet to the door of her room, and beyond it to her mother's room, where *The Black Grimoire* was stashed.

That book is evil, she told herself. But it didn't feel evil. It felt like a friend. Or like a warm pair of socks fresh from the dryer.

Frankie got up quietly and went into the hallway, listening to the sounds of Hailey, Sigmund, Sarafina, and her mom in the kitchen. She heard Vi say, "I want my real return from the dead to be more theatrical. Fog machines, big skirt of feathers. And I want my first public act to be consuming an entire plate of fries with gravy from the interstate diner."

"Jeez." Frankie heard Hailey snort. "Sarafina, didn't you feed her while you were on the run?"

"Silence, Potential," Vi said. "You can talk about slayer metabolism when you have a slayer metabolism."

Frankie padded down the hallway and into her mother's room. In three big strides she reached the bed, then leaned down to sweep her arm underneath it to retrieve *The Black Grimoire.*

The Book of Wants. With it heavy in her hands, it felt smug and self-satisfied, like it had known she would be too weak to resist. There were no words on the cover, but if there had been they would have read, *I Knew You'd Pick Me Up Sooner Or Later, Little Witch.*

Frankie narrowed her eyes. She didn't like smug books. She felt her magic whip up and circle like a nervous cat. It flowed into her fingertips tentatively, like it wanted just a taste. *The Black Grimoire* was a bad idea. Or was it merely a powerful idea? Maybe she was only afraid of it because she hadn't tried it yet.

"I think you'd better give that to me, Mini Red."

Frankie spun. Her Watcher leaned against the door frame.

"Spike! I didn't know you were here."

"Clearly," he said with his arms across his chest, tapping freshly painted black fingernails against his elbow.

"I was just looking at it," she said.

"'Course you were. No way this is a case of like mother, like daughter." Spike sauntered across the room and plucked the book from her grasp. "What were you doing with it?"

"I guess I thought it might have an easy way to mend a broken heart."

"There is no easy way, Mini Red," the vampire said. "There's only whatever way you can."

Frankie frowned. She watched as he flipped the book open and paged through. "What are *you* looking for?"

"Nothing in particular. Maybe a spell for an instant blood warmer."

"It's a spellbook, not an infomercial."

Spike snorted and leaned against the doorjamb, hugging the grimoire to his chest. "Look at you, Mini Red. Growing up before my very eyes. I'm going to blink and you're going to be off at college, at a job, married to some demon who doesn't appreciate you." He looked down and gestured to himself: black shirt, pale skin, platinum hair. "And I'll be here. All of this, always the same."

"But it's good that you're all . . ." Frankie said, and gestured to everything he gestured to. "And you're not the same: You have your new old face!"

Spike rolled his eyes.

"Come on," she said. "What vampire gets a new old face? And when you're done with the new old face, my mom can take it off and whoosh, you'll have a new young face. What's old is new, and then old, and then new again!"

It took a minute, but eventually, he sucked in his cheeks and smiled at her. "Aren't you supposed to be heartbroken?"

"Never too heartbroken to cheer you up." Looking at him, she realized it was hard to imagine a time when he wouldn't be around, even though only a year ago he'd been an infrequent visitor. Spike had wormed his way right into the heart of their family, just like her mom said he did all those years ago when she and Buffy and Xander were young. But eventually he would leave. Someday they would all leave, and she might even live far away and only see her mom on holidays. And that would be normal, even if she couldn't imagine it now.

"Uh-oh," she said. "I'm getting depressed again."

"Well, I've got something to buck you up: My rare book dealer is coming through town. If we go tonight, we can get this nasty little grimoire off our hands."

"Before we do the spell?" Frankie asked.

"Sure. We only need the one. We'll just tear it out and get rid of the evil rest."

The moment he said it, Willow appeared behind him in the hallway. Like she'd somehow overheard. Or like the grimoire had called to her for help.

"What are you talking about?" she asked. "What are you doing with *The Black Grimoire*?"

"Saying goodbye to it," Spike replied. "We can unload it tonight." He handed it to Frankie. Or rather, he tried to hand it to Frankie, but Willow snatched it, calling it into her arms from midair.

"You can't! We're not ready."

"Come on, Willow. It's time. How many black magic book dealers you think there are who can handle something like this? And of that list, how many do you think can be trusted?" Spike held his hand out.

229

"It's not time," Willow growled, and Spike made a grab for it. They grappled for a few moments, grimacing and twisting in a grimoire tug-of-war, until Willow finally lost her temper and magicked the vampire across the room. He hit the wall near the ceiling and slid down in a disoriented pile.

"Mom!" Frankie cried. But her mom wasn't listening. Willow was only listening to one thing now, and it was the thing she cradled in her arms and crooned to like it was a baby.

"It took me so long to find you," Willow said to it.

"Mom?" Frankie said as Spike got shakily up off the carpet. Their argument had attracted attention: Sarafina, Hailey, Sigmund, and Vi gathered around the doorway and peered in.

"What's going on?" Sarafina asked. But Willow didn't answer. She just kept murmuring to the book, her hand skittering over the cover like a pale spider.

"Mom!" Frankie shouted.

Willow's fingers skidded to a halt, and she narrowed her eyes at Frankie. "It's not fair what you ask me to do! To be so close to it. To use it. *Use it*," she said, in a snarling imitation. "But only to help. Push myself, but not too far! Give me a glimpse of massive power, and then squash it back down!"

"Mom, that's not what we're asking."

"Be a goddess and change the world," Willow muttered. "And then go back to being Willow Rosenberg and raise your daughter. Work in a lab. Get aches and pains and stress headaches. Spill your coffee on your new shirt when you're rushing out of the house late. But if I have this book, I don't have to do any of that!"

Tentatively, Frankie took a step closer. Everyone else in the room was frozen. Her mother's eyes had turned completely black, and Willow didn't seem to have noticed.

"Mom, please, just give me the book."

"No, see . . ." Willow opened the book, and the pages parted to the Spell of Many Interdimensional Returns. "We can't get rid of the book, there's more to the spell every time I read it. A new wrinkle, an implication I hadn't noticed before in the text. An ingredient we missed."

"Except you didn't miss it," said Spike. "The book's asking more of her," he said to Frankie. "It's making it harder."

"So she'll lose herself," Frankie whispered. She thrust out her hand. "Give me the book!"

"Yeah, come on, Willow," said Hailey from the doorway. "If you keep the spell in there much longer you'll need six hands to cast it, plus a vial of powdered unicorn horn."

"Shut up, Hailey," Willow said. "It's your fault that they want to get rid of it anyway. You're the one who invited evil into our house."

"She doesn't mean that," Frankie said. But she couldn't look to see if Hailey was hurt. She couldn't take her eyes off her mother.

"I do mean that. And another thing I mean—" Willow turned the page of the spell, to a blank sheet. "I don't think I want to let *The Black Grimoire* go. I think I want to keep it. Forever."

"No, Mom!"

Willow slammed her hand down on the blank page and immediately her body contorted, bending backward as a wave of power thundered through the room. Her fingers disappeared within the pages as the skin and paper melded together and stretched like taffy. She was joining with the book.

Sarafina and Vi reached for Willow's shoulders. The shock they received threw them into the hallway, knocking over Hailey and Sigmund.

Frankie searched the room. There had to be a way to stop the book from taking over her mother. "The spellbooks on the shelves." Her eyes traveled over the familiar spines, good magic, useful magic that she and Willow had read together when she was a child like they were the Sunday funnies. "Spike!" She used her telekinesis to tear a volume from the third row and sent it into her Watcher's hands like he'd called it there himself. "Find the spell to sever a psychic bond."

"Right." The vampire flipped quickly through the pages. "Got it!" He read the incantation, his voice halting but growing louder. Frankie felt the magic speed across the room and timed her attack with it, charging in tandem with the spell to grab *The Black Grimoire* and wrench it from her mother's hands.

Even with the help of the magic it wasn't easy. She had to wrestle it free, and Willow grabbed her shoulder and shoved, her touch sending some of the dark magic into Frankie at the same time.

"You little brat," Willow yelled, but Frankie kept pulling, using her slayer strength and her telekinesis together. When the connection between her mother and the grimoire finally broke, the force threw all of them into the walls. Frankie held on to the book tightly. Her vision swam and her head throbbed. She felt something itching against her wrists. The grimoire had flipped open, and her fingers gripped the pages. She looked down to see her forearms flooding with ink as the Spell of Many Interdimensional Returns worked its way into her skin.

CHAPTER TWENTY-SIX

SCOOBIES! MOUNT UP!

rankie stood in the kitchen as Hailey pressed a cold compress to her forehead. They were all staring at her, Sarafina, Sigmund, Vi. Spike. Her mom was fussing over her like she'd just fallen off her first bike. She kept stroking Frankie's hands and mumbling "I'm sorry, I'm sorry," over and over. But despite a weird feeling in her stomach, Frankie felt fine. She felt good, even. Pumped up. It must have been a bit like how her mom had felt when she was hopped-up on black magic.

"Guys. I'm fine."

"You're not bloody well fine," Spike snapped. "Look at you!"

Frankie looked down at her arms. The Spell of Many Interdimensional Returns was etched into her skin like a tattoo.

"I don't know how this happened," Willow whispered. "I would never hurt you, sweetie. Not on purpose."

"I know." Frankie squeezed her mom's fingers. "But now do you see why we have to get rid of the book?"

Willow's face scrunched. Even after everything that had happened, she still didn't want to let the grimoire go. But she nodded.

"Are you sure we should even do the spell now?" Hailey asked, eyeing Frankie's arms. "It feels like this might have changed things."

Frankie looked down. The spell wasn't going anywhere. It was inside her now. If anything, their situation had improved, because it was out of the book and no longer changing. And it wasn't as though Aspen could steal it. Well, not without cutting off Frankie's arms.

"Nothing's changed except the location," Frankie said. "So the plan is still the plan. We unload the Book of Wants, and as soon as that's finished, we cast the spell to bring Buffy back. I'm done wasting time. Buffy's coming home. Someone needs to go grab Grimloch—we could use the extra muscle."

"I'm on it," Sigmund said He headed for the door and Frankie took a deep breath. It wouldn't be long now.

$$☽ ☽ ○ ☾ ☾$$

Frankie went upstairs to change into clothes that better befit an illicit nighttime exchange of dangerous magical goods, i.e., a loose pair of gray pants and a T-shirt with a bear on it, plus a short tan jacket to hide the spell on her arms. When she came back down, she found Jake in the kitchen. The moment he saw her, he crossed his arms and frowned.

"Show me."

Frankie rolled her eyes and pushed up her sleeves.

"Whoa," he said. "How did you do that?"

"When have you ever known me to be able to do that?" Frankie asked, and let her sleeves fall. "There was a scuffle. A lot of magic being thrown around." Jake's eyes narrowed. "Look, all I did was touch it. And it . . . jumped into me!" She pushed past him to the sink and started to wash her hands, stopping when she realized that what she was trying to do was wash off the spell. "It doesn't change anything, okay? We still have the spell, and we're still going to keep Aspen from getting her hands on the book, and Buffy is still coming home tonight through a shower of hellbeasts."

"Okay, okay." Jake held up his hands in defeat.

Frankie picked up a towel. Jake been subdued since the night of the full moon party, walking on eggshells like he needed to be on his best werewolf behavior. But they were going into the fight of their lives. Frankie needed her old Jake, full of bluster and kind of a doofus. He was the one she could lean on. The one she could fall back on who would catch her like a giant, fluffy, stuffed bear.

"Hey," she said. "Are you okay? You still seem kind of ashamed about what happened to your teammates."

"Well, shouldn't I be?"

"Yes, but, Jake, you're making amends. You're there for them when they need you. You're going to look after them. And honestly, in Sunnydale, there are worse things they could have turned into. Big swimmy fish monsters. Living puppets. Invisible."

"I guess."

"The best thing you can do for them is teach them how to live with their new normal. Because it is pretty normal. Don't make them feel like weirdos."

"It would be nice to stop going so easy on them at practice. I told Perry to run laps yesterday, and then I just ran them for him instead."

Frankie snorted and rolled her eyes.

"I guess you're right," said Jake.

"Good. Because I need my old Jake. The one who'll rush in, claws blazing. The one who'll ask his new pack of lacrosse werewolves to back us up for the spell of the century."

"Huh? Frankie, I don't know. They haven't even been through

their second full moon. I don't think they're ready." He looked down. "And they wouldn't come if I asked."

"All you can do is try. They don't have to fight. It would just be nice to have the extra hands."

Jake paused. He reached for Mr. Stabby, Frankie's favorite sparring stick, where it rested dangerously against the island with the pointy end up. One stumble and someone was bound to need an eye patch. "Bringing good old Mr. Stabby tonight?"

"I guess so. He's not the most practical to bring on patrol, but I doubt some shady magical arms dealer will care if I look like Gandalf."

The front door opened, and Jake stiffened when he saw Grimloch come in behind Sigmund.

"Don't freak out," Frankie warned. "I asked him to come."

"Yeah, but your old Jake would still go rough him up," Jake said, and barreled into the entryway.

But Jake didn't get a chance to do whatever it was he was about to. Because Spike beat him to it.

"Well, well, if it isn't the Hunter of Thrace." Spike marched up to Grim and socked him in the nose. "That was for Frankie," Spike said, and punched him again, two more times.

"And what were those for?" Grim asked, touching his slightly bloodied lip.

"Those were for fun," Spike said perkily. "I don't like you."

"Spike, that's enough." Frankie looked at Grimloch.

"I'm only here to help," Grimloch said.

"We don't need the kind of help that breaks our slayer's heart," said Jake.

"Guys." Frankie stepped in between them. "We *do* need him."

"You sure he's not back with his ex?" Jake asked, visibly bristling.

"He didn't break up with me for Aspen. He broke up with me for reasons. Right, Grim?"

"Right," Grimloch said, and growled.

Frankie turned to the other Scoobies, gathered in the living room. "This spell is going to take all the muscle we have. And we still need a place to cast it. Somewhere with room to move, but away from people. Preferably somewhere we can close off to contain the demons."

"Uh," Hailey said. "This might seem self-serving, but how about the school? Like, in the gymnasium? It's big, we can lock the doors, and it's deserted after hours."

"It'll probably get destroyed," said Oz. "But that's just tradition at this point."

Frankie looked at her Scoobies. They had armed themselves, Hailey with her ax and Sarafina with a startlingly large knife. Sam had a lacrosse stick. Even Sigmund had his bow across his back with a quiver of arrows.

"The school it is," Frankie said. "But first we have to ditch the evil book. We're going to run decoy teams. Vi, Hailey, and Sarafina on one, and Spike and me on the other. If Aspen or anyone from the Darkness is watching, they won't know which team has the real grimoire."

"Wouldn't they assume the real grimoire is with the real slayer?" Sigmund asked.

"That's why Vi is going to take her hood down. The sight of her should throw them." Frankie waited as Vi processed that. She'd been dead for a while now, and flying under the radar seemed to suit her. But after a moment, she shrugged.

"There's no time to rent a fog machine, but this is okay, too."

"Good. Sig, Sam, Oz, and Jake—I need you to prepare the spell space. If it's going to be the gymnasium, we're going to need heavy chains and locks for each set of doors, and the whole thing needs to be ritually cleansed. As soon as we get back, it's go time."

"We're on it," the boys said together and tromped their way out the door. Before he left, Jake tugged Frankie aside.

"And I'll text the lacrosse werewolves."

"Thanks, Jake."

"We're on it, too," said Hailey as she, Vi, and Sarafina followed the boys. "Decoy team one, grab a fake book and remove the hood!" Vi grabbed one of the Rosenberg family photo albums and wrapped it in a blanket. As she ducked out the door, Hailey tugged her sister's hood down. "Good luck," she said to Frankie.

"You too."

Spike stepped out behind them in his black coat. "Meet you in the driveway, Mini Red." Frankie nodded, and the vampire left, leaving her alone with Grimloch and her mom.

"I should stay here," Grimloch said. "With your mother. In case the Darkness come to the house instead."

"That's probably wise," said Frankie. "Try to keep her from doing any spells to magick the book back here."

Willow frowned. "I wasn't gonna."

Grimloch clenched his teeth. "Frankie. I need . . . to tell you something."

She waited. But all he did was look mopey and breathe. "What?" she prodded. When the heavy breathing continued, she shrugged. "Well, can it wait until we get back?"

He said nothing. Just growled a little and bared the tips of his fangs.

"You're being weird," she said.

"I shouldn't be here," he said finally.

"Not at all," Frankie said, shrugging. "I can't afford to have any

238

of our resources just sitting around in a tent. Besides, having you here is just more torture, so it's very in keeping with the current theme of our relationship."

"Frankie," Grimloch started.

She waited again, but when he said nothing more, she ducked out the door and went down the driveway to catch up with Spike.

CHAPTER TWENTY-SEVEN
LIVING THE DREAM AS AN EVIL BOOK CURATOR

As they walked through the dark streets of New Sunnydale Heights, Frankie's slaydar was agitated. It fluttered around in her gut, throwing weak signals like a firefly dying in a jar. Maybe it was trying to warn her about the dark magic coursing through her blood. But she didn't think so. It grew worse with every step she took away from her house.

"Did Grimloch seem odd to you?" she asked Spike.

"If by odd you mean annoying and insufferable, then yes, he seemed like he always does." They were headed toward the familiar turf of the cemetery. That's where Spike said his book dealer would meet them. When they reached the end of the development he crouched and turned to look in all directions. "All right," he said. "Time to move swiftly."

Spike led her through the shadows, across lawns and away from illuminated sidewalks. Frankie spun Mr. Stabby and kept her senses tuned for movement, but there was nothing. No signs of the Darkness. No telltale noises, not even a twinge of the wiggins creeping up between her shoulder blades. Just that nagging ping of her slaydar, like fingers worrying at a fidget cube.

"Are we going to get anything in exchange for this?" Frankie asked, nodding to *The Black Grimoire*, hugged in Spike's arms. "I mean, it must be pretty valuable. Are we going to get money? Like, lots and lots of money?"

"We're talking about the trade of an extremely dangerous and arcane magical artifact," Spike said. "We just need to get rid of it. Also it should be lots and lots and lots of money. And champagne."

"Well, hold on to it tighter. I half expect it to sprout legs and try to run away on its own."

Spike slowed and came to a stop just before the gates of Silent Hills. He peered down one direction and then the other.

"Must be running late."

Frankie scanned the grounds. There were no signs of foul play. "So what do we do?"

"What do you mean 'what do we do'? We wait."

She put up Mr. Stabby and leaned on him like a staff while they hung in the shadows, eyes peeled for any signs of an approaching magic book dealer. "Spike, do you ever wish Hailey'd been called instead of me?"

He gave her a surprised look. "Of course not. Why would you ask that?"

"I don't know." Frankie shrugged. "She's kind of naturally better at everything. And she's Vi's sister, so she makes just as much sense as the new slayer as me. I don't know, part of me just feels like if more people knew she was a Potential they'd be lining up waiting for me to die."

"Don't say that. It isn't true. Also, Hailey would be a bollocks slayer. She'd die instantly, always running in places without thinking and using that bloody little ax all the time, which, let's face it, is not practical—"

"Spike."

Her Watcher sighed. "Hailey would be a fine slayer. But she isn't 'more.' And she wouldn't be better. Being a good slayer isn't just technical skills. It's heart. And you have more heart than . . . than your git of an ex-boyfriend could eat in a lifetime."

Frankie smiled. "Thanks, Spike."

He placed a hand on her shoulder. But before things could turn completely sappy, a vehicle turned the corner and came roaring up the street, flashing its headlights. When Spike stepped out and raised his arm, it honked twice.

"That's what we're waiting for?" Frankie asked. It was a truck, but not just a truck. It was a food truck. A yellow one, with an enormous taco on the top of it.

"That's her," said Spike, and walked toward the truck. "Dorsia Maleferico."

"Her?" Frankie asked. She hadn't expected a "her." "For some reason I thought the broker would be a guy."

Spike gave her a haughty sideways glance. "Look at you, showing your internalized gender bias. Guess it's not just for us oldsters anymore. Look sharp, though, she is a demon."

Ahead, the food truck's window opened, and a woman leaned out. She looked human, at least from the torso up, with midnight-black hair pulled back tight and secured by a food service net. Her mouth was painted bright with hot-pink lipstick. Frankie peered at her, trying to spot any traits that marked her as a demon, but found none. Her skin was smooth and tan, her ears were ear shaped, and her teeth were white and not at all pointy when she smiled.

"William the Bloody," she purred when she saw Spike.

"Dorsia Maleferico," he purred right back. "You look well fed."

"Of course I do, darling; I run a food truck." Her eyes slid to Frankie, who was trying to figure out what Spike meant by well fed. Dorsia looked a little on the thin side, to be honest, but still quite healthy. What did she look like when she was underfed? Was that when the demon came out? "Do you see anything of interest, cher?" the demon asked Frankie. "My fryers are always on"— Dorsia's eyes flashed, reflective for a moment, like a cat's caught by a pair of headlights—"and I have a delicious vegetarian plate: savory beans and cheese, marinated peppers, some soft, herbed rice on frybread."

"She'll pass," Spike answered for her. "She's not a mark." Frankie test-sniffed the air and frowned a little. The vegetarian plate sounded good, and she'd been skirting the edge of hungry ever since Vi had mentioned the diner and those fries with gravy.

Dorsia crossed her arms and leaned upon them to look at Frankie, eyes again flashing a greenish silver. Spike stepped between Frankie and the truck.

"You don't want any of it, Mini Red," he said. "It's . . . expensive."

"Expensive how?" Frankie asked.

"You won't know until you eat it."

"But it is worth every bite," said Dorsia, smiling a bright pink smile. Frankie shook her head, and the demon shrugged. "I heard you had become partial to slayers. Especially the blond leader. I'd hoped it was only a rumor. This one is quite lovely, but she is not as game as your former paramour. Where is the beauty Drusilla?"

"Oh gross." Frankie made a face. "You think I'm a paramour? He's my Watcher, lady, and before that he's my uncle. Also, note his face of advanced age?"

"Hey," Spike barked, insulted. But Dorsia extended a long-nailed hand to toy with his collar.

"I see the new glamour, dug into the skin like it has been stitched by a needle. Well done and appropriately handsome."

"That's more like it." The vampire squared his shoulders. "But much as I love to flirt, it's not why we're here." He hefted *The Black Grimoire* up onto the thin metal counter.

"This *is* it." Dorsia took a long sniff of the cover. Then she straightened and clapped her hands against each other as if clapping off the last bits of flour from cooking. She popped a bit of crispy fried bread into her mouth and began to inspect the book, her pink lacquered nails brushing the spine like she was trying to tickle it. Knowing what Frankie knew about the grimoire and its "wants," she wouldn't have been all that surprised to hear it giggle.

"Mm," Dorsia said finally, placing the book back down. "*The Black Grimoire* will come with me. It knows that it will be safe. It had hoped to find a home with your witch, but . . ." The demon shook her head. "It seems that her magic was corralled, and they were never able to fully bond. A good thing," she whispered, leaning down to Frankie. "For if they had, the world as we know it would likely no longer exist." Frankie smiled weakly. She'd heard her mother referred to as a world ender lots of times, but it never got less disturbing.

"So. We have a deal," Dorsia declared, like the period on the end of a sentence.

"Hang on," said Spike. "That's not just some book we got out of a gumball machine; what'll you give us in exchange?"

"Give?" The demon raised her eyebrow. "You need me to take it, so I will take it. That is the transaction."

"That's no transaction," Spike said, and grabbed for the book.

"Spike," Frankie hissed. "We do need her to take it!" She looked at Dorsia, who stared down at them regally. "But how do we know it'll be safe with you? You seem like a contact from Spike's old days. You know, before the soul? So how do we know you won't take it and team up with it to end the world just like my mom would have?"

"Because, cher," Dorsia replied, leaning down to explain with exaggerated patience, "much as I hate to admit it, I do not have half the power that your mother has. In the hands of a witch like her, *The Black Grimoire* is a sword to the heart of existence. To a demoness like me, it is a trinket. A toy. A bauble." She gestured to the sky, carefree, and Frankie's eyes narrowed.

"Spike's right. You're underplaying it. I don't think it's because you're dangerous with it, or that you'd sell it to some other powerful demon—but you do want it. So what will you give?"

"That's my girl," said Spike, clapping Frankie on the back. Dorsia's bright pink lips pouched together in a sour expression and she picked up the book, giving it a more thorough inspection and muttering to herself in a language that sounded to Frankie like Cajun-inflected French, splashed together with demonic swear words.

"What to give, what to give," she murmured. "What to give for the Book of Wants . . ." She flipped the pages and sniffed the air that wafted from them, and abruptly stopped short. "I give you nothing! This book is incomplete!"

Frankie and Spike looked at each other.

"Yeah," Spike said, "that was an accident, right? Mini Red was just trying to break up an argument, and the spell jumped into her when she touched the page."

"That is not what I meant." Dorsia opened *The Black Grimoire* and pointed to the binding. "I am talking about this."

Spike squinted. Frankie leaned forward. There was a page missing. The ragged edge was just barely visible, where it had been torn out.

"It was like that when we got it," Spike insisted. But Frankie knew better. Willow had carefully, obsessively, turned every page, and none had been missing.

"Wait a minute. Aspen looked through the grimoire when she came to visit Hailey."

Frankie took the book back and paged through it, trying to remember the spells she'd seen and the order in which she'd seen them. But there were so many. Some of them similar. All of them twisted.

"Spike," she said. "Aspen must have taken one of the spells the night she came to our house." She flipped more pages, and his glamour-furrowed brow furrowed still further as he peered over her shoulder. If only she had Hailey's near-photographic memory, she could remember the page that was gone.

She was this close to taking the grimoire and banging it against her forehead when Dorsia reached out and said, "Give it to me."

Frankie handed her the book, and Dorsia took it, and then her hand.

"Open it to the missing page," she said, and Frankie used her free hand to lift the cover. "Now. Pass your palm over the missing spell and repeat after me." Frankie felt something pass between their joined hands. But it didn't feel bad. It felt warm and kind of curious, like the wings of an excited hot climate bird.

"What are you doing?" Spike asked, poised to intervene.

"Just forming a connection," Dorsia replied. "I have no need to do more. This slayer is her mother's daughter."

"Right," Frankie mumbled. "Say that again in a few minutes, after this spell I cast makes *The Black Grimoire* burst into flames."

"Don't be so pessimistic, cher. It doesn't suit you. Now, repeat." She lifted her chin. "Revaler."

"Revaler," Frankie said, and the missing page reappeared.

Not the real page, of course—that was still in Aspen's grubby hands—but more like the grimoire's memory of it: an ethereal and mostly translucent image, floating in an unfelt breeze.

"Am I reading that right?" asked Spike. "It's the spell to bend someone's will. The mind control spell. What would she bloody want with that?"

Mind control. Bending someone's will to your own. Forcing someone to do your bidding. All at once, Frankie's body went cold.

"Spike, we have to go. Now!" She shoved *The Black Grimoire* back into Dorsia's hands and turned back toward New Sunnydale Heights as the vampire sputtered in confusion. "Spike! Hurry!"

"Wait, cher. Take this." Dorsia tossed something to her, something small and wrapped in waxed paper. It smelled delicious, like warm vanilla and butter, but Frankie didn't have time to ask questions. "With that you will create silence," Dorsia explained. "But use it wisely. Its effects are temporary." She nodded, once to Frankie, who nodded back and turned to run, and once to Spike, who had no idea what was happening. "And now our transaction is complete," she said, then closed the food truck window.

"Hey! Mini Red!" Spike shouted, running fast to catch up. "Do you want to tell me what just happened?"

"Not now! We're going back home." She threw Dorsia's yummy-smelling packet to him, and he put it in his pocket for safekeeping.

"What for?" he asked.

"Because Aspen is controlling Grimloch," Frankie said, running faster. "And my mom has no idea."

$$) \; \rangle \; \bigcirc \; (\; \langle$$

Willow leaned on the counter of her kitchen island, sipping a cup of tea across from Grimloch. They had stood by the window until both Frankie and Spike and the decoy team were out of sight. It was only then that they realized they were alone, and had no idea how long the mission would take. The tea was an ice breaker, and she'd brought out some chocolates. But though the demon was polite, he wasn't the best at small talk.

"It's kind of nice being here, just the two of us," she said. "I know you and Frankie aren't together right now, but you were, and I never got the chance to get to know you . . ."

"Indeed," Grimloch mumbled.

"And I think you'll find I'm a fairly open-minded parent when it comes to slayer-demon relationships. As long as you respect her, and treat her with kindness, and don't propose marriage or anything . . ." She trailed off awkwardly. "I mean, I grew up with Buffy and Angel, and I could tell you some stories—"

"Mmph," Grimloch grunted, and Willow started to get annoyed. Sure, they were just passing the time, but he could help. She craned her neck to peer out the window, hoping to see Frankie returning. Maybe even with the grimoire. Maybe Spike's magical antiquities dealer hadn't shown up. Willow looked back down. *It hurt your daughter,* she thought angrily. *You hurt your daughter.* She knew that, and she hated it. But she still wanted to blow the door off its hinges and follow *The Black Grimoire* into the night while floating several feet off the ground.

She tore her eyes away from the door and snapped, "Are you this quiet with Frankie?"

For a moment, Grimloch just toyed with the side of his teacup. "Francesca has a way of filling the silence."

That made Willow smile. "Her name's actually not Francesca. Just Frankie. Frankie—"

"Jane Rosenberg," he said. "I know."

"You care about her," Willow noted. "Then why did you two break up?"

Grimloch walked around the island, aimlessly touching the handle of a cold frying pan.

"You don't have to answer that," Willow said. "I don't mean to pry. I guess I'm not so good at the small talk either."

"Willow," he said, "I'm not . . . I'm not . . ."

Willow waited for him to finish, but when he didn't, she got bored and turned back to the window. Honestly, she didn't know what Frankie found so enticing. Sure, he was a tall drink of water, what Cordelia would have quickly declared as being of "salty goodness," but where Angel had the smoldering looks, he also had a puppylike earnestness that made you want to cuddle him and help him do things. Grimloch? Grimloch seemed like kind of a lump. A judgy lump. A haughty, judgy, demon lump.

"Willow," Grimloch said.

"Yes?"

"I'm sorry."

"Sorry for what?" she asked without much interest.

Unfortunately, she didn't hear his answer. Because before he said anything more, Grimloch picked up the frying pan and swung it at the back of her head.

Frankie and Spike burst into the house moments before Hailey, Vi, and Sarafina. As she and Spike had sprinted for home, Frankie had texted the decoy team, as well as Oz and the boys, to come back, and that Grim could be a double agent.

"Mom? Mom are you here?" Frankie waited. The house was empty.

"Where is she?" Sarafina demanded, snarling. "What has he done with her? I will tear out his spine!"

"Whoa, whoa." Vi put a hand before Sarafina's chest and glanced meaningfully toward Frankie. "It's too soon for spine tearing. I'm sure she's okay. She's the red witch, remember?"

"We don't even know what happened," said Hailey. "Maybe they left together."

They were trying not to scare her, but Frankie was barely listening. She knew already that her fears had come true. She knew even before she saw the shattered teacup and tea spilled all over the kitchen floor, even before she saw the streaks and smears where her mother had been dragged through it and picked up.

"He took her," Frankie said.

"But why would Grim take your mom?"

"Because Aspen is controlling him!" Frankie spun on Hailey. "That sounded accusatory, and it's not what I mean. Look, when we got to the book dealer, she identified a page in the grimoire that had been torn out. It was the mind control spell. Who else could have taken it?"

"Maybe Willow stashed it somewhere," Hailey said quietly.

"No!" Frankie shook her head. How could she make Hailey understand? "I know you think Aspen isn't all bad. But she's bad right now. She used Grimloch to kidnap my mother. And we need to find out where he took her."

The tires of Oz's van squealed as he tore into the driveway. In moments he was in the house, nostrils flared and eyes dark, with Jake and Sigmund right behind him.

"Willow?"

"She's gone," Sarafina answered. "But we will find her, and we will tear out the Hunter's spine!"

Frankie's world began to spin. Her mother was her touchstone, at once so fuzzy and yet so strong. She couldn't truly be in danger. She could never *really* be taken away. Frankie closed her eyes. "You guys, I can't lose my mom."

She felt someone's hands on her—Jake's—and sensed Hailey come closer. She felt the charming, soothing essence of Sigmund as he slipped past to inspect the scene in the kitchen.

"How long do you think he's been under Aspen's control?" Jake asked.

"I don't know," Frankie said. "Maybe since the night she stole the spell."

"That's a long time," Hailey murmured. "At least his breaking up with you makes more sense?" But Frankie couldn't think about that. Knowing that Grimloch hadn't been himself, that Aspen had been bending his will—the idea of it made her skin crawl. He'd tried to tell her. So many times. He'd tried, and she hadn't seen how he was suffering.

"Oh god," Hailey moaned. "This is my fault."

"This is not your fault," Frankie said, and squeezed her hand. "But even if it was—"

"Which is wasn't," Jake emphasized.

"We don't have time for you to feel bad about it. What do you know about Aspen? Do you have any idea where she might have taken my mom?"

251

Hailey's eyes lost focus as she thought. She shook her head. "No. I don't know. I'm sorry."

"Don't be sorry," Frankie said, still holding her hand. "We just need to focus."

"I don't understand," said Sarafina. "Why would they take her? Do they intend to hold her for ransom?"

Vi's eyes snapped to Frankie's. "Aspen's going to use her the way she wanted to use the Scythe."

Frankie nodded.

"Wait," said Oz. "What?"

"Aspen wanted the Scythe to act as a conduit for the slayer power," Frankie explained. "The same way my mom used it when she activated all the Potentials. Aspen just wanted to reverse the flow."

"But we destroyed the Scythe," said Jake. "So no flow."

"No flow through the Scythe," said Frankie. "But my mom was a conduit that day, too. The oracle with the extendable eyes gave us the clue: The power flows through my mom and back again. That's what she said. When we made the decision to destroy the Scythe, we knew that a spell using my mom might still be possible. We just hoped that the Darkness would never figure that out."

"But they did," Spike said angrily. "Who told?"

"That's not important. The only important thing is finding my mom."

"Locator spell," Oz suggested.

Frankie shook her head. "The locator spell takes too long, and with how upset I am I'd probably mess it up anyway. So what else do we have?" She looked around at her Scoobies. "Come on, guys—we're the most powerful club in Sunnydale, we're witches and demons and slayers oh my, so what do we have?"

"We have trackers," said Sigmund, picking up a piece of Willow's shattered teacup. "And we have a trail to follow." He looked at the werewolves and Spike.

"Sigmund, brilliant." Frankie turned to them. "Spike, Oz ,and Jake, we need your creepy noses. Can you pick up my mom's scent?"

"Sure," said Spike. Oz sniffed the air once and said, "I've got it now."

"Then we go. Vi and Sarafina, you're with us. Hailey and Sigmund," Frankie looked at them. "Arm yourselves and get in a car. We'll text you when we find them."

CHAPTER TWENTY-EIGHT

OPENING THE GATE

Willow's head hurt. A lot. And when she tried to reach back and press her hand against it, she couldn't. It felt like she was in handcuffs.

"Hey. She's up."

Willow blinked. Her eyes were swimmy in their sockets, and the light wasn't great. It was orange and flickering, like the light from a campfire.

"Who cares. She's not going anywhere."

That was Aspen's voice. Willow squinted, fighting against dark blotches at the edges of her vision. The leader of the Darkness didn't look innocent and friendly anymore, like she had when Willow had confronted her in the kitchen. Now she just looked . . . wicked.

"Frankie!" Willow gasped. She looked around wildly. There were so many people scattered throughout the room who radiated a slayer's energy. She recognized many from the fight at the empty warehouse. Some carried weapons, mean-looking knives or crossbows. All regarded her with a wary hatred. The Darkness had returned to Sunnydale.

"Frankie," Aspen sneered, and mimed wiping tears. "Frankie, Frankie, Frankie. Is that the only word anybody can say anymore? Your little Frankie isn't here. She can't help you."

But Willow didn't need help. She just needed another moment to gather her wits, and she would blast her way out.

She tried to gather her magic and winced when she felt the sharp cut of the cuffs on her wrists. She was manacled to a rack, set upright against a brick wall. The manacles were thick and bright gold. They glittered in the firelight.

"Yeah, I wouldn't do that," Aspen cautioned. "The rack doesn't like magic."

Willow tried again. The skin inside the manacle ached and stung, like she'd touched it to the burner of a stove. When she looked at the manacles more closely, she saw that the cuffs were edged in silver, a silver liquid that had dried on. She leaned slightly to sniff. Blood. The cuffs were stained with silver blood.

"Magical dampening cuffs," Willow murmured. "What else have you used them for?"

"Torture, mostly," Aspen replied. "But don't worry. I'm not going to do that to you. You"—she came closer and gently grasped Willow by the chin—"are much too valuable."

They were in a brick building with high, industrial ceilings. A black metal catwalk branched overhead, and on one side was a structure that looked like a kiln, or some kind of industrial oven. It was too dark to see out the windows, but the interior was lit by three gold braziers, two small, and one enormous and right in the center, that Willow couldn't help noticing seemed like the perfect size to suspend a rack over and barbecue a witch.

Frankie, she called, trying to reach out with her mind, and felt an even sharper pain reverberate through her arms and up from her bound feet. Fresh red blood appeared at the edges of her restraints to mingle with the dried-on silver.

"Whatever you're doing," Aspen said, "knock it off."

Other members of the Darkness gathered near the main brazier, holding trays of herbs. They tossed them into the flames, sending up plumes of smoke. Willow couldn't feel the magic in the air—the rack had her sealed up tight—but she knew it was there.

"Grimloch," she called. The demon stood a small distance away. "How could you do this? Frankie trusted you. We all trusted you—well, except for Spike." She bared her teeth angrily as he continued to stand there like a lump.

"Don't bother." Aspen removed her long crocheted cardigan to show toned arms adorned in silver armbands. "I told him not to speak."

"And you just do everything your girlfriend tells you to do?"

Aspen looked around at the Darkness. A few of them snorted. Others seemed uncomfortable.

"Grim," Aspen said. "Hop three times and spin around." Willow watched. To her horror, he started to do it, until Aspen raised her hand. "No, don't. I was only kidding."

Willow looked closer. Behind the passive expression and the deadened eyes, she saw the real Grimloch, fighting to get out. She saw it in the way he shivered, and the unearned sheen of sweat sparkling on his brow. His jaw clenched so hard it was a wonder his fangs didn't shatter.

"Wow," Willow said. "I had to go full dark to do magic that evil."

"Keep your judgments to yourself. You don't know anything

about us." Aspen took up a pair of knives and handed them to the slayers beside her. "Kate, Sonia. Make the cuts."

Willow jerked against the rack.

"She's lying to you," she said as Kate and Sonia forced her fingers open and brought the blades to her palms. "She's not going to give your powers back; she's going to take them and use them herself!"

"As long as they're gone," whispered Kate, and she slashed deep. When her blood hit the floor, Willow felt something inside herself snap, so loud and hard that she thought her back might be broken.

She screamed.

Aspen smiled.

"And the gate swings open."

☽ ☽ ○ ☾ ☾

Oz's nose led them to the south side of town and a building in the art district. One of the largest on the block, and Frankie's favorite, constructed out of redbrick so it looked old, like it had stood for a century, unlike everything else in New Sunnydale.

"So what's the plan?" Spike asked beside Frankie. "Is there a plan? Or do we run in guns blazing?"

"Running in guns blazing *is* a plan," Frankie replied, quickening her pace.

"Yeah, but . . . I feel like other Watchers would have a real plan!"

"Then it's a good thing you're not other Watchers."

Frankie didn't want to fan out and surveil the building. She didn't want to map entrances and exits or set up an ambush with silent eye contact and hand signals. Her mom was in there. And since the building wasn't filled with the screams of the Darkness being flayed alive, she was obviously in trouble. Besides, judging by the fury in Oz and Sarafina's snarls, she wouldn't have been able to stop them if she'd tried.

"Jake!" Frankie called. "Text Hailey and Sigmund the location!"

She glanced to her left as Vi caught up.

"You know we're going in outnumbered," Vi said. "You can bet that every member of the Darkness is in there, helping Aspen do whatever it is she's trying to do."

"Every member of the Darkness, and a mind-controlled Hunter of Thrace," said Frankie. "I know."

"Hey," said Spike, "does that mean I finally get to punch him in the face unencumbered?"

Frankie didn't answer. She just took off, racing with Sarafina to see who would have the honor of kicking down the door. As it turned out, they kicked it in together.

"Mom!"

"Willow!"

Frankie collided with the first member of the Darkness she could reach and knocked her back with a hard right cross. "Don't give them time to breathe!" she shouted to the Scoobies.

Her mom was on the wall, shackled to some kind of golden circular torture device. Willow's head lolled, and blood ran in dark rivulets from her hands, wrists, and ankles.

Frankie dodged a punch from another slayer and felt the air move against her cheek. The moment brought her back to earth: These were slayers they were fighting. There was no room for mistakes. Any member of the Darkness could take out any member of the Scoobies. Even her and Vi.

"Don't let them get to her!" Aspen screamed. "I need two minutes! Two minutes more!"

Three slayers charged for Frankie, and she crouched just in time for Jake and Oz to sail over her head, roaring, Oz as a full wolf and Jake with claws out. Their weight knocked down the rogue slayers and then the werewolves leapt away, too smart to engage them hand to hand.

"Aspen!" Hailey shouted as she and Sigmund came through the door.

The leader of the Darkness turned. For just an instant, the expression on her face changed.

"Please don't do this," Hailey said.

Aspen stood before a great burning brazier of gold, light emanating from it brighter than the flames. She looked at Hailey with regret. But then she turned away.

As Aspen started to speak the incantation, Frankie hefted her sharpened sparring stick.

"Frankie, don't!" Hailey cried, but Frankie didn't listen. The Amulet of Junjari had begun to glow against Aspen's chest.

"Fly true, Mr. Stabby," she whispered, and threw it, hard. The flames in the brazier flared as Aspen arched backward with a cry. The weapon barely missed her, but that wasn't why she'd moved. The gem on her chest was burning, and Frankie smelled scorched flesh as Aspen grasped it and her hand began to smoke.

"Stop this," Frankie begged. "You can still stop this, it doesn't have to be this way!"

"It doesn't?" Aspen asked, breathing hard. "You would forgive me? I could be a slayer again? Even after I turned Grim into a mindless drone? Even after I bled the magic out of your mother?"

"Well, when you put it like that," Jake shouted as he grappled with the slayer Frankie had fought in the warehouse that spring. Neha, the lethal spin kicker with the short black bob.

"If you stop, we can talk," Frankie replied. "We can figure it out."

"Stop being such a Girl Scout!" Aspen pointed to Frankie. "Get her!" she shouted to Grimloch. "Kill her!"

One moment he was standing to the side, motionless as a statue, and the next Frankie wheeled backward as Aspen's words compelled him to advance. "Grim, stop!" She ducked as he made to grab her. He was sluggish under the weight of the spell, his remaining will fighting against Aspen's orders. But if Grimloch got ahold of her, he would do what Aspen told him to do. He would kill her.

"Hey!"

Grimloch turned, and Spike, ever true to his word, punched him in the face. But Frankie was the target. There was no deterring or distracting him.

"Hey!" Spike shoved him. "I said 'hey'!"

"He can't disobey, remember?!" Frankie cried, ducking a punch that might have broken her neck.

"Right." Spike took a deep breath and leapt onto Grimloch's back. "Go get your mum," he said as Grimloch swung him from side to side, fighting his way to Frankie despite the extra weight. "I'll take care of this!"

"And I'll take care of Aspen." Vi appeared on Frankie's other side. "She and I have some things to work out."

Frankie wanted a piece of Aspen herself, but she wanted her mom safe more. She ran toward the golden rack, pausing only to roundhouse kick another slayer onto her back and slide through another's legs to pop up behind her. "Eyes!" she declared when the slayer spun around, and Frankie made a *V* with her fingers. The slayer quickly covered her eyes with her hands, and Frankie shoved her aside.

"I hope Spike saw that," she said as she reached Willow. But she doubted it, as he was currently riding Grim like a mechanical bull. "Mom!"

Her mom's eyes fluttered open.

"Frankie."

"I'm here, Mom. I'm going to get you free."

"I tried to call you," Willow mumbled. "I shouldn't have. I shouldn't have lured you here."

"You didn't lure me; I was already on my way." She looked up, fist raised as someone approached, but it was only Hailey and Sigmund.

"Sit tight, Willow," Hailey said. "We'll have you out of those in a flash."

"These chains," Willow said. "I can't cast anything."

Frankie gripped on to the manacles and yanked. They weren't coming loose, not even with slayer strength.

"We need the key," Sigmund said, and looked at Hailey. "Could that be the key you saw?"

"Give me one minute," Hailey said, dashing away.

"Sarafina!" Frankie shouted, and the Sage demon ended her fight with a rogue slayer with a brutal backhand strike. She made it to Willow in a few leaping strides. "Can you lever your knife in here without cutting her? We have to break these locks!"

Frankie looked around the building. Oz was hurt, but he and Jake still had a member of the Darkness on the ropes, thrown against the brick side of one of the dormant kilns. Spike had finally gotten Grimloch's full attention and the two traded blows, their cheekbones already bruised and bloody. As for Vi, she was surrounded, but none of the Darkness seemed to want to attack her. It would have been a hard thing, Frankie supposed, to attack the friend they thought had just returned from the dead.

Sarafina touched Willow's cheek tenderly before shoving the tip of her knife through the manacle's opening and wrenching it to the side. Willow moaned. Sarafina's knife broke. But the cuff broke, too, and Willow's arm fell free.

"We need more knives," Frankie said, looking at the broken blade.

"I have more knives." Sarafina pulled another from somewhere— Frankie didn't know where; the stylish slacks and blouse she wore were quite formfitting, and this knife was even larger than the first.

"Hurry, Sarafina," Frankie whispered, watching the scene unfold between Vi and the rest of the Darkness. "Vi can't hold their attention forever."

)) ○ ((

Vi strode toward Aspen. The Darkness fell back. They asked where she'd been. And how she was alive.

"I'm alive because of them," Vi said. "Because of the Scoobies, and Frankie, the new slayer."

Aspen's eyes burned as she spoke, and that was gratifying.

"Traitor," Aspen said quietly.

"She's leading you into a dead end," Vi said to the Darkness. "She's feeding into your fears so you'll do what she wants. But what she's saying isn't true. Being a slayer is hard. And we've all lost things, and people we love. But it never gave us the right to turn on one another. The blame we put on Buffy Summers, and on the Watchers Council . . . right or wrong, it doesn't justify what we did to them."

"They made us fight," said Kate. "They didn't give us a choice."

In the corner of her eye, Vi saw movement and clocked Hailey moving in the shadows. She was sneaking up on Aspen. Was she crazy?

Vi twitched. Protecting Hailey was half the reason Vi fought. Hailey was the reason Vi's world was worth saving.

And she's a Potential, Vi thought. *And she's grown up strong.*

Vi tore her eyes away from her sister and strode forward.

"Slayers have never had a choice," she said. "But Buffy tried to give me one." She looked around at the other young women, who had all been found after the battle of the First. "Before the spell to activate us, Buffy asked us if we were ready. If we were ready to be strong, to take the power that should have been ours to begin with. And I said yes. Every Potential who was there said yes that day, so if you blame her, then you should blame me, too."

"That wasn't a choice," Sonia objected. "When your back was against the wall, when it was either that or be murdered by the First—"

"That's when hard choices get made!" Vi shouted. "No one just decides, apropos of nothing, to change their lives. To save the world. We make those decisions when we're forced to make them, but we still make them. And we have to own them. What you're doing now to these innocent people, what she's doing to Grimloch who she says she loves . . . that's a decision you're making. That it's an acceptable trade, to get what you want."

Sonia swallowed. Every one of the Darkness stopped to take a breath. Even Kate.

"Oh my god," Spike mused as he held Grimloch's head in a lock with his elbow. "She's going to turn them."

"Is this what you want?" Aspen demanded, arms out to her followers. "To fight and die? To have no lives? To be sent out on missions over and over until you don't come back? When we die, it doesn't change anything—it's expected. There was only ever supposed to be one slayer! The rest of us are extras! Bonus lives to use up until the line resets with her." She turned to point to Frankie and saw Hailey, just as Hailey dipped forward to pick her pocket.

"No!" Vi cried as Aspen grabbed Hailey and lifted her up by the neck.

"Why do they always go for the throat," Hailey gasped.

"Put her down!" Frankie stood. But there were a dozen slayers standing between her and Hailey. There were a dozen slayers standing between Hailey and Vi.

"She wants you to think you've done something there's no coming back from. But it's not true," Vi shouted to the Darkness. "I turned back. They let me turn back."

"You shouldn't have done this," Vi heard Aspen say to Hailey. "I never wanted to hurt you, kid. I thought you understood."

"I do understand," Hailey said through her teeth as she dangled. "And I know that you have a reason to be angry. But I was never going to be okay with this." She looked down into Aspen's eyes. "It doesn't matter how right you are if you do it *wrong*." And then she kicked the leader of the Darkness square in the face.

☽ ☽ ○ ☾ ☾

In the wake of Hailey's kick, the fighting started fresh. Spike and Grimloch resumed their grappling. The werewolves circled the

Darkness. Vi wasted no time going for Aspen, screaming, "You choked my baby sister!"

"Hailey!" Frankie cried. The Potential pushed up from the floor and jogged over, coughing.

"I didn't get the key," she said. "I'm sorry."

"It's all right, child," said Sarafina. "I have knives." She carefully inserted a blade into the last cuff at Willow's wrists and twisted hard. The manacles opened, and Willow fell limp into Frankie and Sarafina's waiting arms.

"Are you okay, sweetie?" Willow looked at Frankie.

"Don't worry about me now," Frankie exclaimed, blinking back tears. "We're getting you out of here."

"Frankie."

The look on Hailey's face made Frankie turn. The Darkness had stopped fighting. Aspen realized it and kicked Vi hard, sending her rolling across the floor.

"What are you doing?" Aspen shouted. "Fight them!"

"Aspen, stop," said Kate. "Maybe this has gone too far." Aspen had gotten around Vi. She was walking toward the largest burning brazier.

"Too far? What would any of you know about too far? I'm the one who made the hard choices. I'm the one who led! I was doing this for us!" Aspen shouted as the Darkness stood, grouped together like stray dogs gathered in an alley. Aspen shook her head and stalked to the brazier. "But I guess there is no us," she said, and grabbed the Amulet of Junjari from around her neck.

"No," Frankie said weakly as Aspen thrust her hand and the amulet into the flames. Willow was wrenched out of Frankie's grasp.

"No, Mom!" Willow was pulled up to float suspended in midair, and the blood that still dripped from her wrists and feet flowed mystically into the flames to join with Aspen's.

The gate that the oracle had warned them about, already cracked open when Aspen's spell began, now swung wide, and Aspen threw her arms and head back as the slayer line coursed through Willow like a thunderbolt.

Vi screamed. The Darkness screamed. Frankie cried out for her mother.

And then it was over. Willow dropped to the ground and Frankie dove to catch her. Vi and the Darkness lay on the ground. The air in the building smelled like the ozone that sometimes followed one of Sunnydale's rare storms.

The Amulet of Junjari glowed against Aspen's palm like a thousand-watt bulb. She placed it back around her neck.

Vi got to her feet. "What did you do?" She walked up to their former leader and gave her a shove. It looked like she'd shoved a wall. Aspen smiled.

"Vi!" Frankie shouted, just before Aspen drew back and struck Vi across the face. Vi flew. She landed hard on the cement and slid to a stop, unconscious.

"My god, she's done it," Spike breathed. He looked at the Darkness. "Stand down!" he ordered as they moved to fight or run. "You don't have any powers anymore! Frankie!"

Frankie looked at her Watcher. At her uncle Spike.

"Get out of here, girl," he said though his fear and disbelief. "Run!"

But Frankie couldn't run. She transferred her mother gently to Sarafina and Sigmund and stood up.

Aspen walked smoothly toward the Darkness, clenching and unclenching her fists.

"You took it all," Kate said breathlessly. "They were right all along. You never wanted to give it back."

"All you wanted was to have yours gone," Aspen replied. "What do you care where it went?"

Sonia and Neha backed away on wobbly legs. So wobbly that they stumbled, like babies just learning to walk.

"Aspen," said Neha. "This isn't right. It's not what you promised. It's not what Geraldine would want."

Aspen hit Neha across the face, and the young woman's jaw dislocated.

"Aspen! Leave them alone!" Frankie cried. But the leader of the Darkness stared at her own fist in wonder before backhanding Sonia so hard that she spun around twice. Every movement carried the weight of a marble statue. Her blows were fast as a striking viper, and seemingly effortless.

Frankie ran straight for her target. *Be smart,* whispered the voices in her head. The voices of her Scoobies. *Use your magic. Don't get hit.*

She ducked the first punch.

"You're still fast," Aspen said, and Frankie swung her fist.

Aspen caught it.

Caught it but didn't break it.

"You're still a slayer." Aspen's eyes narrowed. "How?"

"I don't know," said Frankie, and she used her magic to blast out of Aspen's grasp. "I guess we'll figure it out after I finish kicking your ass."

She ducked and dodged and landed a reverse kick to Aspen's head. The other slayer had forgotten about technique and was fixated on using her new brute strength. Frankie pushed her magic hard, creating distance, using her magic like another pair of fists. But there was no evening the odds. The Amulet of Junjari made her too strong.

267

When Frankie's magic slipped, the hit she took made her see stars. She flew, weightless, all the way across the room to collide with the bricks of the kiln, breaking the mortar. She slammed against the cement floor, and the bricks of the oven collapsed on top of her.

Frankie lay dazed under the pile. Sharp edges dug into her back and shoulders. Her vision swam. Her ears rang. Her skull felt like it had been cracked like an eggshell. She heard Spike scream, and tried to say *No, Uncle Spike, run*, but didn't know if she actually spoke. Through the small cracks of her eyelids she saw Spike, Oz, and Jake attacking Aspen with fists and claws and fangs. Spike's eyes were yellow and full of hate.

Stop, Frankie tried to say. *Stop, she's going to hurt you.*

She had to get up. She had to help them. But the bricks felt so heavy, and her eyes wanted to close. She heard Oz yelp and Jake cry out. She saw Spike land hard on his back, his vulnerable heart bared beneath Aspen's stone fist.

"Aspen!"

Hailey ran past the bodies of fallen slayers to plant herself between Aspen and their friends.

"If you kill them, you'll have to kill me first."

Aspen jerked backward as an arrow shot through the scant air between her and Hailey's heads. Sigmund had his bow in hand, already aiming another arrow. "And if you kill her, you won't get far."

Sarafina slipped out from beneath Willow and drew a large knife. Oz and Jake pushed themselves up from the floor and helped Spike to his feet. Aspen watched their advance with a mix of amusement and wariness.

"You can't kill me," Aspen said.

"Maybe not, but we'll do our best," said Spike.

"Perhaps we will take one of your arms," said Sarafina. "Or scar that pretty face."

Aspen scowled. "Grimloch," she shouted. "Let's go!"

The last thing Frankie heard was their footsteps fading before unconsciousness finally swallowed her up.

PART FOUR

SUPER SLAYER

CHAPTER TWENTY-NINE

CONVALESCENCE

Spike waited in the hall while Oz and Sarafina looked in on Willow. The werewolf and the Sage demon had scarcely left Willow's side since they'd gotten her back to the house, and while that was touching, Spike could have used their help. He'd been the one to carry Frankie up to her bedroom. He'd been the one to steady Jake when he looked like he was about to crumble, and the one to absorb Hailey's tears into one of his few good shirts. He'd tried to pass her off to Sigmund and instead found himself absorbing Sigmund's tears into his other shoulder.

Willow, Frankie, and Vi. They were supposed to be the invincible ones. The world-ending witch and his two slayers. And he hadn't done a thing to stop it. They'd been bloodied, and he'd walked away with nothing more than a bad bruise on one of his enviable cheekbones. Some Watcher he was. Once, Buffy had called him a champion. She'd trusted him to save the world. She would be ashamed of him now.

Oz came out of the bedroom and closed the door.

"How is she?" Spike asked.

"There's no change." The werewolf looked anguished, and Spike frowned. Should he crack a hopeful joke? Give him a bracing clap on the back? What the hell was he good for?

"Red is one of the strongest beings on the planet," he said, "so that's a mark in her favor."

"How's Frankie?" Oz asked.

"Also one of the strongest beings on the planet," said Spike. But there'd been no movement from her room. Nor had there been a change in Vi at the hospital, and that was much more worrisome. With her slayer power gone, who knew if she had any remaining boosts to her healing. She could be just another human, hit by Aspen like she'd been hit by a bus. The doctors had said "intracranial hematoma," and Spike had wanted to punch a wall.

"They'll be all right," he said, to himself as much as Oz.

"But in the meantime, we have an evil super slayer on the loose with a hunter god as her henchman. Should we be running?"

Spike leaned against the wall and crossed his arms. "I don't have the energy to run. Besides, knowing Aspen, she's probably out there playing with her shiny new superpowers, kicking cars to the moon."

"What about the Spell of Many Interdimensional Returns?" Oz asked.

"What about it?" Spike asked. "That spell is currently locked up inside our unconscious slayer-witch, and the only witch with the mojo to cast it is lying in there."

"Isn't there anyone else?" Oz pressed. "You and I are Big and medium-sized Bads, but we could really use some help."

"We can't call Xander and Dawn out of hiding." With how much Aspen hated Dawn, that had been their first phone call, to warn them to run and head for deep cover.

"Don't you have any demon contacts? That one we just gave *The Black Grimoire* away to. Maybe we can get it back."

"We wouldn't want it," said Spike. "That book was nothing but trouble."

"There has to be someone."

Spike looked at Willow's closed door. He looked at Frankie's down the hall.

"There is," he said, and straightened. "I don't know exactly how to reach him. But you're right. It's time we called in the big guns."

$$\text{☽ ☽ ○ ☾ ☾}$$

Frankie awoke to a cool compress against her forehead.

"That feels nice," she murmured. She shifted her feet and felt the familiar sensation of her sheets moving against her legs. The soft cradle of her pillow supported her neck as the cooling compress moved from her forehead to her cheeks.

"Thanks, Mom."

"Uh, no problem, sweetheart."

Frankie opened her eyes.

"Sam?"

Sam gave a little wave and a slightly bashful smile. "Sam," he affirmed. "But I was perfectly happy to be Mom, for as long as you wanted.

"Sorry," he went on as Frankie pushed up onto her elbows. "I'm probably not the one you expected to see. It's just bad timing—Jake, Hailey, Sigmund, and Oz have been taking turns sitting with you. And Spike when the sun's not beaming in." He glanced at the drawn curtains, where afternoon sunlight was spilling through the gaps in the blinds.

"I'm glad to see you, Sam." Frankie ran a hand roughly across her face. "Though honestly I'm glad to see anyone. How's my mom?"

Sam frowned. "She's stable, everyone says. But she's not waking up."

"How long has it been?" Frankie asked.

"Only a night and part of a day." Sam looked at his smartwatch. "A very long night and part of a day. Do you feel okay? Should I call someone?"

"Can you go downstairs and tell them I'm awake? And that I'll be down in a minute?"

"Sure," said Sam. Frankie smiled gamely until he left, and then buried her head in her hands. She remembered everything. Aspen. Her mom, held in midair while the power of the slayers coursed through her. Grimloch, leaving with the woman who held him captive. And her friends. They'd saved her life. They'd intervened, and together they'd been more trouble than Aspen had cared to take on.

Gingerly, Frankie swung her legs out of bed. Someone had wrapped her in her yummy sushi blanket, and she pulled it free of the covers and threw it over her shoulders. Every inch of her body ached. And her head felt big. Larger than normal head size. But when she looked in the mirror, it wasn't any bigger than usual. Her cheek was blackened, though. The bruise ran from her ear to the corner of her mouth.

Maybe Jake would get her a nice frozen bag of peas to press on it.

Taking small steps, she made her way into the hall and across into her mom's room.

"Frankie!" Sarafina stood, and quickly folded her into a hug. "Come. Your mother will want to know you are well."

Frankie wouldn't exactly say she was well. She felt like a walking bag of broken sticks. But she sat on the edge of Willow's bed and took her hand.

Her mom's fingers didn't curl around hers. Her eyelids didn't flutter. Willow lay, motionless and pale, and somehow smaller than Frankie could ever remember seeing her, as if the toll of the magic had shrunk her to the bone.

"Mom?" she whispered. She shook her hand gently. "Mom?"

Frankie glanced at Sarafina and saw her face fall. She'd believed that the sound of Frankie's voice would somehow pull Willow back from the brink.

"She will wake," Sarafina said. "Our red witch will wake."

"How is Vi?" Frankie asked, and Sarafina's eyes clouded.

"She will wake, too."

"The two of you got pretty close, out there on the road."

"There is much about Vi to admire. She is fierce."

Frankie reached out and grasped the Sage demon by the wrist.

"I have to see the others. Will you stay with my mom? Make sure she's not alone?"

Sarafina nodded, and Frankie got up and made her way to the door.

"Did you see my son?" Sarafina asked before she left. "Did you see the way his arrows flew?"

"Sigmund's always been a hell of a warrior," said Frankie. "With or without a weapon in his hand."

"Yes." Sarafina smiled gently. "I am starting to see that."

Frankie took the stairs slowly. It felt like her lungs were on fire when she inhaled, and she thought a few of her joints might have come clean out of their sockets. She was in so much pain that she didn't pay any attention to the squeaky floorboards near the sides, and before she reached the bottom, Hailey, Jake, Sigmund, and Sam swung their heads around the archway and screeched her name.

"Frankie!"

"Ow!" she said preemptively when she saw them coming. "Don't touch me, I've almost been killed!"

They skidded to a halt, faces stricken, and her mouth curled into a smile.

"Well. Don't touch me too much."

They wrapped their arms around her. Jake kissed the top of her head and said, "It's nice to see you're still annoying."

Frankie grinned as Spike and Oz came around the corner, and the new Scoobies disengaged to give the originals a turn.

"Hey, Mini Red," Spike said. "You gave us a scare."

"*You* gave *me* a scare," she retorted. "Throwing yourself at Aspen like that—what were you thinking?"

"The same thing I always think."

"Which is not a lot," said Oz as he came to give Frankie a hug. He drew back to look into her eyes. "Are you okay?"

"If by okay you mean beaten like a dusty rug, then I'm aces. Is there any food?"

"Is there any food," Jake repeated and scoffed. "There's all the food! Sig, Hailey, Sam, and I have been prepping all morning. I have fixings chopped for omelets or frittatas, or I can stuff them into a few cheesy quesadillas if it's too late for breakfast . . ." He hurried into the kitchen and went on, talking mostly to himself. "I'll just make both. If we combine the meals, then you'll be all caught up."

"Gotta love Jake," Hailey said, and Frankie touched her arm.

"How are you? How's Vi?" Frankie almost wished she hadn't asked. Hailey's face was trying to do that closed-book thing, and she was fighting tears so angrily that her eyeballs might have sprouted tiny arms and started punching themselves. Sigmund slipped an arm around her shoulders. He softly kissed her temple, and Hailey blinked in surprise.

"The swelling's going down in her brain," Hailey said. "They thought they might have to release the pressure, but it's going down on its own."

"That's good," Frankie said as she sat down at the table, and Jake slid her a glass of fresh-squeezed orange juice. "That's very good. Where are the other members of the Darkness?"

"Some had to go to the hospital, but none are in the ICU," Oz answered. "They're a little shell-shocked. And scared."

"As they bloody should be," said Spike. He leaned against the kitchen counter. "This is what they wanted. And now they've got it."

Frankie frowned. It was easy now to say be careful what you wish for. But they didn't need ill wishes or *I told you so*s. In the harsh light of day, they would be looking at themselves hard enough.

"They're not the danger anymore," Frankie said. "So they're not our problem."

"Yeah," said Jake. "Now our problem is all of their powers, wrapped up in a very unpleasant Aspen tortilla."

"You probably shouldn't do metaphors when you're cooking," noted Hailey.

"But what do we do, about that tortilla?" asked Sigmund. His brow scrunched thoughtfully as he stood beside Jake, handing off ingredients while Sam stood on his other side prepping plates and forks. "And how is it that Frankie seems to have retained her slayer powers, when the rest of the Darkness did not?"

"All good questions," said Frankie. "But let's handle one thing at a time." She shrugged out of her yummy sushi blanket and dug into the pile of eggs Sam set in front of her while simultaneously grabbing a triangle of quesadilla and dunking it in sour cream. "We have to get Buffy and the others out of that prison dimension. They might still have their powers. The Amulet of Junjari is strong, but I doubt that it has that long a reach."

"We still have the Spell of Many Interdimensional Returns," said Spike. He nodded to Frankie's arms, where the spell remained inked in pretty, looping script.

"You mean the spell that rips open doors and lets all the hell-beasts roam free?" Hailey asked. "That was a dicey idea even before we were down a slayer."

Frankie took another big bite of eggs and a big bite of quesadilla, chewing fast. "We don't have a choice. Aspen just became an evil supervillain, and she only has two objectives. One: destroy us, and two: destroy Buffy and the others." She sighed and turned her eyes up to the ceiling, toward her mom's bedroom. "We have to do that spell. But without my mom, I'm not strong enough to cast it."

They heard the sound of the front door open and close. Frankie and the new Scoobies turned in their chairs as Mr. Giles appeared in the archway to the kitchen and slipped his travel bag down from his shoulder.

"Oh, excellent. I haven't missed lunch."

CHAPTER THIRTY

RETURN OF THE MACK

"**M**r. Giles!"

Frankie bolted out of her chair to greet him. She crossed the distance hunched over and dragging one of her legs, but she still hugged him hard enough to make him say "Oof."

"Little Frankie," he said, and laughed. "You're quite . . . strong."

"Yeah, no more noogies or holding things up high out of her reach," said Jake, and he went to hug Giles, too. "Now that she's a slayer she's got no sense of humor."

"Jake," said Giles fondly. "I didn't expect an Osbourne to be so tall."

Frankie looked up at Mr. Giles. For the first time in a long time she felt curiously safe, and it didn't matter that the feeling was an illusion, that Mr. Giles couldn't instantly solve all of their problems or hold their boogeymen at bay. Her memories of him were intrinsically linked to her memories of Buffy. They were so strongly intertwined that having him there felt like Buffy was there, too.

"How did you know? Did you mystically sense something and know to come?" she asked.

"It was Spike, actually," Giles said, and looked at Spike to nod hello. "Spike . . . good god, you look terrible."

"It's nice to see you, too, Rupert."

"I'm sorry; it's just that you're so—" Giles chuckled. "Old. How delightful. This has already been worth the trip."

Oz came over. He shook Giles's hand and held it. "But that's not why you're here."

The smile slowly left Giles's face. "Take me to her."

$$) \;) \; \bigcirc \; (\; ($$

In her mom's bedroom, Frankie quietly introduced Mr. Giles to Sarafina as Giles lowered himself beside Willow's bed. His expression was soft as he leaned down and gently pressed a hand to her hair.

"Superdad to the rescue," Jake whispered to Frankie, and Frankie grabbed on to Jake's wrist. There was no way that her mom would miss a visit from Giles. She would fight her way back from wherever she was stranded, as soon as she heard his voice.

Except Giles didn't speak. Instead, he reached into his bag and took out three clear crystal orbs and, impressively, spun them around in his palm like David Bowie in that old movie *Labyrinth*. He placed one on each side of Willow and held the last over her chest.

"Willow," he said. "Can you hear me? It's Giles."

Frankie froze. They all froze—Sarafina, Oz, Jake—and waited for Willow to open her eyes.

"Giles?" Willow mumbled, and the sound of their collective exhale made Frankie laugh.

"Mom," she said. "Mom, are you okay?"

"I'm afraid she can't hear you," Giles said when Willow lay motionless. "At least, not yet."

"What are those things?" Jake asked, gesturing to the crystal balls, which had begun to glow a faint silver.

"Think of them as beacons, or microphones. To a person as magical as Willow, they'll be bright as a lighthouse. We just have to guide her consciousness back to them." He leaned closer. "Willow, can you hear me?"

"Giles," she murmured again. "This is a nice dream." Her eyes remained closed, and Frankie's happiness began to fade.

"It's not a dream, Willow. I need you to move toward the sound of my voice."

"Do you have a puppy?" Willow asked.

"I don't have a puppy; this is not a dream. Willow, I need you to listen to my voice, and look for the lights. Do you see the lights?"

"I see ice cream. Are you the ice cream? Is the ice cream Giles?"

Giles sighed. He looked back at them. "This could take a while. It's not always easy, piercing the layers of the subconscious. Perhaps could you leave us alone? It's better if I have space to concentrate."

"Of course," said Frankie, even though she really didn't want to leave. "Can we . . . bring you anything? Do you need anything?" she asked as Sarafina and Oz dragged themselves to the bedroom door.

"A cup of tea would be much appreciated, Frankie." Giles turned that soft, loving-dad expression on her, and she felt as warm as she did in her yummy sushi blanket. "I'm very glad to see you all, you know. I'm sorry it's been so long."

"Hey," said Jake. "If you bring back Ms. R, you get a lifetime pass. I'll go make that tea."

Oz touched Sarafina's arm.

"She's in good hands," he said. "The best hands we know."

Sarafina nodded, and she and Frankie looked back at Willow while Giles whispered, and the crystals glowed. Willow was in the best hands. But what would they do if it didn't work?

☽ ☽ ○ ☾ ☾

"You'd think he was the bloody savior of the world, the way he comes marching in here," Spike muttered as he wiped up some blood he'd spilled on the stove. "Calling me old. I'm sorry I called him at all. Wait till he sees how much better I look in tweed. That'll burn his biscuits."

Frankie and Jake traded a look as they came into the kitchen.

"How long has he been grumbling?" Frankie asked.

"Pretty much nonstop since you went upstairs," said Hailey.

"Well, it's his bloody fault," said Spike. "Coming in here like some long lost . . ." He trailed off. "Probably thinks he's a better Watcher than me. Probably has a million suggestions about how I should read more books and stay home nights thinking about my next cuppa and drive a tiny car and never have any fun—but we have Sigmund for that!"

"Hey, don't drag me into this," said Sigmund.

"Spike, you know you love Giles." Jake clapped the vampire on the back as he put water into the kettle.

"And you're a very good Watcher," said Frankie. "You're just . . . a different kind of Watcher than he was."

Spike straightened, pleased. Then he raised his eyebrows. "Except his slayer was the most successful slayer of all time. And mine are either dead, or *you*—"

"Hey!" said Frankie.

"Or laid up in a hospital bed."

"No, no, no," said Sam. "Don't bring the room down. Vi is

284

going to be okay. Frankie's a great slayer, and you're not that big of a screwup."

"I just hope Mr. Giles can bring my mom back," Frankie said. "I need her." She looked around at her friends. "We all do."

$$\text{)) ○ ((}$$

She looked so small. Nothing like the world-ending force she'd been. Hardly like the woman he'd watched her grow into. This Willow, with her arms prone at her sides, her mouth relaxed and slightly upturned at the corner as if she were waiting, expecting him to say something kind, looked like the long-haired young girl who had wandered into the Sunnydale High School library over twenty-five years ago. She'd looked a little bit coltish, a little bit moony, and just a tad wistfully romantic, as if she was sure something grand would walk into her life at any moment. And something grand did. But nothing like she could have ever imagined.

Willow Rosenberg, who had hidden herself behind computer screens and only loved from afar. Giles hadn't looked twice at her that first day. Or the day after that. Or the day after that. He couldn't have guessed that she would become the best friend of the slayer. That she would become the witch of a generation. That her magic would change everything.

"Giles," she murmured. "Where are you?"

"I'm here, Willow." He squeezed her shoulder. "Do you see the lights?"

"Can you open the Magic Box? I need to buy a new piece of soapstone."

"The Magic Box doesn't exist anymore. Come toward my voice. We can't be lost in memories."

"Memories are like snack boxes," Willow said.

285

"How's that?" Giles asked fondly.

"People like them."

Not all of them, he almost said. Some memories no one wished to linger on. But Willow's memories could be particularly dark. If he lost her in those, he might never get her back again.

"Listen to my voice," he said.

"Will you sing? I like it when you sing."

Giles smiled. "I'm afraid I didn't bring my guitar."

"Well, go ask Oz—he has one."

"Willow." He took her hand. "You must come back now."

"I can't come back now. I'm stretched thin. And there isn't all of me."

"What do you mean?"

"I mean there are lots of mes. And some of the mes aren't here. And some of them are smaller than they should be."

Giles didn't know what that meant. He glanced at the Orbs of Sirus. They glowed steadily silver. No flickering. No flaring. He'd seen a ritual once where the orbs lit in succession, one after the next, chasing each other around the person's physical form as they tried to grab hold of their consciousness.

"You're only afraid. You're hurt. But you're safe now, Willow. You may return. There is no pain here. Only family and friends."

"And tea?"

"And tea." Giles smiled.

"Tea and Frankie," Willow said, and opened her eyes.

$$\mathcal{D} \; \mathcal{D} \; \bigcirc \; \mathcal{C} \; \mathcal{C}$$

Willow sat propped against her pillows as Giles sipped his tea.

"Do you think you're strong enough for visitors? Frankie and the others will want to know you're awake."

"I know," she said. "That's why I'm speaking quietly." She stared at her hands. "I'm not ready to face them. I'd prefer to not be facing you." She glanced at Giles. "Would you mind turning around?"

"What happened is not your fault. Aspen performed a ritual on you; in effect, she stole your magic to do her bidding."

"Not that. I know that." She could still feel that. She'd been the gate through which the slayer power flowed, and Aspen had blown her hinges off. Now she felt all cockeyed and corroded with rust. Open and swaying in the breeze. "I mean before. With *The Black Grimoire*."

"Ah, yes, the Book of Wants. Oz told me about that. I'm surprised you were able to locate it. Some believed it was a myth."

"No myth. It came through town with a black magic smuggler, and Spike and I went to the airfield and swiped it." She pursed her lips. "I blew up a plane. And that was before it had its hooks in me."

"And after?" Giles asked.

"I hurt Frankie." Her face crumpled.

"Frankie's all right." His voice was soft but he didn't try to comfort her. "She has some questionable black magic tattoos. But she seems to be all right. And *The Black Grimoire* is gone."

"Not because I wanted it gone." Willow frowned. "Giles, I was petting that thing like it was Miss Kitty Fantastico."

"That poor kitten," Giles mused. "I still can't believe Dawn almost shot her with a crossbow. You were right to rehome her; it just wasn't safe."

"The point is that I wanted to use it. I mean I *wanted* wanted to. Like I used to want to, before I stopped." Giles looked at her, and she looked down, ashamed.

"Do they know?" he asked, and nodded downstairs.

"Eventually it was pretty obvious. I did mention the petting? But now that the magic's been sucked out of me I feel like myself again.

287

And I don't know how to face them." She shrugged. "I thought after all this time I was cured."

"But there isn't really a cure, is there?" Giles held out his hand, and after a moment, Willow took it and let him help her out of bed. "And this part never gets any easier."

$$) \ ) \ \bigcirc \ (\ ($$

They had gathered around the kitchen table for a competitive game of spades (or at least, competitive on Sarafina's part; she slammed each new trump down so hard that Jake was too scared to lay any of his own) when Willow and Giles came into the kitchen.

"Mom!" Frankie shouted and vaulted up from her chair. She was already much more limber. Being a slayer definitely had its benefits. "You're awake! Are you okay?"

"I'm okay, sweetie. I'm a little disoriented." She pulled Frankie close but held her hand up before anyone could join the group hug. "Wait. I need to apologize to you." She squeezed Frankie's wrist. "For how I behaved with the grimoire. I thought I could handle it on my own. That after all this time I would be strong enough. But I'm not. So I'm sorry I let it go too far without asking for help. And I'm so sorry I hurt you, Frankie."

Frankie wrapped her in another hug. "It's okay, Mom."

"So many years without magic, I started to forget what it was like. I couldn't even remember how it was to have a problem. And then when I started doing magic again, and it went so well, and you all were there . . . I started to feel safe."

Sensing it was time, the others crept closer. Sarafina touched Willow's face, and Oz took her by the hand.

"You are safe," Oz said. "With us around, you'll always be safe."

"Just remember to ask for help next time," said Hailey. "That's the problem with superheroes. Always wanting to do things on their own."

"Superheroes." Willow snorted. "But speaking of superheroes, where's Vi?"

"In the hospital," Hailey said.

"In the hospital, *recovering*," said Sarafina.

"Wait," Willow said. "Aspen's spell—" She looked at Frankie. "Oh my god . . ."

"I'm fine, Mom. I'm still a slayer. One of only two left in this dimension, it seems."

"Just you and the evil Super Saiyan," said Hailey as she stepped away to answer her phone.

"The evil super what now?"

"Just me and Aspen," Frankie said. "Until we get Aunt Buffy and the others back. We have to do the spell, Mom. The Spell of Many Interdimensional Returns."

"The Spell of Many Interdimensional Returns?" asked Giles. He listened while Willow explained, and then shrugged. "I suppose the name was fairly self-explanatory. But your mother won't be able to perform that kind of magic."

"She won't?"

"I won't?" Willow asked.

"Having the slayer power pulled through her body, being used as a gateway for that much magic, will have frayed her mystical form. If not punched holes directly through it."

They looked at Willow, who as usual squirmed beneath the weight of their attention.

"I guess I do feel a little Swiss cheesy," she admitted.

"Well, give her a minute, Rupert," said Spike. "She just woke up."

"Yes, but I'm telling you, this kind of magic takes its toll. And if the Spell of Many Interdimensional Returns does what you say it does, then it will be far more than Willow can take. Performing it could be dangerous, or it could fail completely."

"Then what do we do?" Frankie asked. "I've got this spell just locked up under my skin and no one to cast it?"

"You have to cast it," said Sigmund. The Sage demon walked to them from around the table. "Or rather, Mr. Giles and I will have to cast it off of you."

"I don't have that kind of magic," said Giles.

"Neither do I," said Sigmund. "But we won't need to. With the spell embedded in Frankie, she's already—"

"She's already the source." Giles touched his chin and looked at Sigmund, impressed.

Spike and Jake squinted as Sigmund and Giles exchanged excited chatter. "It's like there's two of them," said Jake from the side of his mouth.

"But wait," Frankie objected. "If I'm casting the spell with the two of you, who's going to be fighting all the hellbeasts and monsters and vermicious knids that come through the dimensional doors?" They were already down one slayer. Having their slayer-witch tied up with magic seemed like an extremely bad idea.

"Hellbeasts and monsters and vermicious knids." Jake looked at Oz, Sarafina, and Spike. "That sounds like our kind of party."

"Guys!" Hailey hung up her phone. "We have to get to the hospital. Vi's awake!"

CHAPTER THIRTY-ONE

THE SLAYER LINE

rankie, Jake, Sigmund, Sarafina, and Willow hurried through the halls of New Sunnydale Memorial Hospital, trying to keep up with Hailey as she whizzed around corners and darted through elevator doors. She was going so fast Frankie thought she might parkour over the nurses' station. But when they reached the intensive care unit, Hailey stopped, like she was afraid to look.

"I know you're out there, twerp," Vi said. "I can see your boots."

Hailey looked back at Frankie and grinned before diving behind the curtain.

"I'm so glad she's awake," said Sigmund while they gave the sisters a moment alone. "Without her enhanced slayer healing, the odds were . . ." He frowned. "And I couldn't bear the thought of Hailey losing someone else."

"Her last someone," Frankie said. "Her last family. Vi is a precious commodity."

"But she's not, though, is she?" asked Jake, and they looked at him. "Not that she isn't precious. Just that she's not her only family."

As if he'd heard him, one of the ICU nurses came around the corner and held up his hands.

"I'm sorry, folks, but there are too many people here. We only allow one visitor per patient to the ICU, and family only."

"But I just said that's what we were," said Jake.

"Even if we are, we're too many, Jakey," said Willow, drawing him gently away. Frankie went, too, but her toes dragged. She knew there were rules, but she badly wanted to see Vi. And Hailey would have wanted them to be there.

"Wait." Sarafina stepped toward the nurse and flashed a beguiling smile. "Surely exceptions can be made. This woman, she is very dear to us."

"I understand that, ma'am, but we cannot have so many people in this area. When your friend is transferred to a standard room—"

"Sigmund," Sarafina said loudly, still smiling. "Perhaps you can better explain to this young man, why it is so important that we see her."

"Hmm?" Sigmund blinked. "Oh. Yes, of course." He joined his mother in smiling and Frankie felt herself go warm all over. Together, his and Sarafina's charm was so strong it was disconcerting. They steered the nurse back around the desk like a pair of smooth, beautiful sharks. By the time he sat back down in his swivel chair he was happily flushed and grinning.

"We can go in now," Sarafina said.

"You guys are this close to creepy, you know that?" said Jake.

"It worked, didn't it?"

"I'm just glad it doesn't work on me."

"It doesn't need to work on you, Thriller," Sigmund said, and clapped him on the back. "I charm you naturally."

They stepped into Vi's room, and Frankie immediately understood the visitor limit. She felt like if she moved an inch she would unhook something vital or damage an expensive piece of equipment.

Sarafina leaned over Vi and embraced her in a gentle hug.

"I suppose I don't need to ask how you got in here," said Vi. "Hey guys. Hey, Frankie."

"Hey," they collectively mumbled. Vi looked terrible. Her face was marked by black-and-yellow bruises. One eye was completely red with burst blood vessels. She didn't look like she had the strength to sit up or lift her head off the pillow. But Vi was a slayer. She should have been a slayer, and back on her feet already.

"So," Vi said, seeing their stricken faces. "I guess it wasn't a dream. And I guess I look as bad as I feel. Where's everybody else?"

"They're fine," said Hailey. "Willow was unconscious for a while. Spike had to call in the original Watcher to lure her consciousness back with these glowy orb things."

"The original Watcher," said Vi. "Giles? Giles is here?"

Willow nodded. "He helped me wake up about an hour ago."

"That's when they said I woke up. Do you think we woke up at the same time? Are you the reason I woke up at all?"

Willow's brow knit.

"I'm not sure. I was doing some very weird things psychically. But I'm happy to take the credit."

"Ow," Vi said as she lifted her arm. "I am absolutely not a slayer anymore. I forgot how much hurting hurts." She looked at Frankie. "What happened to the Darkness?"

"Neha and Sonia were admitted, but not to the ICU. Mostly for observation," Hailey said. "Well, except Neha needs surgery on her jaw. We don't know where the rest of them are. And Aspen disappeared, too. After sucking up all your powers."

"I should try to find them." Vi struggled to sit up. "If they're powerless they're going to need . . ." She fell back on the pillow and winced.

"Stop it," said Hailey. "Stop moving your head!"

But Vi didn't listen. She took a breath and pushed herself up again.

"Here!" Frankie didn't know where he'd gotten them, but Jake had found a few extra pillows and quickly placed them behind Vi's back. "At least lean on these."

"Thanks, werewolf junior." She relaxed and took a few breaths. "But Aspen isn't going to just slip away into the night and live her best super-slayer life in anonymity. She's going to Hulk Smash her way through everyone who's ever pissed her off. Did you warn Dawn?"

"She was our first call," said Frankie.

"Good. My god, she really hates Dawn." Vi lay back and breathed hard. She looked at Frankie, and her eyes moved over the already-fading bruises.

"It didn't get you," Vi said. "You still have your powers."

Frankie nodded. "I'm sorry."

"What are you apologizing for?" Vi asked. "This is what we wanted. I'm lying here mostly dead, but I'm also half the reason Aspen was able to almost kill me. Is this irony?"

You changed your mind, though, didn't you? Frankie wanted to say. *Out on the road with Sarafina, you changed your mind and became a slayer again.*

"But how is it possible?" Hailey asked. "You're not a slayer anymore, but Frankie is. Did Aspen do something to the Darkness so only their powers were taken?"

"Not that I'm aware of," Vi replied.

"Maybe it's because of the way Frankie was made," Willow said, and they all gave her a look. "I mean conceived. Or, I mean made. The line flowed to her differently than it did to other slayers."

"Or maybe," said Vi, "it's because she's where the line is supposed to go. The rest of us were cheaters. We took the power and put it where we wanted it. Not that I don't think we were justified. It was ours, like Buffy said. But maybe Frankie is the line's way of resetting itself."

"But what does that mean?" Hailey asked, shifting uncomfortably. "Is Frankie's power, like, *the* power now? Am I even a Potential anymore?"

"I don't see any reason you wouldn't be," said Vi. "But now that Giles is back, he can take you into the desert and do a few rounds of slayer hokey pokey to figure all that out."

"Some what?" Frankie turned to her mom.

"He shakes a gourd," said Vi.

"Oh." Frankie looked at Hailey. "Well, yes. After this is over, we will do slayer Fyre Fest with Mr. Giles in the desert. But right now, we have to cast the Spell of Many Interdimensional Returns. We have to get Buffy and the others so when I face Aspen the numbers even out."

Overhead, an alarm began to beep, and Frankie tucked in all of her limbs.

"Did I unhook something?"

"It's not me," Vi said.

They turned toward the entrance of the ICU as staff began to hurry in and out, and over the PA system came a calm voice announcing a code green.

"What's a code green?" Frankie asked. "Green's good, right?"

"I'm afraid not in this case," said Sigmund. "Code green means emergency activation. They're preparing to receive incoming trauma patients."

Incoming trauma patients. That could have meant anything. A car accident. A fire. But Frankie's slaydar said it was none of those things. She walked quietly out of Vi's room, passing through mobilizing hospital staff. She made it to the emergency department just as the first of the sirens drew near.

"What's happening?" she asked one of the nurses at the intake station.

The young woman glanced up at Frankie as she worked, half in and half out of her chair.

"Sweetheart, if you're not critical you're going to have to wait for a while," she said. "We have ten to twenty trauma patients headed our way."

"From what?"

"I don't know. They said an attack. Please have a seat now, okay? And we'll help you as soon as we can." She came out from behind the desk and touched Frankie's shoulder reassuringly as she jogged away, speaking into a walkie-talkie.

"Frankie!"

She looked back and saw Jake, wandering out after her.

"Frankie, what is it?"

Frankie turned toward the emergency room entrance as an ambulance pulled up, lights flashing. The driver killed the sirens and jumped out. Emergency personnel ran out to meet them. Another ambulance arrived, and then a third. Frankie stood still, trying to keep out of the way as people hurried all around her. She felt like she was in a dream. The sirens sounded far off, muffled like her ears were stuffed with cotton. She knew what she would see come through those doors, even before the stretchers appeared carrying members of the Darkness.

A doctor leaned over a stretcher and spoke to a patient whose face was mostly blood. Frankie wouldn't have recognized her at all were it not for her signature uneven haircut. It was the tall slayer called Kate. "Ma'am?" the doctor asked loudly. "Can you hear me? Can you tell me what happened?"

"Kate!"

Frankie rushed to her, and Kate peered up at her as through a red mask.

"You know her?" the doctor asked.

"I do." She looked at Kate and squeezed her hand. "I know her."

Kate blinked. She saw Frankie. Recognized her. But Frankie didn't know if she understood what was happening. "She said we couldn't take it back," Kate whispered. "She said we could never have it back."

CHAPTER THIRTY-TWO

THE DARKNESS FALLS

"Aspen goes down. She goes down now. Tonight."

Frankie paced angrily back and forth as the Scoobies old and new stood around her in the living room. They looked at her doubtfully, and she understood why. She didn't know how they would take down Aspen. She only knew that they had to. Seeing what she had done to the Darkness—Frankie couldn't let it stand.

"Frankie," Mr. Giles said gently as she held her arms tight to her sides to keep from punching a hole clean through one of their walls, "you mustn't let anger dictate your actions."

"Don't tell my slayer what to do," Spike said.

"Of course." Giles raised a skeptical eyebrow and put his hands into his pockets. "By all means."

"Mini Red." Spike grabbed Frankie by the shoulders. "Have you gone completely round the bend? Aspen has the powers of a baker's dozen slayers. If you face her alone, she'll take one look at you, rip both of your arms off, throw one through my chest, and then I'll die, staked by one of your arms. And how do you think your mum will feel, watching that?"

He nodded, satisfied, as Giles rolled his eyes and muttered, "Spike, good god."

"That's not going to happen." Frankie tugged loose. "I only have to face her alone for as long as it takes for Buffy and the others to show up. After that, *I'll* be the one with the slayer army."

"That's assuming she doesn't squash us all before we have a chance to cast it," Spike said. "It puts everything at risk. I won't do it."

"Yes, you will," said Frankie. "You won't let me fight alone." She looked at her Watcher. She looked at all of the Scoobies. "I want Aspen's attention. If it's on me, then she won't be anywhere else, hurting anyone else."

"Should we have left Vi at the hospital?" Hailey asked. "What if—?"

"Sarafina's with her. She's strong enough, and fast enough, to get Vi out, if she needs to."

"But that also means we're down another fighter," said Jake. He looked at Frankie regretfully. "I'm used to being the underdog, but no Sarafina, and no Vi, and a severely weakened Ms. R"—he glanced at Willow—"add in a couple of pissed-off hellbeasts, and this seems like not so much a plan as—"

"Suicide," said Oz softly, and Sam squeezed Jake's arm.

"Have you heard from any of the lacrosse werewolves?" Frankie asked. "Are they coming?"

"I don't know," Jake said. "They get that there are demons and vampires and stuff in Sunnydale . . ." He looked at Oz. "They said it explains a lot, actually—but they need time."

"Unfortunately, they don't have time," said Frankie. "Can we count on any of them?"

Jake shrugged. "Maybe O'Shay and Perry," he said, and Frankie frowned.

"Couldn't we just go get Aspen after the spell is cast?" Hailey asked. "With Buffy and the others?"

"Well, that's the other thing," Frankie said grimly. "Even with Buffy and the others, I don't know if we could beat her. But if we open an interdimensional hell door right over her head—"

"Maybe the hellbeasts could do us a favor for a change," Spike said. "It could work."

Frankie turned in a circle. Her friends were scared. But they were also Scoobies. "I know that we can do this. And you know as well as I do that Aspen can't be allowed even one more night of hurting people."

Around the room, arms crossed and uncrossed. Heads hung. Eyes got shifty.

"I suppose we have faced worse." Giles smiled at Willow. "We faced you."

Willow hunched her shoulders as she leaned against him, but Oz raised his hand.

"Actually, I never faced her. I was already gone."

"Me neither," said Spike. "I was on a soul quest."

Frankie looked at Hailey, Jake, and Sigmund. "You guys," she said, "we fought the Countess and won. We averted an apocalypse over the Hellmouth when we smashed that demon beacon. We've faced the Darkness before, and we're still here. But I know this is different. If you can't follow me into this, I understand. But I have to. I'm the slayer."

She waited. And the longer she waited, the more doubt crept in.

Until finally, Hailey said, "Frankie, the vampire slayer-witch."

"First of her name," added Sigmund. "Heir to the sacred slayer line."

"Leader of the new Scoobies," said Sam, and winked.

"And a near-constant pain in my haunches," Jake said. "So I guess we're in."

Frankie smiled so hard she thought her cheeks might break. "Jake. Don't talk about your haunches."

"As long as you promise to save my haunches, if this all goes sideways," he noted, and Sam laughed. "So what's the plan?"

"Step one is to get Aspen where we want her," said Spike.

"That shouldn't be hard," said Frankie. "Right now she's feeling pretty invincible. If we give her an invitation, I'm thinking she'll show up."

Willow flexed her fingers. "I should have enough magic in me to put up a flare. It won't be fancy, but it'll be pretty obvious."

"I can go finish prepping the spell space," said Oz.

"I'll help you," offered Mr. Giles as Oz moved for the door. "Where are we going?"

"The high school."

"Like old times," said Giles. "Thank goodness it's Saturday." He nodded to Willow, and she gave them a little wave as they left.

Spike shook his head. "I'll go start gathering weapons."

"Thanks, Uncle Spike."

"Never let it be said that I don't support running in toward certain death," he sang out over his shoulder.

"I'll go find the right spell for the flare." Willow kissed Frankie on the cheek and touched her arm. "And I'll probably meditate until sundown to try and heal my fractured mystical psyche." She headed upstairs to her bedroom. The new Scoobies stood alone.

Sam gestured in the direction of the vanished adults with his thumbs. "They really take all this impending destruction in stride."

"Different generation," Jake said. He grinned, but in the quiet their newfound resolve began to ebb. Even angry as Frankie was, she would be lying if she said she wasn't afraid. What Spike said about Aspen tearing her arms off and staking him with them was ridiculous, but not impossible.

"I can't believe I ever thought she wasn't dangerous," said Hailey. "She had me so completely fooled."

"She had a lot of people fooled," Frankie said, thinking of Kate.

"If only she wasn't superpowered," said Hailey. "Slayer versus slayer, I'd put money on Frankie any day. But now . . . isn't there any way to, like, suck the extra slayer powers back out of her?"

"You'd have to get close enough to remove the Amulet of Junjari," Sigmund said. "That's what has harnessed the power of the slayers. Not Aspen herself. But considering that it's hung around her neck and she is an ultimate killing machine, I'd say your chances are not good."

"Hey," said Jake. "Super strong or not, Aspen's still only one person. She can probably only kill us one or two at a time, at the most. That should buy us time."

Sam slid his arms around Jake's middle and squeezed. "That's very comforting, Jake. But it does raise a good point—all we need to do, really, is keep Aspen off balance until Frankie, Sigmund, and Mr. Giles can cast the spell. Then boom, we've got more slayers, and Aspen and everybody else will have their hands full with the indiscriminately rampaging hellbeasts."

"Yeah," said Frankie. "But how do you knock a super slayer off balance?"

Sigmund's eyes widened. "Portals," he declared.

The new Scoobies watched him as he puzzled out the rest of his thoughts.

"Traveling via portal is disorienting at best. At worst it can make even the most seasoned of sailors vomit up yesterday's salt cod. If we can keep Aspen moving through portals long enough for the spell to be cast, she won't be able to start a proper fight."

"And how do we keep her moving through portals?" Hailey asked.

"I can cast them in advance. A network of them that we hide inside. But I can't do it alone. That much portal travel will eventually also make *me* lose my salt cod. You'll have to do it, too, Hailey. And Jake."

"What's with the salt cod?" Jake asked. "Who eats salt cod?"

"But how can you do that, Sig," said Frankie, "when we need you to cast the spell off of me, like you said?"

"Your mother will have to stand in for me. I know she's weakened, but your mother weakened is still a stronger witch than I am."

"We'll have to get close enough to Aspen to touch her. Grab her." Hailey's eyes flickered to Jake and back to Sigmund. Sam's grip on Jake's middle tightened, and his tan skin began to pale.

"Close enough to grab her is close enough for her to break our necks," said Jake, pulling Sam closer.

"It's not without its dangers," Sigmund said. "But if we're lucky, she'll be too dazed to do much damage. And we only need to grab her for a few seconds each time. Fast in and fast out, like a boxer."

"That's the same way I intend to fight her," said Frankie. "And I will fight her. As soon as that spell is cast, she's my first and only target. You guys won't have to hold her for long." She and Sigmund nodded to each other, but Sam squirmed again in Jake's arms.

"Are we forgetting about a certain ex-demon-boyfriend-shaped complication?" he asked.

"Dammit," Frankie said. She had forgotten about Grimloch. On purpose. She couldn't bear to think of him, trapped and under Aspen's control. But he would be freed, too, once Aspen was dead.

"It would be easier if we could get Grim back onto our side," said Hailey. "He'd be so pissed off I bet he'd take out a dozen hell-beasts all by himself."

If only, Frankie thought, and closed her eyes as she heard Aspen's voice in her head, ordering Grimloch to kill her. And then another thought rose in her mind.

"I have an idea. It's not perfect, but it should keep Grim from attacking us, at least." She touched Hailey's arm. "And I'm going to need you."

CHAPTER THIRTY-THREE

SO IT'S LIKE THE BAT-SIGNAL

Sarafina and Vi listened as Sigmund and Hailey explained Frankie's plan.

"Well, it's a plan," said Vi.

"And I am to be here for this?" Sarafina asked, aghast. "I am not to fight even one single hellbeast?"

"I need you to stay with Vi," Hailey said. "Please. You're the only one strong enough to protect her if Aspen doesn't take the bait."

"Oh, she'll take the bait." Vi reached out and fiddled with the bag of her IV. "Even before she was all juiced up, an invitation like that would have been hard to ignore."

"How are the other members of the Darkness?" Sigmund asked.

Sarafina shook her head, and Hailey let out a shaky breath. She'd expected that some would probably be lost, but knowing it was a punch to the gut.

"Was it all a lie?" Hailey wondered. "Did she never really care about any of them? Or has the Amulet of Junjari done something to her? Warped her somehow?"

"It doesn't matter," Vi said darkly. One of the machines beside her bed beeped as her pulse jumped. Hailey tensed, and Vi tried to collect herself. "At least Sonia and Neha are safe," she said.

"But will you be, Sigmund?" Sarafina stepped away from Vi's bedside and went to her son. "Shifting through portals, so near to a being with such immense power . . . it is dangerous. Perhaps too dangerous."

"I thought you wanted me to fight."

"You do fight." She pressed a forefinger to his head. "With your brain. I see that now. And I don't wish for that brain to be torn from the rest of your body."

"I don't want that either. The portals I lay will be like a maze. And they'll be the most jarring, vomit-inducing portals known to demonkind. She won't be able to crush our skulls. She'll be too busy retching."

"Sig," Hailey said, "you might be a portal-traveling portal expert, but how are Jake and I supposed to survive that?"

"You'll only have to endure it once. Well, twice. Once on the way through, and again on the way back. The rest of the time you'll simply be reaching out, grabbing Aspen and pulling her through, then shoving her on to Jake in the next, who will shove her on to me, and so on and so forth." He checked his smartwatch. "We'd better get going."

"Yep. Willow's putting up the bat-signal come sundown, and I want to check in on Frankie." Hailey leaned down to kiss Vi on the cheek. "You gonna be okay? Not going to suddenly hemorrhage and bleed out through your ears or anything?"

Vi snorted. "You're not going to have your arms and legs ripped off by my former boss?"

Hailey walked around the bed and nodded to Sigmund. "Time to go."

"But one more thing, Mother," he said, straightening his shoulders. "Since I may be dead in a few hours, I should tell you that should I survive, I won't be marrying a demon of your choosing. Or perhaps any demon at all. I'm going to be making my life decisions for myself, from now on."

Hailey froze. How was he going to cast the portals if his mom dragged him back to DC by the collar of his immaculately pressed shirt? But instead of trembling like a volcano about to erupt, Sarafina crossed her arms and nodded.

"You're not angry?" Sigmund asked. "But I'm not doing what you say. I'm not going to be the Sage demon you always wanted me to be."

"Just take the win, Sig," Hailey muttered.

"I can't," he whispered back. "I have to know what she's thinking!"

"I am thinking," Sarafina said, "that I have raised a son who knows what is right for him. I am thinking that I truly am the 'great' Sarafina DeWitt."

Vi barked laughter and raised her fist to bump Sarafina's as Hailey grabbed a stunned Sigmund and pulled him from the room.

"Well," she said. "I bet that went better than you thought it would."

"Yes," he replied. "I wonder if that trend will continue."

"Huh?" Hailey asked as Sigmund pulled her close, into the kind of kiss that made her knees give out completely. "Whoa," she said as he held her up. "I thought Frankie was just exaggerating about the knee thing."

"Does that mean you'll take me back?"

Hailey recovered her knees and gave him a shove. "This is uncool to do right before we might die. What am I supposed to say?"

Sigmund's face fell. He straightened his glasses. "Of course. I should have—"

Hailey grabbed him and kissed him hard. "I'm kidding, Sig. I've been waiting for you to do that for a long time." They smiled at each other. "Now let's go check on Frankie. After that we'll head to the gym and give Sam and Jake a run for their PDA money."

)) ○ ((

As it turned out, preparing the spell space looked a lot like cleaning the gymnasium. Putting up the basketball hoops. Locking the movable bleachers in place. Jake looped thick chains through the door handles while Sam posted *No Entry—Fumigation in Progress* signs at every entrance.

"No word from the guys?" Sam asked when he'd finished.

Jake shook his head. "It's too soon. And they're still not exactly pleased with me and the fact that I . . ."

"Bit them on the downlow and turned them into werewolves?"

Jake's shoulders hunched with shame. "I know what Oz said, but I don't deserve to be their leader. Not as a pack or anywhere. At our next practice, I'm going to give up my C."

"You can't do that," said Sam.

"I'll earn it back," said Jake. "I just need time."

Sam raised his head as down the hall the doors opened, and in walked O'Shay Thomas and the rest of their lacrosse team.

"Maybe you need less time than you think."

Jake looked up as O'Shay held out the fumigation-in-progress sign.

"So this fumigation business isn't real, right? I thought you said we needed to be here."

"I didn't think you'd come." Jake grinned happily as his teammates—his packmates—surrounded him and greeted him with high fives and chest bumps, shoulder grabs and elbows.

"Of course we came, Cap," O'Shay said. "We never miss a practice."

"And we brought stuff from home," added Zach Connors. He held a shovel. Most of the guys had their protective equipment, and whatever weapons they could scavenge from their homes and garages: hoes, fireplace pokers, baseball bats, and, of course, lacrosse sticks. Perry Reilly had filled his messenger bag with what appeared to be a bunch of bricks.

Jake shook his head. "I don't know what to say."

"Say thank you," said O'Shay.

"Say we're in it to win it," said Perry.

"Say we won't get killed," called Jeremiah Tolbert from the back.

Jake put his hand on O'Shay and Perry's shoulders. "Thank you," he said to them all.

"Okay, okay." Sam stepped in and broke up the scrum. "We've all got work to do." He winked at Jake. "I'll get them set up outside the doors."

Jake nodded and watched them go. Then he headed back inside the gymnasium.

He stepped out of the way as Oz walked the perimeter, sweeping a burning bundle of sage up and down while Mr. Giles walked behind him holding an open spellbook and muttering a blessing. They were trying to lay a protective barrier, to keep the hellbeasts from spilling over into the rest of the school (and the town).

"Did I hear voices outside just now?" Oz asked.

"The lacrosse werewolves," Jake said. "They came. Sam's getting them stationed outside the doors."

"Reserve werewolves," Mr. Giles said, pleased, as he and Oz walked on.

"Okay," Sam said, returning to Jake's side. "There are lacrosse werewolves stationed at every entrance, with instructions to fall back in case of a breach. I left the main doors unchained for Frankie, Willow, and Hailey. And Aspen, too, I guess. After everyone's in, O'Shay will lock them up tight."

"You should be outside with them, Sam."

"What do you mean?" Sam blinked.

Jake looked toward the top row of the bleachers, where a very heavy shield had been erected as a barrier, with several stockpiles of arrows and Sigmund's bows stacked behind. That's where Sam and Sig would be, once the real fighting started.

Only Jake didn't want Sam there at all. He knew Sam was brave. But he hadn't grown up with demons and the forces of darkness like Jake and Frankie had. He didn't really understand what it could cost.

"Look. I know this seems exciting. But this isn't like the Insta-demon, or any of those late nights chasing vampires around the park. This is real. It's not a D and D campaign, no matter how much we pretend like it is."

"Be careful," Sam said, and his handsome face went still as a mask. "You're getting pretty close to being insulting."

"That's not what I'm trying to do. I don't want anything to happen to you, Sam. I'm a werewolf, and I'm with Frankie to the end. You don't have to be."

"That's a hell of a thing to say to me. Sigmund will be here, and he doesn't have any powers that work on demons."

"The portals will work on demons."

"What about Hailey? She's scrappy, I admit—"

"Hailey's a Potential. This is her fight, too."

310

Sam pressed his lips together. Jake shouldn't have said that. He didn't mean that it wasn't Sam's fight. His eyes stung and went cloudy as he grabbed the sleeve of Sam's T-shirt.

"Hey." Sam touched Jake's face. "Listen to me. I'm not leaving."

"But, Sam—"

"*But, Jake.* Not all of the hellbeasts are going to be dragons. Some of them will probably be smaller evil. Like gremlins. Or really angry opossums." He took Jake by the shoulders. "I'm not riding the bench for this, Cap, so let it go. I may be new, but I know what it is to be a Scooby."

Jake wiped at his eyes. "It's kind of scary."

"Yeah. But you'll forget all about that when you're clawing the hell out of your first hornswaggler."

Jake laughed. Frankie and her damn Willy Wonka references.

Jake turned toward the rear of the gym, where Spike had laid out their arsenal of swords, spears, and axes and Oz and Giles stood over a spot on the floor with a paintbrush and a bucket of blood Spike had donated from his meal stash. "What are the old guys doing?"

$$☽ ☽ ◯ ☾ ☾$$

"You should probably wait until Hailey gets here," Spike said to Giles as Giles studied a spellbook in one hand, his other holding the paintbrush and hovering over the blood bucket. "She's got a knack for artwork."

"I know how to paint a bloody magical symbol," Giles snapped, but after a moment he closed the book and dropped the brush into the blood. "Perhaps you're right." He removed his eyeglasses and rubbed the bridge of his nose. Dressed in brown slacks and a light knit shirt, he was a comforting presence despite his obvious stress.

"All the excitement getting to you, Rupert?" Spike asked teasingly. Spike had opted for his more classic look: black jeans and a black T-shirt. Big black boots to run toward Buffy in. "Been a while since you've been in the thick of it."

"I've never been in the thin of it, thank you very much," Giles replied. "Since the attack on the slayers, I've been neck deep in the dark arts, trying to find them and piece together a network of the surviving Watchers Council. While you've been here—" He looked around at the brightly lit gymnasium, striped with the crimson and yellow of New Sunnydale High and adorned with a very cute cartoon Razorback pig. "Having an enjoyable year teaching Frankie. Albeit in that abominable excuse for a library."

Spike looked away.

"What?" Giles asked.

"I haven't taught her enough," Spike said. "It was my only bloody job, and I didn't do it." He looked around the gymnasium, which in a few hours would be torn to shreds and splashed with blood. "I tried. I brought out the guidebook, studied the old Watchers' notes. But she's not ready."

Giles looked at the demon. "That's what the guidebook never tells you," he said quietly. "That's the secret. They're never really ready. But they do it anyway."

Spike pressed his lips together, and Giles placed a hand on his shoulder and squeezed.

"It is abominable, isn't it?" Spike said. "The library. Lights and skylights everywhere so as not to strain their little eyes. And computers. Everything on bloody computers."

"And not enough dust." Giles tapped the pages of the spellbook. "There should be dust, a library should be a house of books, and books ought to have a smell—"

"You know," called Jake from across the gym, "I never noticed before how much you two actually look like each other."

Spike and Giles quickly parted, and Giles put his eyeglasses back on.

"Oh, Jake," Giles said with a polite chuckle. "Do sod off."

$$) \;)\; \bigcirc \;(\; ($$

Upstairs in her bedroom, Frankie had tried on four slaying outfits, each selected for comfort and functionality. She'd put on a super-soft, organic cotton T-shirt, then tried a tank top, then considered a long-sleeved tee with a pocket in the front, for holding a stake. But she was unlikely to use a stake against Aspen and a bunch of assorted hellbeasts, so she took it off again and put the first T-shirt back on. It was plain and black. Less susceptible to bloodstains. She put one of her low-heeled, lace-up ankle boots on one foot and a black zip-up boot on the other and stomped around, trying a few kicks and dropping into a mock leg sweep to see which footwear felt better.

Neither felt great. The anger that had fueled her after the attack on the Darkness had fled, and her stomach was nothing but butter-flies. This was the battle of her life. It was for Buffy, and all the marbles. And no matter what Hailey and the new Scoobies thought, Frankie knew the truth.

Not even on her best day could she beat Aspen.

Frankie looked in the mirror and tugged at her black T-shirt.

"Oh god. I look like Spike."

"Like Watcher, like slayer," Hailey said, poking her head in. "Is it okay if I come in?"

"Sure." Frankie sat down on her bed and stared down at her

boot choices. "I should go with the zip-ups, right? No chance of laces coming loose for me to trip over?"

"I thought tripping over stuff was your specialty," said Hailey.

"Not tonight." Frankie tore off the ankle boot. "Tonight I have to face a whole bunch of slayers rolled up into one very mean slayer. There's no clowning my way through it."

"Hey, you're the slayer-witch." Hailey shrugged. "But personally, I vote for clowning. You don't change up a winning formula on the night of the big game."

"Big game, winning formula . . . Have you been hanging around with Jake? And how are you so calm?"

"It's just an illusion. Before he dropped me off to go pre-cast portals, Sig had to pull the car over so I could throw up into a bush. It really helped."

Frankie looked at her friend more closely. Hailey looked cool as a cucumber, dressed to the nines in Goth chic: black boots, a tiered black-and-gray skirt. Studded bracelets up her arms. But the edges of her winged eyeliner weren't as clean as usual, like they had feathered from sweat, and beneath her tan her skin looked a little sallow.

"Hey," Frankie said. "It's going to be okay. I'm nervous, but I always get nervous. This plan is going to work." Frankie put Buffy's cross around her neck, the one Willow had given her when she first became a slayer. Spike still had the communication cross, wrapped up in his pocket. "The slayers will be rescued, Aspen will be vanquished, and Grimloch will be free." She turned back to Hailey. "And then we should all go out for pie again."

"That was really good." Hailey lifted her nose and sniffed the air. "Did you get some already? What is that smell?"

That smell was buttery, sugary, and caramelly, and had begun to permeate the air of Frankie's room ever since she set the small waxed-paper parcel out on her vanity table.

"That," Frankie said, and pointed to it, "is a silence cookie. I got it from Spike's mystical book dealer in exchange for *The Black Grimoire.*"

"That's all you got?" Hailey got up and went to inspect it, peering between the open folds at the perfectly golden-baked item, lightly frosted with white icing and sprinkled with dark blue and silver sanding sugar. "Seems like you got the short end of the stick. Or is this a cow and magic beans situation?"

"That depends on if it works," Frankie said. "In theory, Aspen eats the silence cookie, and she won't be able to order Grim to kill us. It should buy us some time until—"

"Until I can yank her through a portal and steal the mind control spell."

"Exactly."

"What could go wrong?" Hailey asked with mock confidence as Frankie continued to stare at the cookie. "Are you worried about Grim? I guess he wasn't as big a jerk as we all thought, now that we know Aspen was controlling him." She made a disgusted face. "I can't believe she would do that. It's so gross. So . . . wrong. You've got to be righteously pissed off."

"Yeah," Frankie said. "I'm pissed off about a lot of things." She glanced out her window, where the light had turned a faint and fading pink. "But as luck would have it, tonight I get to work all that anger out on hellbeasts and Aspen's face." She curled her fingers around the waxed paper of the silence cookie and looked down at it.

"Get ready, Aunt Buffy. We're coming for you."

☽ ☽ ○ ☾ ☾

The parking lot was thankfully deserted as Willow, Frankie, and Hailey walked up to the darkened high school.

"No late Saturday activities," Willow mused, looking about nervously. "No over-dedicated study buddies hanging out in the library . . ."

"That doesn't really happen anymore," said Frankie. "We've pretty much run them out."

"That doesn't seem fair," said Willow.

"There's a perfectly good, brand-new, beautiful public library right over there." Hailey pointed across the park. "Within walking distance, great activities schedule, and"—she gestured to the Rosenbergs' magical bodies and to the general mystical battleground that the school was about to become—"it's safer. Speaking of safer, is performing this spell in a gymnasium that sits directly above an active hellmouth really the best choice?"

"It's the only choice," Willow said. "Having an interdimensional door nearby is a spell requirement. It's even listed in the ingredients. The Hellmouth counts." She pulled Frankie's arm over to show Hailey the ingredients list, marked in ink on Frankie's skin. "See? One hellmouth. Right there."

"That book is so evil," Hailey whispered.

They walked up to the main doors, and Frankie looked up into the night sky. It was clear and full of stars, the perfect sky to put a slayer bat-signal up into.

"Ready, Mom?"

Willow cracked open a small spellbook, a newer one, bound in black buckram and with a pentagram embossed in gold. She nervously read over the spell she would use—Frankie noticed that her lips were moving—and reached into her pocket to pull out what looked like a length of black beads, each with an intricate knot placed between them.

"A witch's ladder?" Frankie asked.

"It's mostly for luck," Willow explained. "It's an old spell of

316

Tara's. Just something for my fingers to fiddle with so I don't fidget my way into casting this signal wrong."

Frankie placed her hand over her mother's to steady it. Giles was right; Willow was weak. Nearly tapped out. The magic that usually zapped her instead felt like a sluggish wave lapping at her fingers. "Do you need me to help? Give you some juice?"

"You'd better not." Willow tugged gently away. "My magic is still drained, and when it gets drained, it gets greedy. I don't want to accidentally suck too much out of you so you're not ready for the battle."

"Yes, that would be very bad," said Hailey. She moved Frankie a few steps from her mother and stood half in between, like a human shield. "When dealing with several slayers squared, we at least need one slayer whole." She peered at the book and glanced into the sky. "Just what kind of signal will this be, anyway? Like a stadium light show?"

"I thought about options," Willow said. "A big green shaft of light or a huge middle finger. But in the end I decided on this." Frankie and Hailey backed farther away as Willow squeezed the witch's ladder in her fist and her hair began to float. It took longer to gather the power than Frankie thought was normal, but eventually, Willow threw her hand into the air and shouted.

"Memento Inardesca!"

Light rocketed up from the entirety of her mother's form, and Frankie was shoved back as the pavement cracked beneath their feet. Hailey was knocked clean onto her butt.

"Whoa," Hailey said as Frankie helped her up and Willow stepped out of the bright beam. "I thought you said you were weak."

"That *is* her weak," said Frankie, eyeing the spidering fissures running through the cement.

"Well," Willow said as they stood together looking up at her work. "What do you think? I was aiming for a mix of taunting and luring, but with pizazz."

Frankie tilted her head back. Above the school, the beam of light faded into a swirl of red and silver sparkles, rising high into the sky. They formed no shape and sent no message. But somehow Frankie sensed the impression of the slayer Scythe.

"That's not really the Scythe particles, is it, Mom?"

"No." Willow scoffed. "It's just a tease. Something she would still think of as hers and be sore about losing. Plus, it's only visible to demons and slayers and magic folk, so it won't attract any curious bystanders."

"Nice touch, Ms. R," said Hailey, and Willow looked pleased.

"Okay," said Frankie. "Let's get inside and get ready. It won't be long before she shows up."

CHAPTER THIRTY-FOUR

THE SPELL OF MANY INTERDIMENSIONAL RETURNS

T he Spell of Many Interdimensional Returns. It sounded so cozy. Like the title of an old episode of *Bewitched*. It was hard to believe that casting it would tear holes all the way through hell and back, letting beasts and demons of all shapes pour through like blood through the doors of those elevators in *The Shining*.

Sam and Jake met Frankie, Hailey, and Willow when they got to the gymnasium. Frankie quickly surveyed the space.

"Nice to see a bunch of lacrosse werewolves providing a second line of defense," she said, and Jake blushed.

"Yeah," he said. "They came. They all came."

"Now let's just keep them alive," said Sam.

They walked farther in, and Sigmund gestured wildly for them to keep to the side.

"Careful. I've placed the portals in the center."

The Scoobies walked toward him, slowing to a tiptoed crawl when they drew near so as to avoid accidentally slipping into one. The portal openings were invisible to all but Sigmund, and the way he described passing through them . . . Well, that was the last thing Frankie needed to do right before a battle.

"There are six portals in total," Sigmund explained. "Two that lead back to the gymnasium. Here"—he gestured to the seemingly open air to his left—"and here." He walked a few steps to his right and made the same gesture over again. "Two more connect these portals to my space, and I placed additional escape portals behind your space," he said, nodding to Jake, "and Hailey's. But they should only be used in an emergency, as traveling through them might leave you temporarily incapacitated and/or violently ill."

"Greeeat," Hailey said sarcastically as Mr. Giles called to her and waved.

"I've been told you're quite an artist," he said. "Would you be willing to help us paint this magical symbol upon the floor?"

"Hey, I'm useful!" she said happily, looking at Frankie. She jogged ahead and stared at the open spellbook for a minute, then grabbed the paintbrush and swirled it around the bucket of blood.

Willow peered around the gymnasium. "Seems like a shame to destroy another high school," she said to Oz. "This one is so nice."

"Ah, well. Sunnydale loves to rebuild," he noted.

"We employ a lot of contractors and construction crews," said Jake. He nudged Frankie. "You smell like cookies."

Hailey completed the symbol on the floor of the gym, a ten-foot-diameter circle of blood filled with mystical symbols that ranged from blunt crosses to delicate, curling wards. Frankie didn't need to compare it to the book to know it was a perfect copy. The symbol was placed just before the start of the bleachers, directly below what looked like a hunting stand made out of shields, where she figured Sam would be for the duration of the battle.

"Almost done," Hailey said. "Just one more god's eye . . . aaaand finished!" She straightened carefully and twisted around. "Wait, how do I get out of here now without smearing it?" But before they could consider options, the air over the symbol began to ripple, and Hailey froze as the blood glowed bright red, then scorched itself permanently into the shiny, finished wood floor.

"Well, that's a month of detention," Hailey said.

"Frankie, you'll need to be here." Giles pointed into the symbol. "At the center. Willow and I will draw the spell from your skin and cast it with the aid of your inherent magic. Your magic may be drained in the process, and you won't be free to fight until the Spell of Many Interdimensional Returns has begun."

"Might be a long time to keep Aspen busy," said Spike.

"That's where the new Scoobies come in," Frankie said.

"Hang on," said Oz. "Shouldn't it be us?" He looked at Spike. "We're stronger, and we're"—he paused when Spike's cheekbones came out—"adults."

"They can do it," Frankie said confidently. "And I need you here to catch early demons. And in case anything goes wrong." She squared her shoulders. "Now, Sig, you'd better run us through the portal stuff."

Jake put a hand on Sam's shoulder. "You'd better get up to the shield stand, Sam." Sam nodded. But when Jake leaned in for a kiss, he turned away.

"Don't kiss me goodbye, you insufferable werewolf. You can kiss me hello, when it's over."

Sigmund began to lead the new Scoobies to the center of the gym, but before Frankie went, Spike said, "Hey, Mini Red."

He made a tough expression, and a V with his fingers.

"Poke her eyes out."

Frankie gave him a closed-lip smile.

She joined Sigmund, Hailey, and Jake—very carefully—between the open portals. After Sigmund finished the demonstration, she said, "That doesn't seem so bad."

"Except for the barfing," said Jake.

"Just remember your objective." Frankie made a fist. "Fast grab, fast pull, then on to the next."

"Only not me," said Hailey nervously. "I have to pause for pick pocketing."

"Try to get the mind control spell. But if you can't, you can't. Don't put yourself in more danger. And no one makes a grab for the amulet. She'd kill you for sure; don't be a hero."

Hailey swallowed. "Last time I tried to pick Aspen's pocket it ended with her hand around my throat."

"But not this time," Frankie said. "You can do this."

The new Scoobies stood in a circle. Sigmund DeWitt, the endlessly resourceful brainiac wrapped up in a charming, half-demon body. Hailey Larsson, Goth Potential with natural gifts of style and strength. And Jake Osbourne. Annoying. Werewolf. The older brother Frankie never asked for A year ago she could never have imagined they would be where they were, that they would be her friends, and fighting for the slayer line. That they would be fighting evil. They were teenagers in high school; all they should have been fighting was tooth decay.

"Well," said Sigmund. "I suppose this is it."

"Don't say it like that, Sig," said Hailey. "Like it's the end. This is just something we have to do before we can have pie."

"I can't believe that butthole Aspen gets to have a cookie before we get to have pie," said Jake, eyeing the pastry as Frankie took it out of her pocket.

The silence cookie was definitely magic: It hadn't gotten the least bit squished or crumbly. And it smelled every bit as delicious as it had the moment Dorsia thew it to her. She unwrapped it and tucked the waxed paper back into her pants.

"Hailey," she said suddenly. "If I'm killed, you might be called to be the slayer in the next instant."

"Frankie—" Jake started, but Frankie shook her head.

"Just listen." She looked at Hailey. "I need you to be ready. I need you to finish this, if I can't."

"No," Hailey said. "No way, I couldn't— If you were—"

"I'm not saying this to scare you. And I don't intend to die. Just . . . if it happens . . ." She shrugged. "And know that wherever I am, I'm really happy it's you."

Hailey turned to Sigmund, who looked down somberly, and at Jake, who hadn't taken his eyes off Frankie.

"Okay." Hailey threw her arms around Frankie's neck. *"Don't die.* But I'll be ready."

"We'd best get into the portals," said Sigmund. "Aspen will be here soon, and Hailey and Jake will need time to recover from the initial travel." He put an arm around Hailey to guide her into the portal to Frankie's left, and said, "No, no, Jake, you're this way," when he tried to follow. "I'm going to go through with Hailey and help her to settle. Then I'll travel through the next portal to my space and come through to your side, to check on you."

"I'm so confused," said Jake. But he stepped through the invisible gateway and disappeared.

"Sig, where do these portals go, anyway?" Frankie asked.

"To other isolated places within the school. Were something to happen to the portals, I wanted each of us to be able to return to the battle quickly. Jake has just found himself in the boys' locker room. Hailey will go through to the middle of the grass on the quad, and I'll be in the library, in your training area." He turned Hailey toward her portal opening, and she stepped through, with one last, sad look at Frankie.

"My palms are sweating a little," Frankie said, adjusting her grip on the cookie. "But what do I care? I should be glad Aspen's getting a sweaty cookie." She held it up. "Think I should put a hair on it or something?"

Sigmund chuckled softly. "Good luck, slayer," he said, and he stepped to one side and vanished.

$$☽ ☽ ○ ☾ ☾$$

Frankie stood beside the symbol on the floor as Mr. Giles and her mother prepared her skin to cast the Spell of Many Interdimensional Returns off of it. They rubbed magically charged oil into her hands and forearms, and wisps of black ink broke free to chase Willow's fingers like curious fish.

"That looks kind of cool," Frankie said.

"Yes, it's a very pretty, dimension-breaking spell embedded into my child," Willow replied as she rubbed.

"But see how good it looks? Maybe after you can take me to get a commemorative tattoo," Frankie teased, and grinned when Willow let her hand drop. She looked around at her allies. Sam behind the barrier of shields. Oz and Spike checking and rechecking weapons.

"Spike keeps looking at me like he thinks I'm going to lose," Frankie whispered.

"That's not an insult," Willow said quietly. "That's just because he's scared. Because he loves you."

Frankie snorted. "Spike loves Buffy, beatings, and *Battlestar Galactica*," she quipped.

"Yes," said Willow. "And you."

Mr. Giles turned away and wiped his hands on a cloth. "All right. When the spell begins—"

But he didn't get to finish, because he had to duck and cover when Aspen blew through the main doors, kicking them clear off their hinges and sending them sailing to crash against the opposite wall and fall loudly to the floor.

"Yikes," Frankie said dismally. "What I need magic for, she can now do with her feet."

"Oh man," said Sam. "I brought extra chains, not extra doors."

Aspen walked into the gymnasium with a dead-eyed Grimloch trailing behind. She looked at the charred symbol in the floor.

"Now, what in the world are you up to?"

"None of your business," Frankie said. "Why are you so nosy?" She walked toward Sigmund's cast portals, luring Aspen in the right direction to pass between them. She worried it might seem obvious, but Aspen was beyond caring. Like Frankie had hoped, the former leader of the Darkness felt invincible.

With reason. Sheer power radiated off her. The moment Aspen walked into the room, Frankie's slaydar began to wail. It wailed and wailed, and then promptly ran away.

"Nosy?" Aspen asked. "You weren't exactly sneaky, you know. There's a pillar of sparkles rising a thousand feet over this place. One might think you wanted me here. But not even you could be that stupid." Aspen cocked her head. "Then again, I also wouldn't have said that you could be this frumpy."

Frankie gestured to her shirt. "These are ass-kicking clothes. Durable. Responsible. Don't even get me started on how much you're going to lose on that outfit when it gets ruined. Part of me doesn't want to fight you because of all the waste." Frankie looked at Grimloch as he stood beside Aspen, trapped and suffering. "But the other part of me just can't help myself." Frankie darted forward, mindful of the portal openings, and punched Aspen in the face. It felt like hitting granite. Frankie feinted back and nearly bent in two to evade Aspen's counterpunch, which was so fast she barely saw the fist moving through the air. But she did see the bright glow of the Amulet of Junjari, strung around Aspen's neck.

Frankie stayed low to kick out one of Aspen's knees. Only it didn't get kicked out. Aspen only bent a little, and then reached down and picked Frankie up by the neck.

Frankie was pulled into the air so fast she was actually jarred when she got to the top, and swung back and forth like the bucket of a stopped Ferris wheel.

"I don't know why I didn't get your powers, too," Aspen said as Frankie's legs kicked and dangled. "Maybe the amulet didn't want them because you're so supremely annoying."

"Put her down!" Frankie heard Spike shout.

"No! Spike!" She held her hand out. "Mom! Stay back!"

Aspen looked at Willow, Spike, Oz, and Giles, and then at Frankie, her neck clasped in her hand. "What does this remind me of?" she asked. "Oh, I know. Bowling." She drew Frankie close and squeezed so hard Frankie saw stars. "If I get a strike, maybe I'll let one live."

Aspen drew Frankie back and threw her, sending her flying into Spike and Oz and crashing into the base of the bleachers.

"Oh shoot," Aspen said. "A spare. But I was just kidding, anyway; I was always going to kill everyone."

Frankie groaned and rolled onto her elbows alongside Spike and Oz. "You okay?" she whispered.

"Fine, are you?" asked Spike.

"That really hurt," said Oz.

"I'm glad it hurt." Aspen put her hand on her hip. "Am I

enjoying this too much? Have I become some kind of superpowered sadistic monster?"

"Well, you're not a slayer," said Spike. "But you haven't been a slayer in a long time."

"I'm the only slayer, you idiot vampire," Aspen said, walking toward them. "I'm *all* the slayers."

"Not for long," said Mr. Giles.

Aspen paused. "Mr. Giles? Is that you? And is that what you're doing? That's so cute. You brought daddy home to bring back his Buffy." Aspen smirked. "Let her come. That bitch can't beat me anymore. But I think I'd rather she came back to find you . . . disemboweled." She drew a knife from her jacket and threw it into Giles's stomach.

"Giles!" Willow cried, grabbing him as he staggered back.

Frankie stared at the growing spot of red in Giles's middle.

"Don't worry, Frankie." Aspen smiled. "I won't use a knife on you. I'm going to watch our boyfriend beat you to a paste. Grimloch—"

Frankie burst up from the floor faster than she'd thought she'd be able. She jammed the silence cookie into Aspen's surprised mouth and punched her jaw shut on it.

"What the hell?" Aspen chewed a moment, then spit a few crumbs. "It's . . . really good, actually . . ." And then she stopped speaking. Or, more accurately, she stopped being heard.

"No Grimloch for you," Frankie said, and she kicked her in the face.

Aspen's surprise at losing her voice, and her stubborn, repeated attempts to yell and command Grim, gave Frankie her opening. She attacked with kicks and punches, pushing the super slayer back until she was right where Frankie needed her to be: between the two portals.

"You're much more pleasant without all the talking," Frankie said. "Jake, now!"

Aspen bared her teeth. But she had no time to react when Jake's arms appeared out of nowhere and dragged her through the mouth of the first portal.

As soon as she disappeared, Frankie ran back to the symbol in the floor, where Giles reclined on the lowest bleacher with her mom.

"Mr. Giles," Frankie asked, "what do we do?"

"Should I pull it out?" Willow asked, her hand hovering above the knife.

"No," Giles barked. "Don't pull it out. We do the bloody spell, that's what we do. Spike, get me up."

Spike slipped an arm beneath the senior Watcher and helped him rise. "Never said you weren't tough, Rupert." Spike looked at Frankie. "Better get yourself to the middle of that symbol, Mini Red."

"Right." Frankie stepped onto the symbol. "Oz," she called, "stand ready near the portals. If anyone sounds like they need help, go through."

"You got it," the werewolf said, jogging to the middle of the gym.

Frankie found herself between her mother and Mr. Giles, who grimaced as Spike kept him on his feet.

"All right," Giles said. "Let's begin."

$$) \;) \; \bigcirc \; (\; ($$

Jake wasn't expecting Aspen to be trying to talk when she came through the portal. The way her mouth moved, so angrily and completely without sound, tripped him up for a minute. It was like someone had hit a universal mute button. He watched her eyes roll in her head, disoriented by the trip, the same trip that had made Jake promptly barf all over Matt Larkin's swim locker. He'd leave him a note.

Jake grabbed onto the leader of the Darkness, the rogue slayer who commanded an entire slayer army inside of herself, and felt her muscles tighten like bands of iron. Her lips curled in what he assumed were a whole lot of expletives.

"Oh no, you're not staying." He shoved her hard through the next portal, conveniently placed only a few feet in the other direction. "Sig, she's coming through, and she's pissed!

"Bye bye," he added, waving to the disappearing toe of Aspen's designer boot. Then he took a breath. She'd only been with him a few seconds, but even those few seconds had been terrifying.

"I might barf again," he said, and he turned back to Matt Larkin's locker.

☽ ☽ ○ ☾ ☾

Sigmund crouched, ready to receive the evil slayer package from Jake. He was breathing fast, and his palms were so sweaty he was afraid they would slip right off her. But when she appeared he grabbed on, quickly noting her lack of voice and her increasing pallor as the portal travel made her sick.

"Oh my goodness," he said. "You're not well; let me help." He grabbed her arm and spun her in a fast circle. It wasn't easy. Even disoriented, she was strong. Turning her felt like trying to dance with a statue. But he had to give Hailey every advantage he could. "Coming through on your left, darling!" he shouted, and gave Aspen a shove.

"Be quick," he whispered after she'd disappeared. "Don't get hurt. And send her back."

$$)\ )\ \bigcirc\ (\ ($$

"Dammit, why do you always have to wear so many layers?"

Hailey's heart sank when Aspen emerged through the portal, staggering and stumbling, her eyes rolling so badly that Hailey was nauseated just looking at them. She grabbed on to the leader of the Darkness and quickly stuffed her hands into pockets. So many pockets. Pockets in the leather jacket. Pockets in the jeans. A tiny pocket in the slouchy fabric of the designer T-shirt. She didn't have long. And if she took even one second more than she could—she felt Aspen's hand grip her wrist, and yelped as the bones ground together. She looked up. Aspen's eyes were still and focused.

"Sig!"

One moment she thought her arm was going to snap; the next, Sigmund's torso was reaching through the portal and dragging Aspen back the way she'd come. Hailey dove forward, adding her weight, and they barely managed to get Aspen knocked through. Hailey hit the ground, head spinning so hard she had no choice but to tuck into the fetal position. She heard Sigmund shout to Jake as he pushed Aspen again.

Hailey hadn't even managed one shift in the portal system. And now she couldn't move. Jake and Sigmund were on their own. "Dammit," she tried to say as her teeth clenched.

They couldn't keep this up for much longer.

$$)\ )\ \bigcirc\ (\ ($$

The symbol Hailey had painted, which had then scorched itself permanently into the gymnasium floor, glowed red as Willow and Giles whispered their incantations. Each held one of Frankie's wrists, ready to receive the magic and cast it off her into the . . .

she didn't know what. Into the air of the gym, she supposed. Up onto the ceiling. That would be the smartest place. Let the doors to other dimensions open way up there, and maybe a few soft-bodied hellbeasts would fall and go splat right onto the floor.

"Come on," she whispered. But she wasn't sure who she was talking to. Magic worked at magic's pace. It was working, though: The words and magical symbols tugged against her skin. Ink pressed up against ink, the letters crowding each other like noodles in a spoon of alphabet soup. Except the soup was her body. And it itched a little.

She stared into the middle of the gym, where Oz stood beside the portals, listening. Her friends were alive. She knew that because she could occasionally hear them, and also because Aspen hadn't emerged carrying each of their heads like a demented gym coach passing out basketballs. They were fighting. Doing their jobs. But they needed her help.

Frankie clenched her fists.

"Come on."

☽ ☽ ◯ ☾ ☾

"Uh, is Hailey up yet?" Jake called to Sigmund as the half Sage demon shoved Aspen through to him. They'd moved her between just the one set of portals for a long time, to give Hailey a chance to recover, but it was hard. Aspen wasn't exactly light. Jake could hear the exhaustion creeping into Sigmund's voice. And worse, Aspen was starting to acclimate to the portal travel.

"Not yet," Sig called back. "It . . . it takes time!"

Jake held his arms out to catch the super-slayer package and rebound it. But when he grabbed her shoulders, she grabbed him back.

"Sig," Jake said as he looked into Aspen's very angry eyes. "I don't think we have that time."

"You don't have any," Aspen growled.

"You have your voice back, that's great," Jake said, just before she threw him, through the portal that felt like it wanted to jelly his insides, to land on the hard gym floor.

$$\mathrm{)\ )\ \bigcirc\ (\ (}$$

When Frankie saw Jake fly limply through the portal, she almost broke the connection to the spell. She would have, had it not been for the iron grip of the magic and her mom's orders.

"No!" Willow cried. "If you let go now, we'll have to start over!"

Oz ran to Jake, and Frankie saw his head move. He was alive. But he wasn't the only new arrival. Aspen stepped through the portal right behind him, and she didn't seem the least bit disoriented.

"We have to hurry."

"There is no 'hurry,'" said Willow, between mutterings of magic.

"That," said Aspen, who had apparently regained the use of her voice, "was a typically annoying little trick." She swallowed and touched her stomach. "I need, like, a carbonated beverage. But I'll kill a few werewolves first." She swung her arm up as Oz leapt, and he flew backward halfway across the gymnasium. But Aspen wasn't after Oz.

"Jake!" Frankie cried.

Aspen walked to Jake and leaned down to grab him, before drawing her hand back in surprise. An arrow had sliced through the air and cut the back of her hand. She bared her teeth and looked up at Sam's barricade so quickly it was like a special effect—like watching a vampire change its face. It was a testament to Sam's bravery that he didn't turn tail and run, and instead kept firing arrows between Aspen and his boyfriend.

"I don't know who's back there," Aspen shouted, catching an arrow in midflight and snapping it like a pencil. "But I'm going to kill you, too."

Frankie looked down at her arms, where the spell had crowded so densely that her skin was almost entirely ink. She reached down into her own magic and stirred it up. Her magic wasn't like her mom's, which was a coiled tiger waiting to pounce. Frankie's was much more akin to a house cat. But it still had claws.

The itching of the spell at once became a burn, and Frankie clenched her teeth as the spell began to tear loose. As each new word rose into the air, Willow and Giles spoke it, casting it as it went.

"What are you doing?" Aspen asked. "What is that magic?"

"You'll find out in a minute," Frankie breathed.

Aspen turned to Grimloch, standing by, still and passive as a statue. "Grimloch. Go kill your little girlfriend. Break her arms before she can finish . . . whatever it is she's finishing. And crush the red witch's skull while you're at it." She looked at Frankie triumphantly, and Frankie tensed, ready to do she didn't know what. Break the connection to the spell when they were so close? Let Grimloch attack and break it for them anyway? She looked at Grim, silently pleading with him to fight the mind control.

"Grimloch," Aspen repeated. "Attack them!"

"Why is he not killing us?" Willow asked, just as Hailey and Sigmund raced into the gymnasium through the blown-open doors.

"Sorry I'm late," Hailey panted. "I just couldn't stomach coming back through that portal." She raised her fist. In it was a folded square of paper: the spell from *The Black Grimoire*.

"You," Aspen said.

"*You*," Hailey corrected, "don't have a Hunter of Thrace anymore. Grim, get her!"

Aspen braced as Grimloch charged her, and just as he did, Frankie felt the last of the spell pull free of her skin. Willow spoke the words, and it cast into the air like a lightning bolt. Thunder clapped. Doors between dimensions tore open.

And all at once, it began to rain hellbeasts.

CHAPTER THIRTY-FIVE
IT'S RAINING HELLBEASTS

There was no way to count how many doors had been opened. Some opened in thin air, high in the rafters. Some appeared on the ground. One opened directly in between Sigmund's demon portals, and hellbeasts emerged only to fall through them into the boys' locker room, where, judging from the smear on Jake's chin, they would find themselves surrounded by vomit. Another opened above the basketball net and dropped a small, winged demon directly into the hoop, where it slashed its way free for an easy two points.

Frankie looked down at her mom. Willow was breathing hard, exhausted by the magic.

"It's over? It's cast?" Frankie asked.

"It's cast." Willow smiled. "Go be a slayer."

Frankie jumped out of the magical symbol, once again just a scorched mark in the floor, and headed straight for Aspen. From the corner of her eye she saw Spike gently hand Giles over to her mother's care, and heard him say, "Sorry, old man. Time for me to join the fray."

"Old man." Giles chuckled, leaning on Willow. "Look who's talking."

Spike dove into the fight beside Frankie, colliding with a falling hellbeast that vaguely resembled an angry bipedal cow. Across the gym, Oz was back on his feet, protecting Jake, who was slowly coming to. Grimloch attacked Aspen, but they were both also attacked by hellbeasts and dragged apart.

"Frankie?" Jake asked woozily as she raced past. "Is this the spell?"

"Well, it isn't dodgeball!" She turned and winked. "So get up and fight, you lazy werewolf."

Jake grinned. He took a deep breath and heaved himself up, his claws coming out to rake the shoulder of a muscular demon with a mouth full of razor teeth. Frankie ducked under a pack of hellhounds as they leapt, but when she popped back up they'd forgotten all about her and instead were tearing at the tentacles of a floating green demon as it tried to gore them with a pair of ebony horns.

"Oh good, they'll fight each other."

But it wasn't enough. Not nearly. Hellbeasts and the variety pack of demons were falling at a steady rate. If the doors between dimensions didn't close soon, they were at risk of being killed just by drowning in their sheer volume.

"Mom! How long is this spell supposed to take?"

"I don't know!" Willow shouted back as she weakly blasted tiny, troll-like demons away from Mr. Giles's legs. "A few minutes? At least until it returns what we've been looking for!"

"I just love magic; it's so vague," Frankie said to herself sarcastically. But the thing they were looking for was nowhere in sight. No Buffy. No Kennedy. No slayers except herself, and the slayer of many slayers: Aspen, who fought not one but three demons at once, using her hands to crumple their skulls like paper.

"Aspen!" Frankie screamed. Aspen tossed the last demon away and Frankie took off to meet her head-on. She dodged attacking demons on the way, rolling around one and sliding beneath another. She flipped over the top of one who had a studded shell for a back, while across the gym Aspen simply shoved her way through, breaking necks and tearing out the spines of any demons who were in her path and had spines.

The slayers met in a flurry of strikes and feints. Frankie had to move so fast she barely had time to breathe. Every near strike from the other slayer was a near end, hard enough to kill. She couldn't afford to make a mistake. She couldn't afford to trip over things. But that didn't mean she couldn't be Frankie.

"Whoa!" she cried as she bent back and flipped. "Eep! Yikes!"

"Stop making those noises!" Aspen growled as she punched and missed.

"I will if you stop trying to kill me," Frankie said, and she yipped again as Aspen's stone fist passed a millimeter from the end of her nose.

"Not only will I not stop—" Aspen punched and kicked. She landed a glancing blow to Frankie's shoulder, and Frankie cried out as her joint left its socket. She grabbed her shoulder with her other hand and stumbled back as Aspen advanced. "But I won't stop at you. I'll kill you, and then I'll kill your mom, and Hailey, and your stupid werewolves. I'll kill all your friends, and your Watcher, and then I'll kill Grim, and that'll be your fault, too." She shoved Frankie hard, and she fell onto her butt.

"My fault," Frankie said as she brutally forced her own shoulder back into place. "Buffy's fault, everybody else's fault . . . When are you going accept some personal responsibility?" She jumped up, arms aching, the sounds of the battle raging around them. She heard the cries of demons and saw her mother blasting hellhounds as Jake and Oz fell back to help her. Sigmund and Sam fired arrows from behind the barricade, but demons were barreling up the bleachers. Spike was bloodied and nearly exhausted as he kicked through a tall gray demon in bone armor, only to be tackled to the floor by a giant snake. And Hailey, fighting gamely with her hand ax, made for an uneven fighting team with Grim as she tried to give him orders with the spell.

"Personal responsibility," Aspen said as she grabbed Frankie by the collar. "Look around you. These aren't my hellbeasts. This is your mess. This is—"

Her voice cut off as another bolt of lightning crackled through the air. Aspen watched in horror as Buffy Summers dropped from the sky and landed in a crouch on the gymnasium floor.

Aspen eased her grip on Frankie's collar, distracted, and Frankie drew her arm back.

"You are in so much trouble," Frankie said, and when Aspen turned to look at her, she made a *V* with her fingers and jabbed her in the eyes.

$$\text{)} \text{)} \text{ ○} \text{ (} \text{ (}$$

"BUFFY!"

Frankie raced across the gymnasium to the slayer, who had freshly regained her feet, and her own dimension, as other slayers dropped through around them. They looked a little haggard, a little sweat stained. Their clothes were smudged with dirt. Andrew, it seemed, had fallen directly into the fetal position. But in true Buffy form, it took her almost no time to assess the situation.

"You sure know how to throw a welcome home party." She put a hand on Frankie's shoulder and turned to look at Willow and Giles, at Spike and Oz and Jake. Her appearance, and the arrival of the other slayers, created a brief lull in the fighting as even the demons slowed, sensing the new strength on the scene.

"Buffy, look out!" Willow pointed as a bat-winged demon swooped overhead. Buffy and Frankie ducked, and Willow used her magic to zap it out of the sky.

"Thanks, Will." Buffy looked at her. "Home for not even two seconds, and already it's work, work, work."

"Leave it to Willow to start the party without us," said Kennedy, cracking her knuckles. Her gaze settled on a horde of demons attacking Sigmund and Sam behind the barricade. "I call those ones," she said, and she took off up the bleachers. "Goddess," she called to Willow as she passed. "Sword!" Willow reached down with her magic and sent one into Kennedy's hand, and the ever-ready brunette slashed through three rows of hellhounds as she climbed.

As if that was their cue, the other slayers went to work, weapons or no weapons, slaying demons like they hadn't slain a demon in months. Some, like Rona, fought grimly, like she hated it, using fists and daggers. Chao-Ahn fought with speed, using a two-sword method to create distance and push demons back to the perimeter.

"They're amazing," Frankie said.

"Hey." Buffy gave her a nudge. "They is you. So let's get in there." Her gaze hardened as it landed on Aspen, who was bent over rubbing her eyes. "I think I see a slayer who needs a lesson."

"Careful," said Frankie. "She's not just one slayer anymore. She's lots of slayers. She stole the rest of the Darkness's powers, and now she's basically a slayer-god."

Buffy squared her shoulders. "I've fought a god before. Of course, I died right afterward." She looked at Frankie. "Wanna kick her ass together?"

Frankie grinned. "I've never wanted anything more."

"Grim! Attack the one with the wings," Hailey called out. "No, not that one with the wings! The big one with the wings!" She swung her hand ax and took off the head of something that looked suspiciously like one of those gremlins from the old eighties movies as Grimloch jerked back and forth, trying to follow her increasingly confusing commands. "Sig!" she shouted up to the barricade, currently being defended by a short but very angry brown-haired slayer. "This isn't working!"

Sigmund peeped his head out over the shield.

"You have to be specific!"

"I'm trying! It's hard to control a hunter god and fight a demon horde at the same time!"

He ducked down to avoid the swipe of a claw and came back up with a crossbow that he fired into the attacking demon's chest.

"We need to find a way to free Grimloch's mind!" Sigmund shouted. "To free him from the spell!"

"Can you just tear it up?" Jake asked as he grappled with a demon that looked like a stone gargoyle come to life.

"No!" Willow interjected, dragging a very clingy Andrew back to the relative safety of the spell symbol. "That could kill him!"

Hailey thought quickly. Now that the slayers were there, the tide of the battle had turned—they weren't winning exactly, but death was no longer imminent. Still, they had to do something. The gymnasium was crawling with demons, and occasionally, new ones would squeak through the open dimensional doors. Mr. Giles was wounded, perhaps mortally, Willow was weakened, and now that Buffy was back, Spike seemed to be not so much fighting as attention seeking, pulling off huge, epic kills on the biggest demons he could find. They would all breathe easier if Grimloch was himself again. When Grim was Grim, well, he could really *Roadhouse*-rip a demon's throat out.

Hailey used her ax to fend off a roving hellhound and called to Grimloch. He came to her, and she held the spell up before his face.

"Okay, listen to me," she said. "I am ordering you to act just like you would if you were in control of your own mind." She waved the paper and studied his eyes, dull as rocks inside his head. "I'm commanding you to not be under this spell!"

This is never going to work, she thought dismally, just before Grimloch grabbed her by the shoulders.

"Thank you, Hailey," he said, and squeezed her.

"You're welcome," she replied, watching him return to the fight and begin killing. "You're so very welcome."

$$ \text{☽ ☽ ○ ☾ ☾} $$

"Well," Buffy said as she and Frankie walked toward Aspen, "how do you usually like to start these big fights?"

"I don't know," Frankie replied. "I kind of just . . . tend to fall a lot." She frowned. "You already missed my signature move—I did it right when you came through the ceiling."

"Oh, that V-finger eye-gouge thing?" Buffy turned to her. "That was nice."

"Well, isn't this cozy," Aspen drawled. She studied Buffy with a critical eye but found nothing to insult in the slayer's ensemble. "You don't look nearly as dead of starvation as I hoped. And you"— she looked at Frankie—"I can't believe you told mom on me."

"I'm not your mom," Buffy said. "And I wasn't your boss. I was your leader."

"You were our executioner," Aspen said, and Frankie clenched her fists.

"Oh . . . shut your piehole with that noise," she said. "That's just the propaganda you used to brainwash the Darkness. But it's pretty clear what you were after the whole time."

For a moment, standing in front of Buffy, Aspen seemed small. Full of doubts. But then she shrugged and said, "Well, when the little brat's right, she's right," and she drew two long-bladed knives.

Frankie and Buffy sheared off as she attacked—Buffy spun deftly out of harm's way, and Frankie dove and rolled like a barrel. When she popped back up, she attacked Aspen from the back, while Buffy faced her at the fore. It should have been easy. But Aspen had the strength and speed of a dozen slayers, and fighting her was like fighting someone with eight legs and six arms. Buffy managed to kick the knives from her hand, but in the process she took a glancing blow to the jaw and flipped through the air to land and slide across the finished hardwood.

"Buffy!" Frankie dove between Aspen's legs and kicked her off balance as she slid to her aunt and helped her up.

"I meant to do that," Buffy said, and winced. "I wanted to see how strong she was."

"And?"

"Ow." She rubbed her face. "While she was pummeling me, I did notice she's wearing a gaudy piece of jewelry."

"The Amulet of Junjari," Frankie explained. "It's what she used to steal the slayer power."

"Then let's steal it back." Buffy squared her shoulders and charged in again.

"You make it sound so simple," Frankie muttered, but went with her.

They attacked from angles, using the same timing to force Aspen into defense. But they weren't landing meaningful blows.

"Buffy, Frankie!" Willow called when again they were both knocked back. "You have to beat her now! The spell is about to end!"

"What does that mean?" Buffy and Frankie asked together. But Willow had no time to answer. The air inside the gymnasium contracted and made a sound that reminded Frankie of ice cubes cracking. The dimensional doors were being forced shut. She didn't know what would happen when they did, but she didn't want to wait to find out.

Buffy touched Frankie's shoulder. "Want to show me some of your fancy slayer-witch stuff?"

"I don't have much of it right now," Frankie said. "Casting the spell took it out of me." She looked at Aspen. The Amulet of Junjari bounced on the chain around her neck. "But maybe I don't need much." She turned to Buffy. "If you can keep her busy, I can take that amulet off right over her head."

"You can do that?"

"Okay, I don't actually know. But now is the time to try things!"

Buffy didn't argue. She ran back to Aspen, getting a few assists from Spike, Grimloch, Rona, and Chao-Ahn as they helpfully tackled stray demons in her path, then leapt into the super slayer with a flying roundhouse kick. From the expression on Buffy's face, Frankie knew she had never seen that kick do less, but she didn't let up, punching and feinting, subtly shifting Aspen's position to give Frankie a clear view of the amulet.

Frankie reached into herself with her mind and shook her magic awake. Her trusty telekinesis. It was always there when she needed it. But she didn't need to blast Aspen back a foot or throw a recycling bin at her. She had to be precise. She had to grab on to that thin golden chain and thread it over Aspen's head before she had a chance to notice.

Frankie took a breath. She kept her eye on the gold and raced in.

It wasn't easy getting her magic to grab the chain while dodging Aspen's elbows and fists. Twice her magic caught it and lost it. Twice she nearly got hit. But finally, her magic latched on like a fist and yanked the amulet skyward.

Aspen reached up to catch it, and Buffy grabbed her arms and dragged them back down. But even with her slayer strength, the super slayer was going to break free.

"Rona! Chao-Ahn! Dominique!"

Buffy called to the other slayers and they came, throwing themselves onto Aspen in layers. And still, they struggled to hold her.

"Frankie," Buffy said with the same wide-eyed, overwhelmed expression that Frankie had worn so many times herself. "Can you . . . hurry up?"

"I'm trying!" Frankie's magic pulled at the amulet. "It doesn't want to come off!" About to lose her grip, she jumped up against the pile of slayers and grabbed the green gem with her fists. With both her arms and her magic she tried to force it over Aspen's head, then gave up on the magic and just pulled, trying to break the chain against the super slayer's neck.

"Let go of that, you little—" Aspen growled as the amulet burned the skin of Frankie's hands. With a great heave, she exploded from beneath them, sending Buffy and the others flying in all directions—but not Frankie, who she caught and slammed to the floor. Frankie rolled onto her stomach and thought she heard the faint tinkling of the amulet as it skittered across the gymnasium, just before Aspen's boot came down on her spine.

"Frankie!"

Frankie didn't know which of the Scoobies screamed. It sounded like all of them. Spike. Jake. Her poor mom, who would never recover from the sight. Only . . . Frankie wiggled her toes. Her back hurt, but . . . her back *hurt*, so didn't that mean her spine was still attached?

"Hey," she said. "Why am I not dead?"

She looked across the gym. The Amulet of Junjari lay at Hailey's feet, and the Potential bent down and picked it up.

"Give that back!" Aspen shrieked and ran at her. Frankie struggled up onto her elbows as Hailey froze, watching Aspen approach like an oncoming train.

"Put it on!" Frankie shouted. "Use the powers! Be a slayer!"

Hailey looked at her, hesitant. But she had to. She had to, or Aspen would kill her.

As Aspen jumped, Hailey clenched the amulet in her fist.

"No way," she said. She turned, and threw the Amulet of Junjari cleanly through the torn-open door to another dimension.

And Aspen, single-minded, dove in right after it.

The moment she disappeared, the gymnasium began to quake.

"It's the spell," Willow shouted. "The Spell of Many Interdimensional Returns! It's ending!"

"Again, Will," said Buffy, "what does that—?"

But Buffy never got the chance to finish. The air in the gymnasium gave one final, brutal crack, and the doors between the dimensions sealed themselves up tight. Any hellbeasts trying to wriggle through were promptly chopped in half. And the newly returned slayers, and Andrew, disappeared.

"What?" Frankie cried. "What happened?" The Scoobies finished off their demon kills and ran to the symbol in the floor. "Where did they go? Do we have to do this all again?" Frankie looked around at the wreck of the gymnasium. There were demon corpses everywhere. Through the blasted open doors, she saw

O'Shay Thomas and Zach Connors peek their heads into the gym. They were holding bloodied shovels, but they were alive.

Willow bent down to the scorched markings in the wood. "The spell was designed to return the lost things to their homes." She paused a moment. Then she smiled.

"I know where they are."

CHAPTER THIRTY-SIX

1630 REVELLO DRIVE

The grass was soft against her back and stars winked down from the night sky. It was nice. The air was sweet. It was quiet. She didn't know where she was, but it felt like . . . home. It felt like Sunnydale. Only that didn't make any sense. One minute she'd been in that gym, fighting beside the slayers and Willow and Spike. Even Giles had been there, just like old times. And then she was here, on the grass. Had they not won? Had she died? *Again?*

Buffy sat up and looked around. The grass was green and carefully mowed. It was bordered by a sidewalk lit by streetlamps. She still wore the same clothes she'd been in since the attack in Halifax, the same jeans and shirt she'd worn the whole time they'd been trapped in that prison—well, except for that day when they'd all gotten bored and traded. She sighed. There was breath in her lungs. And a heartbeat in her chest.

She stood up. Wherever she was, it was pleasant, a small green space with a few stone benches and some young, newly planted trees. She walked to what seemed like the main streetlamp and stood beside the first stone bench to run her fingers across the gold plaque.

"Revello Park."

She looked around. Of course. She'd been here before. This was the park they'd put up where her old street had been. This used to be Revello Drive. And she guessed that the spot where she'd just woken up had once been the site of 1630.

Her head turned at the sound of an approaching car. No, not car. An approaching van, and she smiled when she saw Willow leaning out of the passenger window. Frankie leaned out over her like she was on her lap, and then somehow there was Jake, shoving his way out over them both. The van roared its way up to the curb and jerked into park, and the next thing she knew she was being charged by old friends and new. As they wrapped her in a massive hug, most she knew by feel and by sound: the soft, cuddly sounds of Willow and the spot of silence that was Oz. The bouncing and slight whining was Jake. Spike's cold fingers were gentle on her shoulder. Frankie's little slayer fingers were less so, but she could take it. And then there were the new kids: a thoughtful-seeming Black boy with glasses who was too polite to embrace her for more than a second, and the tall, tan girl in black, who'd held a dozen slayers' worth of power in her fist and thrown it away to save them from danger.

"These spells are so literal," Frankie grumbled. "Why couldn't it just let you stay in the gym?"

"It wasn't so bad," said Buffy. "Though I hope everyone else's homes provided a similarly soft landing."

"Chao-Ahn's family home has been the same for a century," said Giles, limping as he approached across the pavement. "As have Rona's and Dominique's. I'm not sure about Flora's, but I think

Kennedy's was converted to apartment buildings. She might be being chased out of somewhere with a broom right about now."

"Giles!" Buffy broke away to support him as he wavered, blood from his stomach wound darkening the front of his clothes. "You shouldn't be up!"

"Yes, next stop is the hospital." He smiled gently. "But I had to make sure you were all right."

"Let's get him back to the van," said Oz, and he and Spike each took an arm. Willow and Frankie snuggled up beneath each of Buffy's.

"I can't believe you're here," said Willow.

"I can't believe you took so long," Buffy teased. She looked around happily as they walked. "And is it just me, or are there way more Scoobies than usual?"

PART FIVE

BUFFY:

THE NEXT GENERATION

CHAPTER THIRTY-SEVEN

THE BATTLE'S DONE AND WE KIND OF WON, SO WE SOUND OUR VICTORY CHEER

After they deposited Giles in the hospital, they returned to the gym to see how much of it they could salvage. There had been significant breakage of doors and bleachers. Scorches and claw marks marred the floors. And nearly every foot was splattered by blood or demon guts.

Sarafina knelt beside the hulking body of one of the muscular horned cow-type demons.

"I didn't get to fight a single one of these," she said, and frowned. "Can you not do the spell again?" she asked Willow. "One more time?"

"No," Willow said, then leaned down to kiss her. "Well. Maybe on our anniversary."

"They're cute," Buffy commented, watching from a distance. She turned to Oz. "It's good that you're here, too, Oz. I think Willow will always rest easier when you're around."

"That goes both ways," said Oz. "And it goes your way, too. So no more disappearing through interdimensional portals."

"Not if I can help it."

"Where did you go, anyway?" Hailey asked, toeing a dead demon to make sure the twitching was just leftover nerves. "I mean, when you disappeared from the gym. Willow said the spell brought you home, but that was a park."

"It was where my old house used to be." Buffy crossed her arms. "Which was a nice touch. Though if it had brought me to the exact location I would have been deposited a few hundred feet in the air, and you would have arrived to find a Buffy pancake."

"That is lucky," Frankie agreed. "The book we got the spell from was extremely evil." She looked around. "Hey, has anyone seen Grim?"

"Grim?" Buffy asked. "As in, Grimloch the Hunter of Thrace?"

"Yeah, you know him: big, hot demon," Hailey explained. "He and Frankie are . . . well . . ." She looked at Jake, Sigmund, and Sam, and the three boys quickly mimed fingers kissing, hearts breaking, and boo-hoo tears.

"Thank you." Frankie narrowed her eyes. "For that very succinct summary of our relationship."

"I'm sure he just needs to be alone for a while," said Hailey. "He just got over being mind-controlled, you know?"

Frankie could understand that. But she wished he would have hung around so she could make sure he was okay. Buffy put a hand on her shoulder before wandering off to help Willow and Spike. When she felt another hand on her shoulder she thought Buffy had come back, but then the hand shoved her and she turned to see Jake.

"Hey. You okay?" he asked.

"Yeah. Though to be honest, I can't believe we all survived." She looked in particular at Sigmund and Sam and the lacrosse werewolves, who seemed dazed but waved at her happily. They'd been cut by claws, and Sam had been bitten by something that she hoped had no werewolf-style transformative powers, but other than that, they were fine.

"Well, we did," said Jake, as the new Scoobies gathered around them. "The slayers are back, and Aspen's vanquished—"

"Thanks to Hailey," said Sigmund.

"Thanks to Hailey." Frankie nodded, and Hailey blushed. "And thanks to all of you. You really held her in those portals."

"Oh crap," said Jake. "I still need to go clean my barf."

"That's very charming," said Sam with a grimace. "Luckily, there's still a lot to do here." They surveyed the battlefield. There were so many dead demons. And no one seemed to have the energy for getting rid of them. Even Spike, still determined to show off for Buffy, was mostly just moving them back and forth into piles.

"This is a lot of demon composting," Frankie said. "And my eco-magic is kaput. Can we just compost the rest of them right here and let Principal Jacobs figure out what to do with all the dirt?"

"Mystery dirt would be better than the mystery demon guts we left floating in the pool," said Jake.

"Mom?" Frankie called. "Can we go?"

"I guess," said Willow. "My magic should recover in a few hours; we can sneak back and take care of this then."

Frankie nodded, just as Andrew burst through the doors of the gymnasium.

"Thank god you're still here," he said, stumbling toward them to land in Spike's confused arms. "I was unceremoniously dumped in the middle of a grocery store. It was bright and cold, and I think that's where my old house was?"

Buffy rolled her eyes. "It's all right," Spike said. He clapped Andrew on the back. "You can come with me to my apartment. Get cleaned up."

"Your apartment?" Andrew asked as Spike led him away. "You

have an apartment? Not like a crypt? Is it a really cool vampire man cave? Is there, like, a black leather couch?"

Spike raised an eyebrow at Willow as he passed. "You owe me," he said, and Willow snorted. She looked at Frankie.

"He says that, but we all know that after ten minutes it'll be all hero worship and blooming onions."

As they walked out of the school, Frankie heard Hailey's voice and turned to see her and Sigmund, walking with their heads bent close together. She saw Jake and Sam, leading a pack of new werewolves. She saw her mom and Buffy, laughing beside Oz and Sarafina.

Frankie smiled. Things were just as they should be.

CHAPTER THIRTY-EIGHT

WHERE DO WE GO FROM HERE?

In the aftermath of the battle, the Rosenberg house once again found itself full to the brim. With Hailey inhabiting the former guest room, Buffy took over the basement, and even though Andrew was camping out at Spike's place, the two of them were always there—Andrew hovering in the kitchen with Jake, and Spike trying to seem like he wasn't hovering over Buffy. The DeWitts and the Osbournes crowded the driveway with vans and hybrid vehicles, and Sam was usually there, too. Sometimes he even brought a few brand-spanking-new lacrosse werewolves.

"This place is overstuffed," Hailey declared as she closed her bedroom door to drown out the sounds of the boys in the kitchen so she and Frankie could have a moment of privacy. "Vi and Mr. Giles are going to be out of the hospital this afternoon, and where are we going to put them? The hall closets?"

"Mr. Giles has dibs on the couch, and I think Sarafina volunteered Sigmund's bed for your sister," said Frankie. "So maybe we'll have to stuff Sig into the hall closet."

"I bet he'd tidy it up while he was in there. We could just keep moving him from closet to closet, and then we wouldn't have to clean. One more thing checked off the list."

Frankie bounced down on the edge of the bed.

"Returned the surviving slayers to the proper dimension." She held up a finger. "Vanquished Aspen the queen of all buttholes." She held up another.

"I don't know how I feel about that." Hailey squinted. "It's making me want to do a PSA about how you shouldn't throw balls and shiny things carelessly because puppies and little kids might chase them."

Frankie smiled. "You don't have anything to feel bad about. Following the amulet was Aspen's choice. And besides, if she caught it, then it's unlikely there was anything over there that could kill her. She'll go from queen of the buttholes to queen of the hellbeasts in no time."

The girls exchanged an uneasy glance. The remaining slayers and the Watchers Council were to meet to decide whether to try to extract Aspen from the other dimension. Frankie couldn't even begin to imagine all the ways it could go wrong, but she was sure to get mixed up in it. She blinked. She was sure to get mixed up in every big, apocalypse-threatening event from now on.

"What's up?" Hailey asked. "You look like you're about to puke."

"I guess I just realized . . . I'm a slayer."

"You just realized that? We figured that out literally an hour after I got to Sunnydale."

"No." Frankie laughed. "I mean . . . I don't know, I guess part of me still felt like once Buffy and the real slayers were back, I wouldn't be one anymore. Like I was a slayer on loan. A substitute slayer who just makes you watch movies and doesn't assign any homework."

Hailey grinned. "You're not a slayer on loan. You're the slayer in *line.* Frankie Rosenberg, also a witch, who stepped into a big pile of slayer shoes and rescued the legendary Buffy Summers. And that's only what you did *first.* Think of all the stuff you'll do next."

"That's what's making me want to barf." Frankie looked down at her shoes and the ankles of her fuzzy unicorn socks below the rolled cuffs of her jeans. "But what about you? You're still a Potential. And with my mom being a slayer power sluice, we can probably figure out a way to get you your powers without also killing me."

"Yeah." Hailey rubbed her palms against her long black skirt, making her studded bracelets jangle. "Maybe. But . . ."

"But what?"

"It's just . . . when I had the Amulet of Junjari I had this flash— all this power, and what it meant—and I swear that tiny rock felt like it weighed about a million pounds. All I could think was *no way.* For now, being a Scooby is plenty badass enough for me." Hailey twisted the length of her hair around her hand like a rope. "It's kind of sad, though, isn't it? Things turned out pretty much like the Darkness wanted, only they didn't live to see it. Your mom's a big swinging two-way slayer gate. Everything's going to be different now for every Potential that comes. They all get to decide to activate or not activate. They could all give their powers back. Even you."

Even her.

"What happens when my mom isn't around anymore?" Frankie wondered aloud. "Like, what happens then?"

"I don't know," said Hailey. "Good thing your mom's so tough. We won't have to find out anytime soon."

"Vi should be happy that you're deciding to hold off," Frankie said.

"Yeah. It is the perfect get-out-of-the-hospital present for when she arrives to further cramp our style in"—Hailey checked an imaginary watch—"two hours."

"Enjoy it while you can." Frankie listened to the people she loved, crammed inside the house. "The battle's over, and pretty soon everyone will have to go back to their normal lives." Sarafina would go back to DC, at least for a while. Buffy would want to go see Dawn and Xander. Mr. Giles would leave to get back to work reassembling the decimated Watchers Council. And Vi. Vi would want to leave, too.

Frankie swallowed. "I think the only question left is whether that means you're going to go with your sister or if you're going to stay."

"You already know the answer to that question," Hailey said, and Frankie's heart sank until Hailey cocked an eyebrow. "But we have to go shopping for new curtains. Yellow flowers?" She gestured to them and made a disgusted face. "You guys . . ."

Frankie threw a pillow at her, and both girls fell back, laughing.

☽ ☽ ○ ☾ ☾

"Dammit, Jake, keep the blinds shut! Or do you like the smell of burning vampire?"

"I'm sorry!" Jake cried as Spike batted at his smoking sleeve. "I didn't mean to!"

"No fighting in the kitchen," Willow ordered as she slid the final grilled cheese sandwich onto a platter piled high with them. "This is getting ridiculous," she said to Oz as he ladled tomato soup into bowls, careful not to confuse the soup with Spike's blood heating in the double boiler. "We just went to the grocery store yesterday."

"I'll go again after lunch," said Oz. "And I can cook some things at my place and bring them over so yours isn't always getting wrecked."

"Dammit, Jake, you did it again!"

"I'm sorry!"

"Okay, come get sandwiches and get away from the windows!" Willow wiped her hands on a towel and scowled at the boys as they trudged over to load their plates. "I know it's crowded in here, but that just means we all need to be extra polite. Jake, be mindful of your shoulders nudging the curtains. And, Spike, you could always hang out on this side of the kitchen, you know."

"Or you know," said the vampire, "you could always cast the same spell you cast over the high school over your house, so I wouldn't have to live in constant fear of combustion." He took a triangle of grilled cheese and bit into it with a self-satisfied crunch.

Temporary peace descended as everyone got busy eating, and Willow stepped into the backyard for a few breaths of fresh air. When she got there, she was surprised to find Buffy doing the same thing. The slayer stood with her back to the house, arms crossed, blond hair hanging down her back as she looked out at nothing in particular. When she heard Willow, she half turned so Willow could see the curve of her cheek.

"This is quite the circus you're running around here."

"I think 'running' is a mischaracterization," said Willow. She went to stand beside her best friend and crossed her arms so the tips of their elbows briefly touched.

Buffy smiled.

"It brings back memories, though, doesn't it?"

Inside, the shouting had started again, and Willow thought she heard something get broken.

361

"Yeah," she said. "All those little Scoobies, running me ragged and giving me an ulcer worrying about their impending deaths. I have Oz and Spike to help—" Buffy gave her a look. "Well, I have Oz to help. But I don't know how your mom did it."

"Mom had Giles," Buffy said. "And she had the delightful distance of denial." She sighed. "But yes, I think we may owe my mom a very big, posthumous apology." She nudged Willow with her shoulder. "Are you okay?"

"Are *you* okay?" Willow countered. "You're the one who was just pulled out of a hell dimension."

"I've been in worse hell dimensions. Except for Andrew's constant rounds of Six Degrees of Kevin Bacon, it wasn't that bad." She looked at Willow. "And you're the one whose kid just got called into all of this."

Yes. Frankie. Her kid was a slayer. And because she was a slayer, her life would be harder and full of danger, with fewer choices than other people had. But it would also be a life of purpose. And she supposed, if anyone had to be called, Frankie was the one most surrounded by people she could trust to help her.

"I'm trying to think about you," Willow said. "When I think about Frankie. Buffy Summers, the slayer who survived. Who proved that a slayer's life doesn't have to be short or tragic."

"God, I'm sorry, Willow."

"For what?

"I don't know. I'm not her mom, but you know I've always loved that kid. And somehow I feel like I am her mom now. Like it's my no-good slayer genes that are making her act up. Play with sharp objects and hang out with boys in leather."

"Okay, the only 'boy in leather' is Spike, and he's her old man Watcher now."

Buffy smiled mischievously. "You really did that to him, huh? That old face?"

"I really did."

"Good." Buffy tossed her hair back. "Let him get a taste of aging for a change. Too bad he still looks . . ." She cocked her head. "Really good."

"Don't tell him that; he'll become insufferable. And don't feel bad about Frankie," said Willow. "I actually think the line got it right. She's got a lot to learn . . ."

"But she's got good teachers," Buffy said.

$$) \ ) \ \bigcirc \ (\ ($$

That night, Frankie snuck out of the house to do some patrolling and to get a few moments alone with her thoughts. She treaded softly down the stairs and headed toward the kitchen, where that evening her mom and the original Scoobies had gathered around the table with Buffy, Vi, and Sarafina, telling tales long into the night. When she got downstairs and peered in, all that remained were a few wineglasses, and a mostly empty bottle of scotch. But in the living room were three distinct lumps: Mr. Giles beneath a blanket on the couch, Vi beneath one on the sofa, and Oz, collapsed into the easy chair.

Frankie crept closer to make sure Vi and Mr. Giles were resting comfortably. They'd both been drinking only tea, having been so recently in the hospital, but she still thought it was unwise for them to stay up so late. But what did she know? She was a teenager. Let the adults make their own stupid adult decisions. She tugged the blanket up higher on Mr. Giles's chest, and he turned slightly and winced in his sleep when the stitches in his stomach pulled taut.

"I hate coming back to bloody Sunnydale," he murmured. "Always almost bloody dying . . ."

Frankie smiled and waited for him to settle, then gently removed his eyeglasses and set them on the coffee table.

"You hate coming back to Sunnydale," she whispered. "But you love to see them. Even Spike."

She turned and slunk toward the door as he nuzzled deeper into his pillow and muttered, "No, not Spike."

Outside, Sunnydale was quiet. As if it, too, was worn out from hosting so many out-of-town demons and hellbeasts. She moved quickly through the warming late spring air and used Mr. Stabby as a walking stick, heading in the direction of Marymore Park. Because she said "patrol," but even she knew what she really meant, and who she was really patrolling for.

It wasn't long before she caught it: the familiar sensation of being hunted. They were near the edge of the forest. She could make a break for it and lead him on one last chase.

Frankie turned around.

"Hey," she said as Grimloch walked toward her. "I've been wondering when you'd start stalking me again."

"I would have come sooner, but you haven't been alone."

"For the last several days, I haven't not been in threes and fours. I was hoping to get to know Kennedy and Rona and the other slayers, but honestly now I'm kind of glad the spell zapped them back to their own places." She looked at his handsome face. The dark hair he kept tucked behind his ear. "Are you all right?" she asked. "Are you going to be all right?"

"I will be," he said. "With some time. And distance."

"That's what I thought you'd say," she said gently.

"I didn't mean to break your heart, Francesca," he said. "That was Aspen."

"That's good to know." That was Aspen. But that didn't mean they were back together. Breaking up had been the right thing. "It still sucks though."

"It does." Grim smiled a little, finally, showing the tips of his fangs. He moved closer, so they were almost touching. "You will have many loves, Frankie," he said. "I shouldn't be the first of them."

"This is goodbye, isn't it? You're leaving tonight."

"I was only waiting to see you," he said. "To thank you. And to apologize, for everything I did—"

"That wasn't your fault. That wasn't you."

"I struck your mother. I attacked you—"

"No, you didn't. My mom knows that, and so does everyone else."

He smiled again, head low.

"I'm going to miss you, Grim," she said. "And I'm glad . . . I'm glad I knew you."

Grimloch turned to go, but not before looking at her in that way he had. There was no heat in that look this time. It was only bemused. Fond. And that was just fine.

"Hey, I know you shouldn't be the first of my loves," Frankie called as he walked away, "but what about the second? The third? The thirtieth?"

Frankie saw his shoulders shake as he chuckled. "Maybe I'll be the last."

She crossed her arms and laughed softly as he disappeared across the park. "Stupid, hot demon."

"You're out pretty late."

"Buffy!" Frankie spun. She hadn't heard the other slayer approach. Not a single snapped twig, not a whisper of disturbed air. Not even a ping off her lazy slaydar.

"So there goes Grimloch," Buffy noted as she came to stand

365

beside Frankie. "Tall, handsome, billowy coat . . . I had one of those once."

"Didn't you have two of those once?" Frankie asked, and Buffy smirked.

"Spike's not tall."

"What are you doing out here? I thought after the marathon reminisce-sesh you'd be passed out with your old stake in one hand and hugging Mr. Gordo with the other."

Buffy raised an eyebrow. "You paint quite the mental picture. But I couldn't sleep. Being penned up in a hell dimension with Andrew will do that to a person. So when I saw you come out here, with your super-sized stake, I thought I'd join you on patrol. I didn't mean to eavesdrop."

"That's okay." She gazed in the direction where Grim had disappeared. "Seeing him . . . it was just one more thing I had to do."

"And now patrol?" Buffy asked. "Show me around that fancy new half-empty cemetery?"

"Really?" Frankie rose onto her toes. Patrolling with Buffy sounded like, well, like living out one of her childhood fantasies.

"Sure." Buffy began to back away, out of the park. "Shall we say, slayer who bags the least demons has to buy the other slayer breakfast?"

"You're on!" Frankie said happily. "Just promise not to laugh if I fall into an open hole or like . . . stake myself."

"If you stake yourself with *that* thing, we'll be trying to explain to your mother why you're a Frankie kebab."

Buffy turned and ran into the night, and Frankie followed, catching up and falling back, jumping hedges and flipping over fences as Buffy pushed her to see what she could do. They staked vamps and it felt almost unfair, with Frankie poking them in their yellow eyes and Buffy kicking them from behind. It felt different from when she trained with Spike. It felt exhilarating.

"This is so much better," she said as she waved away the dust from their fourth vampire. "I mean, you're back, and everything's going to be okay. Before, I just kept messing up. I didn't know what to do. When you were gone . . . it always felt like there was this dark cloud looming over my head."

"When I was gone the world needed another slayer, and it got one," Buffy said. "My being here doesn't magically make you better. You already did that." She put her hands on her hips. "Not that you don't still have things to learn. And you should probably be introduced to the rest of the organization. Or what remains of it."

"You mean," Frankie breathed, "you want me to come with you?"

"Don't get too bright eyed." Buffy tucked her stake into her pocket. "We still have to ask your mom."

☽ ☽ ◯ ☾ ☾

"Only for the summer," Willow said when Frankie asked her. "And I can put a locator spell on you at any time, so don't get any ideas."

"Mom, thank you!" Frankie squealed. She hugged her tight, and then more gently when Willow said, "Ow."

"I'll be totally safe, I promise. And supervised. There will be so many other slayers, and Watchers, there, I'll be in the least danger I've been in all year. It'll be like I'm at slayer boarding school." She sat back on her bed, and Willow smoothed the strands of Frankie's bright red hair.

Willow frowned.

"You're going to grow up even faster now," she said.

"I won't; I promise. I'll only grow at the normal slayer rate. I can even pound a bunch of coffee if you want me to try and stunt myself."

Willow rolled her eyes and pulled Frankie into another hug. "It seems like only yesterday you were trying to learn to magically sort the recycling."

"I'll still sort the recycling," Frankie said into her mom's shoulder, then looked up when Hailey leaned against the door frame.

"So it's true. You're leaving with Buffy. I knew it from the way Spike's moping around down there."

"Poor Spike," Willow said. "He won't know what to do without you."

"I don't think I'm the main source of his moping," said Frankie. "And it's only for the summer. I'll be back in New Sunnydale before the Hellmouth knows I'm gone."

"Poor Spike," Hailey echoed as she plopped down on the foot of Frankie's bed. "I wish I could've been a fly on the wall for his and Buffy's big reunion. Did you see them go off together there for a minute at the gym?"

"Do you think he kissed her?" Frankie asked.

"You guys," Willow chided, but it was too late. Frankie and Hailey were lost in conjecture.

"Do you think she let him?" Hailey countered.

"Well, maybe she kissed him first. I mean, she has been locked away in a prison dimension . . ."

"Ahem," Buffy said. Frankie, Willow, and Hailey turned to see Buffy in the doorway, with none other than Spike.

"Sorry," said Frankie. "We were just . . ."

"Gossiping like teenagers?" Hailey suggested, and grimaced.

"It's okay." Buffy crossed her arms. "But what I do with lips of Spike is between me and lips of Spike."

Frankie and Hailey nodded. But they glanced at the vampire for clues.

"Don't look at me." Spike stuffed his hands into his pockets. "These lips of Spike are sealed."

☽ ☽ ○ ☾ ☾

When Spike returned to his apartment, Andrew was blessedly in the shower. He hadn't stopped showering practically since he'd been rescued. Kept saying he could still smell the hell dimension. But really Spike thought it was just so he could keep borrowing more of his clothes.

Spike reached into the refrigerator for a bag of O negative, then opted for a bottle of bourbon instead. He was in a right foul mood. He wasn't even in the mood to drink. For a moment he remembered the way Buffy used to stick her tongue out and shudder whenever she had a pull. Adorable.

He got a glass and sat down at his kitchen table, listening to the shower run. And run. And run some more.

"Hey! Don't use up all the bloody hot water!"

"What?" Andrew called.

"I said, don't use up all the bloody hot water!"

"I'll be out in a few minutes, roomie! We can find something to stream on TV. There's this show I watch where two brothers slay demons and stuff, and they're both kind of badasses but super bonded . . . It'll be like watching our twins!"

Spike resisted the urge to sneak into the bathroom and flush the toilet.

He poured the bourbon, and someone knocked on his door. "Come in."

When Buffy walked into his kitchen, Spike nearly knocked over his glass. "Didn't know it was you."

"If you had, would you not have said to come in?"

"No—" He looked around. He was dressed, and Andrew was keeping the place clean. "Come in, whatever you like. I don't care." She cocked her head at his attitude, and he held out the bottle. "Want a drink? Want to do your little *blegh* tongue thing?"

"I haven't done my little blegh tongue thing in years," Buffy said. She looked at the bottle and shuddered as she stuck her tongue out. "But *blegh*. I don't know how you can drink any more after last night." She looked around. "This is a nice place."

"Nice and full of Andrew," said Spike. "You taking him with you when you leave?"

"That's the plan." Buffy crossed her arms, and her long blond hair fell to her elbows. "Me, Giles, and Andrew. That's why I'm here, actually. To say so long."

"Right, then." Spike took the bottle and walked away to shove it back onto the counter. "Been good seeing you."

"Oh my god. Are you really going to be this childish? We haven't seen each other in years, and this is how you want to leave it." She rolled her eyes. "I am not even surprised."

"Look, it's not even about you, slayer." He sighed and half turned, just showing his profile. "Or at least, it's not entirely about you. I have had a life, in the years between."

"I know. You've been training Frankie. And you've done a good job."

He snorted. "She hasn't exactly absorbed my teachings. No style, no flair—"

"So she hasn't bleached her hair and put on five pounds of

leather. She gets the job done. And she's alive. Dead demons, living slayer. The only two things on the Watcher checklist."

Spike shrugged in his black T-shirt, one of the few that Andrew hadn't commandeered and somehow stretched the collar out of. "I'm about done with the Watcher checklist. Think it's time I went off on my own again. Frankie doesn't need me anymore; she's got you. And Giles. She's been outgrowing me from the start." He looked down into his bourbon. "And she's clingy," he added, brows raised. "Has this cockamamie idea that I'm her father figure, as if that was even possible. It's this bloody old face Willow stuck me with—"

He stopped when Buffy walked through the kitchen and touched his cheek. Tenderly, like she was testing it to make sure it was real.

"I like this look," she said. "It's distinguished."

He looked up in surprise. She was looking at him the same way she always did when he wasn't being evil or ridiculous, and if he'd had blood to blush with, he would have turned pleasantly red as a beet.

"Or at least, I like this look when it isn't giving you some kind of vampire midlife crisis," she said, and drew away.

"What are you talking about?"

"Frankie is not ready to be without her Watcher. I wasn't ready to be without Giles until I was in college. Until after my mom died. But you think you're such a great teacher that a few semesters with you and Frankie's all set? Please."

"For your information, I imparted more knowledge in two weeks than Rupert managed in two—"

"This isn't Watcher versus Watcher," Buffy interrupted. "Though that would be fun to see. I'm saying she needs you. And Willow would feel better about it, if you were there."

Spike blinked. "There," he repeated. "With you. You're saying you want me to come?"

"I'm saying you have to. Giles and Andrew and I are leaving in the morning, but Frankie has to finish another two weeks of school. You'll have to be the one to bring her to us."

Spike straightened. Did she mean it? Were he and his slayers headed off on another adventure?

"Maybe we can go see Angel over the summer," Buffy went on breezily. "He's always good for a lesson or two."

"Angel?" he asked, as Buffy smirked and walked to his door. "Hang on, you're just saying that? You wouldn't really make me . . . make us . . ." She waved to him happily as she left, and Andrew trotted into the kitchen with a towel on his head and wearing Spike's bathrobe.

"So do you want to order pizzas, or should I just make ants on a log with some nice red wine . . . ?" He picked up the remote control. But not even a night with Andrew could ruin Spike's reinflated mood.

"Pizza," he said, and smiled into his bourbon as Andrew began to dial.

$$) \;) \; \bigcirc \; (\; ($$

Frankie and the new Scoobies sat together on their stone bench in the quad, watching the students of New Sunnydale High make their way in from the parking lot, some happy, some sad, some yawning from not enough sleep, and some wired and jittery after too much coffee.

"They look so . . . normal," Jake said with a squint, his arm slung across Sam's shoulders.

"And that's bad?" asked Hailey from where she leaned against Sigmund.

"It's just weird," said Jake, "knowing how much goes on around here. Knowing that not even a week ago there were a dozen doors to other dimensions ripped open between the basketball hoops."

"But would you rather they know?" asked Sigmund. "Would you rather they understood that they were attending a school that sits literally atop one of the most active hellmouths on the planet?"

"Probably better that they don't," said Sam. "But all the same I don't think it would make much of a difference." The Scoobies turned to look at him. "I mean I don't think they would leave. We didn't."

"True, true," Jake muttered.

"But we know how to fight it," said Frankie.

The slayer looked at her friends. They'd saved the world. And they would do it again.

But they still might not pass trig.

"Speaking of how to fight it," said Jake, "just what are we supposed to do if that thing starts showing its teeth while you're gone?"

"I'm not lost beyond time, Jake. Just message me or call the Council. I'll arrive with more slayers and a Watcher SWAT team. You won't have to lift a finger."

"Or," said Sigmund, "maybe we *won't* call. Sam and I did just fine firing arrows from our barricade, and Jake's nearly got control of his inner werewolf. Plus members of his new pack."

"Jake and the lacrosse werewolves," Sam said, and kissed him.

"We're planning a group pilgrimage to Weretopia," said Jake proudly.

"As for Hailey," Sigmund went on. "'Twas Hailey who slayed the beast."

"Hey," said Frankie as Hailey beamed. "Don't get too cozy without me. I'm only leaving for the summer." She looked out toward the sports field, where a ground crew had gathered and trucks were unloading small, heavy equipment: Bobcats and bulldozers. Principal Jacobs chatted with a few people in yellow hard hats, directing them where to move the mysterious dirt that had somehow gotten into the gymnasium. Rumor had it that she intended to start a school and community garden, which Frankie thought was a great idea, though considering the origins of the dirt, they would probably have to monitor the crops for signs of evil.

She stared out across the quad and thought back to the battles they'd fought on the grounds. The Countess, dismembered on the sports field. The battle of the Hellmouth, where the basement was flooded by demons of Sunnydale's past. And the Spell of Many Interdimensional Returns that had rained demons upon the gymnasium, and returned the missing slayers to the world.

The high school was one unlucky building. It was hard to believe that in a few weeks she would leave it, to go and train with the slayers and the Watchers Council. But when she got back, who knew what new tricks she would have to show the Scoobies—and the Hellmouth.

"Just for the summer," Jake said, and narrowed one eye. "You're not going to be seduced by all their glamorous slayer lifestyles and fancy Watcher gadgets."

"Not going to get too cozy in some grand London flat?" asked Sigmund.

"Or get dragged into debt by designer footwear and fashion?" added Hailey. "Though seriously, you should bring us back some of that. Like boots. Like black Prada boots."

Frankie grinned.

"You won't get too dazzled by the slayer and Watcher originals?" asked Sam. "And forget all about us back in boring old Sunnydale?"

Boring old Sunnydale. Sunnydale had been many things— murderous, destroyed, uncommonly snowy—but it had never been boring.

"No way," Frankie said, and grabbed Jake's hand. "Sunnydale pride. And Scoobies Forever."

ACKNOWLEDGMENTS

How do I say goodbye to the Buffyverse? Haha, I don't! You'll have to drag me out of here kicking and screaming with my grubby little fingers hooked into the Hellmouth! BUFFY FOREVERRR!!

I'm kidding. And I'm not, because Buffy truly is forever. So many amazing Buffyverse tales remain to be told, and it has been my absolute honor to be at the helm for this one. It's also been 100 percent fun, every step of the way.

There are not enough thanks in the world for the folks who brought me onto this project: everyone at Team Buffy Hyperion, but especially my editor, Jocelyn Davies, who can pun with the best of them. Thank you to Elanna Heda, for being a total Scooby. Thank you to the cover designer, Tyler Nevins, and the artist collective ILOVEDUST for continuing to give this series such a badass look. Thank you to Guy Cunningham and Karen Krumpak for a wonderful copyedit and a deep dive into Buffyverse continuity.

Thanks of course to my wonderful former agent, Adriann Zurhellen. As I write this, she's been gone for less than a week and

I miss her already! But by the time *Against the Darkness* comes out, I'll no doubt have much to thank my new agent for: so thank you Emily Van Beek, and the team at Folio Literary Management.

And as always, thanks to the Buffy fans. As we bask in this time of glory, awash in new Buffy stuff, thank you for welcoming Frankie into the fold. Getting to talk Buffy with you and trading favorite episodes, quoting favorite lines, and sharing favorite Buffy memories has been one of the coolest experiences of my life. I hope I get to talk Buffy with you for a long time to come. But for now, Buffy: The Next Generation has come to an end. So be well, happy binge-rewatching, and go put marzipan in your pie plates, Bingo.